Deceived

BERTRICE SMALL

Deceived

KENSINGTON BOOKS
http://www.kensingtonbooks.com

For the newest man in my life, my grandson,
Chandler David Small

Prologue

ENGLAND, 1760

"*Marry?*" Valerian Hawkesworth, the Duke of Farminster, looked startled. "What on earth do you mean, I am to be married, Grandmama?"

The Dowager Duchess of Farminster looked directly at her only grandchild and repeated her previous words. "You were affianced as a boy to the daughter of one of your father's friends, a distant cousin, I believe. You were to marry the girl when she turned seventeen. Since there is no one else engaging your affections, Valerian, you will sail in three weeks' time for the island of St. Timothy in the western Indies to claim the girl. A sugar plantation is no small dowry, dear boy, and it is past time you set up your nursery."

"*A colonial?*" The duke looked dubious.

"Oh, do not be such a snob," his grandmother scolded him. "I am certain the girl has been as well educated as any of the silly misses you know. And whatever she may lack in the social graces, I will tutor her myself. She will make you a grand duchess, dear boy, and having lived on an isolated island all her life, she will undoubtedly be more comfortable in the country, content to remain on your estate to give you several sons and daughters."

"Why was I not told about this arrangement before now?" he demanded irritably. A trip to the western Indies was going to take several weeks. Then he would be forced to remain on this island another few weeks before he could marry the girl and travel back to England. Why, he could be gone three or four months. He would miss the racing season. "Hellfire and damnation!" the duke swore softly.

The dowager duchess's mouth quirked with her amusement. "Your father made the arrangement long before he and your mother were drowned returning from France with your sister. Your grandfather knew of it but put it from him until just before he died a few months ago. It was then he reminded me of this betrothal. We both agreed it was past time you were wed. Since there was no one else, it seemed best to keep to these preplanned nuptials. I sent a letter to Robert Kimberly, your prospective father-in-law, a few weeks back, saying that you would be arriving at the end of March to wed your bride." She handed him a leather folder containing a copy of the betrothal contract.

Valerian Hawkesworth's deep blue eyes scanned the heavy parchment with its clear, precise wording. He was indeed betrothed to a Mistress Charlotte Kimberly, born April the sixth, in the year 1743. The chit was approaching her seventeenth birthday, the time set forth in the document for their marriage. He frowned, and glanced up at his grandmother. "What does she look like?" he said.

The dowager duchess shook her head. "I have not the faintest idea, dear boy, for I have never laid eyes on the child." Then, seeing the mutinous look in her grandson's eyes, she continued. "I am certain that she is lovely. Robert Kimberly brought his bride to England on a wedding trip. She was a very pretty girl, as I recall, and he a handsome young man. Their offspring cannot be unpleasing to the eye, dear boy. Just before the Kimberlys departed England, Mistress Kimberly discovered that she was *enceinte*. Your father and Robert Kimberly drew up a marriage contract between their children then. Of course it was not known if the child Mistress Kimberly was to bear would be a son or a daughter, but it was decided between the two men that Robert's first daughter, whenever she was born, would be your wife. You will see that the girl's name is in your father's hand, and not in the hand of the rest of the document. Two years after the daughter was born, young Mistress Kimberly died in childbirth with a son. Charlotte Kimberly became her father's heiress, for although he eventually remarried, there were no other children of his body. Your parents and sister were drowned shortly afterward, and the entire matter was forgotten until just before your grandfather's death. It was he who reminded me of the marriage contract, and asked that I see you fulfill your obligation. You can really have no strong or reasonable objection, Valerian, as your heart is not engaged elsewhere."

"No," he reluctantly admitted. Then he said, "You mentioned that we might be distantly related, Grandmama. How?"

"As I remember the tale," the dowager duchess began, "and I should have to consult the family Bible, dear boy, to be entirely accurate, but this is what I recall. The first Duke of Farminster was created so by King Charles upon his restoration. Your ancestor had grown up with the king, and gone into exile with him. They were bound by their friendship, loyalty, and by the curious coincidence of having the same birth date. The Earl of Farminster, who became the first duke, had a younger brother who remained behind in England to protect the estates, and two younger sisters. These young women were married. The eldest to a Kimberly, and the younger to a Meredith. Both men were royalists who remained in England working for the king's restoration. When it came, your ancestor saw that his brothers-in-law were rewarded. The island of St. Timothy was given to them by the king and they emigrated to become sugar planters. The last Kimberly, Robert, ahhh, now I remember, married the last Meredith, Emily. It is their daughter, the heiress, who will be your wife."

"But Emily Kimberly is dead, and Robert remarried," the duke said. "What else do you know, Grandmama?"

"Nought, dear boy. The rest you shall learn yourself when you reach St. Timothy."

"The girl might be dead," the duke suggested hopefully.

"We would have been notified," the dowager countered.

"Not necessarily," the duke replied. "After all, this alliance was almost forgotten but that Grandfather remembered it before he died."

"That is true," his grandmother agreed. "The unimportant, albeit wealthy, daughter of a colonial planter might be forgotten by a duke, but that same girl's family would hardly forget that their child was promised to that same duke, and one day to be a duchess. No, Valerian, you cannot escape your fate. You will sail on the *Royal George* from Plymouth in three weeks' time for St. Timothy. You are expected."

"How did my father meet Robert Kimberly?" the duke wondered. "Certainly the families did not keep up their contact over the years."

"To a certain degree they did," the dowager said, surprising him. "But Robert Kimberly came to Oxford, which is where he met your father first. They shared quarters for two years before Kimberly returned to his island home to marry his first wife, Caroline Meredith. There were no offspring from that marriage, and after her death, Robert wed the younger Meredith daughter, Emily, who bore him his daughter, and died with their son. The third wife I know nothing about." The dowager patted her grandson's arm comfortingly. "Now, cease your fretting, dear boy. You do not have to remain on St. Timothy any longer than it takes to marry the girl, assure her family she will have a wonderful life as your duchess, and return to England to settle down. You have run rampant long enough, Valerian. It is time for you to do your duty."

"She will not hold a candle to you," he told his grandmother, a twinkle in his eye, as he smiled down upon her.

"Flatterer!" the dowager responded, but she smiled back at him. Mary Rose Hawkesworth had been considered a great beauty in her youth, and she still was with eyes the same dark blue as her grandson's, a rose and cream complexion, her fair hair now silvery white. "I shall expect my first great-grandson within the year," she told him, and the duke laughed aloud.

"I shall do my best, Grandmama," he promised her, "but she had best be a pretty chit."

"All little pussies are alike in the dark when you stroke them nicely, Valerian," the dowager said wickedly. Then she laughed at the surprised look upon her grandson's face.

Part I

ST. TIMOTHY
PLANTATION, 1760

Chapter

❦ **1** ❦

"**I** have only just heard of your husband's death, Mistress Kimberly. May I tender my condolences to you and your family?"

"You may, Captain Young," Oralia Kimberly said quietly. "Tell me, what brings you to St. Timothy? I have not seen you since Robert and I took our last voyage to Jamaica, two, three years ago."

"Three years," he reminded her, and then remembering why he was there, he handed her the letter. "I was entrusted with this letter in Plymouth, Mistress Kimberly. It is for your late husband. It has a mighty fancy crest on it, if I might be so bold to say."

"Why, so it does, Captain Young," Oralia Kimberly replied, a small smile touching her lips. Barnabas Young was a notorious gossip, but then how else could one learn what was going on in the outside world if it were not for people like him? "I do not recognize the hand," she said. "I believe I shall save it for Aurora to open, as she is her father's heiress."

"I hope he left Missy Calandra and Master George a bit too," the captain said, fishing none too delicately.

"Oh, indeed he did," the widow assured him. "Robert was most generous to my children even if they weren't his own. Why, Calandra is to have five thousand a year, not to mention an outright bequest of a thousand pounds, Captain Young. And, of course, George has done even better, being the young man in the family." There! Now the old seafaring Yankee gossip would have something to talk about as his ship made its way among the islands. *And* her children would be known as good marriage prospects. She and Robert had been so content with their family that they hadn't considered the future. Now, of course, widowed, the children without a fatherly protector, Oralia Kimberly had to think of her two daughters and her son. Of course Aurora wasn't really her child, but she had raised the little girl since she was barely three and thought of her as her own. She was certainly the only mother Aurora could remember. "Will you stay for dinner, and for the night?" she politely asked the captain.

"Thank ye kindly, Mistress Kimberly," he replied, "but 'tis not even noon yet. I have several other stops to make before I take on my cargo in Jamaica and head for England. I hope to get several voyages in before your stormy season hits. I've delivered your letter, and now I'll be heading off again." He tipped his hat to her and made a small bow. "Good day to ye, then, Mistress Kimberly."

"Good day, Captain Young, and thank you," she replied. Oralia Kimberly watched as the seaman made his way down the hill road back to the harbor of St. Timothy. She could see his great-masted ship riding at anchor in the bay. She looked again at the letter he had delivered. It *was* an extremely fancy crest that decorated the missive. Turning the letter over, she inspected the same crest in the sealing wax, and then, breaking the seal, she unfolded the paper. Waiting for Aurora had merely been an excuse to avoid opening the note in Captain Young's presence. She would have been hard pressed to keep the contents a secret with the nosy sailor standing before her. Her brown eyes scanned the page, and then she gasped. *"Gracious! Oh, my!"* she exclaimed. Then she sat down and fanned herself with the parchment. "Oh, Robert, why did you not tell me of this?" she said aloud to her dearly departed spouse.

"What, Mama? Are you still scolding Papa? I do not believe he can hear you now." Her son George gently teased his parent as he entered the airy morning room, removing his broad-brimmed hat, for he had been out in the fields, and the day was already hot.

Oralia Kimberly handed her son the letter.

"Damnation!" George swore softly when he had read it. "Does Aurora know of this, Mama?"

His mother shook her head in the negative. "I remember Robert mentioning to me some years back that he had arranged a marriage for Aurora one day, but he never brought it up again. Quite frankly, it slipped my mind. Ohhh, George! Just think! Aurora is to be a duchess!"

Her son burst out laughing.

"*George!*" Oralia Kimberly glared at her son.

Stifling his chortles, he replied, "Well, Mama, you must admit it is an interesting concept. You must let me be here when you tell her the news that even as we speak her betrothed husband is on the high seas, prepared to sail into the welcoming anchorage of her innocent, girlish heart." Then he burst out laughing again, quite unable to restrain himself.

"George," his mother said, "you are quite impossible! Do you not understand the importance of this? Aurora is to be the Duchess of Farminster. This island is her dowry. What will become of the rest of us, especially of you."

George Spencer-Kimberly shrugged. "I doubt the duke will dispossess us simply because he gains possession of the island, Mama. I am certain that I will remain on as the plantation's overseer, and I have the generous bequest that Papa left me, not to mention a yearly income as well. And you will certainly remain. Our about-to-be relation would hardly send his pretty mother-in-law packing."

"Of course you are correct," Oralia responded. Then she brightened even more. "And Calandra can go to England with Aurora, be presented to society, and find a titled husband! Of course she cannot seek as high as Aurora's husband, but a not too wealthy earl would be delighted to have a girl with five thousand a year. I am, of course, furious with Robert, God rest him, for not telling me of this match, but all in all, it is very fortuitous for the entire family, isn't it, George?"

"Only if Aurora cooperates," her son replied.

"Why would she not *cooperate?*" his mother asked. "What girl in her right mind would turn down a duke?"

"Aurora would," the young man replied, and then sat himself next to his mother. "You and Papa spoiled both the girls, Mama. Cally is charming, but a vain and acquisitive little minx. As for Aurora, she is probably the most headstrong girl in the world. If it is not to her liking, then she will not do it. God help the man who tempts her to the altar, Mama. And she will, I suspect, marry only if it is her idea first. Aurora is not a girl to sit coyly by, waiting for any man."

"Oh, George, what are we to do?" his mother said, and her eyes filled with anxious tears. "This duke is coming all the way from England to marry your sister. It would be scandalous for her to refuse him under such circumstances, especially after Robert arranged it."

"Does his letter say upon which vessel he will take his passage?"

"The *Royal George*," Oralia answered him. "It was to sail from Plymouth on the tenth of February."

"It's an elegant, sleek modern ship," George noted. "It should be arriving no later than March ninth, provided they do not run into any heavy weather, but coming south at this time of year, it should be smooth sailing for the bulk of the voyage, Mama. It carries little cargo, for it is a passenger vessel. It will probably go on to Barbados, St. Kitts, and Tobago after it stops here for our duke."

"And how long will this duke stay with us?" Oralia wondered, then answered her own question. "He will probably want to return fairly quickly to England. That means we won't have long to prepare for the wedding, or to pack Aurora's trousseau, or Cally's possessions. Oh! This is simply impossible!"

George grinned. "When do you intend telling Aurora, Mama?"

Oralia's pretty face grew determined. "Immediately, George! Your sister must be told right away so that she has time to get used to this change in her life. Aurora will be sensible. I know she will be sensible. You are right that she is headstrong, George, but she is an intelligent girl, and logical to a fault. This news will certainly come as a shock, I have no doubt, but when all is said and done, Aurora will see the wisdom in her father's decision. She will not want to disappoint him, I know, even if Robert is no longer here with us."

"I can but hope and pray that you are right, Mama," he replied, but George was not certain at all. Aurora was intelligent, and that, in his opinion, was the problem. A simple, biddable girl would cry a bit upon learning she was to marry a stranger and leave her family. Then she would rally and do her duty. Even Calandra, his younger sister, while hardly simple, would see the advantages to the kind of marriage Aurora was to have. Cally would pounce upon a duke with delight. He did not think Aurora would. No. She would consider the situation, and then decide what was best for her, for the family. Yet, was not this best for her? George considered. He left his mother and hurried off to wash, for it was almost time for the midday meal. In the upstairs hall he ran into Calandra.

"Sally tells me Captain Young was here this morning," she said to him. "Was he?"

George nodded. "He brought a letter, Cally."

"From where? England? Who was it from? What did it say?" she demanded of him. Calandra Spencer-Kimberly was a very beautiful girl, and used to getting her own way in most things.

"I have absolutely no idea," her brother answered her. "I believe Mama intends to tell us later, when we are all together."

"It must be important, George," Cally decided.

"Let me go and wash," he said. "It's damnably hot out in those fields, and you had best get dressed, or you will miss whatever news Mama has for us, little sister. Where is Aurora?"

"She took Martha and went swimming," came the reply. "I think it's shocking that she still swims in the sea, George, and naked too. Only little children should swim naked, for they know no better. I hate swimming! I always felt so sticky after swimming in the sea."

"You dabbled in the sea," he teased her. "You never liked it like Aurora and I like it, Cally. Well, if Martha's with her, they'll be back in plenty of time for the meal, and Mama's news."

The siblings parted, each to their own room, meeting later in the dining room of the house, where their mother and stepsister already awaited them.

"How can you look so cool on such a hot day?" Calandra grumbled, her hazel eyes taking in Aurora's appearance.

Aurora Kimberly laughed. "Because I've spent the morning shamelessly frolicking in the sea, Cally. It's wonderful, and you should join me instead of lying in bed until almost noon each day."

"My skin is too delicate to expose to the hot sun," Calandra replied. "You know I burn like a lobster, Aurora."

"You don't have to stay out as long as I do," her stepsister replied. "Just a quick swim to cool off, and then back into your clothes. You could swim in the afternoon, when the sun isn't as strong, or in the very early morning just before dawn."

Now it was Calandra who laughed. "You know I'm no fish like you," she teased. "Besides, I'd be mortified if anyone saw me. One day some wicked pirate is going to catch a glimpse of you in the sea and carry you off, Aurora. You had best be more careful."

"No pirate ship could get into my cove," Aurora said smugly, "and there is no one else about to see me, Cally, isn't that right, George? George knows my little cove, don't you?"

"It's safe enough," her stepbrother agreed.

They sat down at the beautiful mahogany dining table, Oralia at its head, her son to her right, and her daughters on her left. A servant ladled clear turtle soup into their dishes. Beyond the table the French doors were opened, the light muslin hangings blowing in the trade winds. The sea, calm, and blue-green, spread itself before them.

Calandra gobbled her soup, then said eagerly, "What was in the letter you received from England today, Mama? Who wrote to you?"

Oralia was not surprised by her daughter's question. Calandra's servant, Sally, had undoubtedly seen Captain Young arrive. "The letter was not addressed to me, but to your father," she told her daughter, keeping her voice calm and well modulated. "It seems that Robert made an arrangement with an old friend in England many years ago that his son and Aurora marry one day. The young man is on his way from England now, and will arrive on the *Royal George* in a few weeks' time."

"He'd best not get off the boat," Aurora said fiercely.

"Aurora, this is no younger son coming to wed you because you are an heiress and he needs a living. This young man is Valerian

Hawkesworth, the Duke of Farminster. He is wealthy, and just the sort of man the heiress to a sugar plantation should marry."

"My God, Aurora!" Calandra's eyes were wide, and not just a bit envious. "You are going to be a duchess!"

"No, I'm not, Cally," came the stubborn reply.

"Aurora, I realize this is a shock to you," her stepmother said. "It was very foolish of your father not tell us of this arrangement at all, particularly before he died so suddenly."

"Papa's horse threw him, Mama," Aurora reminded Oralia. "He could have hardly anticipated that."

"No," Oralia responded, "he could not have anticipated it, but the marriage contract says you are to marry when you are seventeen. You will be seventeen on the sixth of April. Robert might have said *something*. I do not know when he expected to tell you, my dear, but he is gone, and the duke is on his way to St. Timothy expecting to marry you. Now you know, and we will not discuss it again for a few days so that you may get used to the idea of of it all." She smiled at her children, and then said, "Serve the chicken now, Hermes."

"I am not going to get used to it, Mama!" Aurora protested. "I have absolutely no intention of marrying an English duke I never met, and probably won't like anyhow. And I shall have to live in England all the time, and probably go to court to meet that German king. I do not like Germans, Mama. Do you remember that German overseer we once had? He was a horrible man!"

"One cannot judge an entire nation by one man, Aurora. I thought I had taught you better than that. Besides, the king is an old man and will probably not live much longer. His son, Prince George, is said to be kind and lovely. A real Englishman. It will be a young and delightful court that you join, my dear."

"Not I," Aurora said ominously.

"We will discuss it in a few days," Oralia said.

"We will discuss it now, Mama," came the reply. "I am not going to marry a stranger and go to live a life that I should hate in a wet, cold country I have never even seen."

"I would," said Calandra. "To marry a duke, and go to court, I would marry the devil himself! You really are a fool, Aurora. What an opportunity your father has given you, and you are not one bit grateful. If Papa had betrothed me to a duke, I'd wed him in a trice!"

"A stranger, Cally? You would marry some stranger you had never set eyes upon? I think it is you who are the fool!" Aurora said.

"Marriages are always arranged," Calandra answered her stepsister. "So you have never set eyes upon this man. He cannot, surely, be the beast from some fairy tale! And, remember, he has never laid eyes on you either. I'm certain he is wondering during his long days at sea if you are the sort of girl he *really* wants for a duchess, but he will do his duty, for his father made this match."

"He will gain a sugar plantation and this island for his troubles," Aurora noted.

"And you will gain a duchess's coronet!" Calandra countered.

"I don't want it," Aurora said irritably.

"I wish I had your opportunity, you silly creature," Calandra snapped at her stepsister. "You really are quite spoiled!"

"Do you want this duke, Cally?" Aurora asked the other girl. "Then have him! You marry this Valerian Hawkesworth!"

"Aurora, that is quite impossible," her stepmother said.

"*Why?*" Aurora demanded. She brushed a tendril of hair from her face where it had fallen. "Have you seen this marriage contract that Papa arranged? What exactly does it say, Mama?"

"Say? Why, I have no idea," Oralia replied.

"George! Go to Papa's library and look in the strongbox he kept by his desk. I will wager a year's crop you will find this marriage contract in that box. Bring it here at once," Aurora commanded her stepbrother. Then she looked directly at her stepmother in a way that discomfited the poor woman. "We will see if there is not some way I cannot wheedle my way out of this situation. Why, the nerve of this duke! He has ignored us all these years, and now, with not so much as a by-your-leave, madam, he announces he is coming to marry me!"

Calandra giggled. "I will wager a year's crop, if it were mine to wager, that your duke would be horrified to learn what manner of girl you are, Aurora. Men, I am told, do not like forward and fierce women such as yourself. You will have to improve your manners."

"Hah!" her stepsister responded. "The man who marries me will have to accept me for myself. I will not be molded and posed like some clay figurine. Besides, Cally, how would you know what a man wants in a woman. You haven't been off St. Timothy since you arrived from Jamaica, when my father and your mother married. You don't know any more about men than I do!"

"We're totally backward and gauche, the pair of us," Calandra lamented. "I don't know why Papa insisted on making us wait until we were seventeen to have a season in England. Why, he wouldn't even let us go to Jamaica for a visit. We will seem like savages when we are finally allowed out into polite society." She pushed her plate away fretfully. "I find I am no longer hungry, Mama."

George reappeared, clutching a parchment. "You were right," he said, handing it to Aurora and sitting back down. "It was in Papa's strongbox just as you said it would be. Hasn't anyone looked through that box since Papa's death? It is chock-full of papers."

Aurora didn't answer him, instead, opened the missive and read it over carefully. Then, suddenly, a very wide smile brightened her face, and she chuckled wickedly. "Here it is! The answer to my problem, Mama. This contract betroths *Charlotte* Kimberly to Valerian Hawkesworth. Now, while it is true I was christened Charlotte Aurora, Mama, Calandra was christened Charlotte Calandra. Remember that when you married Papa and came with George and Cally to St. Timothy, it was decided that rather than have two Charlottes, each of us would use our second name to avoid jealousy, or the appearance of favoritism toward either of us. This marriage contract does not say *Charlotte Aurora Kimberly*. It plainly says only *Charlotte Kimberly*. So, if Cally wants to marry this duke, she can. He certainly won't know the difference, having never laid eyes on me in his life."

"No! No! Aurora! We couldn't do such a thing," Oralia protested.

"Why not?" came the quick response.

"Well, for one thing," her stepmother said with what she hoped was perfect logic, "the duke is expecting to marry the heiress to

St. Timothy, and not a girl with a thousand a year, a thousand pounds in gold, and some jewelry. Calandra's dowry simply wouldn't be good enough for the Duke of Farminster."

"Mama," Aurora countered with equal reason, "if this duke is coming from England to marry Charlotte Kimberly, then it would appear he is a man of principle. If he cannot marry Charlotte Kimberly, I do not believe he will return quietly to England without protest. I am not the attraction for him. How could I be? He knows me not. It is the island and the plantation that hold an appeal for this man, and he will not be satisfied to go home without them. So he must have a Charlotte Kimberly to wife. Cally wants a duke for a husband. I do not know what I want, but I do know I will not be driven to the altar. Cally's inheritance from Papa shall be mine, and I would have one other thing. I want the Meredith plantation house that belonged to my mother's family. Cally will then be this duke's Charlotte Kimberly, and this island and the plantation will be turned over to her husband upon their marriage. Everyone will be happy. The duke will have the island, and Cally will have the duke. It is a perfect answer to our problems."

"You are so very clever, Aurora," her stepmother admitted, "but what if the duke learns of your deception? If indeed I would even allow such a thing. Could it not be considered fraud? No! No! I will not permit such dupery. It is dishonest!"

"Then you face the possibility of having the duke demand we turn over St. Timothy's plantation to him anyhow, and we shall all be dispossessed, homeless, abandoned by all. After all, he is keeping his part of the bargain by coming to marry Charlotte Kimberly. If the bride will not cooperate, do you really expect him to bow, and graciously withdraw, leaving us to our home? Nonsense, Mama! He will be mortally offended. Why, George may even have to fight a duel to death to assuage this duke's honor. Then the duke will demand reparation for his embarrassment and broken heart. Well, it shall not be my fault. I have offered you a reasonable solution to our problem. Don't you want Cally to be a duchess? She'll be a perfect one with her classic features, her marble-white skin, and raven's-wing hair."

Oralia Kimberly bit her lower lip in vexation.

George Spencer-Kimberly shook his head in admiration at his stepsister's devilish cleverness. Then he looked toward Calandra. She was absolutely holding her breath in anticipation.

"Say yes, Mama!" she half whispered, her tone almost desperate.

But Oralia Kimberly held firm. "No," she said. "I cannot permit such a thing. Be reasonable, Aurora. Your father planned this marriage before your birth. If he were alive, we should not be having this conversation at all. I will discuss it no further." She arose from the dining table and hurried from the room.

"I want to be a duchess," Calandra whined.

"You will be," Aurora assured her stepsister.

"You heard what Mama said," George reminded them.

"Mama will change her mind, I promise you," Aurora said with a mischievous grin. "She will have little choice when the duke's ship sails into the harbor and I am still refusing to marry him. When that moment comes, her resoluteness will collapse entirely, for she will be considering what I have said over these next few weeks, George. No matter how honest and good she is, she cannot help but consider how marvelous Cally will look in a duchess's jewels; or of how much she will enjoy visiting Jamaica, and boasting of *her* daughter, the Duchess of Farminster." Aurora laughed, and then she stood up from the table. "We really must begin considering your wedding gown, Cally."

Calandra pushed her chair back. "Do you really think we can persuade Mama, Aurora?" She stood.

"You just leave it to me, little sister" was the answer.

"Do not call me little sister! We are both to be seventeen," Cally protested.

"But my birthday is April sixth, and yours is June first. That makes me the elder by two months," Aurora teased her stepsister.

"Oh, you!" Calandra giggled. Then she said, "What do you think this duke is like, Aurora?"

"He is undoubtedly most arrogant, and overweening proud" came the reply. "Not once in all my life has he communicated with me, nor, do I believe, did he ever write to Papa."

"Did you ever consider," George said quietly, "that perhaps he did not know he was to be married either? There are letters in Papa's strongbox from a James Hawkesworth. I told you that I don't believe anyone has looked through that box since Papa died. Certainly Mama didn't. God only knows what else is there. Shall we go and look?"

"Yes! Yes!" his sisters chorused in unison, and the trio made their way from the dining room to the late Robert Kimberly's beautiful paneled study.

Settling themselves on the floor, they dragged the box into their midst. Opening it, George Spencer-Kimberly pulled forth a packet of letters tied with hemp twine. Undoing the binding, he opened the first of the letters which was on the bottom, and perused it.

"This is the first letter from James Hawkesworth. He seems to be the Third Duke of Farminster. He writes to tell Papa that his son, Charles, has been drowned with his wife and daughter in a boating accident. His grandson, Valerian, he says, was not with them, and although the boy is devastated by the loss, he will recover. He says he is glad that his son made this match between their families, and that he will make certain that the obligation is honored when little Charlotte is grown. He asks after her."

"How touching," Aurora said dryly.

"I think he sounds like a nice old man," Cally ventured to add.

"So," her elder sister said, "we know that Valerian Hawkesworth's parents and sisters are dead, and that he was raised by his grandfather."

"And grandmother," George corrected her. "James Hawkesworth mentions his wife. He wrote to Papa twice a year. In June, and in December. From the tone of his letters, Papa obviously wrote him back, passing on news of the family, and how you were growing up, Aurora."

"Does this old duke ever refer to me as Aurora?" she asked.

"I will have to read through all the letters," George replied, "but from what I can see, it would appear not."

"What does he say about the grandson?" Aurora's aquamarine-blue eyes were thoughtful, and her brow just slightly furrowed.

"Not a great deal. Wait, here is something! It's in the last letter, which was written June last. There is no December letter."

"Of course not. The old man obviously died," Aurora noted. "Well, come, George, and tell us what the June letter says."

"It is not very long. You know, it would appear that the old duke wrote Papa in his own hand, and did not use a secretary. The writing is quite spidery."

My dear Robert,

I have not been well these last months. It would seem that passing one's seventieth birthday takes a toll on the health. From my calculations, it would appear that little Charlotte has celebrated her sixteenth birthday. The contract between our two families calls for the marriage of your daughter and my grandson to be celebrated next year after Charlotte's seventeenth birthday. Valerian has grown into as fine a man as one could wish. I will tell him soon of the arrangement made between his father and you all those years ago. He will come for your daughter next spring, but we shall have to correspond before that, of course. My good wife sends greetings to you and your family. I remain, as ever, James Hawkesworth, Third Duke of Farminster.

George lay the letter aside and said, "You see, Aurora, your duke knew nothing about this marriage between you. He was as much in the dark as you were."

"There is no further correspondence?"

"Only the letter Mama received this morning," George replied.

"Where is it?" Aurora demanded to know.

Calandra jumped up, crying, "Here! On Papa's desk! Mama has lain it there by force of habit." Her hazel eyes scanned the missive quickly. Then she read:

"To Robert Kimberly.

It is with grieving heart that I write to tell you of my husband's passing in early November. His heir, our grandson, Valerian, has assumed his duties as the Fourth Duke of Farminster. I see from James's correspondence with you that the time approaches for the marriage between your daughter, Charlotte, and Valerian. My grand-son will sail February the tenth from Plymouth aboard the Royal George. *We look forward to receiving Charlotte into the family, and I will do my best to see she is made comfortable. And please reassure Charlotte that I will personally advise her, and train her in her new duties as Duchess of Farminster. Please know that you and your family will always be welcome at Hawkes Hill Hall. I remain, Mary Rose Hawkesworth, Dowager Duchess of Farminster.*

"Oh, my!" Calandra sighed. "Doesn't it all sound grand? I wonder what a duchess's duties are, Aurora. Do you think I can do them?"

"Just more manners, I suspect," Aurora reassured her stepsister, "and you are wonderously clever at learning the civilities, decorums, and etiquette of society, Cally. I cannot be bothered with such folderol."

George had been going through the previous duke's correspondence as his sisters spoke. Now he said, "There is no mention of you being called Aurora, my clever little sister. The bride is mentioned only as Charlotte in all the correspondence."

"But what if Papa referred to her in *his* letters as Aurora?" Calandra suggested. "What will we do then?"

"Since this duke wasn't aware of the marriage plans his family made," Aurora said slowly, "it is unlikely he has ever seen the letters Papa wrote to his grandfather. I question if the old duke even kept the correspondence between them. His lady wife does not seem overly familiar with the situation, I divine."

"Papa kept the letters he received," Calandra pointed out.

"Yes," Aurora agreed, "but it was more in Papa's interest to keep them in the event the Hawkesworth family attempted to cry off, or conveniently forget the betrothal and marry off their heir to a wealthier heiress. Papa's letters from the duke would have given him grounds for an action in the courts should he have felt the Kimberly honor besmirched. You know how proud Papa was of the family."

"We can find no evidence the duke knows he was betrothed to Charlotte Aurora," George said. "I believe it is worth taking the chance of marrying him to Cally. How can he possibly find out that a switch has been made?"

"And if he does," Aurora said, "it is to be hoped that by that time he will harbor some tender feeling for Cally, and that she will have borne him an heir. Besides, he will have St. Timothy Plantation. What will he have lost by our little ruse?" She smiled at her stepbrother. "I am so glad you agree with me, George."

"I do not know if I agree with you at all," the young man answered her, "but I do know that once you have set your mind to something, Aurora, you will not change it easily, if at all. I think you are being foolish, because I believe you to be frightened of this sudden shift in your life. Papa wanted you to have this marriage, but if you will not have it, then I can do nothing more than attempt to see the family is not endangered by your foolish action. The duke shall have a Charlotte Kimberly to wed even if it is not the correct Charlotte Kimberly."

"Papa would be very proud of you, George," Aurora told him. "He always said he wished he were your natural father instead of just your stepfather. He loved you and Cally every bit as much as he loved me. That is why he legally adopted you and gave you his name as well as that of your own dead father. I wish he had left you St. Timothy instead of leaving it to me. Then nothing would have ever changed."

George reached out and took Aurora's hand in his. "I might bear Papa's name, little sister, but I am not of his blood. It was blood that made his decision for him. As you have already said, he was proud of his family. I am well provided for, God knows, and he has requested in his will that the duke continue my tenure as manager and overseer of St. Timothy. I am good at it, Aurora! There is no reason the duke will not honor Papa's request, and as long as the plantation remains prosperous, he will have no cause for complaint, will he?"

Calandra settled herself back down on the floor with her two siblings, resting her head on her brother's shoulder. The trio had been together for almost their entire lifetime, and loved one another dearly. If Oralia and Robert Kimberly had worried that their children would not get on, it was a notion dismissed in the first few minutes of their meeting, when Aurora had struggled from her nanny's arms and run down the dock to welcome her new stepmother and siblings to St. Timothy. It seemed to those watching that the child was greeting her natural mother, brother, and sister, who had been away but a time. There had never been any jealousy between any of them.

"Then we are agreed," Aurora said. "Cally will marry the duke, bringing with her the plantation as a dowry. I will have Cally's portion from Papa, and my mother's family home. And George will have what Papa left him, and remain as manager."

"You are absolutely certain this is what you want?" George questioned her. "Once Cally has been introduced to the duke as his bride, there can be no going back, Aurora. You do understand that?"

She nodded. "I want to marry a man who loves me, George, not a man who is obligated to marry me. I know there are some who would think me a fool for it, but I do not care. I will go to England with Cally and the duke and see if I can find a gentleman who will love me. If I do not, then I shall return to St. Timothy to my own home."

"Very well, then," George Spencer-Kimberly said. "Then it is indeed agreed between us that this is the course of action we shall take. I hope that the duke never finds out our little ruse."

"What of Mama?" Cally said. "She says she will not cooperate."

"Aurora is right," George replied. "When the duke's vessel sails into the harbor, Mama will have no choice but to go along with us. If she does not, she risks everything. I do not like making her unhappy, but if Aurora will not have her duke, then this is the best direction for us to take if we are to preserve the family."

The brother and his two sisters joined hands.

"Together," said George.

"Forever," said Cally.

"As one!" Aurora responded, finishing the pledge of allegiance they had made up as children and repeated whenever they did something together that they considered important.

"Then it is settled," Cally said, her eyes sparkling.

"Yes," Aurora agreed.

"And you shall be the duke's duchess," George chuckled. "What a treat London society has in store for it."

"I shall be a wonderful duchess," Cally told him. "I shall have all the beautiful gowns I want! And jewelry! And I shall dance till dawn every night with all the handsome gentlemen!"

"First, however," her brother reminded her, "you will have to produce an heir for the duke. That will be your primary duty. It is your insurance should Valerian Hawkesworth ever find out you are not who you should be, little sister."

"Fiddlesticks, George! It will make no difference if he finds out one day. He will have St. Timothy anyway. There is plenty of time for babies, and being stuck in some country mansion just as isolated as our island home is not my idea of being a grand duchess. Any woman can have babies! I want to go to London and see the king! Do not distress yourselves. I shall make my duke fall madly in love with me. Then he will allow me to do whatever I want, for he will desire to please me at all times else I withdraw my love from him." She giggled. "Ohhh, I cannot wait to be a duchess!"

"What a heartless little hussy you will be." Aurora laughed. "You had best not let Mama hear you speaking this way. It will give her a terrible attack of the vapors, I fear."

"I love Mama," Calandra admitted, "but it will be so nice not to have her telling me what to do all the time."

"You will have the old dowager telling you what to do instead," her brother teased her.

"Another reason for staying in London," Calandra countered.

And the three of them laughed, while outside the study, a sudden afternoon squall blew in from the sea to pepper the windows with warm rain.

Chapter

2

The Duke of Farminster stood at the rail of the *Royal George* as it made its way around the island of St. Timothy. The only bay suitable for landing was on the far side of the island, away from the shipping lanes. In the last few days he had been treated to all manner of topography as they sailed among the islands of the western Indies. Many of the islands were mountainous, some were flat, but this island seemed to have a broad plain all about it, with a spine of rolling hills in the center running the length of the island. The cane fields were lush and green, and he was not just a little impressed.

"They're harvesting. It's the season," the captain said, coming to stand by his side. "The island is about eighty square miles in size, about half of Barbados, and smaller than Grenada. Do you know anything about it, your grace?"

"Precious little," Valerian Hawkesworth replied. "I know the two families who were given the grant by King Charles were related to mine by marriage. My bride, and her father, are the last of them."

"The families kept in touch with England, then. Many of them don't, y'know. They go native," the captain noted disapprovingly.

"No, our branches kept in touch. My father and Mr. Kimberly were at Oxford together, which is how the match came about between myself and Miss Kimberly. Is there a town on the island, Captain Conway?"

The seaman shook his head. "Nay, your grace. St. Timothy was Kimberly and Meredith property. They grow sugar cane, and nothing else is done with the land. Besides, who would live here, and what sort of business could a man employ his time with on an island like this? Other than the family, and a few bond servants, there are only blacks."

The duke nodded in response and gazed out over the blue-green sea. The island was beautiful, but was it profitable? Was this Kimberly girl really a good match? His grandmother has assumed that the Kimberlys were rich, but were they? The island's whole subsistence depended upon a good sugar crop. He would, he decided, want to go over the books, and speak with Mr. Kimberly as soon as possible. If the plantation did not make an excellent profit, they must consider the possibility of a cash dower. The ship entered the bay. He could see the warehouses and docks along the shore.

"Do they ship their sugar to England from here?" he asked Captain Conway.

"They ship to Barbados, and from there to England. The cargo ships can't be bothered with a small island like this one, and don't call. It's the same all over the Indies, but St. Timothy is in an excellent location, your grace. It can ship cheaper than the plantations in Jamaica because the trade winds blow more convenient here than there."

"I can see I have a great deal to learn," the duke replied.

"Do you intend remaining here, then, your grace?" That would certainly be odd, the captain thought, unless, of course, this nobleman had murdered someone and needed to be out of England for a time.

"No, but if this plantation is to come to me through my bride, sir, it would be advisable for me to know about how it is run. I would not like to lose Miss Kimberly's dowry through ignorance or carelessness. I do not run my stud farms like that, and I will certainly not allow this plantation to be run that way."

Interesting, the captain thought. A milord who actually involved himself in the making of money. "You will have no difficulty then, your grace," Captain Conway said. "St. Timothy is run by Mr. Kimberly himself, aided by his stepson, Mr. George Spencer-Kimberly, a fine young man, I can tell you." He bowed to the duke. "You will excuse me, your grace. I must go and see to our landing."

The duke bowed in return, and watched the captain hurry off. Miss Kimberly had a stepbrother who helped run the plantation. Well, if he did indeed prove to be a fine young man, and he was interested in remaining on St. Timothy, there would be nothing to worry about when his father-in-law went to his reward many years hence. I wonder, Valerian Hawkesworth thought to himself, what kind of an income Kimberly has settled on my bride in the years until she comes into her inheritance.

His eyes went to the large house upon the crest of a high hill overlooking the harbor. It was very white, and appeared to be open in front. It was a style of architecture with which he was unfamiliar. It didn't look like any house he had ever seen. He would be interested to see it close up. The low boom of a cannon startled him.

"Not to worry, yer grace," his cabin steward told him, coming to the duke's side. "It's just that little gun of ours letting yer in-laws know yer here. Not that yer young lady isn't watching us from her window right now, for I'll wager she is," he chuckled broadly.

"They're here!" Calandra shrieked excitedly. "Did you hear the arrival cannon? Look! Down in the harbor! The *Royal George* is sailing in right now! Oh, I think I am going to swoon! My duke is here! *He's here!*" She collapsed into a chair, fanning herself with her handkerchief. "I do not think I can bear the excitement!"

"I am not going to allow you three to bully me," Oralia Kimberly said, but there was no iron in her voice. "You cannot do this! It is dishonest, and it is wrong! *George!*" She appealed to her son.

"I am sorry, Mama, but we have been over and over this for the last month. Cally will marry the duke. It is the only way. If you attempt to tell the duke the truth, I shall say Papa's death unhinged you and you do not know your own stepdaughter, or daughter, any longer. Then we will lock you away until the duke and Cally are wed and departed for England. Now, I must go down to the docks to greet our guest." He turned on his heel and left her.

"You are cruel, George!" she cried after him, but Oralia knew it was no use. The three young people had decided a course of action between them, and they would follow it through. If she interfered, George was quite capable of following through on his threat; and even if the duke believed her, Aurora was equally capable of telling him that she didn't want to marry him. Then where would they all be?

Aurora caught Calandra's eye. Her look plainly said, *See! I told you we would win*. "Come, little sister," she said sweetly, "you cannot greet your duke looking like that. We'll have to hurry. Will you excuse us, Mama?"

Oralia waved them away. "Yes, yes," she said. She needed time to compose herself, for while this deception might not distress her children, she was quite upset by their actions. If only Robert had not died, she thought despairingly for the thousandth time in the last four weeks. But Robert was dead. She had no choice but to follow her children's lead. Perhaps they were right. What real harm was there in what they were doing? Would it not be wickeder to force Aurora into a marriage she didn't want? Especially when Calandra was so willing to take her place? Her daughter a duchess! Oralia bit her lip in vexation. No! They were wrong! But there was no help for it. What would Robert think of all of this? She shuddered. She knew what Robert would think, but, "Damnation!" the word slipped out, Robert wasn't here, and it had always been next to impossible for her to control the three children. Robert had been the one to do that, and now he was gone from her side, leaving her to cope with an impossible situation. I will not cry, Oralia thought desperately. *Calandra a duchess!*

Upstairs the two girls and their servants were all hurrying to get ready for the Duke of Farminster's arrival. Calandra bathed in her tub, behind a painted screen. The air was heavy with her favorite scent, a mixture of tuberose and gardenia. Sally, her personal maid, was, under Aurora's direction, laying out her young mistress's clothing. Finally satisfied with her selection, Aurora withdrew to her own bedroom to change her clothing.

"Yer a fool, and yer papa would be furious if he knew what you was doing," her servant, Martha, said. "There is still time to change yer mind, Mistress Aurora. A man is a man, and while some are better than the others, in the end they're all alike, I say."

"Martha, do not scold me over this," Aurora replied. "I really don't want to marry anyone at this time. Even if this duke were willing to wait a year or two, what if I don't like him? No, this is a better solution all around, for me, for Cally, for all of us."

"And what if you do like him?" Martha demanded.

"I hope I shall like him as a brother-in-law, as a friend, but now that he is to be my sister's husband, there is no chance of anything else, Martha. Certainly you understand that."

The servant pursed her lips in mute disapproval. She had come to St. Timothy as a bondswoman shortly after Aurora's birth. Because she was not a criminal, and because she was mannerly, Emily Kimberly had purchased her to care for her newborn daughter. Martha's offense in the eyes of English law was that she was poor. When her parents had died she had been evicted from the family cottage by their landlord. It had been the local vicar who had suggested she indenture herself for a period of seven years, and give herself a chance at a better life in the new world. Martha had followed his advice, putting herself into the hands of the vicar's brother, a decent man who saw his bondspeople placed with good families who would not abuse them. She had served as Aurora's nanny when she was a child, and remained on when her term of servitude ended, as a free woman and Aurora's personal servant.

"I've set out a fresh gown for you," she told her young mistress.

"Oh, don't be cross with me, Martha," Aurora said, hugging the older woman. "It really is all for the best, you know."

Martha shook the girl off. "Now, don't you go thinking you can wheedle me like you can Mistress Oralia and Master George, because you can't. If your papa were here, you would have to do what you was told, and no nonsense about it. Now, go wash. I put your basin and sponge in the dressing room. I've set out that pretty blue-gray cotton gown for you to wear like you said. Even with those lovely lace engageants, it's too plain. I don't know why you want to wear it to meet this duke."

"Because I don't want to outshine Calandra," Aurora said. "We want the duke's whole attention upon her today."

"You had best tell her not to giggle so much," Martha remarked sourly. "It makes her sound like a little fool, not that she ain't for going along with you in this foolishness."

Aurora hid her smile as she entered the dressing room. The window at its end looked out on the bay, and she could see the ship slowly making its way toward the docks. St. Timothy had a deep water mooring, and a ship could come close to the shore, unlike other islands, where the ships had to moor in the harbors itself and the passengers or goods ferried to and fro. Slipping out of her gown, she sponged herself off with the perfumed water Martha had set out. Then, drying herself, she put on the blue-gray cotton gown with its round scooped neckline, and graceful skirts that fell over her stiffened petticoats. The lace engageants, or ruffles, fell from her three-quarter sleeves.

"Come and fasten me up, Martha," she called. Then she gazed at her image in the long mirror. Her skin had a faint golden and rosy look to it that set off her aquamarine-blue eyes and brown-gold hair. While she protected herself from the sun most of the time, she was not fanatic about her skin like Calandra. Calandra was inordinately proud of her marble-white skin which she went to great lengths to protect, never going out in the sunlight without a broad-brimmed hat upon her head, her arms covered, lace mittens upon her hands. Aurora had to admit, however, that the fair skin, hazel eyes, and black hair Calandra possessed made quite a striking appearance.

"Come along, miss," Martha said, interrupting Aurora's thoughts, "come, and let me do your hair proper."

Proper to Martha meant an elegant little chignon in the back of Aurora's head, and two ringlets apiece upon either side of her face. Calandra favored the chignon, and a single long ringlet on the left side of her face, convinced that her left side was her better profile, and needed attention drawn to it. Calandra was sweet but vain, Aurora thought to herself. She's just what I imagine a duchess should be. Her eyes strayed again to the windows of her bedroom, and she wished that she had a spyglass to seek out George as he greeted the duke.

George Spencer-Kimberly watched as the *Royal George* was made fast to the docks, and when the gangway was lowered he hurried up it. "Captain Conway, it's good to see you again, sir! You've brought a passenger for us, I believe." His eyes strayed to the tall gentleman by the captain's side. Black hair. Black, no, dark blue eyes. Rugged features. Hard body. Not quite what he had been expecting in an English duke. He had thought a softer type, but this man did not look soft. For a brief moment George Spencer-Kimberly reconsidered the deception about to be played on this man and wondered if it was wise, but it was too late to turn back now.

"Aye, Mr. Kimberly," the captain said. "I've your passenger for you, sir. I would have thought your father would be here to greet him."

"My father passed away unexpectedly the day after Christmas," George replied. "A sudden burst of thunder, and a lightning bolt too near his horse. The beast reared up, throwing Papa, killing him instantly."

" 'Pon my soul!" the captain exclaimed. "What a tragedy!" Then, remembering his duty, he said, "Mr. Kimberly, may I present to you, his grace, the Duke of Farminster. Your grace. Mr. George Spencer-Kimberly."

The two men shook hands, the duke taking in the measure of the young man before him. Not quite his own height. Stocky. Pleasant-looking with blue eyes and brown hair. A firm handshake, the hands slightly callused. No idler this young fellow.

"Mr. Kimberly, allow me to present my condolences to you. Had I but known of your loss, I should have delayed my journey," Valerian Hawkesworth said politely.

"Since we knew nothing of you, your grace, prior to your grandmother's letter, we could not have stopped you," George replied, his eyes twinkling with ill-disguised humor. "Were you yourself aware of your, um, obligation to my sister?"

The duke laughed, appreciating the younger man's wit. "No, sir, I was as taken aback by the situation as I have no doubt your sister was. Am I right?"

George nodded with a grin. "There is a cart for your man and your baggage. I brought a horse for you, sir. We can talk as we ride up to the house together."

"Agreed!" the duke responded, then he turned and spoke to his valet, instructing him as if the man had not already heard George. When he had finished he said to Captain Conway, "You will stop to board my bride and myself when you return to England as we discussed?"

"Aye, sir," the captain replied. " 'Twill be in two and a half weeks. If there's any delay, I get a message to you."

The two men departed the vessel.

Unable to help himself, George said, "You don't intend remaining long on St. Timothy, do you? I think Mama will be quite distressed."

"The *Royal George* is the finest passenger ship traveling between England and these islands, Mr. Kimberly. I do not wish Charlotte's wedding voyage to be less than comfortable. If we do not return to England on its return trip, we shall have to wait several months for it to come again. I believe at that point we shall be facing your stormy season. I would not distress your mother, but I think it best my bride and I leave as soon as we can." The duke swung himself into the saddle, gathering the reins into his hand.

"I think," said George as he mounted his own horse, "that I should explain to you that my stepsister is not known as Charlotte. She is known by her second name, Calandra."

"Why?" Valerian Hawkesworth asked.

"When our mother married our stepfather, Cally and Mama's daughter were just under three years of age. Both had been christened with the same first name, Charlotte. Our parents decided that the girls would be known by their second names, Calandra and Aurora. That is why the marriage contract, at least our copy, gives the bride's name only as Charlotte," George finished, tensing just slightly as he waited for the duke's comment.

"Indeed," the duke said dryly. "So my bride is known as Calandra? 'Tis an elegant name. Is she an elegant girl, Mr. Kimberly?"

"My stepsister is certainly an attractive girl, and I suppose with the right gowns and hairstyles she might be elegant one day, but Cally is just an innocent island maiden. You will have to be the judge of that, your grace."

"You will call me Valerian, and I will call you George, sir," the duke answered him. "And what is your sister like?"

"A pretty chit," George said. "Aurora is a law unto herself though." He chuckled.

The horses moved up from the harbor along the dusty dirt road to the house on the hillside. Now the duke could see the building better. The open front was in reality a spacious veranda. The ground floor windows were long. All the windows belonging to the house had heavy wooden shutters on either side of them. To protect them in the fierce storms he had heard about from Captain Conway undoubtedly. On either side of the roadway the land was thick and lush with green growth such as he had never seen. Vines entwined with brightly colored flowers attracted his eyes. The trees were filled with scarlet, green, blue, and gold birds of a most exotic nature. The heat was pleasant, but he had never before known anything like it, and the winds that seemed to constantly blow were softer, sweeter, and had just a hint of dampness.

"Is your manager, and your overseer satisfactory?" the duke asked George. "How have you managed since your stepfather's death?"

"My father," George replied, "ran St. Timothy himself. He didn't approve of those men who allowed others to handle their affairs, leaving them free to pursue a life of pleasure. I was five and a half when we first came here from Jamaica. On my sixth birthday my father took me out with him when he made his rounds. I went with him every day after that. I am nineteen now, and have been handling the plantation's books ever since I ceased my formal education at the age of sixteen. My father meant for me to eventually run St. Timothy in its entirety. With his death, however, the ownership passed to Cally, and will pass to you upon your marriage to my stepsister. If you wish to bring your own man to take over the running of the plantation, I will give him my full cooperation, Valerian. You have my word on it."

"There is no need for a stranger to be introduced here, George," the duke responded. "I will never live here, for my life is in England, but I agree with your father in the matter of absentee ownership of an estate. I would like you to remain here, if it pleases you, to run the plantation as your father did. When I have gone over the books, we will decide upon a fair rate of remuneration for your services. After all, you will one day want to take a wife, and will need to support her. The plantation will one day become the property of one of the children Calandra and I produce. Perhaps a second son would favor it. We will both rest easy knowing St. Timothy is in good hands. Do you think this arrangement will be satisfactory to you?"

"Aye, Valerian!" George said enthusiastically. This was really working out quite well, he thought to himself, pleased, and Mama would be delighted to know she should not be discommoded in any way. "There is one thing you should know," George continued. "The old Meredith plantation house, which is located on the other side of the island. It came to Papa through his second wife, Emily Meredith. Papa left it to Aurora along with an income. There is no real land with it. Only the land upon which the house sits, but Papa thought she would want her own home should she marry one day. Her inheritance, and her income along with the house, make her a good choice for a respectable young man of good family. Mama is sending her to England with you and Cally."

A husband-hunting sister-in-law? Valerian Hawkesworth frowned. He did not need or want such an encumbrance on his honeymoon voyage home. "I shall speak to your mama about that," he said. "Of course Miss Spencer-Kimberly will be welcome at Hawkes Hill."

They rode up the driveway to the house, where two young men hurried up to take their mounts.

"Your servants are not black?" The duke was curious.

"Our house servants are bondsmen and bondswomen. Mama prefers it that way. Few leave us when their term of servitude is up. We have slaves peopling the fields and the sugar house. I have also trained several intelligent blacks as foremen, and clerks to work with me. They are most trustworthy men. We do not mistreat our people as so many others do. My father would have freed his slaves if he could have. Since he could not afford to do so, he did the next best thing. He treated them with humanity and kindness."

"We will speak of this later," the duke said, brushing the dust from his breeches and coat.

"Come into the house, Valerian," George said, leading the way.

The foyer was high-ceilinged and cool, the duke found. The woodwork was all white, as were the walls. It was very inviting. He followed George into a bright room with yellow and white striped wallpaper. The furniture was beautifully carved and fashioned mahogany, the chair and settee seats neatly caned. There were no draperies on the long windows, only tiers of mahogany shutters. The wide pine plank floors were covered with a large and beautiful blue and beige Oriental carpet, one of the finest he had ever seen. Three ladies awaited them. The elder, gowned in black silk and white lace, arose, smiling.

"Valerian, may I present my mother, Oralia Kimberly," George said politely. "Mama, the Duke of Farminster."

Oralia held out her hand to be kissed, and then, withdrawing it, said, "You are welcome to St. Timothy, your grace." The hand gestured. "My daughters."

His dark blue eyes quickly swept over the two girls. One wore a simple gown of blue-gray, and her look was almost bold. The other was gowned in white silk with pink painted rosebuds. She did not look at him, but rather blushed prettily as Oralia drew her up.

"This is your betrothed, your grace, my stepdaughter, Charlotte Calandra Kimberly," she said. "Greet the duke, my child," she gently pressed the girl. "He has come a long way for this moment."

Calandra looked up, her dainty pink mouth making a tiny "O" of pleasure as she gazed upon the man who was to be her husband.

He was divinely handsome! She held out her hand, saying in a soft voice, "How do you do, sir. I bid you welcome to St. Timothy's." And she curtsied.

He took her hand in his. It was an elegant little hand. Then, slowly raising it to his lips, his eyes locking onto hers, he kissed it. "Your brother tells me that you prefer being called by your second name, Miss Kimberly. Calandra, Duchess of Farminster, has a pleasing ring to it, do you not think?" And he smiled warmly at her.

I shall swoon, Cally thought, but then Aurora pinched her, and she drew in a breath, saying in what she hoped was a detached voice, "It does when you say it, your grace. Since I have learned of our betrothal, I have not dared to even think of it. It was all such a surprise."

"For me also," the duke replied, "but now that I stand in your exquisite presence, I am no longer surprised, simply overwhelmed by the beauty that is to be mine."

"Ohhh," Cally gasped, the giggle she had been about to utter destroyed by Aurora's relentless pinching fingers.

"And may I present my daughter, Aurora, your grace," Oralia said, taking advantage of Calandra's speechlessness to bring the other girl forward in front of the duke.

Aurora looked him straight in the eye, saying, "Sir, I echo my sister's welcome to St. Timothy."

He kissed her hand too, replying, "I thank you, Miss Spencer-Kimberly. I confess that had I been presented with the both of you and told to choose a bride, I should be hard pressed to do so."

"How fortunate it is, then, sir, that you do not have to choose. The choice had been made for you, is that not easier," Aurora said.

"You are quick-spoken, Miss Spencer-Kimberly," he replied.

"Indeed, sir, I am," she answered, not in the least quelled. Arrogant bastard, she thought. I was right to foist him off on Cally. She will be the perfect complacent little wife for him.

"Come and sit by me, your grace," Oralia said, gaining hold of the situation before it got out of hand. "Was your voyage a pleasant one? George, ask Hermes to bring us some refreshment. We make a lovely drink with our own rum and fruit juice," she told the duke, smiling. Oralia patted the place beside her on the settee as she seated herself. She then nodded to Calandra to seat herself on the other side of the duke.

The young girl was trembling with excitement. Aurora bent and murmured softly into her sister's ear, "Calm yourself, Cally. He is, after all, only a man. And try not to giggle."

Calandra nodded. She could not take her eyes from the duke's face. *He was so handsome!* She would wager a sugar crop that Aurora was sorry now for switching places with her. This man, of course, would want children, but she would deal with that eventually. She could have children. She concentrated on the positive. She was amazed that fortune had smiled on her in this manner. And for the first time in their lives, she felt genuinely sorry for Aurora. To have so carelessly given up a duke!

Hermes arrived with a silver tray, bringing with him lemonade for the two girls, and rum and fruit punch for the others. The duke remarked, surprised, that the beverage was cool.

"There is a stream that runs by the kitchen house," Cally told him breathlessly, eager to join the conversation between her mother and the duke. "Jugs of rum and fruit juices as well as milk and cream are kept there to cool. St. Timothy is a well-run plantation."

"So I have noticed, Miss Kimberly," he replied. "Perhaps tomorrow you will ride out with me and show me the estate."

Cally's pretty face fell. "I do not ride well," she said.

"George and Aurora will show you the island," Oralia said quickly. "Calandra must avoid the sun, for her skin is delicate, and has always been so. Not my chicks, however."

"In England the sun is not as strong," Valerian Hawkesworth said. "I will help you to improve your riding skills, Miss Kimberly, and we shall ride to the hunt together. Would you like that?"

"Oh, yes!" Cally said enthusiastically, thinking silently she would rather die than be bounded all over the English countryside on the back of a nasty horse.

Aurora swallowed back a guffaw. Cally was afraid of horses and always had been. Riding was pure torture for her. She hated it. Well, the duke would learn that soon enough, but Aurora doubted he would be too disappointed, for in the long run Cally would make him an excellent wife. That was all he really wanted. A pleasant companion and a good breeder. That was what all men wanted. Or so her father had always said, and when he did so in Oralia's presence she would look sad. Papa and her stepmother had lost two sons before the doctor who had once lived on the island in their employ had said she could try no more else the next pregnancy kill her. He had gone back to England shortly after that, having taught one of the bondsmen and a slave man enough of his skills to be of service to the inhabitants of St. Timothy.

"Aurora is a fine horsewoman," she heard Mama say. "I would like her to travel to England with you and Calandra so she may experience society, and perhaps find a husband of her own. She has a fine dowry, your grace, and is, as you see, a pretty young girl. She will be company for Calandra, and a comfort, too, as my daughter has never been off this island in her entire life, and is apt to be frightened."

"You will call me Valerian, ma'am," he began. "While Miss Aurora is certainly more than welcome at Hawkes Hill, and my grandmother will be more than delighted to take her entrance into society upon herself, I would prefer that your daughter travel to England on the vessel following the *Royal George*. The return to England will be our honeymoon voyage, and you will understand that I prefer to make that trip in the company of my bride alone. I shall not allow Calandra to be afraid, ma'am, but we must have time to get to know each other."

"Can you not do that over the next few months here on St. Timothy?" Oralia asked him. "You will certainly be given your privacy, Valerian."

George caught Aurora's eye, and waited for the duke to answer.

"I intend returning to England almost immediately, ma'am," the duke replied. "The *Royal George* is the finest passenger ship making the trip between England and the western Indies. If we do not board it on its eastbound return, we shall have to wait for several months to catch it again. By that time your stormy season will be upon us. This is an excellent time of year to travel this particular route, and I want Calandra's ocean voyage to be a perfect one. The *Royal George* will stop at St. Timothy in two and a half weeks' time to pick us up. I have previously arranged with Captain Conway to bring the Anglican minister from Barbados with him. He will marry Calandra and me that same day here in this house. I will then rely upon your kindness to return the minister to Barbados even as we sail for England."

"Oh, my!" Oralia said, distressed by his words.

He was sooo masterful, Cally thought admiringly of the duke.

"I realize that this comes as somewhat of a shock, ma'am, but you must know that I knew nothing of this marriage until shortly after my grandfather's death last autumn. I do not want to miss the racing season. England will be coming into summer, which while nowhere near as warm as here, will give Calandra a chance to grow used to our climate before the winter. It will also give me the opportunity to introduce Calandra into society. The Prince of Wales is a fine fellow, and there has been talk recently of his marrying. There will be much gaiety, and Calandra will enjoy it until such time as she is with child."

"She hasn't a proper wardrobe," Oralia protested. "There has been virtually no time to prepare a trousseau."

"St. Timothy's is not aware of the latest fashions," he replied. "I will have a brand-new wardrobe made for my wife in London. And one for Miss Spencer-Kimberly as well that will be awaiting her upon her arrival the following month." He patted Oralia's hand comfortingly. "You must not fret yourself, ma'am. I will take splendid care of your daughter. After all, she is to be the Duchess of Farminster."

Cally jumped up, clapping her hands with delight! "Oh, yes, Mama! Imagine! A brand-new wardrobe for me, and one for Aurora too! The latest London fashions!" She turned to the duke. "Will I have wonderful jewelry too, sir? And a coach and four? And a wench to help my Sally? Will we see the king? Will your horses race? May I have pin money to wager upon them?" Her pale cheeks were pink with excitement.

"Calandra!" Her shocked mother could barely speak.

Aurora and George were astounded, for they had never before heard Cally so enthusiastic. They didn't know if they dare laugh.

Valerian Hawkesworth, however, did laugh. It was a deep rumble of mirth that filled the room. What an enchanting child, he thought, this girl he was to marry shortly. His late father's meddling had, it seemed, turned out well after all. He arose from the settee, taking Cally's hands in his and smiling down at her indulgently. "Yes, my precious Calandra," he said boldly. "You shall have everything that your little heart desires from me, and more, I promise you!"

He had spoken her name. "Ohhh, Valerian!" she murmured, looking up at him for a moment before the thick, dark lashes brushed her snowy white cheeks. Then she said, "I shall never be fearful of anything as long as you are with me." She gazed up at him again, her hazel eyes limpid. "Would you like to see our garden?"

George Spencer-Kimberly choked back a snicker even as Aurora rolled her eyes heavenward unbelievingly.

"What a lovely idea!" Oralia pounced upon her daughter's suggestion. "I will call Sally to bring you a hat and your mitts, my child." She stood up. "Come, Aurora, George. Let us leave these young people alone." Then she hurried from the drawing room, her son and stepdaughter following.

"Oh, la, sir! You have quite stolen my heart!" Aurora mocked her stepsister, fluttering her lashes at George.

"Quite, Miss Kimberly! Quite so!" George responded, kissing Aurora's hand with a loud smacking noise, and twirling her about.

"Stop it, the pair of you," Oralia scolded.

"But Cally is being so silly," Aurora said.

"She's a young, inexperienced girl, and but following her heart. She is quite overwhelmed by the duke, and I think that he is taken by her, for which I thank the good Lord. *Especially*"—and here she lowered her voice—"especially considering what you two have done. I can only hope, Aurora, that you have no regrets *now.*"

"None, Mama" came the quick reply. "Cally is quite welcome to the duke. I find him arrogant and odious."

"He is to be your host in England. You will have to be mannerly," Oralia said, and then, "Oh! You cannot travel alone to England!"

"Martha will be with me," Aurora reminded her.

"No! No! It will not do, my child. Martha is a servant. No respectable young woman of good family travels alone but for a servant."

"I am just as happy to remain here, Mama," Aurora told her. Oralia shook her head. "You must be married eventually, Aurora. Most of the planters' sons are dissolute creatures involved with their slave women, and with St. Timothy you would not have a great deal of choice despite your dowry and income. The heirs are looking for heiresses, and must find them in England, or France, where their wicked practices are not known, and they appear respectable to a discerning parent. No. You must go to England to find a mate. There your little fortune will be acceptable to some baronet of good breeding." She thought for a moment, and then she said, "George shall go with you! That is the solution to our problem. It is quite acceptable for you to travel under the protection of an elder brother. And perhaps George will find a nice young wife while he is in England. We must ask the duke if he knows which ship follows the *Royal George*, and then see that the passage is booked on it for you both."

"The harvest will not quite be over if I leave so soon," George protested. "And who the devil will oversee the planting, Mama? I cannot leave now. The duke has asked me to remain as his manager and overseer. I have responsibilities to him, and to my sister."

"You have a greater responsibility to Aurora," his mother responded meaningfully. "She must have her chance too!"

"I do not have to follow on Cally's heels to England, Mama," Aurora said sensibly. "Let her and the duke settle into married life. George can finish the harvest and see to the new planting. Then in late autumn he and I can depart for England. It will be over a year before the new crop is ready to harvest, which will give him plenty of time to be a young gentleman of fashion, perhaps even a macaroni, in London. And I shall have a lovely visit with Cally before we have to return home to St. Timothy for the next harvest." She smiled at her stepmother. "Isn't that really a better plan, Mama? Let the duke sweep Cally off to England and her new life without our interference. He will have little love for his in-laws if they land on him too quickly."

"But you will be almost eighteen then," Oralia objected weakly.

Aurora laughed. "Oh, Mama, I'm certain there will be someone willing to overlook my vast age in exchange for my dowry."

"You are quite impossible," Oralia said. "I wonder if you will ever find a man to put up with you." But she smiled as she spoke.

"I'd rather be with you here on St. Timothy" came the reply.

"Does Aurora's plan suit you, George?" Oralia asked her son.

"Aye, it does," he agreed.

"Then it is settled," Aurora said, and they all agreed it was.

Chapter

⚜ 3 ⚜

The duke's valet, Browne, awakened him quite early, as his master had requested he do. While the sky was light, the sun was not yet up. The air was warm and quite still for a change. He bathed and dressed quickly, for he was to ride with George and Aurora before the sun became too hot for his inspection. By ten o'clock in the morning George told him the heat would be too much for him, as he was unused to it.

Browne handed him a deep saucer. "A bit of tea, sir. The cook was kind enough to make it up. The family stock is really quite palatable. We may not be in civilization, but it ain't bad here but for the heat. I hardly closed my eyes all night."

"You'll be quite used to it by the time we leave, Browne," Valerian Hawkesworth said with a smile. He drank the fragrant tea, setting the saucer down on a small table when he had emptied it.

"Master George sent up this hat for you to wear, sir." Browne handed the duke the broad-brimmed straw head covering, remarking, "It surely ain't fashionable, is it, my lord?"

Clapping the hat on his dark head, the duke picked up his riding crop and left his bedroom. In the airy downstairs foyer he found his two companions waiting. He was a bit surprised to see that Miss Spencer-Kimberly was wearing breeches. "You do not ride sidesaddle?" he said.

"Of course not," she said. "The terrain is rough on the island. It is not some tame London park, your grace. Do all English ladies of fashion ride seated, their leg thrown awkwardly over their saddle's pommel? It is an extremely uncomfortable way to ride. I firmly believe that is why Cally never took to a horse. She is of a delicate nature, and felt unsafe seated so unnaturally. Still, I could never get her to ride astride. She thought it not feminine." The look she gave him challenged him to agree with her stepsister.

"I believe," Valerian Hawkesworth said, neatly sidestepping the issue, "that as we are to be related by marriage, Miss Spencer-Kimberly, that you should call me something other than *your grace*. I shall call you Aurora, and you may call me Valerian."

"Oh, may I?" Aurora said, her eyes wide, her voice unnaturally sweet. She fluttered her lashes at him.

"Sister, behave yourself!" George scolded her. "Valerian isn't used to your sharp tongue and teasing ways." He grinned at the duke. "She's quite a minx, I fear. Papa never quite knew what to do with her. He doted on both the girls, and both are spoiled."

"I think I know what I should have done with her," the duke said, his dark blue eyes hard. "I suspect Aurora has never felt a hard hand on her bottom. It reforms the worst jades."

George saw the fire in her eyes and said quickly, "We must be off. The sun will be up before we know it! Come along now."

"I know nothing about sugar except that it is sweet," Valerian said to his companions. "Tell me about it as we ride."

"It's a never-ending round-robin of labor," George said. "We have four large fields on this side of the island, and four on the other side, which once belonged to the Meredith family. We rotate the fields. This year we are harvesting on this side of the island, and the other side is fallow, but being constantly fertilized, for cane takes a great deal of nourishment from the soil. We harvest every eighteen months. In a year, before the one side is ready for harvesting, we replant on the other side. The fallow fields need to be weeded in the between times. During the rainy season, usually between May and December, we plant. In the dry season, usually from January to May, we harvest our crop. We are never idle."

"How is cane planted?" the duke asked.

"We propagate, using cuttings from the tops of mature plants. The slaves dig holes and fertilize. Our father's father planted in long trenches, but now everyone holes because it prevents the soil from eroding and conserves moisture. Once the cane is planted, it is a constant round of fertilizing and weeding until the cane is cut."

"How many slaves do you have?"

George thought a moment, and then he said sheepishly, "I don't know. Enough to do the work, of course."

"How many new slaves are required to be bought each year? I have been told that the mortality rate on sugar plantations is extraordinarily high due to the hard work and harsh conditions," the duke remarked. As they approached the fields, he could already see black men and women at work, cutting and stacking the cane.

"The mortality rate on St. Timothy is relatively low but for old age and an occasional accident." Aurora spoke up now. "Papa hated slavery. Had he been able to run the plantation without slaves, he would have done so, but he realized it was not realistic. He did the next best thing. He gave them decent housing and food. We have trained one of their own to doctor them. Field slaves work hard, but our slaves are not overworked, and Sunday is a day of rest for everyone on St. Timothy, free, bond, and slave alike. Consequently, our slave women bear live children who grow up to work in the fields next to their fathers. I cannot remember the last time a slave was bought. It is not like that on neighboring islands and plantations. Under English law the slaves have absolutely no rights at all. A master can kill a slave for no cause and still be within his rights. It's horrible! Those poor blacks are worked around the clock until they die, and their owners care not. The slavers call regularly from Africa, bringing new consignments of unfortunate souls to be used, and then disposed of without thought. It is outrageous! *But we do not do that here on St. Timothy.*"

She spoke with such passion that she surprised him. He had thought her merely sharp-tongued and spoiled, but Aurora, it would seem, had a conscience. As he did not like slavery either, it pleased him.

"Actually, treating our people humanely works to our advantage," George told the duke. "They are used to working together, have made themselves into several field crews, and for their own amusement compete against one another. When the harvest is in, we reward them all, the lion's share going to the most productive crew. It's certainly better than working them to death and then having to teach and break in new men. I have four black foremen, and each of them has trained an assistant. And my clerks are all black men. And another advantage to our way is that since at least three generations of our slaves have been born on St. Timothy, there is no incentive to rebel, and there is no longing for Africa, from whence their ancestors came. St. Timothy is our home, all of us, black and white."

"How many hours a day do your field slaves labor?" Valerian asked George as they stopped a moment to look over a field that was already half cleared.

"We are in the fields by six o'clock in the morning, and toil until noon when the sun is so vicious. They return to the fields about two o'clock, and stay until sunset."

"Is there much malingering?"

George shook his head. "When a field hand goes to the doctor, it is because they are genuinely injured or ill. These are honest people, and their families would not allow them to feign illness."

"Do many run away?"

"Where would they go?" Aurora said. "British law says a slave has absolutely no rights. If a black cannot show papers of manumission, it is assumed they are runaways. They are jailed until their owners can be found, and if they are not, they are resold. No one has run from St. Timothy in my memory, for they are safer here, and better treated than anywhere else in the colonies."

They rode into the fields toward a group of centrally located buildings. The field hands greeted them as they passed them by.

"These buildings house the cane mill as well as the boiling and refining houses," George explained. "The cane is cut as close to the ground as possible, the leaves stripped, and then the cane is cut into three- to four-foot lengths, bundled up, and brought to the mill. Within the mill the slaves crush the cane to extract its juices. We then boil the juice, clarify it, and it crystallizes into sugar. We take a little of the molasses, which is what is left after we clarify the cane, and make our rum with it. It's a long, tedious, hot process. Only the strongest men can work here."

"You make enough rum only for your personal use?"

George nodded.

"Would it be possible to make more rum?" Valerian asked.

"I always wanted to do that!" George said enthusiastically. "There is a good market for rum outside the islands. We would need to build a facility to bottle it. Papa never wanted to do it, but I think we need to diversify, and build up our resources. If we lost a crop to a hurricane, we would have the means to plant again, and to survive. Papa said we would have to borrow to build, and he wanted no part of the island endangered by moneylenders."

"Do you have enough slaves to start such a process?" the older man queried the younger. "Or would it be necessary to buy new slaves?"

"We can train men to oversee the process, but we can use the younger women to do the bottling, Valerian," George responded. "Bringing new slaves to the island could cause trouble."

"I am completely unnecessary to this conversation," Aurora said suddenly. "George, you do not really need me now. I am going for a swim before the sun is too high."

"*You swim?*" the duke was astounded.

"In the sea," she told him pertly, and then, turning her horse away, she moved off back through the fields.

"She can really swim?" Valerian asked George.

"Like a fish," he said. "Even better than I can, much to my embarrassment. She's a bonny girl, Valerian, and a wonderful companion, if a brother might brag a bit. She can shoot a pistol too."

"Good Lord!" the duke exclaimed. "And is Calandra like her?"

George laughed. "Nay, she is not. Cally dislikes swimming almost as much as she dislikes riding, and the sight of a pistol renders her faint. Yet she is a game girl, and has kept up with the two of us for years. Cally, however, can play the pianoforte, and she sings like an angel. She has a wonderful eye, and paints the most exquisite landscape miniatures. These are talents much more suited to being a duchess, I would assume. They are both wonderful sisters!''

"I had a sister once," Valerian said as they resumed their ride. "She was drowned with my parents returning from France. My mother was half French. After her father died, and she was married to my father, my French grandmother returned to her girlhood home. My parents had taken Sophia for a visit. A wicked storm blew up in the Channel even as they were in sight of England. Their ship went down, and all aboard her were lost. Sophia was eight." He smiled softly. "I yet remember her, but were it not for her portrait in the family gallery, her face would elude me today. She was a pretty child, and, as I recall, very mischievous. She once drove all the chickens on the home farm out into the fields to *free* them because she said she could not bear to know they would be eventually eaten. She had a kind heart, my sister."

George nodded his understanding. "Cally and Aurora once freed a turtle that was to be used for soup for the same reason," he said.

The two men rode on, George taking his companion to the top of the gentle hills that divided the island lengthwise. He pointed out the fields, and the old Meredith plantation house that would now belong to Aurora. From their vantage point Valerian could view the entire island, and the sea in which it sat.

"What is that island?" the duke asked. "It looks quite wild."

"It's St. Vincent, and is inhabited by the Carib Indians. They do not bother us, nor we them," George answered. "They have lost so much to the British, French, and the Spanish, even the Dutch, that they are content to live peaceably as long as they are left to themselves."

"And where is Barbados?"

George turned. "You can just make it out today, for it's a bit hazy. St. Timothy is between the two islands."

Valerian Hawkesworth gazed out over the island. It was like an emerald set on an aquamarine cloth. Above them the bright sun glittered in an azure sky. It was absolutely beautiful in a way he had never known, or even imagined. In a nearby tree he spotted several medium-sized birds. They were teal green with sapphire-blue tails and wing tips. Each had a cap of bright orange, and bone-colored hooked beaks. He pointed toward the small flock, asking George, "What are they?"

"Tiomoids, a variety of parrot native to this island" was the reply. "Pretty, aren't they?"

"I've never seen anything like them. Oh, I've seen parrots in England, but usually they're blue and gold, or white. I've never seen any like these."

"They don't seem to be anywhere else but here," George said. "They're harmless. They don't ravage the cane, so we leave them be."

They returned down the hills, but when they had reached the fields again, a tall, neatly garbed black man came running, calling out to George Spencer-Kimberly.

"What is it, Isaac?"

"You are needed in the counting house, sir. I was sent to find you. Will you come?"

George turned to Valerian. "I must go. If you would like, tomorrow we can go over the books."

"Can we not do it this afternoon?" the duke asked.

"I think Cally might find herself offended if we did," George answered with a twinkle in his eye.

Valerian laughed. "You are right. I must remember that I am to be a married man, and can no longer think only of myself."

George nodded. "Just follow the road back to the house. You won't get lost. There is only one cutoff, and that leads to the beach. Your path goes straight. The other turns to the right."

"I think I can find my way," the duke said as he moved off.

When he came to the narrow track that led right, however, he turned his horse onto it. He wanted to see the beach, and ride along the edge of the sea for a bit. St. Timothy was such a fascinating place. He felt a longing to go exploring such as he had not felt since he was a young boy. He didn't expect he would lose his way so completely that he couldn't find his way back to the plantation house. The jungle deepened for a short way, and then began to thin out once more. He could hear the waves on the shore, but it was a soft sound.

As he was about to move out onto the sand, something caught his eye in the water. It was a head. He saw Aurora's horse tethered. Then his eyes went to her clothing which was piled neatly next to a cloth that was spread on the white beach. Was she swimming nude? He was surprised, and perhaps shocked, although he was not certain of that. He knew he should turn around and return to the main road, but he didn't want to. Instead, he remained hidden in the shadows, watching as she swam closer to shore.

She stood, and his question was answered. She was completely without garments, and she was utterly the most beautiful creature he had ever seen at that particular moment. The crystal-clear waters came almost to her knees. She reached about to gather her hair into her hands, and then wrung it out as she walked from the sea onto the beach. Lying upon the cloth, she spread her hair out to dry. Valerian sat silent, hardly daring to breathe. After a while Aurora turned over, again arranging her hair in a manner intended to dry it. She remained that way for another short period.

What I am doing? the duke thought. I am like a boy spying on the dairymaids, and yet he could not move away. She had long legs, and her skin was pale gold all over. A bunch of luxuriant little curls, golden brown in color, burst forth from the junction between her legs. He wanted to plunge his fingers into that tempting tangle and explore her most secret places. He watched her arise from the beach, and his eyes fastened eagerly upon her breasts. They were small, and perfectly round in shape, their nipples pert and upstanding. Her narrow waist led to surprisingly shapely hips, perhaps a trifle more statuesque than he would have suspected beneath her skirts. She turned, then bent to retrieve her shirt. Her buttocks were so sweetly formed, he longed to fondle them. It was then he realized how uncomfortable he had suddenly become. His male organ was swollen hard, and almost unbearably painful.

God, he thought irritably! This girl is to be my sister-in-law, yet here I am, spying on her like some debauched bastard. How the hell shall I ever look her in the eye again? He watched as Aurora pulled on her breeches, stockings, and shoes. Suddenly he was angry. It was her fault! She was a teasing little wanton! What sort of respectable girl went about swimming naked for all to see who could see? He could only hope the wench would not cause a scandal when she came to England. He would have to find a respectable husband for her as quickly as possible, but somehow the thought of another man with Aurora angered him even further. Valerian Hawkesworth turned his horse back toward the main road before she caught him looking at her. If she found him out, she might tell Calandra, and he didn't want his bride upset by a momentary weakness on his part.

The days flew by. He spent the mornings with George, learning about how a sugar plantation was run, monitoring the books. He found his wife's dowry a productive one. The Kimberlys, Robert in particular, had been very prudent, the duke discovered. Proceeds from the sales of the sugar crops were deposited with London banks. Kimberly had provided generously for his widow, and for his two stepchildren, whom, Valerian learned, he had formally adopted. Both Aurora and George would be considered excellent marriage prospects. He expected to have no trouble finding a husband for his sister-in-law, provided, of course, she behaved herself. But other than her proclivity for swimming naked in the sea, he could find little fault with her, except perhaps her quick tongue. And the sea surrounding England was generally too cold to swim in at all. Valerian Hawkesworth was beginning to feel expansive in his good fortune.

He spent the afternoon and evenings with Calandra, her mother, and sister. His bride-to-be was very lovely, if perhaps a trifle dull, but then that was to be expected. She had spent her entire life on St. Timothy, which, while beautiful, offered little in the way of cultural stimulation. Calandra could read, and she could write, but she was, she admitted to him, hopeless at sums. She spoke a little French, but where she excelled was in the arts. Her embroidery was exquisite, as were the miniatures she painted; and as George had said, she sang sweetly, and played the pianoforte in the drawing room quite well. All in all she would be an asset to Farminster. His grandmother would smooth out her rough spots, and Calandra would be quite acceptable in society.

His sister-in-law, on the other hand, was far more stimulating to speak with, and quite the bluestocking. She had read everything in her father's library several times over. She wrote with a very fine hand, and had taught herself Latin. Besides English, she spoke both Spanish and French fluently, having had access along with George to a tutor for several years. He had seen her ride and swim. And one afternoon he had seen her best her brother at target shooting. She had a keen eye for mathematical figures, but none of the female accomplishments of her stepsister. She could neither sing nor play, nor paint nor embroider, and while she would not hurt Calandra's feelings by scoffing at such things, it was obvious she had little time or patience for them. Aurora and Calandra were fascinating opposites, yet they loved each other dearly, he could see.

Cally's wedding gown was ready. The servants sewed diligently on the clothing she would take with her until she might obtain that fine London wardrobe. The duke was pleased that Aurora and George would be coming in eight months' time rather than on his heels. He had Aurora's measurements taken, and promised that a wardrobe would be sent to her in time to travel to England. And George, too, was to share in his brother-in-law's bounty. It would be winter when they arrived, the duke reminded them, and they would both need warm, fashionable clothing.

"You will send to me to let me know on what ship you intend traveling. I would suggest the *Royal George,* or its sister ship, the *Queen Caroline.* I will send my carriage to meet you."

"You are so kind to us, Valerian," Oralia said.

"Would you not come too, ma'am?" he asked her as he had several times previously. "We would welcome you at Hawkes Hill, and hope that Calandra will be with child by then. I know she would welcome her mother, particularly under those conditions."

Oralia shook her head. "When Robert brought me here from Jamaica, I vowed that I would never again set sail upon the sea. I have neither the head nor the stomach for it, it seems." She laughed.

"Then we must return to St. Timothy often so you may know your grandchildren, ma'am," Valerian said generously.

Oralia beamed even as Calandra giggled.

He had begun to worry about Calandra. How many walks had they taken in the plantation house gardens? But she had yet to allow him any intimacy but the privilege of holding her hand. On the several occasions he had attempted to kiss her on the lips, she had turned away so that his lips barely brushed her cheek. If she would not allow him an innocent kiss, what was to happen when they were married? Aurora, he suspected, would have long ago succumbed to his kisses. He didn't know why he had thought it, but he did. Then, having thought it, he put the idea from him guiltily. Certainly Oralia had, or would shortly, explain to Calandra her marital duties. Then it would be up to him to instruct his bride in the more practical aspects of those duties.

The night before the wedding Oralia joined both her daughters in Cally's bedchamber. "Aurora, I think it best you leave us," she said.

"May I not remain?" her stepdaughter replied. "You are going to speak to Cally of the physical side of marriage, aren't you, Mama? I might as well hear it now, as you probably won't be with me when I marry."

"But you are not departing for England for several months," Oralia replied. "We will speak then, Aurora."

"I would rather hear it all with Cally, Mama."

"Oh, please let her stay," Cally begged prettily.

Oralia shrugged. She was uncomfortable enough as it was. It was actually a very practical idea to get this little speech all over and done with just once. "Very well," she acquiesced. "Marriage has many aspects to it," she began. "A good wife respects her husband. She keeps his house, and if he so desires, she may even offer him her counsel. But a woman's chief duty, my girls, is to give her husband children. In order to do this, she must cojoin her body to his and receive his seed into her womb. For some women this is a pleasant duty, and she may even enjoy her husband's passion."

"Did you?" Aurora asked frankly.

Oralia blushed. "I did with your father," she said low.

"But not with mine?" Cally asked.

Oralia bit her lip, but then said candidly, "Your father was not as gentle a man as was Robert Kimberly. While all men are basically alike in their forms, each is different in the manner in which he makes love to his wife. You must be prepared for this, both of you. Cally, I believe your duke will be kind and patient. Permit him the freedom of your body, for it is his right. You must not deny him."

"What will he do?" Cally asked curiously.

"Each man has an . . . um . . . um . . . an . . ."

"Appendage?" Aurora suggested.

"How on earth did you know *that?*" her mother gasped.

"I remember seeing George had one when we swam together as children," Aurora said calmly. "It was a bit small, however."

"They grow as the male grows," Oralia told them weakly, thinking this was probably the worst thing she had ever had to do in her life. "This appendage is the means by which a man joins his body with his wife."

"How?" Cally said.

"There is an opening in a female's body," her mother said. "It can be found between your legs. As a man's desire grows, this appendage will thicken, and grow. It is then ready to enter your body, which your husband, if he is thoughtful, will prepare for his entry."

"How?" Cally again.

"He will stroke you," Oralia said.

"Like a cat?" Cally sounded disbelieving.

"You know what you need to know," Oralia said. "Valerian will answer any other questions you have, Calandra."

"How does a baby get into my body?" Cally persisted.

"Your husband will deliver his seed into your womb by means of his appendage. This seed will grow if you are fertile at the time it enters your body, for you will not always be fertile to his seed, and the seed evolves into a baby. It generally takes about nine months for a child to come to full term. At that point it will push itself from your body through the same opening by which it entered it."

"Will it be a son or daughter?" Cally was not yet satisfied.

"You will not know until the child is born," her mother said. "Now, Calandra, Aurora, I think you have more than enough information. It is time for you to go to sleep. Tomorrow is a very important day for you, Calandra. You will marry, and you will leave St. Timothy as the Duchess of Farminster. You must get your rest."

"Let Aurora stay for a while," Cally asked her mother. "It is the last night we will have each other's company for a long time, and when we meet again, everything will be different."

Oralia nodded, understanding, and then, standing up, she left the room. She and Robert had been so fortunate in their marriage and in their children. She wanted that for both of the girls.

When she had gone, Cally said, "I wonder what part of me he will stroke." Then she giggled nervously. "It is all quite silly."

"Men, I have noted, have an appreciation of women's breasts. Perhaps he will stroke your breasts," Aurora said. "Have you ever touched yourself, Cally?"

"Have you?"

Aurora nodded. Then she undid the ribbons on her nightgown, exposing her upper torso to her sister's view. "Undo yours," she commanded.

Cally complied with the request. "I've never done this before," she whispered. "Is it naughty?"

"Probably," Aurora responded, her hands cupping her round little breasts. "Do what I do, Cally."

Cally's bosom was only slightly larger than her sister's. Her breasts were cone-shaped, and had large nipples. Shyly, she slipped her hands beneath them, all the while watching as Aurora began to rub her nipples with her thumbs. Cally followed suit. Her nipples grew hard beneath her touch, but she felt more irritation than anything else. Aurora, however, closed her eyes and sighed. She slipped one hand down her body, pushing her nightgown away, until her fingers were lost in the tight curls of her bush. Cally watched wide-eyed as Aurora thrust a finger between the folds of flesh and began to rub herself.

"What are you doing?" she said, half shocked.

"You do it too," her sister said softly. "Ummmm, it feels so good. If this is what a man does to you, I can hardly wait to marry!"

"I cannot do *that*," Cally protested, but she was fascinated.

"Yes . . . you can," Aurora murmured. "Oh! Oh! Oh! That was so nice, Cally. Go ahead! Try it. You'll feel so good afterward!"

Nervously, Calandra followed her sister's instructions. Soon her body began to tingle in a way she had never known before, and she did not think she liked it. Her fingers were slickly sticky with some kind of juice her body seemed to be emitting. Then she gave a little shudder. "Ohhh!" she cried. "Ohhhh!"

"There now, wasn't that nice?" Aurora said mischievously.

"I don't think I liked it at all," Cally said, arising from the bed where they were both sitting to wash her fingers off. "How did you ever learn such a thing?" She scrubbed her hand fiercely.

Aurora shrugged. "I don't really know. I just did it one day, and I liked it. Valerian will probably touch you that way. I think the gooey fluid that comes from that place is what Mama meant when she said he would prepare you for his entry. I imagine the appendage goes in far more easily when it is greased than if you were dry."

"I think it is nasty, and I shall not do it!" Cally said.

"Oh, don't be silly, Cally. Of course you'll do it. You have to if you're going to have a baby, and, as Mama says, it's your first duty to the Hawkesworth family to give them an heir. You'll probably like it better when Valerian does it to you. Has he kissed you yet?"

"I wouldn't let him," Cally said.

"Well, you'll have to after the wedding," Aurora told her sister in practical tones. Then she arose from the bed, retying her night-gown. "I'm off for bed, sweeting. Happy dreams, little sister. I will miss you. See you on the morrow."

"Aurora!"

She turned.

"I love you!" Cally said.

"I love you too," Aurora replied, and then left her sister.

In the downstairs foyer Calandra's trunks sat waiting. The wedding would be first thing in the morning, when the *Royal George* arrived. Then the newlyweds and their two servants would depart for England after a wedding breakfast. The minister would be returned to Barbados by means of a St. Timothy boat, and the day would progress just like any other day on the island, except that Cally would be gone.

The household was up early. The baths were filled, and all involved bathed. Tea was brought to each bedroom. Cally's maid, Sally, was so sick with her excitement that she vomited twice.

"What's the matter with you?" Martha asked the younger woman.

"I'm going 'ome!" Sally said. "I'm going to see England again, and be personal maid to a duchess!" Sally's term of bondage had ended several years earlier. She had always been homesick for England, but had never had the means to return. She had been transported for debt. The only means of support she had was here with Calandra. Now she had been asked to accompany her mistress, and she was thrilled. "Don't tell me, Martha 'enry, that you won't be 'appy to see England again."

"You ain't going to remain personal maid to a duchess long if you don't put those H's back on your words, Sally me girl," Martha told the younger woman sternly. "I thought we had learned you better these past ten years. A duchess's servant got to talk more posh. You want to end up back in the same London slum from where you came?"

"Gawd, no!" Sally exclaimed. She looked worried. "Maybe I ought to stay put right here on St. Timothy."

"Don't be a ninny," Martha said. "Just remember to speak careful, and learn everything you can from the Hawkesworth family servants. You've got the next couple of weeks to make friends, and ask questions of Browne, the duke's valet. And by make friends I don't mean you should go and seduce the poor fellow. And if anyone should question your authority, and try and steal your place, just remember to be tough and remind 'em that you've been with *her grace* since she was a child. Few will challenge an association like that. Be pleasant, but don't trust anyone until you got a real good lay of the land. The dowager duchess will have a favorite serving woman. Make friends with her and defer to her judgment. With a strong ally like that, you ain't got nothing to worry about."

"Oh, Martha! I'm going to miss you!" Sally's plain face was woebegone. Her gray eyes were teary.

"Go on with you," Martha said gruffly, but she was feeling a bit weepy too. When Sally departed, she would have no close woman friend of her own class. But it was only for a little while, she reminded herself. Her eye went to the windows, and then she said, "Look out in the harbor. The *Royal George* is sailing in, and the bride not ready!"

Cally's wedding gown was brought forth. It was a beautiful garment of cream-colored satin. The round neckline was edged in matching lace that matched the engageants falling from the three-quarter sleeves. The skirt opened in the front to reveal a brocade underskirt embroidered in a delicate floral pattern with gold thread. The skirt was gathered full at the hips with flounces and ruches, and lay over its underskirt and several stiffened petticoats. Calandra's dark hair was gathered into a chignon, and one long curl was coaxed to lie over her left shoulder. She wore no jewelry except for pear-shaped pearl earbobs and a small gold cross on a fine gold chain. Carefully she slipped her stocking feet into low-heeled cream brocade shoes with small gold rosettes. Then she looked at herself in the long mirror.

Calandra Hawkesworth. It had a noble ring to it. *Calandra, Duchess of Farminster*, she thought, and preened before the glass. Yes. She looked like a duchess. She was going to be a great success in England. "I am beautiful," she said aloud to no one in particular.

"You are, and that's the truth," Martha told her with a smile, "but don't you forget when you get to England, that pretty is as pretty does, Miss Calandra. I'll want to hear good things of you when we arrive."

Oralia came into the bedroom and stopped, her hand going to her heart as she viewed her daughter. "Oh, my, my, darling! It is perfect. You look regal." She handed Cally a small spray of star-shaped white orchids. Then she asked, "Where is Aurora?"

"Here, Mama." Aurora entered by the door that connected her room and Cally's. Her gown was almost identical to her sister's except that it was pale rose-colored silk. The visible underskirt was of cream brocade, hand painted with tiny blue forget-me-nots. Her matching shoes had pink rosettes, and her brown-gold hair was fashioned with twin ringlets on either side of her head. Her only jewelry was a gold cross that matched her sister's.

"Oh, how lovely you look!" Oralia said, pleased. She presented her stepdaughter with a bouquet of pink hibiscus and green ferns.

George popped his head in the door. "Captain Conway and the Reverend Mr. Edwardes have arrived. The bridegroom is waiting eagerly. Are you ladies ready?"

"Escort me down, George, and then you may come and get your sister," Oralia said, gesturing to the two servants to accompany her.

The two sisters were alone for a brief moment.

"You're certain you're not sorry?" Cally said. "This is a wonderful and generous thing you have done, Aurora, but even I know Papa would not approve."

"I am not sorry," Aurora assured her, "and Papa would want me happy first and foremost. You know that. Now, you be happy, Cally."

"Ohhh, I just know I will! I am going to be a duchess, and live in England. I cannot wait to get there and become a part of society!"

"And Valerian? Do you give no thought to him?" Aurora was just slightly troubled by Cally's childish attitude.

"Valerian? Well, he will be my husband. What else is there?" Cally replied. "I'm certain we shall get on quite well."

George returned. "Come, my little sisters. 'Tis time."

They left the bedchamber, and Aurora descended the staircase first, moving slowly so that everyone would have a chance to see and admire Calandra. Of course only the servants were there to see, besides the ship's captain and the Anglican minister who stood with his back before the open door of the house. To his left stood the duke, dressed simply but elegantly in pale fawn-colored breeches, full at the top and fitted above the knee, below which he wore white stockings. His coat was of black velvet, and his waistcoat a white brocade embroidered with black thread garlands. He had silver buckles on his shoes, and lace at his throat and cuffs. Reaching the minister, Aurora stepped to the left and turned to see her stepsister.

Cally moved gracefully, her little hand upon George's arm. When they arrived before the Reverend Mr. Edwardes, Valerian stepped forward, and George gave his sister's hand into that of the duke and stepped into Valerian's former place as George had two roles to fulfill in this wedding. He was to give the bride away, and he was also the best man.

"Dearly beloved, we are gathered here together today in the sight of God and this company to join together this man and this woman," intoned the Anglican minister.

How long had it been since she had been to church? Aurora wondered. The minister had come from Barbados for her father's funeral, and before that? She could not remember. Her father would have liked to have had a clergyman on St. Timothy, but without a congregation it would have been good money wasted, he always said. The slaves had their own religion, and a family of five plus their servants was hardly worth the bother. So the minister was sent for only when he was needed. Hardly an ideal arrangement, Aurora thought. When I go to England I shall go to church every Sunday, she decided. *England*. What fate was awaiting her there? Only time would tell. Her mind wandered here and there for the next few minutes, and then she heard the minister say, "I now pronounce you man and wife." He joined their hands. "Those whom God hath joined together, let no man put asunder. Amen." Then the Reverend Mr. Edwardes smiled at the couple. "You may kiss the bride, your grace."

Knowing her shyness, Valerian quickly and lightly brushed Calandra's lips with his own. She looked very surprised.

Oralia kissed her daughter and then the duke. "I am so very happy for you both!" she said, her eyes filled with tears.

The newlyweds were then congratulated by their relations, Captain Conway, and the servants before they adjourned to the dining room for a wedding breakfast. While they ate, the trunks were being carried from the house, put into a cart, and taken down to the harbor to the ship. When the last toast was drunk, Captain Conway arose from his place.

"I do not wish to rush your grace, but the sooner I can weigh anchor today, the sooner we will reach England."

"Of course," the duke agreed, standing and drawing Cally up with him. "You will want to change, my dear. Sally, take your mistress upstairs, and do not dawdle."

"Yes, yer grace," Sally said smartly. She and Martha had been invited to the table, being old and treasured retainers.

In a surprisingly short time the new Duchess of Farminster returned, dressed fashionably in a gaily flowered Pompadour taffeta travel dress, a broad-brimmed straw hat with blue ribbons, and lace mitts upon her pretty hands. "I am ready," she said in a breathless voice.

Oralia began to cry. Both her daughter and stepdaughter rushed to comfort her. "I am being foolish, I know," she sniffed.

"Now, Mama, you must reconsider your decision and come to England with Aurora and George in late autumn," Cally said.

Oralia shook her head. "I do not like to travel," she replied. "When you have had a baby or two, or three, bring them home one winter to St. Timothy for their grandmama to see before she dies."

"Now, Mama," Aurora said, struggling not to laugh. "You are not going to die for many years to come. You are far too young. Give Cally your blessing, and a kiss so they may be under way."

Oralia sighed, but did as her stepdaughter suggested, kissing first Calandra, and then Valerian Hawkesworth. "Take care of my darling child," she instructed the duke.

"I will, ma'am," he promised her.

Cally then hugged her stepsister, her brother, and finally Martha. "I shall look forward to seeing you in a few months."

George grinned. "Together," he said.

"Forever!" Cally responded.

"As one!" Aurora finished their pledge.

Valerian Hawkesworth looked puzzled, and the trio laughed.

"Your wife will explain to you," Oralia said. "Now, go, before I cannot let you go!" She put her handkerchief to her mouth.

The duke helped his bride into the open carriage, and with a wave they were off down to the harbor, Captain Conway, Browne, and Sally following in their own conveyance.

"I do not know if I can bear it," Oralia said softly.

"Be of good cheer, ma'am," the Reverend Mr. Edwardes said. "It is God's will that a daughter leave her mother's house for a husband. Your daughter has married incredibly well. Be thankful!"

"George," Aurora said quickly, "would you be so good as to take our kindly minister down to the boat and have Franklin sail him back over to Barbados. The winds are brisk today, and I believe he can be home in time for lunch. It was so good of you to come to St. Timothy to marry Cally and Valerian, but we cannot keep you further from your parish duties, Reverend Edwardes." She smiled sweetly.

"Happy to come, Miss Aurora," he replied. "I hope I shall next see you wed to some fine young man. We have several suitable gentlemen in my parish, among whom might be one who would suit you."

"Perhaps I shall come over to Barbados for a visit after my brother and I return from England next year, sir," she replied.

"Your dear mama will be all right, won't she?" the minister inquired solicitously. "Losing a daughter is hard, I know. My good wife and I have married off four in as many years."

"Mama will be fine," Aurora assured him.

"Come along, sir," George said brightly, understanding that Aurora wanted the man gone before Oralia might say something revealing. He took the rector by the arm. "I shall see to his fee," he murmured to his stepsister, and then he hustled the Reverend Mr. Edwardes out the door before another moment could pass by.

Part II

ENGLAND, 1761

Chapter

4

"Is it always this cold in England?" Aurora asked Captain Conway as the *Royal George* prepared to dock at Dover. She shivered, drawing her hooded cape about her. The deep green wool was lined in rabbit, the hood trimmed with lynx. There were several flannel petticoats beneath her gown, and she was wearing knitted woolen stockings, but she was still chilled to the bone. She shivered.

"It's January, Miss Aurora," the captain said, "and in England January is always a cold month. Then, too, it's particularly icy out here on the water. It will be better once you're ashore, and your blood will thicken soon enough so that you won't feel the cold."

"I hope so!" Aurora responded. *England.* It was the most colorless place she had ever seen. The sea was dark, as were the buildings on the shore. The sky was gray, and there was snow everywhere. She had heard of snow, but of course until then she had never seen it.

George joined her at the rail as the captain excused himself. "Are you as cold as I am?" he asked her.

Aurora nodded. "There is no color," she remarked. "It's quite grim. I cannot imagine Cally likes it much, although her letter, when she wrote, did not offer any complaint."

"Mama lives for her letters," George replied. "We must see that

Cally writes her more often. She cannot be so overwhelmed with her duties as a duchess that she has no time to write Mama."

"Do Wickham and Martha have everything packed and ready for us to disembark? Do you think the duke will meet us?"

"He'll probably send a coach to take us up to London," George said. "And, yes, the trunks are ready."

They returned to the salon to warm themselves. Very shortly the *Royal George* docked, its heavy lines securing it to the shore. The gangway was lowered, and the passengers began to depart the ship. Actually there had been few passengers on this crossing: a children's tutor returning to England on the death of his mother, two young women from Barbados who were being sent to school, and their chaperon, a rather quiet older woman coming to visit her daughter, who was married to a clergyman in Oxfordshire. They had all been mightily impressed by the two siblings from St. Timothy, who, the captain had informed them, were coming to England to visit their sister, the Duchess of Farminster.

As George and Aurora stepped to the head of the gangway, they saw Cally waving madly to them and calling their names. She stood next to a magnificent traveling coach, and was accompanied by a gentleman, not her husband. They hurried off the ship, Wickham and Martha following.

Cally hurled herself enthusiastically at her brother and stepsister. "Darlings! I thought you would never get here!" She hugged them both, kissing them on their cheeks. Her scent was overwhelming.

"Where is Valerian?" George questioned his sister as the baggage was being loaded on a smaller coach in which the servants would travel. "I thought perhaps he would come with you."

"*Valerian?* I really don't know where he is," Cally said in unconcerned tones. "Possibly he is down in the country. Dear brother, we were misled. He may bear the title of duke, but the man is a farmer! Imagine! A farmer! He would rather spend his time with his horses and cattle and sheep than in the society of elegant people."

"No matter, Cally," Aurora said sharply. "You still bear the title of duchess, and do not, as far as I can see, want for anything."

"Oh, Aurora, it is good that you have not changed. Did I not tell you, Trahern? Her wit is wonderfully sharp." She had turned to the man accompanying her. He was very tall, and slender, and fair. "Trahern, this is my sister, Aurora. Aurora darling, this is Charles, Lord Trahern. I brought him especially for you."

"How embarrassing for both me and for Lord Trahern," Aurora answered her stepsister, annoyed. "I think you know, Cally, how very much I dislike *anyone* choosing a gentleman for me." Her meaning was very pointed, and for the briefest moment Calandra looked uncomfortable.

Then she giggled. "Oh, you are so naughty!" she simpered. Lord Trahern's thin lips had twitched with amusement when Aurora had delivered her put-down of her stepsister. Now he caught Aurora's gloved hand, and raising it to his lips, kissed it. "Miss Spencer-Kimberly, I am delighted to meet you, even if you are not delighted to meet me." Calandra had been babbling for weeks about this sibling, and what a good match she would be. God knows he needed a wife with an income, but this girl was far too intelligent to be fooled, unlike dear little Calandra, whose sole interests were bound up with her own pleasures and her own desires. He returned Aurora's hand.

"Cally," George said, "you may be used to this weather, but we are not. Let us get into your coach. Where are you taking us?"

"London!" Cally said brightly. "It's a long drive, but we will go straight through. Trahern was kind enough to arrange for extra horses for the coach along the way. Come along now!"

It was a good fifty-mile drive. They stopped three times to exchange horses on both the coaches. Twice they stopped to eat, use the necessary, and get warm by an inn fire. They had docked just after dawn. When they arrived in London it was already dark, and Aurora was still cold and exhausted. Cally had chattered almost the entire way. She babbled about society, and fashion, and the latest gossip.

"The king is to be married this year," she said.

"The king to wed? He's too old," George said.

"Ohhh! You don't know, do you? Well," she answered her own question, "how could you. The old king died in late October. We have a nice new king, and he's going to marry some German princess, Charlotte of Mecklenburg-Strelitz. He's very handsome, the king.'' She giggled. "Dull, but handsome. Do you know how the old king died?'' She lowered her voice. "He was on his *commode!*'' And she giggled wildly again. *"His commode!* Of course they hushed it up so the common people would not hear and make a mockery of it, but naturally they did. All of Europe knows that old King George died sitting on his commode!''

"How mean-spirited of you, Cally,'' Aurora chided her stepsister.

"Oh, Aurora!'' came the protest. "You are so serious. You must become gayer, or you will never succeed in finding a husband for yourself. Men in polite society do not like bluestockings.''

After what seemed an interminable time, the coach pulled up in front of Farminster House. Servants ran from the mansion to lower the coach's steps, open the door, and help the occupants out. Aurora sighed with gratitude as they entered the warm house. Behind her she could hear her stepsister giving orders to the servants about the baggage.

"Welcome to England, Miss Spencer-Kimberly,'' she heard a voice say.

Looking up as she drew her gloves off, she saw the duke descending the stairs. "Thank you, your grace,'' she responded politely.

He took her two cold hands in his warm ones and replied, "I thought we had agreed all those long months ago that you would call me Valerian, Aurora. Lord, you are frozen, I fear. Come into the drawing room, and I will have tea brought. My grandmother has come up from Hawkes Hill with me to greet you. She is waiting for you.''

Ascending the staircase, they entered a magnificent drawing room with a gilded ornamental frieze around its paneled ceiling. The carpets were thick and colorful. The walls were hung with fine portraits, and the mahogany furniture, unlike that in the Indies, was upholstered richly. Heavy velvet draperies hung from the windows, and in a huge fireplace flanked by great stone lions a great warm blaze burned. By the fire sat an elderly lady with snow-white hair. She arose to greet them.

"Grandmama, this is Miss Aurora Spencer-Kimberly," the duke said. "Aurora, this is my grandmama, the Dowager Duchess of Farminster."

Aurora curtsied prettily. "How do you do, ma'am," she said.

Mary Rose Hawkesworth looked sharply at Aurora. Why was the girl's face familiar? She looked nothing like that foolish Calandra. "How do you do, Miss Spencer-Kimberly," she answered the girl. Then, seeing Aurora shiver, she said, "Come by the fire, my dear. You are, of course, not used to our English weather."

"I fear not, ma'am, although Captain Conway assures me that my blood will thicken, and then I shall not feel the cold as deeply."

The dowager chuckled, and led the girl to a seat by the fire. Her grandson pulled the bell cord on the wall, and when a servant replied sent the fellow for hot tea. Out in the foyer Cally could be heard laughing, and then she called for her stepsister.

"We are in the east drawing room," the duke responded.

Cally burst into the room, George and Lord Trahern in her wake. "Hawkesworth!" she said, surprised. "What brings you in from the country?" Then her eye spied the dowager. "Oh! Grandmama has come too. Good evening to you, ma'am." She offered the dowager a scant curtsy.

"Calandra" came the frosty reply.

"We did not expect you, Hawkesworth," Calandra said.

"Obviously not, my dear," he answered her. "Good evening, Trahern." Then he turned and said, "Welcome to England, George." The brothers-in-law shook hands. "Come now, and meet my grandmother."

There was something terribly wrong between Cally and her husband, Aurora thought. They were civil to each other—barely—but there was a coolness between them. For some reason, she felt sorrier for the duke than for her stepsister. The young woman chattering brightly in this room was not the sister she remembered. She could tell from just looking at George that he felt the same way. The butler arrived bearing a large silver tray upon which was a teapot, tea saucers, and a plate upon which were delicate triangles of buttered bread and thin slices of fruitcake.

"*Tea?* Ohhh, no, no, no, no, no!" Cally trilled. "We would celebrate my brother and stepsister's arrival with champagne! Bring some up from the cellars!" she ordered the butler.

"Cally, I am so cold," Aurora told her. "I want tea!"

"Oh, very well, but the rest of us shall have champagne!" Cally declared. "Aurora, I hope your attitude stems from exhaustion, and that you are not going to prove to be a dull guest."

"It was not my understanding that George and I had come to provide entertainment for you, Cally," Aurora snapped.

"Good for you, girl!" the old dowager said softly.

"Trahern," the duke said suddenly. "I thank you for accompanying my wife to Dover, but I would assume that you have an engagement elsewhere this evening. We will excuse you."

Charles, Lord Trahern, bowed to the Duke of Farminster, a small sardonic smile upon his mouth. "Good evening to you, then, your grace," he said, bowing. Then he left the room.

"I did not want him to go!" Cally said angrily, stamping her foot.

"He overstayed his welcome" came the response from her husband.

"You are always spoiling my fun!" Cally whined. "And now you have given me the headache. I am going to bed, Hawkesworth, and I do not wish to be disturbed by *anyone.*"

"Of course, my dear," the duke said smoothly, and he bowed to her. "Shall I escort you to your room?"

"No!" Cally said sharply, and she departed the drawing room.

There was a long silence. George Spencer-Kimberly looked exceedingly uncomfortable. The dowager looked annoyed. There was a look on Valerian Hawkesworth's face that Aurora could not fathom. She said, "What has happened to my stepsister? I do not know her any longer."

"She has, I am afraid," said the dowager, "been seduced by society. I have seen it happen before with these young girls." She poured a generous dollop of fragrant tea into a deep saucer and handed it to Aurora. "It is worse with Calandra, for she had no contact with real society before she came to England. She tells me she lived on St. Timothy her entire life, and never even visited

Barbados. Why on earth did her father not at least take her to Barbados?"

"I believe our father did not quite see Cally and me as growing up into young women," Aurora said quietly. She took a sip of her tea. It was hot and satisfying. She took another sip, and then set the saucer down upon a small table. "We did not even know of this marriage arrangement Papa had made until we received your letter, ma'am. Only then did my brother, George, open Papa's strongbox, and we found the betrothal agreement. Had Valerian just arrived without prior warning on your part, we should have been even more surprised than we were."

The dowager nodded. "My late husband and your father were obviously cut from the same cloth," she said. "No need to trouble the ladies until we must, my James used to say." She shook her head. "As if women cannot manage on their own. Well, we can, but I suppose to keep them happy, we must pretend we cannot." She peered at Aurora. "You look a far more sensible miss than your sister, child. Are you?"

"We are different, ma'am, I will admit, but we are sisters, and do love each other. Cally calls me a bluestocking. If loving learning makes me such a creature, then I suppose I am."

"And are you as eager to make your mark on society as is your sister?" the dowager asked Aurora.

"I think I am a trifle afraid of society" was the reply. "From the little I have seen of England so far, it is most overwhelming. The drive from Dover was interesting, but once we reached the city I found myself becoming a trifle uncomfortable. I suppose it is because I am not used to so many people, and so many buildings. I believe I shall prefer Hawkes Hill," Aurora concluded.

"I've lived in England my entire life," the dowager woman replied, "and I, too, prefer Hawkes Hill." She smiled, but her eyes were again scanning Aurora's face. Why did the girl look so familiar? "Valerian!" she called to her grandson. "Bring Mr. Spencer-Kimberly over here so I may get a better look at him."

The duke complied with her request, flashing a quick grin at his companion. "Now you're in for it," he said low.

The dowager looked the young man over carefully. Medium brown hair. Hazel eyes. A stocky build. Of average height. There was nothing in particular to distinguish him, but he did wear his clothes well, and he had a pleasant countenance if only average features. "I believe," she said, "that we can find a most suitable wife for you, Mr. Spencer-Kimberly. Not here in London, of course. Too many flibbertigibbets and fortune hunters. But down at Hawkes Hill. A good, sensible country girl who will be a good breeder even in the heat of the Indies."

"I would be most grateful for your guidance, your grace," George replied sincerely, a friendly twinkle in his eye.

"Harrumph, and pretty manners to boot." The dowager chuckled. "You are certainly a different cut from my grandaughter-in-law, I must say. I am amazed the same woman raised you. It must be in the blood." She rose to her feet. "I am going to show Miss Aurora to her bedroom, Valerian, The child is about to fall asleep on her feet, and has had a long day. Come, girl, we will leave the gentlemen to their own devices." She exited the drawing room with Aurora stumbling sleepily in her wake.

The butler came to clear away the tea things.

"Bring whiskey," the duke ordered him.

When they were finally settled by the fire, heavy crystal glasses in their hands, George looked directly at his brother-in-law and said, "What is the matter between you and Cally, Valerian? I've never seen her behave as she behaved today, and it is obvious that something is wrong from the way you treat each other."

For a moment Valerian Hawkesworth considered telling his companion that whatever the problem was, it was not George's concern, but then he said, "It was a mistake to marry a girl I did not know. It is my fault. Had I remained on St. Timothy for some months instead of being so eager to return to England for the racing season, I should have discovered that your sister is still more of a child than a woman. She would not permit me to consummate our marriage until we had reached England. She feared, she said, in such close quarters as we had aboard the ship that the other passengers might hear us. I acquiesced reluctantly. However, Calandra does not like *the act* as she so coldly refers to it, yet I swear to you that I am not a cruel or thoughtless lover. She hates being down in the country, and fled to London without my permission three months ago. I thought if I left her here until you and Aurora arrived that perhaps she would get this passion for constant amusement out of her system, but I fear she has not. Her dressmaker's bills are outrageous. She commissioned a new coach to be built for her. Its interior is completely lined in scarlet velvet, and has crystal accoutrements. She went to Tattersall's and purchased two snow-white and two pure black horses to pull the damned thing. Do you know how much that cost me, George? And I would be more than willing to indulge her if she were willing to do her duty by Farminster and give me an heir, but she will not! I would not shock you, nor would I appear indelicate, but on the few occasions that I have managed to make love to Calandra—and believe me, George, it is no more than a dozen times in all the months we have been married—your sister lays silent, her head turned away from me as if she cannot bear to look at her husband. It is not easy to rouse one's passions with such a cold wife. Frankly, I prefer not to, but what choice have I? She is my wife."

George shook his head, astounded by the duke's revelations. "Valerian, I do not know what to say to you. I could have never imagined that Cally would behave in such a fashion with you. I am truly sorry."

Valerian Hawkesworth shook his head. "It is not your fault, George, and I am glad that you and Aurora are here at last. We will remain in London a few weeks, but then we will return to Hawkes Hill. Calandra will come, too, even if I have to drag her by the hair on her head. I have had enough of her childishness! Enough of her friends! Men like Trahern, whose reputations are not the best. Calandra seems to have no sense where her friends are concerned. The time has come, however, for her to do her duty by Farminster and give me an heir. She will not return to London again until she has!"

The two men talked awhile longer by the fire, sipping the amber whiskey in their glasses until it was gone. Then the duke escorted his brother-in-law to his bedroom, and bid him good night.

"Wickham," George said when he was alone with his servant. "Do you know what room Miss Aurora is in?"

The valet nodded. "Aye, sir."

"Go and learn from Martha whether my sister is still awake."

The valet hurried out, returning a few moments later. "She's still up, sir. Follow me." And he led his master down the hall to Aurora's room, knocking on the door, and then opening it for his master.

George entered the room to find his sister sitting up in bed in her nightgown, a nightcap on her head, sipping more tea. "Still cold?" he asked her, noting the down coverlet on the bed.

"I'm finally warming up," she said. "What did the duke have to say? What is the matter with Cally? Martha, bring my brother a chair, and then remain to hear what he has to tell us."

George sat in the chair that the servant supplied and then told the two women what the duke had reported to him. "Valerian has been very patient, and most understanding, I feel," he concluded.

"We should hear what Cally has to say," Aurora told him.

"It will be but her opinion of how she is treated, and have nothing to do with the facts of the matter," George responded. "You yourself were shocked by her behavior today, Aurora."

She nodded. "I was," she admitted, "but this is all so unlike Cally." She sighed. "Still, the dowager's words to me but confirm the duke's more intimate tale to you. What a coil."

"You should have married him the way your papa planned," Martha said grimly. "But you would have your own way, and now look what has happened."

"It is too late for regrets," Aurora said. "Let us sleep on it, and then we will see how we may help Cally and the duke to mend fences. Surely there is something we can do."

"The last time you three did something . . ." Martha began.

"Don't scold us, Martha," George said, arising. Then he bent and kissed his stepsister. "Good night, Aurora." As he opened the door, he gave Martha a quick kiss on the cheek too, and then was gone.

"Young devil!" Martha muttered, but she wasn't angry.

Calandra had not changed her habits of childhood, and would not awaken much before noon, Sally informed them. She was prettily attired in gray with a white lace cap, and looked very smart. But like her mistress, she, too, had changed. She was superior and sharp with Martha, which did not please the older woman.

"Gotten a bit above herself, I'm thinking," Martha said dourly. She settled a breakfast tray on Aurora's lap. The tray was set with exquisite fine china and heavy silver service. It contained poached eggs in a heavy cream sauce with peppercorns grated over the top, lovely pink country ham, fresh bread, butter, and honey. "I've set the tea on the sidetable, miss," Martha said.

Aurora ate with greater appetite than she would have thought she had. Everything was absolutely delicious, and seasoned to perfection. When she had finished every single scrap, and was sipping her saucer of tea, there came a knock upon the door. Outside was the duke's man, Browne. The duke wondered if Miss Aurora would like to take a carriage ride to see some of the city. Her brother, of course, would accompany them, Browne said seriously.

"Tell him yes," Aurora said to Martha.

Her bath was filled, and she bathed, then dressed, Martha carefully arranging her hair, which was clean and free of salt for the first time in weeks. The servant then set her mistress's fur-lined cape upon her shoulders, drawing the hood up carefully, and handing her a pair of fur-lined gloves.

"Now, you make certain you keep warm," she cautioned.

George arrived, and escorted his stepsister down into the wide foyer where the duke was awaiting them.

"Good morning," he greeted the pair. "The carriage is waiting for us outside. As I am certain that you will want to spend some time with Calandra this afternoon, Aurora, I have arranged for us to have a drive through Hyde Park. You must yet be tired. Is there anything in London that you would like to see?"

"Could we go to the British Museum?" she asked.

"Of course," he said, not telling her that the museum was open only three hours a day, and that tickets must be obtained weeks in advance. He was certain he could pull a string or two so she might visit this relatively new wonder.

Farminster House was located on the west side of Grosvenor Square. It had been built in 1740. Of redbrick with stone dressings, it stood three stories high, atop which were attics for the servants.

"If it were warmer," the duke said as they settled themselves in the vehicle, "we should ride in an open carriage, but I believe you will be able to see enough through the windows of this coach."

The horses stepped smartly around the square and onto Upper Grosvenor Street, which led right into Hyde Park. Aurora was delighted to see how close they were to this beautiful greensward with its watercourses. From Upper Grosvenor they turned onto Park Lane. The park, the duke explained, had once been a royal hunting ground, but had been opened to the public in the previous century. Deer of several varieties could still be found within Hyde Park's brick walls. The late Queen Caroline had been something of a landscape gardener, and working with the finest architects of her day had done many things to increase the beauty of the park. Among her accomplishments was having the river Westbourne damned to form the Serpentine, an exquisite lake.

"We will just drive about the perimeter of the park today," Valerian said. "It is still too cold for you to walk abroad. My grandmama would be quite put out if I should be responsible for your getting a chill. Not to mention how angry Calandra would be, for she has great plans, I am certain, to take you about to all the most fashionable parties."

"I do not believe I shall find the parties as fascinating as I will find the museum," Aurora replied. Then she said, "George has told me of the estrangement between you and my sister. I will do my best to convince Cally of the errors of her ways."

Valerian Hawkesworth shook his head. "You are kind, Aurora,

but I fear your task an impossible one. I know you little better than I knew Calandra when we were married, and yet I believe you would have made me a far better wife than your sister. What a pity that you were not the heiress I was to wed."

Aurora flushed a bright pink.

"Forgive me," the duke said hastily. "I have embarrassed you, and I certainly did not mean to do so." He took her gloved hand in his. "Will you forgive me, Aurora?"

She nodded, unable to speak. Please God he never learn the way he had been deceived. He would never forgive her, and worse, his anger could be directed against George and their mama.

"I find your grandmother a delightful lady," George said, attempting to bridge the uncomfortable gap. "I wish Mama could meet her."

Returning to the house, they found Calandra was awake and calling for her sister. Aurora excused herself and went to join her sister. Cally was sitting up in bed, an exquisite lace nightcap covering her dark hair. She was sipping a saucer of tea.

"Where were you?" she demanded.

"Valerian took George and me for a drive about the park."

"How dull," Cally said.

"He is going to arrange for us to visit the British Museum," Aurora continued. "I cannot wait to see the exhibits."

Calandra rolled her hazel eyes heavenward. "Aurora, what am I to do with you? If you are to catch a husband, you must not show so much intellect. Men do not like women of intellect. Besides, you will strain your eyes in a boring museum. You must maintain a feminine composure, and be charming. The gentlemen like that. I have become quite popular among the gentlemen in polite society. You must too."

Aurora laughed. "You are indeed in your element, Cally, but what of your duty to Valerian? You must give him an heir or two before you utterly exhaust yourself with all this frivolity."

"If I have a baby I shall ruin my figure," Cally said. "Lady Standish told me that her waist size increased by an inch with each child she gave her husband. When she was my age her waist was eighteen inches. Now it is twenty-four!"

"A man expects his wife to give him children," Aurora patiently continued. "Have them and be done with it. Valerian seems to me to be a good man, and I do like his grandmother. You are fortunate in your new family, Cally."

"I do not like the dowager. She hates me, Aurora! And she disapproves of me, but I do not care about that," Cally said.

"She will approve of you completely when you have given her grandson an heir, Cally," Aurora replied. "The Hawkesworths are an old and noble family. There is no reason for them to die out. You must cease being selfish, little sister, and do your duty."

"There is a ball at the Duchess of Devonshire's tonight," Cally said. "We have all been invited. Trahern will be looking for you. He is quite splendid, isn't he?"

"I find him a bit repellent," Aurora said. Then, "You will consider what I have said to you, Cally, won't you? Mama would not be very pleased with your behavior, you know. I do not know what I shall write to her. She cannot be fooled for long even if we are an ocean apart. After one inane correspondence on the many sights in London, I shall have no excuse but to tell her about this change in your sweetness of temperament. Now, I have warned you."

"Oh, do not be mean to me!" Cally cried, and she attempted to squeeze a few tears from her eyes.

"You never could do that correctly." Aurora chuckled. "I am not in the least sympathetic to you. You have been awful, and now you must cease being so dreadful, Cally."

"You are going to be no fun, I just know it," Cally grumbled. "I don't know why you bothered to come to England at all."

"I suspect it is a good thing that I did," Cally told her. "Remember, had it not been for me, you should not be a duchess."

"That is a terrible thing to say, Aurora!"

"But it is the truth."

"You are sorry now, aren't you?" Cally sneered. "You are sorry you did not marry him as Papa planned. Well, you had your chance. I am the Duchess of Farminster, and I intend remaining the duchess!"

"When," Aurora demanded, "when did I ever ask for the return of a gift, Cally? This marriage was my gift to you. I do not want it back. I never wanted it, but you have a duty to Valerian Hawkesworth, and you must fulfill that duty. Only then can you indulge your own desires and behave like a spoiled child!" She arose. "I do not want to go to your damned ball!" Then she stormed from the room.

"You had best mend your fences with her," Sally said. "She has the power to unseat you, your grace."

"You forget yourself," Cally said coldly, handing the tea saucer to her maid. Then she sat back against her pillows, her eyes calculating, her demeanor thoughtful. Finally she said, "The new ball gown. The turquoise one with the gold lace. Bring it to my sister with my apologies, and say I should like to see her in it tonight."

"Your grace," Sally replied, "that gown is far too sophisticated for a virgin who is husband hunting."

"You are right," Cally said. "What do I have that is suitable?"

"There is the silk gown in Appleblossom's Love, your grace. It has little silk flowers about the neckline, and lovely lace."

Cally nodded. "Take it to her. It is far too sweet for me. I don't know why I ever bought it in the first place."

Sally fetched the gown in question and brought it to Aurora's bedroom. When Martha opened the door, she said, "Her grace thought that Miss Aurora would look lovely in this, and hopes she will wear it tonight to the Duchess of Devonshire's ball. Have your mistress ready to leave at ten o'clock."

"Ten o'clock!" Martha exclaimed. "Respectable people are abed at that time of night, Sally."

"In London, in polite society, folks in the upper crust have balls at ten o'clock of an evening. You'll get used to waiting up till three or four o'clock in the morning. I did." Martha took the garment, shaking her head in wonderment as Sally hurried off down the hall. "Dancing almost to dawn. It can't be right!" Martha muttered after the retreating figure.

"I told Cally I'm not going to any ball," Aurora told her servant. "Oh, Martha, Cally has become so selfish!"

"Always was selfish," Martha answered. "There just wasn't so much temptation back on St. Timothy. Now, don't you fret yourself, miss. This dress is the prettiest I've ever seen, and by the look of it, not worn even once! You're going to look lovely in it, and no nonsense about not going. Of course you're going. Your mama would be mighty upset if you didn't take advantage of every opportunity offered you while you are in England." She hung the ball gown in the dressing room.

"Are you glad to be back in England, Martha?" Aurora asked her.

"I don't rightly know yet, miss. I was twenty-five when my parents died and I left. I'm over forty now. The best part of my life has been being in service to your family, miss. I'm happiest, I suppose, wherever you are."

Aurora hugged the older woman. "Oh, Martha, I do love you!"

The servant flushed, pleased. "Now, don't go getting all mushy on me, Miss Aurora," she half scolded.

The clock on the mantel struck one.

"Oh, I must join the others in the dining room. The dowager told me last evening that luncheon is at one o'clock! Is my hair neat?"

"As a pin," Martha replied. "Hurry along, miss!"

Aurora reached the dining room just as the others were being seated. Curtsying to the dowager, she apologized for her lateness.

"Nonsense, child, you are punctual to the minute" was the reply. "Valerian tells me that he took you for a turn around Hyde Park this morning. Did you enjoy it?"

"Very much," Aurora said. "I was frankly relieved to find such a lovely place so near Farminster House."

"A little bit of country in this otherwise bustling city," Mary Rose Hawkesworth said with a smile. "That is why I insisted my husband buy a house in Grosvenor Square. If I have to come to London, I must be near the park. Of course, I have always come to London as little as possible," she finished with a chuckle.

"Calandra tells me we are going to the Duchess of Devonshire's ball tonight," Aurora said.

"Indeed, are we?" The dowager was surprised. "Your sister has obviously forgotten to inform me. I shall speak to her after luncheon. She is not old enough, even if she is married to my grandson, to be your chaperon. You must be accompanied by a respectable matron lest any obtain the wrong impression of your character."

"I am relieved, ma'am," Aurora said frankly. "Cally seems to want to foist her friend, Lord Trahern, off on me, and I do not like him. With you by my side, I believe together we can repel him."

The dowager laughed, and then she grew serious. "You are wise not to be taken in by Trahern. He's a handsome devil, I'll give you that, but a bounder on the prowl for a wife with a good income."

"He will not get mine," Aurora said firmly. "I shall not leave your side, ma'am."

"Why, girl, you must if you are to dance with some of our more eligible gentlemen," the old lady said.

"Only with your approval," Aurora answered her. "I will rely on your knowledge of the men involved, and your judgment of their characters."

Mary Rose Hawkesworth nodded, and began to sip her soup. Why was the girl familiar, she asked herself for the fiftieth time since she had met Aurora yesterday evening? She had seen that face before. But where? And what a pity it wasn't this sensible miss Valerian had married instead of that bubblehead, Calandra Kimberly. Calandra. Her friendship with Lord Trahern was disturbing. The Dowager Duchess of Farminster was not so old she had not heard the gossip about Trahern. It was most unsavory. She knew Calandra was not cuckholding her grandson with the cad, for Calandra was too cold a woman, not at all to Trahern's taste. He was, of course, clever, witty, and amusing, and those traits would attract Calandra. She would want to keep in his good graces, for Trahern knew absolutely everyone, and since he had not caused any serious scandal, was welcome in all the best houses as an eligible man. Calandra was silly enough to believe that if she could make a match between Trahern and her stepsister, she would gain the devil's friendship forever.

Well, it wasn't going to happen because she would not let it happen. And it wasn't going to happen because Aurora was much too intelligent to be taken in by a man like Lord Charles Trahern. The dowager began to consider eligible young men in London now who might be suitable husbands for Aurora. None, however, came to mind. Perhaps when they were back in the country, she considered. Actually, her grandson would be a perfect husband for Aurora, and she would be a perfect wife for him. What a pity that fate had deemed it otherwise. If instead of sending Valerian off to St. Timothy a year ago she had invited Calandra and her family to England, perhaps things could have been changed. They would have seen that Calandra was unsuited to the position of duchess, and that Aurora was more than suitable.

"What are you thinking of so hard, Grandmama?" the duke said.

"Nothing of import, dear boy," the dowager replied.

Chapter

5

Aurora was not certain if it had been the best or the worst month of her life. London was a very exciting, but also a very exhausting city in which to live. Valerian had managed to obtain two tickets to the British Museum, which was located in the newly purchased Montagu House, Bloomsbury. George had begged off, not really as interested as his stepsister was in antiquities, and so the duke had escorted Aurora. The museum had its beginnings when Sir Hans Sloane, a physician and collector, had suggested to Parliament that they might be interested in buying his works of art, antiquities, and natural history collections for less than half the price it had cost him to assemble them. Parliament was delighted to accept, and the Foundation Act was passed to cover the cost of that expense, and future such expenses. The Harleian Collection of Manuscripts was purchased in that same year from the Duchess of Portland. The museum had opened two years prior, and was very popular.

Aurora enjoyed her visit immensely, but to her surprise, she equally enjoyed the ancient Ceremony of the Keys that took place each night at the Tower of London. To this ritual she was escorted by the duke, her stepbrother, and the dowager duchess, prior to attending a ball. Calandra had chosen not to attend, rolling her eyes at them and complaining that Aurora's interest in sightseeing was becoming increasingly boring, and her intellect had been commented upon most unfavorably by several of Calandra's friends. Aurora had just laughed and gone off to Tower Hill with her party.

Standing upon a roof, they watched as the chief yeoman warder, in his red cloak and Tudor bonnet, a lantern in his hand, marched toward the Byward Tower, the keys to the ancient fortress displayed in his gloved hand.

"An escort for the keys," he loudly called out, and four yeomen of the guard fell into step beside him as he marched through the gates of the Byward Tower and over the causeway connecting it to the entrance gate beyond the Middle Tower. The chief yeoman warder locked the gate and then continued on to lock the gates of Byward Tower, finally approaching the Bloody Tower. There the sentry on guard came forward, challenging: "Halt! Who goes there?"

"The keys," replied the chief yeoman warder.

"Whose keys?"

"Queen Elizabeth's keys."

The sentry then presented arms even as the chief yeoman warder removed his cap and called out, "God preserve Queen Elizabeth!"

"Amen!" replied the yeoman accompanying him and the sentry.

"How exciting it must have been in those days," Aurora said afterward as their coach made its way to another of the seemingly never-ending balls. She had found to her surprise that she did not really enjoy this continual round of social events Calandra so loved. She knew she had been a great disappointment to her stepsister, but she just couldn't help it.

None of the young men who had been presented to her had taken her fancy in the least. Many were young and eager, and woefully ignorant for upper-class gentlemen. There were rakes and roués and older men looking for a second or third wife. Her comfortable little income made her eligible, but the truth was, most of the men she met looked down on her because she was a colonial, and not English born. The fops, however, were the worst. They were openly rude, and behaved as if they were doing her a great service to even speak with her. Aurora did not think she liked high society. And the women were little better. The girls her age looked sideways at her because she was considered a rival. Their mamas, in whispers, reminded all who would listen that Miss Aurora was the sister of that silly and possibly not-quite-respectable Duchess of Farminster. The way that woman carried on with Lord Trahern, and right under her husband's nose too. Well, the sister might look as innocent as the new-driven snow; and she might even have a respectable income if one were to believe the rumors; but was she really all she seemed? And what respectable family would consider such a girl for one of their sons? One could not be too careful, the mamas of the girls Aurora's age commented in an effort to turn attention to their own offspring. Aurora was not so foolish that she didn't realize what was happening.

The duke had extended their London stay longer than he had originally intended. Now, however, he was ready to return home to Hereford. Calandra was furious. She did not want to go, but she found no allies even among her own brother and stepsister. They had both had enough of London, and were delighted to be leaving the city. Calandra sulked. Valerian was adamant. Cornering his wife's maid in the hallway, he said,

"Are you happy in your position, Sally?"

"Oh, yes, yer grace," Sally replied, bobbing a curtsy.

"Do you wish to retain your place, then?"

"Yes, yer grace." Sally shifted her feet nervously.

"In whose employ are you?" The duke towered over the servant.

"H-her grace's," Sally half whispered. She was suddenly afraid.

"No, Sally, you are not in her grace's employ. You may serve her grace, but you are in my employ. You take my wage. You live under my roof, and you eat at my table. You even have a small clothing allowance from my generosity. Do you understand the difference between being *in service* and being *in my employ?*"

"Y-y-yes, yer grace." She had to pee.

"Then since you are content with your lot, I may assume you wish to remain in my employ. In order to do that, Sally, you will report to me any foolishness your mistress may contemplate. Tomorrow we leave for Hawkes Hill. We will remain there until *I* decide to come up to London again. That will not be until your mistress has given me an heir or two. If your mistress should attempt to run away again, you will warn me in time to prevent her from doing so. If you do not, Sally, you will find yourself back in the same slum from whence you sprang. Do you understand me, girl?"

"If *she* finds out I'm spying on her, she'll kill me!" Sally told the duke. "She's got a real mean temper when she's crossed."

"You will be clever, Sally, and she will not find out," he soothed the maid. "And as long as you obey me, girl, there will be a place for you in my household. I wield more power here than your mistress, and you are no fool. You know it to be so."

Sally nodded, and then the duke stepped aside to allow her to pass. He had been patient with Calandra, but now he was through being patient. She took his forbearance for stupidity and weakness. Decamping from Hawkes Hill and coming up to London without his knowledge had been outrageous. She believed herself off his leash, but she was not. The lead he held her by was a long one. The time, however, had come to rein her in and bring her to heel. Once they reached home he was going to be in her bed every night. He would use her until she bloomed with his child. That was why he had married her. To get children from her. With George and Aurora as his allies they would bring Calandra around to a more reasonable frame of mind.

Aurora. He was thinking about her far more than he should, and he knew it was wrong. But she was everything he had ever desired in a wife. She was intelligent and kind. She had wit, not to mention beauty. She knew her duty, which was certainly more than he could say for his wife. He was glad, nay, relieved, that no one had taken her fancy here in London. What fools men could be. It would be difficult when his grandmother found Aurora the right husband, and he had no doubt that she would. She already had a match in mind for George, the dowager had told her grandson. Valerian Hawkesworth sighed deeply. He needed to go home.

It was a journey of several days' duration from London to Hawkes Hill in Hereford. There were several coaches involved. The dowager had one in which she traveled with her personal maid. There was one for Martha, Sally, and Sally's assistant, Moll, who shared their accommodation with the duke's valet, Browne, and George's man, Wickham. Calandra and Aurora had their own vehicle in which the duke and George might ride when they were not a-horse. There were three baggage carts. There were fresh horses awaiting them at all the inns, brought from the duke's estate. A skeleton staff would remain at Farminster House. The rest of the servants had departed the day before for Hereford.

On the morning of their departure Moll came to Martha. "Sally says her ladyship is having a tantrum and carrying on something awful. Could yer mistress come, please?" She curtsied to Martha, who thought the young girl a nice child with promise.

"We'll both come," Martha replied. "Go tell Sally."

"I knew she would do this," Aurora said. "She half as much said so yesterday. What are we to do, Martha? I am not certain we shouldn't write to Mama and beg her to come to England."

"Yer mama won't come, miss. She don't like the sea, but I have an idea. You just tell her high and mightiness that if she don't behave herself, you'll tell the duke of the deception played on him. That's fraud. The duke can annul the marriage or get a divorce, I don't know which. Either way, where will Miss Cally be then?"

Aurora's eyes twinkled. "Cally would rather die than lose her title," she said. "I would not have thought such duplicity was possible in your character, Martha."

"I still got a few surprises up my sleeve, miss" was the reply.

They could hear Cally shrieking as they approached her bedroom. "I'm not going! I have already told you! I am not going! The king is giving a ball tonight, and I will not miss it! Everyone will be there!"

"But we, however, shall not," Aurora said, entering her stepsister's bedchamber. "We shall be tucked up asleep in some comfortable inn on the road to Hawkes Hill before the first musician can tune his violin, Cally. Why are you not dressed? We are leaving in less than an hour. You really are quite impossible, sweeting." She turned to Moll. "Come, girl, and help your mistress. Sally, are the trunks ready yet? Everyone else's have already gone down."

"*I am not going!*" Calandra snarled, her hazel eyes darkening. Her hand reached for an ornament to throw. She gasped as Aurora grasped her wrist strongly, thereby preventing her from further mayhem.

"Leave us, all of you, just for a moment," Aurora said. "My sister and I need to speak together privately." She released Cally's wrist.

The three servants left the room.

"Why are you on *his* side?" Cally demanded.

"Because he is right and you are wrong," Aurora answered her bluntly. "You were married to a duke not so you might spend the rest of your life in a round of endless pleasures, but so that you might bear him children, Cally. I may be considered headstrong, but no one has ever said I did not do my duty. Now you must do yours."

"It was your duty to marry him, not mine, but you would not marry him," Calandra responded, rubbing her wrist.

"Because I was headstrong." Aurora laughed, "But you did marry him. He fulfilled his part of the bargain. Now you must fulfill yours."

"I will not do it! And there is nothing you say, Aurora, that will make me. I am the Duchess of Farminster. You are only my stepsister. You have no power over me!" Cally said meanly.

"Ahhh, little one, but I do," Aurora replied softly. "If you do not come quietly with us to Hereford, I will tell Valerian of how we deceived him."

"You wouldn't dare!" Cally whispered, disbelieving.

"I will have no choice," Aurora answered her. "If you will not do your duty as Valerian's wife, then I must tell him of the fraud we perpetrated upon him. This will allow him to either annul your marriage or divorce you with just cause, which he certainly has. You have been a disobedient wife, and you refuse to give him heirs. What good are you to him? You have, I regret to tell you, Cally, become a great embarrassment to George and me. Only the vast span of the ocean has kept me from informing Mama of your bad behavior. She would not approve of it. She would want me to act toward you as I am now doing. She would not want you to ruin us all. Do you understand me, Cally?"

"I hate you!" Calandra spat out.

"No, little sister, you don't really hate me, but you are angry that

I have found a way to curb your wicked conduct. You were always a poor loser at games, Cally, and this is the biggest game of all. The most important we shall ever play."

"No wonder the men didn't like you," Cally said cruelly. "They said you were uppity and high-flown for such an unimportant little colonial. Too much of a bluestocking, Trahern said he heard."

"Lord Trahern's gossip is of little import to me, Cally. I found your friends shallow, dull, and wretchedly obvious. As for the ladies, they were little better, and most of the girls my age were insipid and silly. Very much like you have become, I fear. I think I shall find a nice country gentleman far more to my taste, even if he isn't a duke. However, if you wish to retain your title, little sister, you had best let Moll dress you. The trip is a long one, the dowager informs me. We want to make it as pleasant as possible. Shall I call your servants back now?" She smiled at Calandra.

What would she do, I wonder, Cally thought, if I told her to go to the devil and called her bluff. But Cally knew what Aurora would do. She never in all their lives had made an idle threat or refused a reasonable dare. She will expose me. Expose our deceit even if it means we will all be ruined. She has a dowry and an income. I have nothing if I am not the Duchess of Farminster. I should have to go back to St. Timothy and live in the old Meredith plantation house with Mama for the rest of my life. *Alone. Thousands of miles from London.* She shuddered.

"Cally?"

"Oh, call my servants in, Aurora. You have won this round, but I will find a way to repay you for this betrayal, I promise you!"

"You will feel better when we have reached Hawkes Hill," Aurora said soothingly. "You are exhausted with all your social life."

"Oh, go to the devil!" Cally said sourly, "And get out!"

Their trip was not unpleasant. Cally sulked and hardly spoke to her, but the landscape outside their carriage while winter still was yet lovely. Their vehicle was comfortable and warm, and very well sprung. The horses were changed at midday when they stopped to refresh themselves at the prearranged inn. Their accommodations were clean and quite satisfactory. There were hot, tasty meals and warm featherbeds with down comforters. Hot water was brought at night to wash, and again in the morning.

When her stepsister's mood refused to lighten, Aurora asked the dowager's permission to ride in her coach with her. She was a far better companion, and very knowledgeable about the country through which they were traveling.

"The road we travel upon was originally built by the Romans," the dowager informed Aurora. "Do you know about the Romans, girl?"

"A little bit, ma'am. They were an ancient peoples, warlike, considered a great civilization in their time. I did not know, however, that they built roads too."

"All over England, girl!" She smiled at Aurora. "How is it you know about the Romans? I doubt that bubblehead of a sister of yours knows about Romans, or much of anything else either."

"Cally was not particularly fond of her studies as George and I were, but she plays the pianoforte beautifully. Has she played for you? She can sing too, and paint," Aurora defended Calandra.

"How did you convince her to come along so meekly?" the dowager demanded. "She's been sulking ever since we left London, but she came."

Aurora laughed, pretending to make light of the matter. "Why, ma'am, I just told her if she didn't behave herself, the duke would divorce her, and then she wouldn't be a duchess anymore."

"Hah!" the dowager barked a sharp laugh. "You certainly know the bubblehead's weak spot, don't you, girl? Aye, that was a good threat. Calandra likes being the Duchess of Farminster." She looked sharply at Aurora. "I shall have to be careful choosing a husband for you, girl. If he is too weak, you will have no respect for him, and if he is too strong, you will kill each other. You present me with quite a challenge."

"As my family knows, ma'am, I will marry only for love. Titles and wealth mean little to me. Nevertheless, I will appreciate your efforts in the matter. Perhaps together we shall be successful."

Her gloved hands were folded meekly in her lap, but Mary Rose Hawkesworth was not in the least fooled.

"Are you as stubborn as your sister, then, miss?" she asked.

"I will admit to being stubborn," Aurora replied, "but you will find me far more reasonable than Cally, I think."

The dowager chuckled, genuinely amused. It had been a very long time since she had been so taken with someone as she was with Aurora. Again she considered the pity of it that it hadn't been Aurora her dear grandson married instead of the foolish Calandra. Changing the subject, she said, "I believe I have the perfect wife for George, although I will certainly present him with several young ladies that I consider suitable marriage prospects. Still, I have my own personal favorite. I shall tell you about her if you do not tell your brother. He should make up his own mind, of course."

"I promise, ma'am," Aurora said.

"Her name is Elizabeth Bowen. She is the eldest daughter of Sir Ronald and Lady Elsie Bowen. Sir Ronald is a baronet with a small estate matching ours. He is the vicar at Farminster village church."

"Would her family be willing to have their daughter move an ocean away from them, ma'am?" Aurora wondered. "You know that Valerian appointed George to remain in his position as St. Timothy's manager."

"The Bowens will thank God if Betsy and George are taken with each other. Lady Elsie proved a fecund wife, but she has given her husband five daughters before their son was at last born. Five dowries, and the estate entailed upon the heir. Those poor girls don't have large portions, and cannot expect great marriages. A young man with an income such as your brother's will be considered a treasure."

"How will he meet her, ma'am?"

"We shall have a ball at Hawkes Hill once we are settled in again. That should please your sister," the dowager said. Then she yawned. "I am exhausted with all this traveling. I will certainly be glad to be sleeping in my own bed tonight." She closed her eyes, and very shortly began to snore softly.

Aurora looked out the window of the coach as it rumbled along the road. The landscape was rolling. Here and there the symmetry of the land was broken by isolated hills. They had crossed a great number of brooks, streams, and small rivers along the way. The countryside was heavily wooded, stands of oak and elm and beech vying with orchards that come spring would blossom, and come late summer would give forth a bounteous crop of apples and pears. There were arable fields, their plow ruts frozen with winter's cold. By summer they would be golden with wheat. Herefordshire's greatest wealth was in the sheep and cattle now grazing on the late February hills. The cattle were bred for meat, which for the most part would end up in London. The sheep gave a good wool crop regularly that was woven in the area's many small water-powered mills into fine cloth and yarns.

Most of the farms and small towns they passed by had timber-framed houses with thatched roofs. The churches, even those in the little villages, were, however, constructed of stone, as were the castles and the great houses of nobility. Cally had complained that Hawkes Hill was a big old-fashioned stone house with a slate roof, and nothing to recommend it at all. The dowager, however, had told Aurora that the house dated back to Tudor times, and indeed had been constructed on the ruins of an earlier house that had burned.

The Hawkesworth family had been barons on the estate for longer than anyone could recall. The earldom had come into being when one of the ancestors had done a great favor for King Henry VII. This first Tudor king was noted for being tightfisted. Raising a man in rank was a cheap enough thanks for the king, especially when the man already possessed a large estate. The dukedom, of course, had come through Charles II.

Suddenly the coach began to slow itself, and when it had almost stopped it turned off the high road onto a narrower track. The vehicle bumped along, but the dowager continued to snore on contentedly. Aurora smiled, and drew the lap robe up a bit farther so the old lady would not catch a chill. They were obviously approaching Hawkes Hill Hall. The carriage finally came out of the trees, and Aurora could see the roadway stretching ahead of them across a greensward, and, beyond, upon a hill, was set the hall. It looked almost like a castle with its dark gray stone turrets and towers.

Aurora gently shook her companion. "Ma'am, I believe we are approaching home," she said.

"Eh? What?" The old lady's eyes flew open, focused, and then she said, "Yes, that is Hawkes Hill. I hope you are going to be very happy here with us, Aurora. At least until you depart a bride."

"Or return home to St. Timothy," Aurora replied.

"Do not say such a thing," the dowager scolded her. "I should consider myself a complete failure, and unable to face your dear mama, if I did not provide you with a good husband, child."

As the travelers drew up to the house, they found servants waiting to welcome them and take the luggage down from the baggage carts. Calandra swept grandly by everyone, Sally and Moll in her wake, disappearing into the building. The duke ushered his grandmother and his guests inside.

"Welcome to Hawkes Hill," he said to George and Aurora. "Grandmama, will you be joining us for dinner this evening?"

The dowager held her hands out to the fireplace, then said, "I think not, dear boy. It has been a long trip, and I think I should prefer a tray in my room. I know you understand."

"Yer grace?" Moll had joined them. "Her grace says she'll take dinner in her room too; and she don't want to be disturbed neither, she says to tell you, sir." The maidservant curtsied, flushing.

"Tell her grace that I acquiesce tonight, but tomorrow is another matter. Say it just like that, Moll," the duke instructed the girl, his demeanor serious.

"Yes, yer grace." Moll curtsied again, almost running from the drawing room where they were all standing.

"Impudent chit!" the dowager muttered. "And to send that poor child to deliver such a message. Valerian, you must do something!"

"I fully intend to, Grandmama." He turned to George and Aurora.

"Dinner in the country is at seven," he said. "Peters will show you to your rooms." He bowed.

The dowager had gone on ahead of them. George and Aurora followed the butler back into the entry hall. Beyond the staircase they could see a large room, probably the old hall, Aurora thought. She was really looking forward to exploring this wonderful house. *It might have been yours,* a wicked little voice in her head reminded her. She pushed the thought away. She had made her choice, and she had to be content to live with it. It was, after all, what she had wanted. *Wasn't it?*

"You and the old girl get on quite well," George whispered as they mounted the broad staircase. "You were in her coach all but the first day. Cally is obviously still in a bad mood."

"The dowager was far better company than our sister," Aurora told him. "Besides, I like her. She is intelligent and has wit."

"What are we to do about Cally?" George persisted.

"Cally is not our concern," Aurora told her brother. "We helped to get her home, and now the rest is up to the duke. She is his wife. Besides, Lady Mary Rose has plans for you, George. She has lined up a bevy of eligibles from which you must pick a bride." Aurora chuckled wickedly. "I cannot wait to meet the girl who will ensnare you with melting eyes and maidenly sighs."

"And what about you, miss?" he demanded.

"First you, George," Aurora laughed, giving him a gay wave as she entered the bedroom Peters indicated was hers. "I'll see you at dinner, brother dear!" And she blew him a kiss.

"Well, miss, and here you are at last," Martha said. " 'Tis a grand house this Hawkes Hill. Just look at this room. Isn't it lovely?"

Aurora looked around, and had to agree with her servant that it was a lovely room. The walls were covered in a creamy silk. The woodwork was painted pale green. The hardwood floors were covered with a rose and green Oriental carpet. The marble fireplace was flanked with a winged angel on either side. The cream and celadon striped draperies were of heavy silk, tied back with heavy gold roping. The mahogany bed had tall turned posts and an arched canopy of cream satin. The matching bed drapes were sprigged with rosebuds. There was a magnificent mahogany chest against one wall; a piecrust table before the windows flanked on either side by upholstered chairs; and by her bedside was the prettiest little side table Aurora had ever seen, atop which was a crystal candlestick with a beeswax candle and a small silver snuffer.

"And," Martha said, sounding most pleased, "there's a separate dressing room for your clothing, miss, as well as a little room for me so I don't have to climb those stairs into the attic."

"Then you think we'll be happy here?" Aurora teased her servant.

"We'd have been happier if you knows what," Martha replied tartly. "Miss Calandra's rooms are at the far end of the hallway. She ain't hardly spoke to you since we left London."

"She's still angry at me, I fear, for threatening her as I did," Aurora said. "I far more enjoyed riding with the old dowager." She sighed. "It is unusual for Cally to have such a prolonged attack of the sulks, but she'll come around in time. After all, I'm all she'll have unless she makes some friends among the local gentry."

"They won't be tony enough for the likes of our duchess," Martha decided. Then she said, "Would you like a bath, miss?"

Aurora nodded. "It is to be just George, Valerian, and me at the dinner table, but I think I should make an effort, don't you?"

Martha agreed. Going to the wall, she yanked on the bellpull. It was answered shortly by a housemaid. "My mistress needs a bath," Martha said. "Would you be kind enough to have hot water brought?"

"Yes, ma'am," the housemaid said politely. A personal servant outranked her.

At five minutes before the hour of seven, Aurora descended back down the wide staircase, going to the drawing room where the duke had said they would meet. Her gown was of lavender silk, the underskirt a broad stripe of lavender and cream. The rounded neckline was edged in tiny purple silk violets, and her sleeves dripped lace.

"Good evening, Valerian," she said, curtsying prettily. "I am early, then, for I do not see George, who is always on time."

"How pretty you look, Aurora," he replied by way of a greeting. He was dressed in white knee breeches, a black velvet coat, and a waistcoat of black and white striped silk. "No, your brother has not come down yet. Do you find your room satisfactory?"

"Oh, yes! And Martha is more than pleased to have her own little room next to mine. It was most thoughtful."

"Excuse me, your grace." George's valet, Wickham, stood politely in the door of the drawing room.

"Yes, Wickham?"

"Master George begs your pardon, yer grace, but he's got the headache fierce, and is already, beggin' yer pardon again, tossin' his guts. He can't come down to dinner. Not that I didn't warn him to wear a hat today when you was ridin', but would he listen?"

"Do what you must to cure the poor fellow," the duke said. "I hope he will be better by the morrow."

"Thank you, yer grace," Wickham said, and withdrew.

"Poor George," Aurora sympathized with her absent brother. "He gets these headaches out of the blue now and then. The worst of them cause his stomach to turn as delicate as a maiden's. It's better since he is grown, but when we were children he got them every few months. Mama had to sit by his bed and rub his aching head."

"Tell me about your growing up on St. Timothy," the duke said, escorting her into the magnificent dining room and seating her on his right. "Peters, remove the other table setting. Master George will not be joining us. He has been taken ill." He turned back to Aurora.

"You must be bored to death with hearing about our childhood," Aurora laughed. "Surely Calandra has spoken at length on it."

"Your sister speaks only about society, her place in it, fashion, and the latest gossip," Valerian replied bitterly.

"But surely on your voyage . . . you were several weeks at sea," Aurora said.

"Our honeymoon voyage was dull, to say the least. Your sister spent a great deal of time alternately boring and impressing the other passengers, depending upon their level of gullibility, with her mindless chatter which revolved about her title, the wardrobe she would purchase when we reached England, and the high place she would take in society. Most nights she was overcome with seasickness, or so she said. I slept in Sally's cabin, and Sally slept on the trundle beneath Calandra's bed."

"Oh, Valerian, I am so sorry," Aurora said, and without thinking reached out to touch his hand comfortingly.

His fingers closed about hers. "You could not know, Aurora. I apologize for being less than delicate with you."

"I do not understand Cally at all. She is entirely different from the sister I grew up with," Aurora responded, her cheeks pink, and then she gently extracted her hand from his. She could feel every pulse in her body pounding at his touch, but she hoped her discomfort did not show. She had begun to suspect that her comparisons of the gentlemen she had met in London to Valerian Hawkesworth were detrimental to her finding a husband of her own to love. She must not be attracted to this man, nor he to her. Valerian Hawkesworth was Cally's husband.

"Let us forget my wife for the moment," he told her. "Tell me of what it was like to grow up on St. Timothy."

"It was wonderful," Aurora began. Perhaps her recollections would help him to understand Cally better, and allow them to forge a deeper, more loving relationship. "I remember nothing but St. Timothy, although George says he thinks he remembers Jamaica. Robert Kimberly formally adopted us immediately. He filed the papers in Barbados. He is the only father I have ever known." Well, at least that was the truth, Aurora thought to herself. "There was never any rivalry between any of us. I have been told that brothers and sisters often fight, but we never did. When we were small, we made up a motto, and we have adhered to it all of our lives. You heard us speak it the day you and my sister departed St. Timothy. *Together. Forever. As one.*"

The duke nodded. "Cally never explained it to me," he said. "I think it is charming. Go on."

"There is really little to tell," Aurora continued. "Our home was filled with love. Mama was the gentler parent, and it was easy to get around her. Papa was the sterner one, but he was never cruel, never beat any of us, and getting around him was a victory." She laughed with the memory. "We had a tutor for lessons. George and

I excelled, and were in frequent competition. Cally did not like learning a great deal. She was better at female pursuits like embroidery, painting, and music. George and I rode a great deal, but Cally has never really liked horses, as I told you previously. My brother and I loved swimming together, but Cally does not like the water, and always feared for her delicate skin in the sun. When we were small, the three of us would paddle about in the shallows beneath Martha's eye, but from the time she was about six, Cally did not enjoy being naked, and refused to swim with us. And when we were eight, Martha decided that George and I could not swim together unless he wore his drawers and I wore a chemise. We did not understand why at the time, but we obeyed her directive. Martha can be very severe, and Mama told us we must obey her."

"And you never left your island kingdom?" the duke said.

Aurora shook her head. "No. There was no need to leave it. We had everything we needed there."

"And no one came to visit?"

"Rarely. Mama's family in Jamaica had disowned her when she ran away with her first husband, our father. He was of good family, but the black sheep, I fear. He was killed in a duel. Poor Mama. She always believed she could reform him, but it was not to be. He had been dead over a year when she met Papa. Her first husband had left her practically impoverished. A cousin, who knew Papa, took pity on Mama and invited her to dinner the same night she had invited Papa. Mama says it was love at first sight. They were married a month later, shocking Mama's family once again. They would not even come to the wedding, and voiced their opinion about Kingston that Mama would once again suffer for her impulsive behavior. I do not believe they would have been welcome on St. Timothy even if they had come. No, we had few visitors on the island. An occasional planter or sea captain. No one else."

A simple meal was served as she spoke. A clear soup, a lemon sole, a roast of beef with Yorkshire pudding, a dish of carrots, and another of turnip. For all her chatter, Aurora managed to eat with a hearty appetite, much to the duke's amazement. Her appetite was quite astoundingly prodigious for a girl with such a small frame. In

London they had rarely taken a meal together, Calandra preferring to serve her guests meals on trays before departing for a ball, and when they had had dinner at another house he had been nowhere near Aurora to see her eat with the gusto with which she was now eating. Where did she put it all? he wondered.

"Tell me about your childhood," she said as she spooned up the last of her sherried trifle from a Wedgwood dish. "You lost your parents when you were young, didn't you?"

"Like you," he said, escorting her back into the drawing room, "I had a happy childhood, cut all too short when my parents, and sister, Sophia, were drowned returning from France. My grandparents then took it upon themselves to raise me. I was tutored until I went off to Oxford. I came home after two years. I prefer my country life, my horses, the cattle and sheep I raise. I have my own mills, and Hawkes yarn is becoming quite well known throughout England. I have formed a small company and market it myself. Your sister was quite horrified when she learned of it. She considers farming and trade beneath a gentleman, but the king loves farming too." They sat together upon a tapestried settee. "Will you miss London, like Cally?" he asked her.

"No," Aurora told him. "Like you, I am a country mouse." The scent of him was filling her head and making her dizzy.

"Then perhaps you will ride with me in the morning. If your sister keeps to her schedule, we shall not see her much before two in the afternoon," he said dryly.

"It has been a long journey," Aurora replied. "I think perhaps tomorrow I shall stay abed until at least nine o'clock."

"Of course," he said. "We shall ride later, and I will show you one of my little mills. Perhaps George will be up to coming too." What was that fragrance that surrounded her? It was so clean and fresh.

"That would be nice," Aurora murmured. His big hand lay almost next to hers upon her skirt, his upon his knee. She could feel the heat from it. *She had to get a grip upon herself!*

There was a long, deep silence between them. He did not know what to say, and feared to speak to speak at all lest he break the spell between them.

Finally Aurora forced herself to her feet. "It has been a tiring day, Valerian," she said. "I believe I shall go to my room now." *Were her knees going to hold her up?*

"Let me escort you," he said, jumping up and taking her arm.

She wanted to tell him it wasn't necessary. That she was perfectly capable of finding her way out into the hall and walking up the staircase to her bedroom. There was no danger in it. Martha would be there waiting for her, but somehow Aurora could say nothing except "Thank you, Valerian." His fingers gripped her elbow in a firm yet gentle grasp. It was ridiculous, but she felt safe with him somehow, and there was really nothing wrong in his polite actions. The problem was with her. He was engendering feelings within her that she had never before experienced, and she must get a hold of herself at once. She must remember that this man was her sister's husband. If their marriage had not been a happy one to date, it soon would be. It had to be! Cally would have a child, and everything would be all right.

They mounted the stairs together. Behind them the servants were snuffing out the candles. Reaching the door of her bedroom, Valerian stopped, and releasing his grip on her arm leaned forward to kiss her on the forehead.

"Good night, Aurora," he said. "Pleasant dreams." Then he walked off down the corridor to his own rooms.

She stepped through the doorway into her chamber. Her heart was pounding. When he had moved toward her she had thought she would faint, and then his lips had touched her forehead. She had been actually disappointed. Aurora knew she ought to be ashamed of herself, but she somehow couldn't bring herself to be. I must never again be alone with him, she thought. It is too dangerous. He is unhappy, and it is all my fault, but I cannot change anything now.

"You're as white as a sheet," Martha said, coming up and taking Aurora's hands in hers. "And you're cold as ice. What has happened?"

"Nothing," Aurora lied. "Nothing at all. I am just beginning to feel the effects of our journey, and am exhausted. I want to go to bed."

"Very well, miss," Martha said, but she did not for one minute believe that everything was right with her young mistress.

Chapter

6

It was past ten o'clock in the morning before Martha awakened her mistress the next day. Gently she shook the girl, and when Aurora had finally opened her eyes, the serving woman said, "I've brought your breakfast, miss." Then she plumped the pillows up behind the girl's back and placed a tray upon her lap. "The duke asked if you would ride with him this morning, but I told him you was still sleeping, and much too tired for all that activity today. I hope I did right, miss."

Disappointment commingled with relief. "You did, Martha. I am far too fatigued. I think I shall take a leaf from Cally's book and remain the morning in bed."

"An excellent idea, miss. The dowager's Jane tells me that's what the old lady is going to do too."

"Have you spoken with Wickham? Is George recovered?"

"Recovered, ate a huge breakfast, and gone off with the duke," Martha reported with a smile. "Now, there's some nice oat stirabout I sweetened with honey on your tray, and a soft-boiled egg. You eat every bit of it up, miss. You need your strength."

It felt good to be cosseted, Aurora thought as she spooned the oat cereal, rich with honey and heavy cream, into her mouth. She had certainly imagined last evening. Valerian Hawkesworth was too much of a gentleman to make advances to his wife's sister. She was simply overtired. They had had the voyage from St. Timothy, and then she had not really had a moment's rest since they arrived in England. Cally would not hear of it, and was constantly on the go, George and Aurora in her wake. The country was going to be a lovely change of pace.

She stayed the morning in bed. Calandra was nowhere to be found, and Aurora assumed she would still be in her chambers. George and the duke had not returned. The dowager kept to her bed. Aurora found her way to the duke's library, and, taking down a book on the history of the Hawkesworth family, settled into a chair by the fire to read. Peters, the butler, interrupted her at one point to ask if she would like him to bring her a tray with some luncheon.

"What time is it?" Aurora asked him.

"Almost one o'clock, miss," the butler replied.

"Is no one else taking lunch, then?"

"The duchess and the dowager duchess have called for trays in their chambers, miss. The duke and Master George have not yet returned. They were to ride over to Malvern mill, and that is a bit of a distance. They have undoubtedly stopped at one of the farms to eat. There is only yourself up and about."

"I am hungry," Aurora considered aloud.

"A nice pot of tea with your meal, miss?" the butler said.

"Yes, please," she answered. "Thank you, Peters."

The butler bowed slightly. Miss Aurora had nice manners, he thought to himself as he departed the library. What a pity her sister did not. The young duchess was the most demanding and ungrateful woman it had ever been his misfortune to know, and her servant, Sally, wasn't much better. He hoped they would not ruin young Moll, who was his granddaughter. The girl would be useless in service if they did.

Aurora read all day until the light began to fade in the library. Peters brought her luncheon. A footman added more logs to the fire twice. Finally a maid entered the room and began lighting the lamps. Aurora put the book back on its shelf and hurried upstairs to dress for dinner. If the duke and George had returned, she had not heard them come into the house. Cally, she knew, had not sent for her, else Peters would have come for her. She wondered how long her sister would sulk and allow her anger to burn.

She found George and Valerian awaiting her when she entered the drawing room. Cally and the dowager were still recovering from their journey. George was talkative, and full of enthusiasm over what he had seen that day.

"I believe we can apply some of the principles used in setting up the knitting mills to the bottling factory we shall build on St. Timothy," he said. "First, however, we ought to get a contract for the rum. Do you know of anyone in the Royal Navy who might help us, Val?"

Aurora let them talk, eating her dinner quietly.

There came a lull in the conversation between the two men as the dinner was drawing to a close, and the duke said, "Have you seen Calandra today, Aurora?"

Startled to hear her name spoken, she looked up. "What? I do beg your pardon, Valerian, but I was daydreaming, I fear."

"Have you seen Calandra?" he repeated.

"No, I spent my morning in bed and my afternoon reading in your library," she responded, not quite looking at him.

"Do you find my library satisfactory?" he said.

"*Satisfactory?* Why, it is the most incredible library I have ever seen!" she enthused. Then, "I hope you do not mind that I invaded your privacy, Valerian."

"Not at all. What did you read?" The dark blue eyes were willing her to look directly at him, but she would not.

"I came across a history of the Hawkesworth family. It is quite fascinating," she told him. She could feel him staring, and turned to her brother. "You must visit the library, George. There is a whole section on Greek history, and I know how you love that."

"I should like that!" George said, his voice excited.

"Why do you not take George to the library now," Valerian suggested. "I must leave you and go up to see Calandra." He rose from the table and bowed politely to them. "I bid you both good night."

Valerian Hawkesworth mounted the stairs purposefully, but instead of entering his wife's chambers, he entered his own. There, with Browne's help, he disrobed, washed, cleaned his teeth, and rinsed his mouth. He refused the silk nightshirt Browne offered, instead wrapping himself in a quilted silk robe the color of his best claret. Then he dismissed his valet courteously. Browne departed, his ageless face impassive, knowing what was to come, and knowing he would never divulge even the slightest hint of it to the other servants. Let the women gossip. He would not.

Entering his wife's bedchamber via a connecting door, the duke saw Calandra seated at her dressing table, Sally brushing her mistress's long black hair. He heard the servant counting off the strokes. Walking across the room, he took the silver brush from Sally, saying, "You are dismissed for the night, Sally. And Moll too." He began to ply the brush, taking up the count from where the maid had left off. "How many do you usually do?" he asked Calandra.

"Two hundred," she replied as the door closed behind her two serving girls.

He continued counting until all the strokes were accounted for, as he did not wish to antagonize Calandra. Perhaps, just perhaps now that they were home, now that Calandra surely understood he would not tolerate any more nonsense from her, perhaps now she would yield herself to him willingly and give him the children he desired. "Two hundred," he finally said, putting the brush down on the table and drawing her up and about so she faced him. He bent to kiss her.

A look of acute distaste passed over her face, and she pulled away from him. "Really, Valerian, must you?" she said coolly.

"You are my wife," he said quietly.

"And that gives you the right to impose your animal nature upon me? How unfair!" Calandra said.

What was the matter with her? he wondered. He had not been brutal or cruel with her on the rare occasions he had exercised his husbandly rights. The duke drew a deep breath. "What is it about intimacy between us that troubles you, Calandra?" he asked her.

He must be patient. "Do you find me unattractive? What can I do to please you, my dear?"

"If you truly desire to please me, Valerian, then I would ask that you leave me in peace and allow me to return to London to my friends."

Suddenly he was jealous. It wasn't that he really cared about this shallow girl who was his wife, but his pride was at stake here. Grasping her by the arms, he said angrily, "Is it Trahern? Do you find him attractive? Is he your lover? You will take no more lovers until you have given me my heir, Calandra! Until then, you will go nowhere!"

"*Trahern?*" She sounded genuinely surprised. Then she laughed. "I suppose he is attractive enough, but he is not my lover. I have no lovers. You are the only man who has ever known me in the biblical sense. I simply do not enjoy *the act*. I hate it when you push your member into my body, grunting and groaning until you release that unpleasant, sticky discharge of yours. If I never had to do *that* again, I should be a happy woman. I suppose that is why you are here tonight."

He was astounded by her admission. "Is it just me, or is it all men you despise in this sense?" he asked her.

"All men," she said frankly. "I do not like *the act*. I do not like being crushed beneath someone else's body. The scent you produce when you do it is unpleasant to my nostrils. The whole process is utterly disgusting. There is no delicacy in it at all, and I don't want to do it ever again. If you attempt to assault me, I shall scream the house down, Valerian. Now that I have explained myself, I hope you will go away and leave me free of such actions from now on."

He needed a drink, but there was none available to him here. Drawing in another deep breath, he said in a voice far calmer than he himself was feeling, "When did you know you felt this way, Calandra? Did your mother not explain to you that the act of copulation between a husband a wife was the manner in which they obtain children?"

"I felt this way from the moment you first touched me," she said quickly. *Too quickly.*

"No," he disagreed, "you are lying to me." His grip on her arms tightened again. "Tell me the truth, Calandra!"

"I was a virgin when we married!" she cried out. *"I was!"*

"I know that," he said, his voice a shade calmer. *"Tell me!"*

"When I was a little girl, perhaps eight, there was this planter from Barbados who would stop several times a year on his way to and from Jamaica. He brought Mama all the gossip of her family and friends, for even though she was estranged from them, she still enjoyed knowing what was going on in their lives. He was a great big man, the planter, and he always seemed to favor me over Aurora, taking me up onto his lap, cuddling me, pinching my cheeks, and saying I was the prettiest little girl in the world. Then he began to seek me out when no one else was around. He would take me on his lap and put his hand beneath my gown, touching me where I didn't even dare touch myself. I didn't like it, but he would soothe me with a kiss and a sweetmeat, and then release me, telling me that *this* was our little secret, and asking me not to tell anyone. Once he set me between his legs and took his member from his breeches and asked me to touch it. That was the day Martha came upon us. She took me from the man and told him that only if he promised her he would leave immediately and never return would she keep his disgusting secret. Then she took me away and questioned me as to what had happened, and for how long had it been happening. She said I must never tell anyone or else I would be considered *damaged goods*, and no decent young man would want me for a wife." Calandra gave a bitter little laugh. "But I knew by then I never wanted to be touched by a man again if I could avoid it."

"You knew what was involved in a marital relationship then," the duke said, "and yet you still married me? Why, Calandra?"

"I wanted to be a duchess," she answered him simply, and then, "and when I first saw you, you were so handsome, I thought that I could overcome my aversion, at least long enough to give you children. Then, I believed, you would take a mistress, and I should not have to endure your attentions for the rest of my life. I really did think I could do it, Valerian. *I did!*"

"You will have to do it, Calandra," he told her. "It is either that, or I must have the marriage annulled on the basis of your refusal to give me children. I am sorry, but I must have heirs!"

"You cannot cast me off," Calandra cried to him. "I like being a duchess! I think you are very cruel to me. If you try to annul our marriage, I shall tell people that you practice wicked and filthy perversions, and I shall ruin you so no decent parent will give their daughter into your safekeeping for a wife. You will never have children, Valerian! *Never! Never! Never!*"

Valerian Hawkesworth had a fierce temper that he rarely allowed to get out of control. Now, however, it exploded into a white-hot fury. "You dare to threaten me, you coldhearted marble Venus?"

Calandra stepped back, startled by the rage she saw in his deep blue eyes which were now practically black with anger.

The duke, however, reached out to grasp a handful of her long hair, wrapping it about his fist, yanking it close to him so that they were face-to-face. *"You will give me an heir, Calandra,"* he told her. "Since you wish to remain a duchess, you will do your duty by my family." His free hand grasped at the neckline of her nightgown, and he ripped it open. She shrieked, but before she might set up a greater cry, he threw her to the bed, and taking a handkerchief from his robe, he tied it tightly about her mouth. Then, standing, he removed his robe.

Valerian was furious with himself. Never in his entire life had he behaved this way with a woman. Any woman. Her threat, however, had been a powerful one. Even if he succeeded in annulling their union, her accusations could indeed ruin his chances for another marriage, even to Aurora. The scandal would be incredible, and his family would be barred from court. The new king was a moral young man with plans for marriage to a respectable princess. It was his own fault. He should have sent for the Kimberlys to come to England so he might get to know them before he married Calandra. He should have been suspicious when she refused to even let him kiss her in the plantation gardens. She had been his betrothed wife, not some debutante he was seeking to seduce. *He should have known something was wrong.* It was all his fault, and now there was nothing to do but that she give him the children he wanted whether she desired his attentions or not.

"You will not have to endure my passion," he told her, "once you are with child." He looked down on her. She was very beautiful, but he felt absolutely no lust for her at all. His member lay limp. Calandra gazed scornfully at it, silently taunting. He could have sworn she was trying to smile. The bitch was mocking him! At that moment he realized that he hated her. Hated her as much as he now knew he loved Aurora.

Aurora. His mind went back to that day on St. Timothy when he had accidentally come down to the beach and seen her frolicking in the blue-green waters of the sea. Then she had come up onto the beach all golden in color. As warm as the sunlight itself. He remembered her long legs, her perfectly round little breasts the size of ripe peaches, the pretty tangle of curls at the junction of her thighs that had glistened with little crystal drops of water. *And he had desired her then*. Even as he desired her now.

Cally whimpered, her eyes riveted to his groin where his member now thrust forth, hard as iron, and ready to plow her furrow. Dispassionately, he looked first at her, then at his manhood. Coldly pulling her legs apart, he leaned forward to pinion her arms and pushed himself into her. His desire for Aurora was great, and he quickly spilled his seed into his wife. Her look of revulsion soothed his troubled conscience. He remained with her long enough to assure she did not flush the seed from her body, and then, untying the handkerchief from her mouth, he arose from her bed.

"We will do this every night until I am convinced you are with child, Calandra," he told her with brutal frankness. "If you attempt to cry out, I will gag you once again. You will cause no upset within my house. Once you have given me a healthy son, then I shall leave you in peace for the rest of your days. You may go to London. You may go to Paris. You may go to hell for all I care. But you will go nowhere until I have my heir. Is that understood?"

She nodded, stunned by his determination.

"And tomorrow you will appear at the dinner table. I will tolerate no more sulking on your part. Is that also understood?"

"Yes," Cally whispered.

The duke picked up his dressing gown, and, wrapping it about himself, departed her chamber through the connecting door. Within the privacy of his own rooms he sagged against the chifforobe. He felt absolutely drained, and disgusted with himself, but what other choice had he had? He had heard of women like Calandra who disliked the sexual act entirely. Some women, he knew, preferred other women as lovers, as some men preferred those of their own kind. There were those who had lovers of both sexes, and then there were those very few like his wife for whom physical passion was repellent. What a pity she had been spoiled as a child by the planter from Barbados, who had touched her as no decent man should a little girl. That monster would have eventually raped Calandra had not the vigilant Martha discovered them.

Had Calandra been born with some inner distaste for lust and for love? Or had that youthful experience hurt and frightened her? If he had behaved differently, could he have taught her the joys of passion? He wanted to believe he could, but in his heart he knew that he could not. He had never been rough with his wife until that night. He had been patient and gentle with her. When he had finally gotten into her bed, it had been three nights before he had taken her virginity. Valerian Hawkesworth did not know what else he could have done. Now neither of them had a choice in the matter. He needed an heir, and Calandra wanted to remain Duchess of Farminster. It was a heavy burden he had to bear, and he would have to bear it alone. With a sigh he took off his dressing gown and put on the silk nightshirt that Browne had left at the foot of his bed before climbing between the lavender-scented sheets.

He had seen the shock in Calandra's eyes when his manhood had responded to his secret thoughts of Aurora. He wondered what his wife would think should she learn the object of his desire was her own sister. Hellfire and damnation, how he wanted her! But he would never have her except in his lonely dreams. He would have to cooperate with his grandmother to find Aurora a husband, and he would have to stand by as she was married to another man. A stranger who would get to plunder Aurora's sweetness as he never would. He hated the thought. Closing his eyes, he attempted to sleep.

In the morning the ladies always took breakfast on trays in their bedchambers. At luncheon, however, the duke was surprised to find his wife joining them at table. While a trifle paler than normal, Calandra looked none the worse for wear. Greeting him politely, she took her place, smiling brightly at those assembled.

"I am almost recovered from our journey," she said, and turned to the dowager. "And you, ma'am? You are looking well today."

Mary Rose Hawkesworth's thin eyebrow rose imperceptibly. "I am still tired," she said, "but then, I am a great deal older than you are, my dear. Still, I could not bear my own company another minute. Aurora, I am told you have been amusing yourself with our library."

"It's a wonderful library," Aurora responded. "Cally, how pretty you look," she told her sister. "I was worried about you."

"You need not have fretted," Cally replied. "How typical of you, Aurora, to spend all your time in a library. You will ruin your eyes and get wrinkles, I fear." She turned back to the dowager. "We must plan a ball, ma'am, if we are to launch my sister and brother onto the sea of matrimony. You know all the country folk to invite."

"Indeed I do. I thought, perhaps, Calandra, that the first of May would be a delightful time. All the villages celebrate with Maypoles, dancing, and bonfires. Would that suit you?"

"Can we not do it sooner?" Cally asked.

The dowager shook her head. "I am afraid not. There is a great deal of planning to a ball, Calandra, as you will see, since I expect you to help me plan it. Eventually you will plan all your balls yourself, but as this will be your first fete at Hawkes Hill, I will help you. There is much to do."

"Like what?" Cally was genuinely curious.

"Well, for starters," the dowager said, "the ballroom must be refurbished and thoroughly cleaned, the floors polished to a high gloss, the crystal chandeliers all washed and polished and set with freshly dipped candles. A menu must be selected and planned for those invited to dinner beforehand. We can seat only fifty. There are, of course, invitations to be issued, and they must all arrive on the same day else any guest feel slighted by learning another had received his or her invitation first. The gardeners must be certain that there are plenty of fresh flowers from the greenhouses for the hallway, the drawing room, the dining room, the ballroom. What cannot be supplied by our greenhouses must be begged from neighbors. We will have to hire young men and women from the village to help out as maids and footmen, and in the kitchens. And musicians, of course! Some of our guests may be invited to remain overnight, and so there must be bedrooms prepared for them."

"There is a great deal of detail to it, isn't there?" Calandra said, suddenly not quite so enthusiastic. "Can we not hire someone to do it all? And what of a seamstress? I will certainly need a new ball gown. I can hardly greet my guest in an old ball gown."

"Since none of our guests will have seen any of your ball gowns, Calandra, I do not understand why you need another one," Valerian said dryly.

She glared at him. "Do not be such a pinchpenny with me, sir. I will not embarrass myself by appearing in an old ball gown."

"Then you shall not," he said, "nor shall any of my ladies. A seamstress shall be called in to make ball gowns for you and Aurora and Grandmama. It is only fair, I think."

"What a fine idea!" his grandmother said, a twinkle in her eye.

"I do not really need another gown," Aurora said, "but I will not refuse your kind offer, Valerian. Perhaps, Cally, you will let me help you and Lady Mary Rose to repay my lord duke's kindness."

"Oh, yes! You were always better than I in matters like this," Cally said, delighted that her sister had volunteered her services. Perhaps she would not be angry at Aurora any longer. "Mama always said you were good at planning entertainments."

Well, thought the dowager, I will have some help in this endeavor, for she had quickly seen that Calandra was going to be absolutely no help at all to her. Aurora, on the other hand, would certainly be of value, and, the dowager suspected, probably had an eye for detail.

The following day was Sunday, and they traveled down into Farminster village to church. It was March, and a brisk breeze blew across the fields. Some of the trees were beginning to show signs of leafing, their buds plump and exhibiting green. Here and there, clumps of bright yellow daffodils were in bloom. The coach horses stepped smartly down the road, drawing up before St. Anne's. A footman jumped down from the rear of the coach where he had been riding, and opening the door, lowered the steps. Holding out his hand, he helped the ladies to exit the vehicle. The gentlemen had ridden, and were even now dismounting.

The dowager led the way, nodding to this side and that as the villagers greeted her, the women curtsying, the men doffing their caps as she and her companions passed. Now and then she would stop a moment to greet someone by name. As they reached the porch of the stone church, her sharp eye spied the women she had been seeking.

"Ahhh," the dowager said, smiling toothily, "my dear Lady Bowen. How'd ye do? And your lovely daughters too, I see, and Master William. A lovely day, isn't it? Have you met my grandson's wife, the young duchess?"

Lady Bowen was a tiny, birdlike creature with pale blue eyes and sandy-brown curls. She curtsied. "How nice it is to see your ladyship again," she twittered, for she found the dowager formidable. "No, I haven't met the duchess yet." Her eyes darted between the two girls.

Mary Rose Hawkesworth drew Calandra forward. "Calandra, Duchess of Farminster, Lady Elsie Bowen, the vicar's wife."

Lady Bowen curtsied while Cally nodded coolly as she had seen her London friends do when presented with someone of a lower station.

"And this is the duchess's sister, Miss Aurora Spencer-Kimberly," the dowager continued, more pleased when Aurora held out her hand, curtsied prettily, and greeted Lady Bowen politely, than she had been with Calandra's high tone and slightly insulting manner. She turned, calling, "Valerian, come and bid Lady Bowen a good morning before we go in to services, and bring George." And when the two men came and the duke had done his grandmother's bidding, the old lady introduced George to the Bowens. First Lady Bowen, and then her son, William, a freckle-faced lad, who if the gossip had it correct was a little hellraiser, and his mother's despair. "And here, dear George, we have Miss Elizabeth, Miss Isabelle, Miss Suzanne, Miss Caroline, and Miss Maryanne Bowen. Such pretty girls, Lady Bowen," she complimented their mother, "and all very accomplished, I am told. You are a fortunate parent indeed, and will certainly find husbands for them all when they are old enough."

"Oh," Lady Bowen twittered, "Betsy is quite old enough now!"

"Is she indeed?" the dowager purred, and then with a nod she beckoned her family into the church.

"Really, Mama!" Elizabeth Bowen was outraged, and not just a trifle embarrassed by her mother's enthusiasm.

"Well, you are old enough for marriage," her mother protested, "and I am told that Mr. Spencer-Kimberly is looking for a wife. He will return to the western Indies, where he has been raised to continue to manage St. Timothy island plantation when he finds a suitable mate. He has an inheritance *and* an income, I am told. Would it be so terrible if he found you attractive and offered for you, Betsy?"

"How on earth do you obtain all this information, and so quickly?" Betsy Bowen asked her mother. "Why, the duke and his family only just returned this week to Farminster, Mama."

"I have my sources," her parent replied smugly. "Remember, Betsy, you are not the only eligible in the neighborhood, and I have heard whispers of a ball in May at the hall. A fine young man like Mr. Spencer-Kimberly will be snapped up quickly, my girl, and your dowry is not so large that you can afford to turn up your nose at such a prize."

"Mama! Mama! The organist is about to begin the processional," William Bowen cried to his mother.

"Gracious, thank you, Willie. Come, girls! We are late!" And Lady Bowen, skirts flying, hurried into the church with her family. Quickly taking their places in the front two pews, opposite the duke's private pew, they took up their hymnals and began to sing. Betsy Bowen could not resist glancing over into the duke's pew at George. He did look nice, and he had greeted her, and each of her sisters, most politely by name. He didn't appear at all high-flown or overproud. If only Mama wouldn't embarrass her by pushing her at him. I had best take matters into my own hands before that happens, she thought to herself.

When the service was over and they walked from the church, Betsy managed to maneuver herself so that she was walking next to George Spencer-Kimberly. "Do you ride, sir?" she asked him. "We have such lovely countryside hereabouts."

"Perhaps you would show it to me," he responded, "if, of course, your parents would permit it, Miss Elizabeth." He liked this girl already. She wasn't silly or flirtatiously vain like the girls he had met in London. She was straightforward, and looked to be sensible.

"Mama, Mr. Spencer-Kimberly would like to ride with me one morning if he has your permission," Betsy called to her mother.

Lady Bowen was astounded. Good Lord, how had Betsy elicited that invitation? Pray God she hadn't been forward, and Mr. Spencer-Kimberly thought her a lightskirt. "I shall have to speak to your papa, Betsy," she told her daughter, and then, "Will you come to tea today, Mr. Spencer-Kimberly? We should be so pleased to receive you. Five o'clock, at the vicarage."

"I should be pleased, ma'am," George answered Lady Bowen.

"Oh, Lord," Betsy muttered beneath her breath.

"I promise not to hold your mama against you, Miss Elizabeth," George murmured with a low chuckle.

Startled, her eyes met his, and Betsy blushed, then said, "You understand, don't you?"

He nodded. "I have a doting and anxious mama too." Then he bowed to her, tipping his hat. "Until this afternoon," he said.

He is really too good to be true, Betsy thought, amazed at her good fortune. If he really is wonderful, we shall be engaged by the time that ball is held in May, else I lose him to some other girl! She stood watching as George rode off with the duke.

"How did you get him to ask you riding?" her sister Isabelle asked, coming to stand beside Betsy. Isabelle was fifteen. "Mama is ready to have an attack of the vapors, else he think you loose."

"I simply asked if he rode and said we had pretty countryside,"

Betsy said, linking her arm in Isabelle's as they walked to the vicarage.

"Do you think I'll be invited to the duke's ball?" the younger girl wondered. "Oh, I should so like to go, Betsy! I've never been to a ball in my whole life, and it's bound to be elegant."

"Well," her sister considered, "you will be sixteen on the thirtieth of April, sweeting. If you are included in the invitation, I will take your part with Mama. Papa is always easy to manage."

"Oh, Betsy! You are the very best sister possible!" Isabelle said. Then she waved at the dowager as the ducal coach passed by on its way back to the hall.

Mary Rose Hawkesworth waved back. "Pretty chits, aren't they?" she said to her two companions. "Of course, Isabelle is too young for George, but Elizabeth would be most suitable, and I believe she likes him. Did you notice how cleverly she managed to get him to ask her riding, and now he is to go to tea at the vicarage this afternoon. I am most pleased," she finished, and, smiling, sat back in her seat.

"The church is small," Calandra noted.

"It is a country church, Cally, and quite charming," Aurora said. "Certainly there are none larger on Barbados, I'm certain."

"Who cares about Barbados" was her answer. "We've never been anyway, so we cannot know. The churches in London, however, are much bigger than St. Anne's, and far grander."

"Did you go to services in any of them?" Aurora teased her sister. "I mean, before George and I arrived. In fact, if memory serves me, you did not go with us at all while we were in London."

"You couldn't expect me to get up and go to church after having been dancing until dawn most nights," Cally said irritably.

"How fortuitous, then, that you shall not have that problem here in the country," the dowager said sharply. "We attend church each Sunday, Calandra. It is up to us to set an example for our people."

"I thought the vicar's sermon quite good," Aurora said.

"He preaches well," Lady Hawkesworth agreed.

"It was short," Cally said.

Aurora bit her lip to keep from laughing.

The days flew by. Spring had come in all its glory. George had made a success with the Bowens and now rode daily with Betsy, staying away from the hall, and spending more time at the vicarage as the weeks progressed. It was obvious that romance was in the air even if their brother had not said anything yet to confirm their suspicions.

"I think he means to offer for her," Aurora said to Calandra one afternoon as they wrote out the invitations for the ball. "I will miss him when he returns to St. Timothy, won't you?"

Cally nodded. "We've been together our whole lives except for those few months when I first came to England. It will seem strange not seeing George. Will you go too, Aurora? I don't want you to go. Not now! Especially not now! I couldn't bear it if you left me alone!"

"Why are you so unhappy?" Aurora asked her sister bluntly.

"It is Valerian," Cally whispered. "He is such a beast! I just want to go back to London, but he will not let me. He makes me perform *the act* each night. I have told him I don't want children. I just want to go back to London and have fun!"

"Cally, Cally," her sister chided her. "Children are the fruit of a marriage. If you didn't want children, you should not have married Valerian. I know your husband is a good man. Give him his children and he will let you return to London for the season."

"I want to live there all the time," Cally said. "And if I hadn't married him, you would have had to do so. Besides, I wanted to be a duchess, Aurora, and you didn't! Oh, why do I even talk to you about this? How can you understand? You are a silly little virgin, but one day you will understand how horrible it is to have a man in your bed, pawing at you, and pushing himself into your body. I hate it!"

Calandra's face was a mask of revulsion and disgust, and Aurora was hard put not to shiver. "Mama did not seem to mind having Papa in her bed," she said softly.

"Some women like *it*," Cally said darkly, "but I do not. If I cannot escape this horror soon, I shall go mad."

"If you could just have a child," Aurora said. "I know you would feel different if you had a child of your own, Cally."

The invitations were dispatched, and there was not one refusal. Everyone in the adjoining area was eager to come to Hawkes Hill Hall on May first for the ball being given by the Duke and Duchess of Farminster. Many of their neighbors had not yet met Calandra, for she had fled back to London soon after arriving in the country the previous year. There had been gossip, however, for everyone had a relation or friend in London society. And then, too, the duchess had an older brother, and a younger sister, both eligible, and both, if the tittle-tattle was to be believed, with very nice incomes. It was surprising, however, the scandalmongers chattered, that neither of these siblings had found mates in London. Obviously they were not attractive, or possibly a little too colonial for high society. Such things, of course, could be overlooked by a more practical country lady or gentleman.

Calandra had done little except help with the invitations. Her sole focus had been on the gown she would wear. Aurora had helped the dowager with all the fine details, overseeing the refurbishing of the ballroom, helping to choose the flowers and then working with herself and the housekeeper to arrange them, sending to London for the musicians. The dowager had chosen those fortunate few who would come to dinner; and invited the vicar, Lady Elsie, and their two eldest daughters to stay overnight. George had already informed his benefactress that he intended asking Miss Elizabeth Bowen to be his wife, and the dowager duchess had already ascertained that the Bowens would approve the match if it pleased their eldest daughter. George would speak to them formally the afternoon of the ball.

As the day of the ball approached, Calandra grew more and more excited. Her gown was finished, and, she declared, was a triumph that would be envied by every one of her female guests. Of rose-colored silk, it had a deeply scooped neckline that would allow her alabaster bosom to swell provocatively. The underskirt was of cloth of gold with embroidered silk roses. Gold lace and silk roses edged the neckline. Gold lace dripped from her sleeves. Her gold kid shoes had pink rosettes on them, and her silk stockings were gold and rose stripes. Her dark hair, with its single elegant curl, would be dressed with fresh roses. She would wear pear-shaped pearl earbobs, and a strand of large pearls about her throat. The pearls dated back to Elizabethan times, and had been hidden away during the Commonwealth era. It was a showy touch, for women in this day wore little jewelry, but Calandra didn't care. What was jewelry for but to wear. Not keep in some dark vault!

"Isn't your gown a bit short," Aurora said, noting that the skirt of the ball gown seemed skimpy.

"It is the latest style!" Cally crowed. "A ball gown should come only to the ankle, so one can dance comfortably. We shall be more in style than any of our guests."

"Practical," the dowager said thoughtfully. Then, "A lady does not make her guests feel uncomfortable for any reason, Calandra."

"No, ma'am," Cally replied, flushing with irritation at having been rebuked by the old woman. She fingered the silk on the dress form.

"And what of your gown, child?" the dowager asked Aurora.

Aurora removed the dust sheet from the second form to reveal a gown of aquamarine silk, its chiffon underskirt painted with silver stars. Small silver lace stars decorated the rounded neckline, and the blue-green chiffon and lace sleeves.

"Why, it matches your eyes," the dowager said, delighted. "It is charming. You shall be the two prettiest ladies at the ball, I vow. Do you have the proper panniers and petticoats?"

"Yes, ma'am," Cally responded. "The seamstress brought an excellent selection of both, and we have already chosen."

"And your jewelry, Aurora? What will you wear?"

"Just my little gold chain, ma'am," the girl said.

"I have a pair of aquamarine drops that will be perfect with your gown," the dowager said. "While Calandra will be the finest peahen in the family, you should not appear too plain. After all, we are seeking the proper gentleman for you, am I not correct, Calandra?"

"I certainly agree, ma'am," Cally answered, hiding the jealousy she felt over her husband's grandmother giving Aurora family jewelry to wear. Still, Aurora should have something. Smiling, she said, "And your gown, ma'am? What have you had made for yourself?"

"Nothing as fine as what you two girls have," the dowager replied. "My gown is of a deep blue silk the seamstress said is called Midnight in Morocco. I do not need to show such fine feathers any longer. After all, I am an old woman," Mary Hawkesworth finished. "I have no desire to catch myself a husband."

The Bowens and their two elder daughters arrived in late morning the day of the ball. The younger daughter was almost ill with excitement.

Aurora immediately took Isabelle in hand. "It's just a dancing party," she reassured the girl. "We went to them every night when we were in London. I was constantly exhausted. You will have a marvelous time, I promise you. How pretty you are. You shall take all the beaus, and I am already eighteen. Practically an old maid!"

"Ohhh," Isabelle said, "I am nowhere near as pretty as you are, Miss Spencer-Kimberly. Will you sit with me tonight?"

"Of course," Aurora replied, patting the younger girl's hand.

"Do you think your brother is going to propose to my sister?" Isabelle asked ingenuously. "My parents have been doing a lot of whispering lately, and grow silent when any of us girls are about. Betsy is quite mad over George, you know, Miss Spencer-Kimberly. I think he is wonderful too. I wish I weren't just sixteen."

"But you are," Aurora said, "and there is plenty of time for some handsome gentleman to steal your heart, Isabelle. Now, why don't you call me Aurora." She lowered her voice. "We are almost family."

"*We are?*" Isabelle squealed, and then she too lowered her voice. "Really? Are you certain? Ohhh, I should adore it!"

"Let us let nature take its course, and allow Betsy to be surprised in her own fashion, Isabelle," Aurora suggested. "Come, you must see the gardens. They are lovely right now. Not as exotic as our gardens in St. Timothy, but beautiful in a different way."

Together the two girls exited the house arm in arm.

"What a sweet girl Miss Spencer-Kimberly is," Lady Elsie said to the dowager duchess. "Why, she has put our Isabelle right at ease with whatever she said to her. How kind! What a pity our

Willie is so young. She will certainly make some man a fine wife. Have you thought of any prospects for her?"

"No," the reply came. "Aurora is a young woman of definite likes and dislikes. But she does have good sense. I shall allow her to find her own mate, and she will, I am certain, make a good job of it."

Then together the two women went into the drawing room where George and the vicar were awaiting them. Sir Ronald had a broad smile upon his face.

"My dear," he said to his wife, "Mr. Spencer-Kimberly has requested my permission to ask Elizabeth to marry him. I have, of course, given him it. I think we can be certain that Betsy will not be unfavorable to his proposal, eh?" He chuckled broadly. The vicar was a tall, full-figured man with a ruddy complexion and sandy hair.

"Oh, my dear boy!" Lady Elsie cried, dabbing at her eyes with a lacy handkerchief.

"Go and find the chit, George," the dowager said sharply, "and get it over with before we are all prostrate with the excitement."

Grinning, George bowed to the trio and hurried off to find his intended, who was in the hallway, directing the unloading of her family's baggage coach with particular emphasis on the trunk that held the ball gowns.

"Come along, Betsy!" he told her. "Peters will see that everything is perfect, I promise you, won't you, Peters?"

"Indeed, sir" was the reply. "I shall have the gowns unpacked immediately, and pressed, Miss Bowen."

"Thank you," Betsy called as she allowed George to drag her out the door into the sunshine. "Where are we going?" she asked him.

"You'll see," he said, leading her through the house's beautiful gardens, past the lake, and into a lovely marble summerhouse that overlooked the water. Seating her upon a marble bench, George knelt upon one knee. "Miss Bowen," he began, "er, Betsy. Will you do me the honor . . . the supreme honor, of becoming my wife?"

"Yes," said Betsy Bowen.

"We cannot remain in England," George continued earnestly.

"I must return to St. Timothy very soon. We would have to make our life there in the western Indies, not that we couldn't occasionally visit England."

"Yes," replied Betsy Bowen.

"It is a very isolated life, as I have previously explained. You will have little female company but for my mother and the servants. Of course we can go to Barbados, and Jamaica, to socialize whenever possible."

"George, get off your knees," Betsy Bowen told him. "I love you. I will most certainly marry you. I understand that life on St. Timothy will not be anything like life here in Herefordshire, but I know I will be happy because we will be there together."

He stumbled to his feet. "You will marry me?"

"Yes, George, I will," she replied. Men were so dense. "Where is my betrothal ring? I wish to wear it tonight and dazzle all the girls who have come to cast their nets at you. They will be most disappointed. Shall we have Papa officially announce our engagement? When will we marry? It must be fairly soon, I expect."

"We don't have to return to St. Timothy until late autumn," he said. "From June until then there is danger of severe storms. We should leave probably in early November. That way we will be home in time for Christmas. That would please my mother very much," he told her.

"Do you think your mama will like me?" Betsy wondered.

"I know she will!" he said happily, and then he drew forth a ring from his pocket and placed it on her finger. "It isn't very large, for I am not a rich man," he explained.

Betsy looked down at the round pink pearl which was surrounded by diamonds. She held her hand out, admiring the ring. Then, looking up at George, she smiled through her tears. "It's beautiful!" she said.

"You're crying," he exclaimed, quickly sitting next to her and placing a comforting arm about her shoulders.

"I am so happy," she said. "Will you not kiss me, George? I believe it is the traditional thing to do under these circumstances."

Gently he brushed the tears from her cheek, and then George

tenderly kissed Betsy Bowen's pursed pink lips. It was not the first time they had kissed, and he always enjoyed it greatly when their mouths met. This petite young woman with her dark blond curls, and her big gray-blue eyes, had the most astounding physical effect upon him. She was sweet as sugar water, and as warm as whiskey going down his throat. He had chosen well, he knew. Betsy would be a good and loving wife. Standing, he raised her up. "Let us go and tell your parents and my sisters of our happiness," he said to her.

She nodded, and hand in hand they walked back to the house, where the dowager had already gathered together her grandson, Aurora, Calandra, the Bowens, and Isabelle in the drawing room in anticipation of the announcement to come. Mary Rose Hawkesworth was very pleased with herself. She had engineered George's introduction to Elizabeth Bowen quite well, and it had all turned out exactly as she had hoped. Now, despite her protestations to the contrary, she intended to have a hand in picking a husband for Aurora, but she would be very clever again so the girl would not know of her interference.

The drawing room door opened, and George and Betsy entered.

"We have something to tell you all," George said with a wide smile, and he put his arm about Betsy, leaving no doubt in anyone's mind what his revelation was to be.

Chapter

7

Carriage after carriage pulled up the torchlit drive leading to Hawkes Hill Hall, stopping before the main entry to the house. Footmen raced forward to open the coach doors and draw down the steps. Gloved hands were offered to each vehicle's occupants, steadying them as they dismounted from their transport. Ball gowns were shaken free of wrinkles, real or imaginary. Hairdos were patted to assure perfection despite the ride from home to hall.

Within the front door of the house, in the large main hallway, servants hurried forth to take capes and cloaks. The guests ascended the wide main staircase of the house to where the Duke and Duchess of Farminster were awaiting them, along with the dowager, Aurora, and George. The visitors passed along the receiving line, and finally into the ballroom, gasping at the beauty of it. The crystal chandeliers sparkled. There were flowers everywhere in large stone urns. Usually a ballroom had its corners blocked by painted screens behind which were commodes, should the call of nature make a visit necessary.

"Not in my ballroom," Calandra had declared. "By evening's end the entire ballroom will stink to high heaven."

"You must provide for your guests' comfort," the dowager said.

"There are two large cloakrooms on either side of the ballroom," Calandra said. "I have thoroughly inspected them, and both are quite suitable. We shall use them as necessaries, one for the gentlemen and one for the ladies. We shall have lady's maids and footmen attending to our guests, and the ballroom shall remain free of noxious odors."

"What an excellent idea!" the dowager approved. "The cloaks and capes can be put in the main closet room in the front hall. Very good, my girl! Very good indeed! That's the kind of thinking we need from a Duchess of Farminster."

And so it had been arranged. Footmen and maidservants were stationed about the ballroom at discreet intervals so those in dire need might inquire as to the location of the commodes. At one end of the ballroom a dais had been set up for the musicians, who were currently playing light music. The dancing would not begin until the duke and duchess had greeted their guests. It had been decided not to have a pre-ball dinner for specified guests. Only the family and the Bowens had eaten in the dining room that evening.

Calandra was on her absolute best behavior. She had never given a ball before, but she had closely observed the London hostesses who had, and envied them. Now she was the one giving the ball, and everyone was saying how beautiful everything had looked, and how elegant it all was. Well, of course these country people would be impressed by the simplicity of her arrangements, but if she were in London, it would have been so much better. A tiny wave of nausea swept over her, and she closed her eyes a moment. She should definitely not have eaten the prawns this evening.

"I believe all our guests have arrived, dear," the duke said to her. "It is time for us to open the ball." Taking her by the arm, he led her into the ballroom.

"Let the vicar make his announcement first," Calandra said. "If he does not, there will be a great deal of tittle-tattle about the attention George is paying to Betsy."

The duke nodded, agreeing with his wife, and spoke softly to Sir Ronald. Then in the company of the vicar they made their way to the dais. The conductor signaled to the guests with a flourish of music, and then the duke held up his hand.

"My friends, before we begin the dance, the vicar has a word or two to say to you all."

Sir Ronald cleared his throat, and then without further ado said,

"Lady Elsie and I are most happy to announce the betrothal of our eldest daughter, Elizabeth, to Mr. George Spencer-Kimberly, elder brother of her grace, the Duchess of Farminster. The wedding will be celebrated in late October, as George must return to the Indies shortly thereafter. I hope you will be as pleased for the happy couple as my wife and I are." He then bowed to the assembled audience and stepped down.

Almost immediately Betsy, George, and Lady Elsie were overwhelmed by congratulations from the other guests, difficult for many mamas with eligible daughters. They had all come in the hope that their darlings could attract the attentions of Mr. Spencer-Kimberly. Now, here was that Bowen girl, with her modest dowry, snapping up the finest prize to come into the neighborhood in years, and before anyone else even had a chance. It was really most unfair!

But the music began, and the duke and duchess led off the ball with a minuet, which would be the most sophisticated dance danced all evening. Mostly they would dance the merry and lively country dances. Cally had hired a dancing master to teach her, George, and Aurora so they would not seem backward; but for now she tripped brightly to the sprightly music of the minuet with her husband, and for a brief moment she was happy and content again.

Valerian glanced at her, and thought how lovely she was. If only her heart had not been so cold, he might have loved her. He saw George dancing with Betsy, and thought how happy they looked. He saw Aurora, in the gown that matched her lovely eyes, dancing with Justin St. John, a childhood friend and distant cousin. Even his grandmother was dancing with old General Tremayne, who was now master of the local hunt. It had been well over a year since his grandfather had died, and it was time she began to socialize again.

The evening wore on, and everyone seemed to be having a wonderful time despite the disappointment of George's unavailability. A buffet was served in the dining room, and the guests wandered in and out, the older folk settling themselves on the available chairs and settees, leaving the floor to the younger members of society.

Calandra was enormously popular with the gentlemen, and had

danced every dance, as had Aurora, who was now dancing with the duke.

"You are the most beautiful girl in the room tonight," he told her. "How clever of you to choose a fabric for your gown that matches your lovely aquamarine blue eyes."

"Thank you," Aurora said softly, "but I am not certain that you should be speaking to me this way. Besides, your wife is the most beautiful woman in the room, I think."

"The most beautiful *woman*, yes," he agreed, "but you are the most beautiful *girl.*" He smiled down into her eyes.

Damn him, Aurora thought as a wave of dizziness swept over her and she stumbled in the dance. His arm tightened about her waist as he swung her around in the romp, a dance peculiar to the area. Regaining her balance, she glared at him. "You are clever, Valerian. Be certain that you do not outmaneuver yourself with your quick wit."

Before he could reply, the music ceased, and Justin St. John was at their side. "I believe the next dance is ours, Aurora," he said with a rakish grin. He was a tall, lean man with chestnut-colored hair and eyes the golden brown hue of excellent sherry. He was nowhere near as handsome as his relative, but he was attractive.

"It seems to me, St. John, that you have danced several times tonight with my sister-in-law. You will, I fear, compromise her reputation," the duke growled, his blue eyes growing darker with his irritation.

"Why, Hawkesworth," his cousin mocked him, "you sound like an overprotective papa, or a rival suitor, but, of course, as a married man you could hardly fill the latter position, now, could you?" The look he shot at the duke was challenging.

"Gentlemen," Aurora said coldly, "you both insult and embarrass me with this public display of bickering." Then she turned and left them, going to the dowager's side, her color high.

"They were rivals from the time they were born," the dowager remarked quietly. "At family gatherings, at school." She sighed. "Who began it this time, my girl?"

"I would say they both did," Aurora replied. "Valerian accused

Justin of dancing too much with me, and Justin said Valerian sounded like an overprotective father or a jealous suitor. How dare they both behave as if I were some *thing* whose possession was to be quarreled over. I censured them both, and both deserved it! How are they related?"

"They share a great-grandfather on the Hawkesworth side," the dowager said. "You did well to put them both down, my girl."

Suddenly a commotion erupted at the far end of the ballroom.

"The duchess has fainted!" they heard someone cry.

Aurora jumped up and ran quickly down the ballroom, almost colliding with the duke as they both hurried to reach Cally's side. She lay in a crumpled heap of rose and gold silk upon the polished floor. The duke picked up his wife and lay her on a nearby settee.

"Is Dr. Michaels still here?" he asked.

Aurora knelt by her sister's side, patting her hand and calling softly to her. "Calandra! Calandra! Are you all right?"

Cally slowly opened her eyes. "What happened?" she asked.

A ruddy-faced man pushed his way through the guests. "Now, what has happened to her grace?" he said in brusk tones, taking Cally's hand and checking her pulse. "Someone fetch her maid," he said.

"It was the prawns," Cally told the doctor. "I knew I should not have eaten them. Very little has agreed with me lately, but they looked so very delicious, and I was so desperately hungry."

"I could not help but notice your grace's appetite at the buffet this evening," the doctor responded, feeling her forehead.

"I know it is so indelicate of me," Cally told him, "but of late I cannot get enough to eat, yet I feel constantly empty and queasy."

Sally had been fetched, and now came to stand by her mistress's side. She had a decidedly worried look about her. "Is she all right, Miss Aurora?" Sally asked nervously.

"This is her grace's maid," Aurora told the doctor.

He turned and beckoned to Sally, and when she stood next to him, he whispered something to her. For a moment Sally thought, and then she murmured low to the doctor. The doctor turned to them.

"It is as I suspected," he said quietly to the duke and Aurora. "Her grace is undoubtedly with child. Your lordship will, I can happily say, be a father before the year's end. May I offer you both my congratulations."

Cally began to cry softly.

"Tears of happiness," Dr. Michaels pronounced. "I've seen it many times. Dry your eyes, my dear lady, your prayers are answered."

"If you say one word to embarrass Valerian, I shall kill you," Aurora murmured softly to her sister.

"Do not leave me!" Cally begged her sister.

"I will remain at Hawkes Hill as long as you want me to stay," Aurora assured her sister. "Now, smile at your husband."

Cally obeyed her sister, smiling tremulously at the duke, who had a stunned look upon his handsome face.

Aurora arose to her feet. "Is this not what you wanted, Valerian?" she asked him quietly. "My sister is giving you an heir."

"Yes! Yes!" he said, and then turning to his guests, he told them, "The duchess has just fainted. It would appear, according to Dr. Michaels, that my wife will give me an heir by year's end!"

The room erupted into a cacophony of congratulations.

"Well," the Dowager Countess of Kempe said to the Dowager Duchess of Farminster, "this has been a most exciting and fortuitous evening for your family, my dear Mary Rose. A betrothal and the impending arrival of a Hawkesworth heir. Certainly you must be happy."

"Indeed," the dowager said, smiling broadly. "I am delighted I have lived long enough to see a great-grandchild. Well, I shall," she amended with a chuckle. "Valerian," she called, "I think it is time that we sent everyone home so that Calandra can be put to bed."

The duke did not have to say anything, for the guests heartily agreed, and were already taking their leave of their host and hostess. Calandra was now seated demurely upon the settee, accepting their compliments and their thanks for a wonderful evening. Valerian stood by her side. George and Betsy had been out on the terrace when Calandra had swooned, and had only just come in. Aurora quickly filled them in on the events that had taken place while they had sat beneath the moon, planning their future. They added their congratulations to the many already received.

"Mama will be absolutely delighted to learn she is to be a grandmother," George said.

"Remain until the baby is born," Cally begged him.

"I cannot, sweeting. I must be home to oversee the harvesting of the cane. It is with apprehension that I have left the planting of the Kimberly fields to their foremen under Mother's direction. And Mama should not be alone on St. Timothy with only servants for company for any longer than necessary. I would leave England earlier, Cally, but that the storm season is practically upon us, and I don't want Betsy to experience a rough voyage if I can avoid it. Aurora will be with you, and you will be just fine, little sister."

The guests were all gone now, and Valerian Hawkesworth picked up his wife in his arms and carried her upstairs to her bedchamber. Setting her down in a chair by the fire, he said quietly, "You are now free of my attentions, Calandra. You have my gratitude for what you are doing. Deliver my heir safely, and my generosity and tolerance will be almost boundless," he promised her.

"*Almost?*" She looked seriously at him.

"Whatever you do, madam, I expect no scandal," he said quietly. "As for the rest of the terms of our arrangement, we can discuss them *after* our child is born. We are civilized people, are we not?"

"What if it is a daughter?" she inquired nervously.

"Then after a season in London, to which I will accompany you, we will return to Hawkes Hill to make another attempt."

Calandra shuddered openly.

"Boys run in the family, my dear," he said. "I think you will be fairly safe from my unwelcome attentions." He bowed politely and exited her rooms.

Downstairs again, he found that George and Betsy, as well as the other Bowens, had disappeared, but his grandmother stood in the hallway while Aurora said good night to Justin St. John.

"Will you ride with me tomorrow?" St. John said, smiling down at her in a proprietary way the duke found extremely irritating.

"It is tomorrow," laughed Aurora. "I am exhausted, and shall spend most of the day in bed. The day after, perhaps." She turned to the dowager. "May I, ma'am? Would it be all right?"

"Of course, my dear, but not too early, St. John. Nine o'clock will do very nicely. Remember me to your mama. I am sorry she was unable to attend tonight. You must arrange to bring her to tea some day quite soon. Perhaps when the weather is warmer."

"Thank you, ma'am," he replied. Then he kissed the dowager's hand, and lastly Aurora's, lingering over hers a trifle longer than he should have. "Good night, my lovely goddess of the dawn," he said softly, but not so softly the others didn't hear.

Aurora blushed at the unexpected compliment.

"Get along with you, you young rogue!" the dowager scolded.

Releasing Aurora's hand, St. John replied, "Good night, Cousin Valerian. I had a very good time, I vow. Congratulations upon the impending birth of your heir. You will give the duchess my kindest regards?" Then with a final bow he was gone through the door.

"Impudent puppy!" snapped the duke. "Are you sure, Grandmama, that it is proper for Aurora to ride with that devil. I do not think it wise at all. Two grooms must go with them."

"Two?" Aurora said, surprised.

"One groom will be quite enough, Valerian," the dowager said sharply, looking at her grandson.

"I am far too tired to argue," Aurora said. "I am going to bed. Is Cally still awake, Valerian?"

"She was when I came down," he answered her.

"Then I shall stop in and say good night," Aurora replied, and she hurried up the staircase.

"Come into the drawing room with me," the dowager commanded her grandson. "I must speak with you."

The lights in the drawing room had already been extinguished, but a bright fire burned. Standing just past the closed door to the room, Mary Rose Hawkesworth said to the duke, "Aurora must be married, and St. John is a suitable prospect if he pleases her. I will not allow your boyhood rivalry to interfere, Valerian. Do I make myself clear?"

"You have already decided on St. John, haven't you?" he responded.

"It is not up to me, my boy, it is up to Aurora," she answered him in prim tones.

"Grandmama, do not fence with me. I know you well. You very carefully engineered George and Betsy's rapprochement, and do not deny it. Oh, I will not tell on you, never fear. It is a good match, but I do not believe that Justin St. John is a good match for Aurora." The duke went to the sideboard and poured himself a large whiskey.

"You have a wife, Valerian," Mary Rose Hawkesworth said quietly.

Her grandson spun around, a shocked look upon his face.

"Do not deny that you are attracted to Aurora," his grandmother continued. "Oh, you are usually discreet, but I see how you look at her when you believe that no one else is observing you, and I believe that of the two girls, she would have been the better wife for you; but you married Calandra, and she is now expecting your child. That, my dear boy, settles it. I know that Calandra is a cold-hearted little bitch. I am astounded you have managed to impregnate her, but you have. As you cannot have both girls, and Calandra is your wife, Aurora must be married to another man. Do not interfere with me, Valerian," the dowager warned her grandson sternly.

"Do not interfere with me, Grandmama," he replied calmly. "I am the head of this family, and if I decide that a gentleman shall not wed Aurora, then he shall not."

"And if she loves him, Valerian? What then, my boy?"

"Aurora could not possibly fall in love with St. John," he said with complete assurance.

"Perhaps not, but there will be some man who surely catches her fancy in the next few months. You will have no choice but to stand by and watch as she picks a husband, Valerian," his grandmother said.

"We will see," the duke answered her.

"If you cause a scandal, or hurt either of those girls, I will never forgive you," the dowager threatened him.

"Surely, madam, you know me better than that," the duke said.

The old lady shook her head. "I am not certain I know you at all now. There is no way you can escape your marriage, Valerian. Perhaps if she had not proved fertile, you might have found a way, but not now. Calandra is with child. *Your child.* The Fifth Duke of Farminster will enter this world before the new year. That is an undisputed fact."

He did not respond to her words, and turning, the dowager exited the drawing room for her own chambers. As she passed Calandra's bedroom, she could hear soft laughter, and she smiled. Thank goodness for Aurora. She would keep that flighty chit her grandson was married to on the straight and narrow during her pregnancy, and there would be a healthy child. But afterward? Who knew what arrangement Valerian had made with his wife in order to elicit her cooperation, if indeed she had cooperated with him at all. It was so terribly unfortunate.

Valerian Hawkesworth remained standing in the drawing room where she had left him. He stared into the fire, cradling the whiskey glass in his hands. What did it matter that Calandra and he had little use for each other. There would be a child, an heir, to follow him, and wasn't that what he wanted, as Aurora had asked him earlier. Wasn't it enough? It didn't matter that Calandra would live out her frivolous life in London going from party to party like a bee going from flower to flower. He would have his son. If his mother would not be there for him, his father would. And his grandmother, and his aunt Aurora.

Aurora. His grandmother was right. She would choose a man and marry. The best he could hope for was that she remain nearby so he would not lose her entirely. But he would lose her. He would lose her to a husband, to her own children. Oh, she would be kind to her little nephew, he had no doubt, but Valerian Hawkesworth would not have Aurora. He might have her friendship. Her sympathy. But nothing more, and the problem was that he wanted more. *He wanted her.*

Damn her for stealing his heart! And damn Calandra that she did not want him! If Calandra had loved him, it could have been different. *No.* It would not have been different, he had to admit to himself. He was in love with Aurora Spencer-Kimberly. He had never been in love with his wife, and he never would be. He would never capture the heart of either of these women, but at least he would have his son. It didn't seem enough, but it would have to be, he knew.

As for his cousin, Justin St. John, he wondered if St. John was really attracted to Aurora, or if he was simply playing with the girl to annoy Hawkesworth. He didn't want Aurora hurt, yet how could he forbid her St. John's company? He couldn't. The thought, however, of his cousin making love to Aurora infuriated him. He would watch St. John closely to determine his intentions, and in this effort, he knew, he would be ably assisted by his grandmother. She would not want Aurora harmed, or her heart broken by a cad, even if the scoundrel was a blood relation. The duke turned from the fire and placed his whiskey tumbler on the silver tray from where he had originally taken it. Then with a sigh he left the drawing room, seeking his own bed. *A lonely bed.*

Aurora heard him pass by her bedroom door. By now she knew his step. She was angry at the duke. Angry that he made Cally so unhappy, although she knew that most of the fault lay with her sister. She was angry at him that a compliment from his lips could cause her heart to race. That those intense blue eyes could make her knees go weak when he looked meaningfully at her. She wondered what it would have been like if she had married him. Would he have made her as unhappy as he was making Cally? *No.* Cally's problems stemmed from her inability to enjoy the physical pleasures of the marriage bed. I may be a virgin, Aurora thought to herself, but I know I would enjoy a husband's attentions.

Especially if that husband were Valerian Hawkesworth, the little voice in her head said slyly, and Aurora was suddenly shocked by her own thoughts. She had had her chance to marry the duke, but she had gone out of her way to avoid her deceased father's wishes. She had deliberately deceived Valerian into thinking Cally was his intended bride. No one had forced her to subterfuge. It had all been her own idea. She had bullied Mama into going along with her. George, of course, knew her well enough to realize if Aurora didn't want to do something, she wouldn't, and had in turn done what he believed was best for the family. Both she and Cally had behaved childishly in the whole matter. Now they were going to have to live with the results of their chicanery. It wasn't going to be easy, she knew.

Cally was terrified of being with child, frightened of childbirth, vain about her figure, which she declared was going to be ruined. Had she not been more fearful of Valerian, Aurora believed her sister would have found a way to rid herself of this new life she carried. Fortunately her distaste for the marriage bed was enough to make her behave, because if she lost this child, she would be forced to endure her husband's vigorous attentions once more. If, however, she brought this child to a successful birth, and it was a son—*Oh, pray God it was a son!*—then she would never again have to face her husband's animal lust, she had said to Aurora.

Aurora considered her sister's words. *Animal lust.* It actually sounded rather wickedly delicious. She caressed her round breasts beneath the coverlet, undoing the ribbons that tied her nightgown, and slipping her hand inside the garment to fondle the warm flesh. What would it be like to have a man doing this? She thought of Justin St. John, but his face was almost instantly replaced by that of the duke's. For a moment Aurora felt guilty, but she pushed her guilt aside. It was only pretend, and only she knew what she was thinking. Her nipples grew hard with her thoughts. Sucking her index finger a moment, she began to rub the wetness about the hard little nub, smiling languidly as the familiar tingle began between her legs. Her other hand slipped down to push between the swollen flesh. She was already wet.

Aurora closed her eyes. Her breath was coming in hard little pants, and she struggled to keep the sound low lest she awaken Martha. She imagined a dark head on her breast, and tugged suggestively at her nipple. Would his mouth feel like that, or would it be much more wonderful than she could even imagine? The index finger of her right hand found that sensitive spot hidden within her nether lips, and she teased at it. What would it be like to lay naked in a bed with the man you loved? To feel his weight on you? To have your bare breasts crushed against his hard chest? To have his member inside you? Aurora worked her finger fiercely against her pleasure nub, and suddenly the lovely melting feeling swept over her, leaving her almost breathless with her release. Tonight, however, it wasn't quite enough, and she didn't understand why. It had always been enough before.

Aurora couldn't sleep. What was the matter with her? It was probably the excitement of the ball. It had been a lovely time, made even more so by the knowledge that she had contributed so much to the preparation. She had very much enjoyed helping the dowager, and she had learned a great deal of what was expected of the wife of a well-to-do man with a big house. There had been no parties or balls on St. Timothy. Her father had taken his pleasure in Jamaica or Barbados prior to his marriage, and during the brief period between her mother's death and his remarriage to Oralia. Unless there were other families on an island, society was scant.

It was not so here in England. They were a very social people, and she had to admit that she frankly enjoyed it. Not London society, as Cally had, but this country life suited Aurora very well. In the weeks since she had first arrived, she had ridden with her brother and Betsy, gone on several picnics with the Bowen sisters and their friends, and played tennis on the grass. The country families were friendly, and while proud of their lineage, they were not snobbish like the London society folk she had met.

If I meet a man I can love, and marry him, I shall always live in the country, Aurora decided. *If she met a man.* Well, she had met several nice gentlemen this evening who appeared eager to know her better. Me, or my dowry? she considered suspiciously. Of course, Justin St. John didn't need her dowry or her income. He was, according to the dowager, comfortably off in his own right.

"Sheep," the dowager said. "The family has the largest flocks in the area. Always did. They sell the wool in the open market, and poor Valerian has to pay a higher price to get it for his mills than if St. John would make a private arrangement with him. Of course, the rogue does it deliberately to irritate my grandson." She chuckled. "I keep telling Valerian that the best way to outfox St. John is to increase the size of his own flocks so he wouldn't need his cousin's wool."

So St. John's motives could not be disputed. If he showed an interest in Aurora, it had to be because he found her attractive, she decided. And he *was* attractive. Not in the brooding, dark way that Valerian was, but in a prettier, no, that was not a word one should use when describing a man. Softer? He didn't have that fierce, be-damned-to-you look the duke had. St. John laughed easily, as the tiny lines about his eyes and mouth indicated. It would be interesting getting to know him better, provided, of course, that he pursued his interest in her, but the dowager seemed to believe he would.

Aurora shifted onto her left side. She was finally beginning to get sleepy. Outside her windows, for she had not let Martha draw the draperies, she could see the sky beginning to lighten with the dawn. She really was tired. Her eyelids were very heavy now, and she yawned deeply several times. She tried to think of Justin St. John, but every time she did, Valerian Hawkesworth's handsome face replaced his cousin's. It was disturbing, but she could no longer concentrate, and finally fell asleep, her breathing measured and relaxed.

She slept until well past the noon hour, finally awakening to the sound of a bird outside her windows, singing its heart out. She lay quietly, enjoying the thrilling song. Obviously someone had found his mate, and was ready to build a nest, she chuckled to herself. Languidly she reached for the bellpull and yanked upon it.

"So, you're awake at last," Martha said, bustling into the bed-room. "You're the first up. The old dowager is still snoring her head off, Jane tells me; and the young duchess ain't blinked an eye yet. Tell me about the ball, and that Mr. St. John you met. Is he nice?"

"He seems to be," Aurora said. Then, "I want tea, Martha, and something to eat. I am ravenous!"

"Right away, miss. They say that Mr. St. John is very rich, and he don't have anyone but his mother. She's real anxious he take a wife. A girl would be lucky to get a man like that. Big house, big estate, I'm told."

"It seems to me you've been told a lot more than I have." Aurora laughed. "Does he have a mistress?"

"*Miss Aurora!* What a shocking thing for you to say. Nice girls aren't supposed to know about such women, or such arrangements," Martha scolded her mistress. "Your mama would have a fit to hear you talk like that! I think the young duchess is having a bad effect on you."

"Cally? No, Martha, she isn't. I take everything Cally says with a very large grain of salt. I just wondered why a man as eligible as Mr. St. John hadn't taken a wife yet. It's a reasonable question, I believe. If there is some lady who has captured his heart hiding in the shadows, I would be foolish to waste my time, or allow my heart to be broken. While the dowager thinks him suitable, the duke thinks him a cad. Such divergent opinions pique my curiosity."

"I think I'd listen to the old lady, miss. She does favor you, even more than the young duchess, if you'll forgive my saying so. She wants what's best for you, and will see you ain't hurt."

Martha hurried from the room, returning about a half hour later with a large tray which she set upon the piecrust table by the windows. Helping Aurora into a pretty peach silk dressing gown, she seated her at the table and began removing the silver domes covering the dishes and plates. There was a dish of eggs poached in sherry and heavy cream, a thick slice of country ham, flaky little croissants, a crock of sweet butter, a dish of new peas, a honeycomb, a silver bowl of freshly picked strawberries with a companion bowl of clotted cream, and a pot of tea. Aurora fell upon the food as if she had been starving, and in short order had cleaned up all of the plates and dishes. Sitting back in her chair, she sipped her saucer of tea, a contented smile upon her beautiful face.

"Delicious," she pronounced, "and please tell Cook I said so when you return the tray to the kitchens."

"He'll be pleased to have a compliment, I can tell you, for the young duchess does nothing but complain 'cause he don't fix her fancy meals like in London. Never a word of thanks he gets from her. I don't know where Miss Calandra's manners got to since she's come home to England," Martha grumbled.

"She is just very impressed by what she considers high society," Aurora defended her sister. "Eventually she'll know better."

"Hmmph" was Martha's comment. "Ought to be grateful for what you have done for her, miss, and behave properly like she was taught to do instead of affecting all those la-di-da ways, and Sally as bad."

"I think I shall return to bed," Aurora said. "I am still very tired. Ask Peters if there will be dinner tonight, or if we are to eat on trays. I hope it's trays. It would be lovely not to have to get dressed, and just lay about. I want to finish reading the history of the Hawkesworth family. With all I've been doing these last weeks to help the dowager plan the ball, I have had no time to myself."

"Don't know why you're reading about this family, miss. You ain't going to be part of it," Martha remarked sharply.

"The duke and Mr. St. John are related through a great-grandfather," Aurora said innocently. "I would like to understand the familial connection, Martha. Besides, you know how much I love history, and this family's history is really wonderful."

"I didn't know the duke and your Mr. St. John was related," Martha said, surprised.

"Well," Aurora teased her maid, "I cannot believe the below-stairs grapevine was so negligent that it didn't inform you of such a pertinent fact about Mr. St. John, who is certainly not *mine.*"

"Not yet," Martha said with a grin. Then she picked up the tray with its empty dishes. "I'll take these down. Are you available for the duchess if Sally asks?"

"Not today, if I can avoid it, Martha. I do not think I can cope with Cally's discontent and whining. And now that she is with child, none of us will have any peace, I suspect, until that poor baby is born. You will remember that Cally has never been an easy patient."

Martha shook her head. "Gawd help us," she agreed as she departed the bedroom carrying the silver tray. "It's going to be as if she was the first and only woman who carried a child, and every little inconvenience will be magnified out of proportion." The door closed behind her.

Aurora chuckled at Martha's astute evaluation of the situation. It was going to be a very interesting few months to come, she decided.

Chapter

8

"It isn't fair!" Calandra, Duchess of Farminster wailed. "It just isn't fair ! I look like some shoat ready to be slaughtered. I can bear no more. I cannot! I want this child to be born!"

It was a glorious late September day, and Cally was sprawled in a chaise upon the lawns leading to the garden. She was one of those rare creatures that pregnancy did not become. Her alabaster skin had grown sallow. Her raven's-wing-black hair was lackluster. Her face and hands were puffy, and unless she remained reclining for a good part of the day, her feet had a tendency to swell. Worse, with almost three more months until she delivered, her belly was quite distended.

Restlessly, her fingers plucked at a small tray of sugar comfits, discarding one, then another, and finally popping the third choice into her mouth. Her hazel eyes narrowed as she watched her sister playing tennis with Justin St. John. Aurora looked absolutely beautiful in the simple Indian calico print gown. It was really a house dress, but equally suitable to such a rough-and-tumble game as tennis. When had Aurora's waist been so supple and slender as it was now? For a brief moment Cally hated her, and then she felt guilty.

Aurora had been so patient and kind all the summer long, and Cally was not so big a fool that she didn't realize it. Still, she found it irritating to watch her sister having such a good time when she could not. Not that it was the sort of good time Cally was truly envious of, for it was not. And the beaus! There had been any number of them Aurora had flirted with and then discarded. But those young men she refused always remained to become her friends. Cally didn't understand it. One thing remained constant, however. Justin St. John. He was not discarded, and Cally doubted he would have gone if he had been. It was becoming very obvious that he intended to make Aurora his wife.

Cally didn't blame her sister for playing the field, for taking her time, for holding back before agreeing to marriage. If only I had really known what was involved in being married, Cally thought, I should not have been so quick to jump. If I hadn't, it would be Aurora who would be lying here, her belly all blown up, while I flirted with all the gentlemen. But then, of course, I shouldn't be a duchess, Cally considered. Still, she was beginning to wonder if it was really worth it just to be the Duchess of Farminster. In retrospect, all she had needed was a rich, doting husband who would let her live in London and become one of its celebrated hostesses. *A rich old husband.* A man with grown, or half-grown children who would not make unpleasant demands upon her person, but would be satisfied that she was young, and beautiful, and desired by all his friends, who would, of course, envy him his young and beautiful wife. It would be easy to love a man like that, Cally decided. If only she hadn't listened to Aurora. Aurora was really to blame for all of this nastiness.

Cally's eyes narrowed again. Aurora would be sorry soon enough. Justin St. John looked to be very much the same sort of animal that her own husband was. He would make *demands* upon Aurora, and Aurora would surely suffer, hopefully, even more than Cally had. And, Cally knew, St. John would not take Aurora to London. He would keep her down here in the country, giving her child after child until her beauty was ruined. And I shall be up in London having a wonderful time, Cally thought. Yes! I shall have my revenge eventually. And St. John didn't even have a title! He was simply a wealthy man with good if nebulous connections to the Hawkesworth family, or so Aurora said.

"Are you all right?" the dowager asked as Calandra suddenly winced in pain. The old lady was seated next to the young duchess, acting her usual role of chaperon.

"The little beast just moved again," Cally said. "I hate it when it does that. Fortunately, it is not too often. I feel as if I had swallowed a roast boar whole, ma'am."

"Being *enceinte* can be uncomfortable at times," the dowager sympathized, although frankly she was sick and tired of Cally's complaints. All the little wretch did was whine, and she was openly counting the days till she could leave Hawkes Hill and return to London. Valerian had made no bones about the fact that when his wife recovered from her childbirth, she could depart. Farminster House would be put at her disposal, along with a suitable staff. She would have an allowance, which hopefully she would live within, and unless the child was a girl, she would not have to return to Hawkes Hill unless she desired to come. A wet nurse was already engaged to feed the baby.

Aurora ran up and flung herself on the grass. She was flushed and laughing. "You really are a poor loser, St. John," she mocked.

Justin St. John sat down beside her. "No girl should play tennis like that, Aurora. You play like a boy."

"If I were, would you expect me to let you win?" she demanded.

"Ma'am, I turn to you for a judgment in this case," he said to the dowager duchess.

"No! No! St. John, you will not get me to take sides in this matter," Mary Rose Hawkesworth chuckled. "You were beaten fair and square. Your backhand is deplorable. Why, I vow that I could have beaten you myself had I been of a mind to play."

He clapped his hand over his chest, a pained expression upon his face. "Ma'am, you have wounded me grievously," he declared.

The dowager rapped his shoulder sharply with her fan. "You are not that delicate a flower, St. John," she scolded him. "Will you stay for supper? Valerian should be back from the mills shortly."

"Thank you, ma'am," he said. "I should like that."

"Cally, will you join us too?" Aurora asked.

Cally shook her head. "I am not comfortable sitting straight up any longer," she complained. "You have no idea, sister, how discomforting a thing it is to carry an unborn child within your own body."

Aurora patted the sticky-fingered hand that lay upon Cally's skirts. "Would you like it if I rubbed your shoulders and feet for you later tonight before you go to sleep?" she inquired solicitously.

"Ohhh, would you?" Cally smiled. "That would be so nice. You are the only one in this whole house who understands how miserable I am, sister. Thank God I have you, else I should die of loneliness."

Mary Rose Hawkesworth bit her tongue to prevent a pithy retort. The entire household had been turned upside down to ensure Calandra's comfort and satisfy her every ridiculous whim. And she positively abused Aurora's kindness, although Aurora never complained. If I remain here another minute, the dowager thought, I shall say something quite cutting. She arose from her chair. "It has become a bit cool for me," she lied. "I think I shall go inside, my dears. Please remain and enjoy yourselves. Perhaps I shall take a nap."

She walked slowly across the lawns to calm herself, but she was still angry at Calandra's selfishness, and knew she could not nap. Entering the house, she decided to walk in the picture gallery. Viewing the family portraits, seeing the faces of those who had come before her, remembering the family history, was always enjoyable. She must bring Aurora here one day soon, if she could get her away from Calandra. Aurora had so very much enjoyed reading the history of the family. She would certainly enjoy putting faces to the names in the book.

It was a long gallery that had been added to the house several hundred years earlier. It had been created from a windowed hallway that originally connected one wing of the house to another. Tall windows ran along one side of the gallery. They faced southwest. The wall opposite was paneled in warm wood. The wide-board floors were well polished and laid with beautiful Turkey carpets of red and blue. Afternoon sunlight now flooded the room displaying the portraits at their very best. Mary Rose Hawkesworth smiled as she entered the gallery.

There was her late husband, looking dashing, and quite handsome. There was their son, Charles, and his sweet wife, Henrietta. There were even separate portraits of Valerian, and his sister, Sophia, as children. The dowager moved deliberately, looking at each face of each lord and lady represented. Here now was the First Duke of Farminster, his wife, and his children. There were his parents, the last earl and countess, and their children. The daughters, the first duke's sisters, were lovely young women. She smiled back at the portraits, and then, suddenly, the Dowager Duchess of Farminster gasped. Unbelieving, she peered at the name plate upon the portrait. It read: CATHERINE HAWKESWORTH KIMBERLY, 3 MAY 1630–28 OCTOBER 1700. The young woman in the portrait was the girl who had been married to the Kimberly who had been given St. Timothy by King Charles II. *And she was Aurora's image!*

That is why Aurora has seemed so familiar to me, the dowager realized. How many times have I seen this portrait in passing over the years? She looked at the painting next to Catherine Hawkesworth Kimberly. It was of Anne Hawkesworth Meredith, who looked very much like her elder sister. What can it mean? Dear God, what can it mean, the dowager thought. But she already knew what it meant. Valerian was married to the wrong girl, and she could not, at least not now, tell him the truth. *If it was the truth.* But she knew it was. Who could confirm it for her? Aurora's servant, Martha. She would tell the dowager the truth, if pressed, and she would not allow her young mistress to be hurt. Mary Rose Hawkesworth hurried from the portrait gallery, and going to her bedroom, she sent her maid, Jane, to fetch Martha, ascertaining first that Aurora was still outdoors.

"Yes, my lady, you sent for me?" Martha stood politely before the dowager, curtsying.

"You may leave us, Jane," the dowager said quietly. "Please keep watch as I have asked, and let me know the moment Miss Aurora comes into the house."

Jane nodded, and hurried from the room.

The dowager looked at Martha in what she hoped was a stern

but not confrontational manner. "I want the truth," she said quietly.
"Is your mistress the girl who was *really* betrothed to my grandson?"

Martha hesitated a moment, and then she sighed. "Yes, my lady,"
she said. "It's her who should be the duchess, and not Miss Calandra.
I warned her that no good comes of lies, but she didn't listen."

"Tell me what happened," the dowager said. "Was it the stepmother's idea? Why on earth was this deception played?"

"Oh, no, my lady! Mistress Oralia wanted no part of it at all.
Only at the last minute, when it became apparent that Miss Aurora
would have her way, did she give in, but she never wanted it, nor
did she agree willingly." Then Martha went on to explain to the
Dowager Duchess of Farminster the truth of the entire matter. She
concluded by asking the old lady, "How on earth did your ladyship
find out?"

The dowager smiled softly. "Aurora has seemed familiar to me
from the moment I met her," she told Martha. "Then this afternoon
I was in the family portrait gallery, when I came across the painting
of the first duke's younger sister. She is Aurora's image, as is her
sister, who was married to a Meredith. Calandra does not bear even
the faintest resemblance to these ancestors. The Hawkesworths are
not dark usually. Valerian gets his coloring from his French mother."

"Forgive me, lady, but are you going to tell?" Martha questioned
the dowager nervously.

"How can I, Martha? Calandra was married legally, although if
she were not with child, I should tell, and have my grandson annul
the marriage based upon the fraud involved. However, Calandra is
with child, and the child is innocent of its mother's deceit. No. I
shall not tell my grandson; nor shall I tell Aurora, although I am
angered by her deceptive actions. And you will say nothing either,
Martha, of this conversation. Perhaps, however, your load has been
lightened by the fact it will now be shared, eh?"

"Oh, my lady, I knew it was wrong, but what could I do? I am
a servant, and even Mistress Oralia and Master George was forced
to go along with my mistress. She can be terribly stubborn!"

The dowager patted Martha's plump hand and smiled encouragingly at her. "Go along now, Martha. Somehow it will work itself out."

Martha curtsied and departed the room.

Well, the dowager thought gloomily, her new knowledge was nothing more than an irritant. Nothing had really been accomplished by confirming her suspicions. What a fool she had been! She had been so distraught by her James's death that she hadn't been thinking clearly. She should have sent for Mistress Kimberly and her charges to come to England. Perhaps then Aurora could have been convinced that marrying Valerian Hawkesworth was not a fate worse than death. But no. Cornered, the girl had created an ingenious scheme, and it had almost worked had it not been for her little stroll through the portrait gallery today. If Mistress Kimberly had come to England, perhaps the dowager would have seen the portrait sooner and discovered that they were in the process of being deceived. Now I shall have to live with this information, she considered irritably. What a coil!

At dinner, however, her mood was barely noticed because of the sparring between Valerian and St. John over Aurora. Dear God, the dowager thought, annoyed. They are like a pair of schoolboys, and there sits Aurora, encouraging them by her very jibes. The girl must be married, and as soon as possible, before she tempts Valerian and there is a scandal! It was obvious to her that Valerian was attracted to Aurora despite his marital state. And why not? The girl was clever and amusing. She held his interest with her intellect and not simply her beauty, unlike poor Calandra, who honestly believed that beauty counted for everything. Yes, Valerian was intrigued every bit as much as his cousin was. As for St. John, it was quite apparent he wanted the girl too, and sensing the duke's interest in Aurora, baited him as had always been his habit when the two fought over something. St. John had a very wicked sense of humor, unlike Valerian, but an equally strong will. Yes, there was going to be a scandal if the dowager could not prevent it.

The meal, she suddenly realized, was over. "Take Aurora for a stroll through the gardens, St. John," the dowager said, encouraging her young relative to action. She sent a fierce look toward her grandson.

"It has surely grown chill," the duke replied, ignoring his grandmama's silent warning. "Perhaps Aurora does not want to stroll in the evening air."

"I like the evening air," Aurora spoke up. "I will take a shawl and be quite cozy." She arose from her seat.

"And I am quite capable of keeping Aurora warm should she grow cold," St. John remarked, his amber eyes dancing with devilment.

"Behave yourself, boy!" The dowager playfully rapped his knuckles with her ivory fan. "I'll have no naughtiness!" But she chuckled as she spoke. "If your intentions are honorable, however, my dear St. John, that is an entirely different matter," she finished. Then she watched with a smile as St. John escorted a blushed Aurora from the dining room. Her look was one of satisfaction.

"Hellfire and damnation, Grandmama," the duke swore irritably. "You would do well peddling maidenheads on the London bridge. Aurora is far too good for my cousin. Why do you encourage him?"

"Control yourself, sir," she said sternly. "Your interest in your sister-in-law becomes too obvious. You cannot have her, Valerian. You have a wife, and I know you would not disgrace the Hawkesworth name or dishonor Aurora by offering her a lesser position in your life than Calandra now holds."

"*I love her,*" he said low, his face agonized.

"I know," his grandmother responded. "That is the tragedy, dear boy. You love her, and she would have made you a better wife than her sister, but fate had other plans for you both. Calandra, for all her faults, is expecting your heir, and Aurora must be married off as soon as is possible to prevent you from yourself, Valerian. St. John is an ideal candidate for her. He may not be titled, but he is a member of this family and a wealthy man. Aurora's dowry, while a good one, is not good enough for a title, I fear. If she weds St. John, she will be near her sister, and that, I believe, is to the good."

"Calandra will leave Hawkes Hill as soon as she is recovered from the birth of our child," he reminded the old lady. "You know that is our bargain, and I will keep to it."

"Perhaps she will not want to go if Aurora is near," the dowager said hopefully. "In any event, Aurora must be married whether her sister remains here or departs back to London."

"I do not think I can bear to see her married to another man," the duke admitted. "What a weakling I am, Grandmama!"

"Then Aurora must return to St. Timothy with her brother and his bride when they leave in early November," the dowager said firmly.

"*No!*" He shook his head vehemently. "I would rather she be wed to St. John and here, where I could at least see her, than send her back to St. Timothy, where I would never see her again."

"You will have your child, Valerian, my boy," the dowager said softly. "He will need you, for he will, I believe, have no mother. Let the child become your world. You will be happy, I promise you."

Valerian Hawkesworth sighed sadly, a sound so filled with pain that it almost broke his grandmother's heart, particularly that she knew the truth, thanks to the portrait in the family gallery and Martha's forced honesty. I will forget I ever knew about this deception, she decided silently. Then she turned her head to gaze out through the dining room windows onto the garden, where Aurora walked with Justin St. John. They were merely shadows in the twilight, and she hoped that St. John would press Aurora to marry him. She wished she could hear what they were saying, and then she smiled at herself for being a nosy old lady.

"Do you sense we are being watched?" Aurora said, her voice tinged with amusement. "I can almost feel the dowager's eyes on the back of my neck." She chuckled. "I do like her so much!"

"She has come to love you," St. John said, "as have I."

"Are you about to propose to me again?" she teased him. "How many times will this make, St. John? Five? Six?"

"This will be the seventh time, Aurora, and seven has always been a fortunate number for me." He stopped walking and drew her into the circle of his arms. "This time I will not take no for an answer, my dear." He ran a finger down the side of her face, and then caught her chin between his thumb and his forefinger. "I want you, Aurora. Do you understand what I mean? *I want you!*" The amber eyes blazed at her.

This suddenly forceful St. John intrigued her. What had happened to the slightly bored sophisticate he had been until a moment before? This man had a dangerous edge to him, and she was fascinated. "You want me? Do you mean you want to make love to me, St. John? What a naughty suggestion to make to a respectable maiden such as myself," she answered him, her tone slightly mocking.

He laughed softly. "You do not fool me, Miss Spencer-Kimberly. Beneath that elegant and respectable missishness lies a fierce passion that has never been stoked, but when it is, it will threaten to consume us both. I want to make love to you, Aurora, and you want me to make love to you." His arms tightened about her. "Don't you?"

Her heart was suddenly racing, and her knees were threatening to give way beneath her. His words. The intensity in his voice. It was very exciting. She had always been careful of her reputation, never allowing a gentleman to kiss her or hold her hand, and now she wondered why not. Were not women supposed to have feelings of sensuality? She certainly did. Raising her aquamarine eyes to his, she answered breathlessly, *"Yes!* I do want you to make to love to me, St. John. Are you shocked?"

He shook his head. "No," he said. "I can recognize a passionate virgin when I see one, Aurora."

Instantly she was enraged. How dare he insult her in such a fashion. Pulling away from St. John, she slapped him. "Cad!"

"Bitch!" he replied, yanking her roughly back into his arms. Then he kissed her, pinioning her arms back behind her so that her struggles were virtually useless.

Her first kiss. And she would remember it the rest of her life. It was not the soft and gentle thing she had always imagined. It was hard, and fierce, and demanding. For a moment she reveled in its savagery. Then she kicked him as hard as she could.

"Ouch!" he yelped, but he did not let her go. Instead, he kicked her feet out from beneath her so that they fell to the grassy path below. Restraining her, he grinned into her face. "You really are a vixen, Aurora." He bent to kiss her again, but she turned her head away from him angrily.

"Let me go," she snarled. "Let me up this instant, St. John, or I shall scream so loud, they will think there is a murder being committed!"

He forced her head back to his and found her mouth again. This time, however, his kiss was deep and intoxicatingly sweet. He knew she wanted to resist him, but she would not be able to avoid her own fiery nature. She was a virgin. A most curious virgin with an ardent bent. He gave her just enough room to breathe before pressing his lips back down upon hers, working against the pink flesh until it began to soften beneath his. A tiny sound of pleasure caught his ear. Her body moved slightly against his. He ran his tongue along her lips, pushing between the twin delights and into the warm, moist grotto of her mouth, finding her tongue and stroking it hungrily with his own.

She was going to explode with the longing now sweeping over her body, Aurora thought muzzily. How could the conjunction of two mouths engender such incredible pleasure? Why had she avoided kissing until now? And why hadn't Cally told her how wonderful it was? Surely her sister could not object to *this*. It was pure heaven! Daringly, she entwined her tongue with his in some primitive mating, and to her surprise he shuddered almost violently, then pulled away from her, gasping for air with a groan. *"More!"* she commanded him.

He brushed his mouth over her teasingly, next kissing her eyelids. Turning her head aside with his palm, he nibbled a ribbon of kisses down the side of her face and neck. She felt the heat of him in the hollow between her neck and her shoulder. She arched her head and throat to give him greater access to her perfumed flesh. *"Wonderful! Wonderful!"* she murmured breathlessly as he moved to her chest and the swell of her small breasts. His hand slipped beneath her back to fumble with the laces of her gown, which he quickly undid in a most expert fashion. She was wearing no corset.

He repositioned them so he might draw her into his arms as they lay upon the grass. His hand pulled gently at her loosened bodice, and her breasts almost fell out of her chemise. For a moment he gazed in rapt awe at the two lovely orbs, and then he kissed the plump flesh passionately, his hand unable to keep from fondling her. "God, you are so lovely," he groaned.

Mesmerized, she watched him as he caressed her, cupping a breast in the warm hollow of the palm of his hand, squeezing it tenderly, leaning over to kiss a nipple. She struggled to keep herself from crying out, but a small "Oh" escaped from between her lips. Somehow she knew that he should not be being quite so intimate with her, and she felt bound to protest. "St. John," she gasped, "I don't think you should be doing this. Oh! Oh! Ohhhh, St. John, do cease this torture!" His mouth had closed over the nipple, and was now drawing upon it. She was afire, and that place between her thighs was beginning to tingle. "St. John, in God's name, stop! It's marvelous, but I don't want to lose my virginity in the Hawkesworths' garden! *Stop!*" She struggled to break away from his embrace.

With a genuinely constrained groan and a deep sigh he released her. "Damnation, wench, you are too exciting for a mere mortal! I ache to possess you, Aurora. Say you will marry me!"

"I will consider it, St. John," she told him softly, for the first time seriously contemplating marriage to him. If this love play were a sample of the delights marriage had to offer, then perhaps she should take him up on his proposal. He did have the right qualifications for a husband. She enjoyed his company, and if he could stir up her passions so quickly, then obviously she must be falling in love with him. After all, what was love anyway? Certainly no one had ever given her a rational explanation of the emotion. She seemed to be on her own.

He groaned again, rolling on his back. There was a genuinely pained look upon his face.

"Do you hurt?" she asked him innocently.

"Yes," he told her.

"Where?" she queried him. "Will it help if I rub it? I rub Cally's shoulders and feet when they ache."

A wicked grin creased St. John's face. "I'm not certain you would want to rub my injured part, Aurora, should you see the state it's in; nor am I certain you should unless we are betrothed."

"Oh, St. John, don't be such a fool!" she scolded him. "Show me what hurts this instant, and I will make it better."

In response, his fingers fumbled with the buttons on his pantaloons, opening them to release his male member. "Ahhhh!" he exhaled as it burst forth from its painful confinement.

Amazed, Aurora stared, her gaze transfixed upon the thick, long peg of flesh that thrust up from the opening in his garment. She remembered seeing George's member when they were children swimming naked in the sea. It had looked nothing like this intimidating object. Fearless, however, she reached out to touch it, but he caught her wrist and held it.

"No," St. John told her. "If you touch me, I'll lose all control, Aurora. Turn about and avert your eyes while I lace you up. I was too constricted, which caused my discomfort. I will be all right now as long as you don't touch me. When we are married I will be delighted if you choose to caress my fine fellow, but not at this moment."

It wasn't easy, but she tore her stare away from him, pulling herself about so that her back faced him. She sat silently as he skillfully laced up her bodice. A thousand questions filled her mind. "Is it normal?" she finally said, breaking the stillness between them.

"In size?" he returned.

She nodded.

"I think so. Hawkesworth's is a wee bit bigger than mine, I believe, but it's how a man wields his member that's more important." He slipped his arms about her and kissed the nape of her neck.

"Will it hurt me?" Aurora couldn't help but lean her head back against his shoulder. I think I will marry him, she thought, but I do not think I shall tell him now. Not quite yet.

"When I relieve you of your virginity, you will feel it," he told her. "For some girls it's a sharp, brief flash of pain. For others no more than a sting of discomfort. It really depends how tightly your maidenhead is lodged, and how thick it is."

"You have obviously done this before," she remarked dryly.

"Yes," he told her, "I have, but never with a wife, Aurora."

"I have not said I would marry you, St. John." She removed his embracing arms and struggled to her feet, brushing her gown off as she did so, and patting her hair back into some semblance of order.

Standing, he took her by the shoulders and turned her about, tilting her face up to his. "You will marry me, Aurora," he told her with a small smile. "You cannot resist the magic I arouse in your tempting little body, can you?"

"Cad!" she smacked at him, but only half seriously.

"Bitch!" he retorted, giving her a quick kiss.

Then they both laughed.

"Button yourself, St. John, or the entire household will know what we have been about, I fear," she told him sternly.

"They will suspect it anyway," he chuckled, buttoning himself.

"You may escort me back into the house," she said loftily. "Then you must go home, St. John. Your mother is surely wondering what has happened to you. I'm certain she does not know what a devil you are."

"Alas," he said as they walked back through the gardens to the house, "I fear she does, my dear. May I come tomorrow and bring you home for tea so she may meet her future daughter-in-law?"

"St. John!" Aurora was exasperated. "I have not said yes yet. You must not presume until I do."

"Patience is not a virtue with me, Aurora," he said.

"Virtue is not a virtue with you," she riposted.

He burst out laughing, admitting, "True. True."

Entering the house, Aurora saw a light coming from beneath the library door. "Good night, St. John," she told him.

He pulled her into his arms and kissed her slowly, smiling down into her eyes, nibbling tenderly upon her lower lip. "Good night, Aurora, my darling. How I long for the night when I shall not have to let you go to a lonely bed." Then he whispered softly in her ear, "I shall insist we sleep naked, and I shall caress and kiss every inch of your lovely body until you beg me to take you. *And I will!*" His hands were fastened about her small waist, and he held her so that her breasts just touched his chest. "I am going to tease and taunt you until the day that you marry me, darling. I know that that little secret place of yours is even now throbbing and wet, isn't it?"

Surprised, she nodded. "I think you are very wicked, St. John," she murmured low. "If you tease me, I shall tease you, and that fine fellow, as you call your member, will ache with longing for me even as it now does, doesn't it?" She daringly ran her tongue along his lips.

The library door opened, and the duke spoke sharply. "Go to your room, Aurora. St. John, go home. I'll have no scandal in my house."

With a chuckle Justin St. John kissed the tip of Aurora's nose, and releasing his hold on her, bowed mockingly at his cousin as he departed.

Valerian Hawkesworth had an angry look about him. "You will remember, miss, that I am your guardian while you are here in England. You will not play the strumpet again, or I will have you confined to your room on a diet of bread and water. Do you understand, Aurora?"

"I understand that you are arrogant, *my lord*, even as I have always believed you to be. You may force my sister to your will, but you will never force me. I shall probably marry St. John, although I have not yet decided to do so, and if you believe that I would compromise my own good name, you are sadly mistaken. I bid you good night." She ran up the staircase and hurried to the dowager's room, knocking politely.

"Yes, miss?" The dowager's Jane answered the door.

"If her ladyship is still awake, I should like to speak with her," Aurora said politely.

"Come in, miss, she's been waiting," Jane replied. She was a tiny woman with a cheery smile who always wore a neatly starched mobcap over her gray curls, and was utterly devoted to her mistress.

Mary Rose Hawkesworth was already settled in her bed, her nightcap with its blue silk ribbons tied beneath her chin. "Well?" she demanded. "Did he propose, and did you accept him, Aurora?"

"It was the seventh time he has proposed," she said with a small laugh. "I have always refused him."

"He has proposed to you seven times, and you refused him?" The dowager was astounded. "Gracious, child, what can you be thinking?"

"I did not refuse tonight, but neither did I accept, although I am of a mind to accept, ma'am," Aurora told her sponsor.

"Why now?" The dowager was curious. Aurora, she was discovering, could be a most unpredictable young girl. Stubborn, Martha had said.

"He kissed me," Aurora replied. "I liked it. I liked it very much, ma'am. He has been so proper and so polite until tonight. He was rather masterful this evening. I found it intriguing, and quite delicious. He is not the fop I thought him to be, and now perhaps I shall accept his offer because I believe he will be a most interesting man to have for a husband. I might even be falling in love with him."

"Ahhhh," the dowager said, nodding with approval, her eye meeting that of her servant. "You will not get a better offer, my child. St. John is well off without your dowry, and so he has no ulterior motive involved in asking for your hand. He has not sought to marry before now, although heaven knows there have been several most suitable young women he might have had. I suspect he has fallen in love with you."

"He has asked me to tea tomorrow to meet his mama," Aurora told the dowager.

"Excellent!" came the enthusiastic reply. "I shall, of course, accompany you. It will show Mistress St. John that I fully approve of any alliance contracted between her son and our family." There was a smile of utter satisfaction upon her handsome face. It was going well, and it was going to work out precisely as she had hoped. "Have you thought about when we shall have the wedding, my child?" she asked.

"I have not told St. John yes yet, ma'am." Aurora laughed.

"But you will, of course, and the sooner the better," the old lady advised her charge.

"Would late spring be too soon?" Aurora wondered. "I suppose we should probably wait a year not to appear unseemly, but I have always wanted to be married in the spring. Cally should be well recovered from her childbirth by then, and can be my attendant witness, as I was for her when she married the duke last winter."

"Spring would be a perfect time," the dowager agreed. "April or May, my child. Mid-May would be beautiful! And who cares what the old gossips say. St. John is eager, and so, I suspect, are you now." Her blue eyes twinkled mischievously at the girl. "I well remember those heady kisses of my youth. None are ever quite so sweet as those."

"I respect your experience," Aurora told her playfully. "Now, however, ma'am, I suspect that you would like to retire. I bid you good night." Impulsively, Aurora bent and kissed the dowager's wrinkled cheek. Then with a quick curtsy she was gone from the room.

Mary Rose Hawkesworth touched her cheek, and a tear rolled down her face. "Why, that sweet child," she said softly.

"She is that," Jane agreed. "A pity she weren't the one we got for Master Valerian."

"Yes," the dowager agreed. "A great pity indeed."

Chapter

9

"Hold still, miss," Martha said as she carefully laced up her young mistress. "'I've never known you to be so fidgety!"

"I've never been invited to meet a gentleman's mother before, and frankly I'm nervous," Aurora admitted to her maid.

"The dowager will be with you," Martha replied. "Just let her do all the talking. Answer politely and try to appear mannerly, miss. Mistress St. John doesn't have to know you ride astride or like to swim naked in the sea. Just be what every mama wants for her son. A well-mannered, loving girl who will devote herself to her husband."

"I haven't told St. John that I'll marry him yet," Aurora protested.

Martha turned the girl about and looked critically at her garb. Apple-green silk gown with a petticoat panel of ivory brocade embroidered with multicolored butterflies; tight sleeves to just below the elbow with creamy engageants; a pretty rounded neckline modestly edged with a lace ruffle. She nodded, satisfied. "Of course you're going to marry Mr. St. John, miss," she said. "That's what we come from St. Timothy for last winter. To find you a husband, and Mr. St. John will make you a fine one. Now, here's your shawl. It's not cold, so you'll not need a cloak." She draped it over Aurora's shoulders, then handed her a pair of lace mitts and a reticule of pale green silk. "There's a handkerchief inside, and a little painted fan if it gets too warm. Now, you hold still a minute while I affix the finishing touch." She put a small bunch of little cream-colored silk flowers in the girl's hair and stepped back. "Yes," she nodded. "It's just perfect. Now, go and join the dowager, and remember what I told you. A modest and mannerly demeanor and a gentle voice will impress Mistress St. John best."

Mary Rose Hawkesworth stood with her grandson as Aurora descended the staircase. "How pretty you look, my child," she complimented her.

"Thank you, ma'am" came the response, and then Aurora looked at the duke and said, "Do you think I look pretty, Valerian?"

"Conserve your flirtatious manners for my cousin, Aurora," he sharply put her down. "I am certain he will be delighted to see how boldly you have dressed for him."

"*Boldly?* What in heaven's name is bold about my appearance?" she demanded angrily.

"The neckline on your gown is immodest," he grumbled.

"It is edged in a lace ruffle, and Martha says it is quite decorous," Aurora snapped back at him. "You surely don't consider yourself an arbiter on women's fashions, sir?"

"Enough," the dowager said, raising her hand, and then, "Come, my dear, or we will be late to Primrose Court." She gave her grandson a hard look and then took Aurora's arm.

He stood watching as the carriage drew away from the house. She had looked utterly adorable, and the thought that she had dressed with the idea of pleasing St. John was infuriating. Did his cousin love Aurora? *Really love her?* Would he make her happy, or would he break her heart when she discovered St. John's penchant for women? All women. St. John would do what so many of their contemporaries did. He would take a respectable wife with a respectable dowry and have several children, all the while keeping a bit of fluff hidden away. Valerian Hawkesworth knew his cousin's bad habits, although St. John had always been so utterly discreet that virtually no one realized what a cad he could be. Of course, the duke admitted to himself, he had taken a wife for precisely the same reasons they all did, and while he did not love Calandra, he had never been unfaithful to her except perhaps in the deepest and most secret place in his heart. With a sigh he returned to his library, and pouring himself a whiskey, sat down.

The ducal carriage quickly left Hawkes Hill behind. It would be almost half an hour's ride to Primrose Court, as the St. John home was known.

"Margaret St. John will be delighted to have Justin finally married," the dowager remarked as they rode along. "You are very fortunate, my child. Primrose Court has a dower house, and Mistress St. John has been eager to move into it. She has spent the last several years preparing it for her arrival. You'll have no mother-in-law in your house."

"But, ma'am, I still have not decided whether to marry St. John or not. I hope the good lady is not presuming I will." Aurora shifted nervously in her seat.

"Now, my child," the dowager said, patting Aurora's hand, "you must cease this maidenly dithering. It is not at all becoming to a girl of your intellect. Of course you will marry Justin St. John. He's an excellent catch, and your mama will be absolutely delighted." She smiled encouragingly at the girl. "I know you are a little frightened, but you do not have to be, Aurora. If your mama is in St. Timothy, the rest of your family is here with you, and everything is just going to be fine." She patted the lace-mitted hand again.

The vehicle traveled on past orchards of apples and pears now being picked. The air was sweet with the scent of ripe fruit. Finally they turned off the main road, going through an open gate and down a narrow tree-lined way that led to Primrose Court. It was a lovely warm, pinkish brick mansion of Tudor vintage that had been modernized over the years to include large windows and a round pillared porch. The coach horses trotted smartly up the graveled drive, finally stopping directly before the house. Immediately servants were hurrying forward to open the carriage door, draw down the steps, and help the passengers out, escorting them into the building.

Justin St. John was awaiting them in the foyer. "Welcome, your ladyship," he said, kissing the dowager's hand. Then he turned to Aurora. "Welcome home, my darling," he told her, and she blushed.

"Oh, St. John, don't be such a fool," she gently scolded him.

"Come into the drawing room and meet Mama," he said with a small smile. How pretty she looked, he thought to himself. She seemed to have gone out of her way for him today. She was going to say yes. He just knew she was going to say yes! His heart raced, and for a brief moment he felt like a schoolboy again. Leading the two women into the salon where his mother was standing to greet their guests, he let his parent greet the dowager first.

Mistress St. John curtsied to Mary Rose Hawkesworth. "How lovely that you could come for a visit, ma'am," she said. "I am so sorry that the ague kept me from your grand ball last May. The neighbors are yet speaking of it, and such a dramatic climax to have the young duchess faint, and everyone to learn she was with child. Is she well?"

The dowager smiled thinly. "As well as any young woman in her condition, Margaret. I have brought the duchess's sister with me today. St. John! Introduce Aurora!"

"Mama, may I present Miss Aurora Spencer-Kimberly," he dutifully said, drawing Aurora forward with a smile.

"How do you do," Aurora said softly, curtsying politely.

"So," Margaret St. John said, "you are the girl who is to marry my son, Miss Spencer-Kimberly. You are going to marry Justin, aren't you?" Her gray eyes twinkled with humor at Aurora's surprised expression.

There was what seemed a long silence, and then Aurora said, "Yes, Mistress St. John, I am. I hope that you will approve."

Margaret St. John hugged Aurora warmly. "My dear, I am absolutely rapturously relieved that some nice young woman has decided to settle Justin down. Come, now, let us sit down and have our tea."

She was in a dream, Aurora thought. Had she really agreed to marry St. John? Yes, she had. The dowager was looking smugly pleased. Mistress St. John appeared delighted as she poured out the tea, and St. John was grinning at her like a fool. Why did I say yes, Aurora wondered to herself. Do I love him? Do I really want to marry him? She sipped her tea silently. Martha would very definitely approve her decorum. She was brought back to reality at the sound of St. John's voice.

"Let's be married at Christmas," he said enthusiastically.

His mother immediately looked shocked. "Justin," she cautioned him, "one cannot arrange a proper wedding so quickly, nor is it seemly. There would be talk at so swift a union, and it would reflect badly upon Aurora, I fear. People would be counting on their fingers, I regret."

"Aurora and I have already discussed this matter, Margaret, and while it is a trifle soon, we thought next May would be lovely. Aurora has always wanted to be married in the springtime," the dowager said.

"May? That's almost eight months away," St. John groused.

"Oh, yes," his mother said to the dowager, "May would be just lovely, and the duchess will have recovered from her childbirth by then and can be at her sister's side. It's a trifle soon, of course, but no one would think badly of us if we arranged the wedding for May. The betrothal must be announced quickly, however."

"Valerian is Aurora's guardian here in England. I will see that he gives a small, intimate dinner next week, and he will announce the engagement at that time. With the duchess *enceinte*, no one will consider it strange we are being so simple," the dowager replied.

"What a pity the duchess's condition prevented them from attending the royal wedding and the coronation this month," Mistress St. John noted. "I understand it was all quite magnificent, and that the queen is a lovely young woman."

"Indeed, Calandra was dreadfully disappointed," the dowager replied, remembering how her grandson's wife had shrieked and carried on when she learned that she could not travel during her pregnancy. It had been three days before she had stopped crying, and she was still not over her disappointment, nor would she ever be, the dowager thought.

The two women now settled down to a good gossip, for although St. John's mother was at least fifteen years younger than the dowager, they had many interests and friends in common.

"I am going to take Aurora on a tour of the house," St. John finally said, and his mother waved them off.

They left the drawing room hand in hand, and he showed her the dining room, the back salon the family generally used, the ballroom, and the original old hall, which was beamed and hung with banners. Leading her upstairs, he took her through a door, and they were in a large bedchamber. "And this is my room," he said softly, drawing her into his arms and kissing her slowly.

For a moment she enjoyed the kiss, and then she drew just slightly away from him. "I don't think we should be here, St. John, nor should we be engaged in such activity."

"When did you decide to marry me?" he asked her, his fingers unlacing her gown as he bent to kiss her again.

"When your mother asked me," she admitted, and slipped her arms about his neck, kissing him back. "Where is my betrothal ring?"

He pushed her down onto his bed, and straddling her gently, pulled her bodice down to reveal her soft, alabaster bosom. His hands reached out to fondle the dainty mounds. Bending his head, he began to lick first the pink nipples, and then each of her round breasts in its turn. She sighed, encouraging him in his pursuit, and he began to suck on her nipples, drawing upon them strongly, biting them tenderly until she was writhing beneath him and almost whimpering.

Finally he lifted his head from the sweetness of her flesh and asked her, "Do you want to know more, my darling Aurora?"

"Yes," she murmured. She was already afire with his passionate attentions to her sensitive breasts. They felt hard and ready to burst.

"This will be so much easier when you do not have so many garments on," he told her. He pushed her skirts up. Beneath the green silk she had on at least half a dozen petticoats, but, thankfully, no panniers. He thrust the material aside enough to slip his hand beneath, and began stroking her leg, which was encased in a silk stocking and tightly gartered. He was going to undress her himself on their wedding night, slowly, deliberately, and purposively, kissing each bit of flesh as he exposed it until his very touch would set her afire. His fingers moved above her garter, touching the very soft skin of her inner thigh. He caressed it lightly, teasingly.

Aurora's head was spinning. His big hands were so gentle, his mouth so deliciously wicked when he used it on her breasts. His hand moved farther upward, brushing softly against her little nest of curls. This, she sensed, was dangerous territory. She stirred restlessly as a single long finger slipped between her nether lips to find her little pleasure button. He began rubbing it provocatively.

"*St. John!*" she squeaked.

"Don't you like it?" he whispered hotly in her ear, his finger continuing its wonderful and erotic friction.

"*Yes!*" Oh, God, yes! This was even better than when she did it to herself. She squirmed with excitement, gasping as she reached the crest of delight. "Ummmmm! Oh, St. John, that is simply too delicious. Oh! Oh! *Ohhhhh!*" She shuddered.

Leaning forward, he kissed her lips, his tongue playing with her. Then he murmured, "One day I shall use my tongue on you there, my darling, but you are not yet ready for such games." The finger slipped away from her pleasure button and began to penetrate her. She gasped with surprise, but he reassured her. "It's all right, my precious. This is where I shall enter your body when we are married." His finger gently inserted itself, moving forward in her hot passage very slowly, very carefully. When he reached her maidenhead, he ceased his action, gently ascertaining that her virginity was well lodged.

She whimpered.

"Hush, darling," he soothed her, and began to move the finger back and forth within her. "There, isn't that nice, Aurora? No, sweeting, do not move else I hurt you without meaning to do so." The finger moved swiftly, and within moments she was crying out with her pleasure, and when the shudders had subsided, he withdrew his finger, putting it into his mouth to suck upon it. His member was like iron, and tightly lodged within his pantaloons. Loosening it, he lay next to her and put her hand upon it. "If you soothe me *very* gently, my darling, it would help."

"But yesterday you said it would hurt you," she murmured, her fingers closing about him. He was warm and throbbing with life.

"That, my darling, was yesterday in Hawkesworth's garden. This is now in my house. Gently, Aurora," he instructed as she loosed him and began to stroke his member. "Ahhh, yes, that is the way." He reached into his coat and drew forth a silk handkerchief. "Take your hand away now, Aurora. My love juices are about to flow forth."

She couldn't help it. Turning her head, she watched as his member erupted forth a creamy stream of thick liquid. He stemmed the flow in the handkerchief, shivering with pleasure until finally it was done. Mopping the residue, he lay the sodden silk aside, then, turning, kissed her mouth even as she reached out to caress the limp flesh.

He smiled at her. "You weren't afraid, were you?"

"No," she told him, and then, "we have been very wicked, haven't we, St. John? Very wicked indeed."

"I haven't half begun to be wicked with you, Aurora," he told her with a chuckle, and kissed her again.

She murmured her approval, but suddenly the clock on the mantel began to strike. Aurora stiffened and pulled away from St. John. "Your mama and the dowager will surely begin to wonder where we have gotten to!" Pushing her skirts down, she sat up. "Oh, do lace me up, St. John!"

Chuckling, he complied, afterward fastening his own buttons.

Aurora looked into the mirror over the fireplace. "Oh, Lord, my hair is a disaster, and I shall never be able to fix it!"

Laughing now, he reached into the drawer of the bedside table and drew forth a small hairbrush with which he repaired her coif. When he had finished, he said, "There. No one will ever suspect that we were toying with your virtue, my darling." He drew her up. "Come, and I shall take you to the strongroom, where I have the St. John betrothal ring. It is a magnificent yellow diamond, oval in shape, and will become you, my darling. Let everyone think what they may. You will be my wife in the spring, Aurora."

"I don't suppose I should ask how you became so proficient in restoring a lady's coiffure," Aurora said tartly.

"No," he agreed, "you should not." Then, taking her by the hand, they left the bedroom.

When they returned to the drawing room, both Mistress St. John and the dowager were both extravagant in their praise of Aurora's new ring. And for the first time she felt a little bit of excitement.

"Is this love?" she softly asked St. John.

"I don't know," he said. "I've never been in love before, but I do know I feel different about you than any other woman I have ever known, my darling. Perhaps it is love."

It was rather flattering, she thought as their carriage made its way back to Hawkes Hill. He had never been in love before he met her. Cally didn't love the duke, nor did Valerian love her. I think I am very lucky, Aurora considered.

"A marvelous stone," the dowager said for the fourth time since she had seen Aurora's ring. "A bit showy, perhaps, but without a flaw. There isn't another diamond like it in all the world. It belonged to an Indian rajah, I am told, and has a name. *The Virgin*, it is called. I am so very pleased, my dear child," the dowager continued. "And I know that your family will be too."

George Spencer-Kimberly was indeed delighted. "When's the wedding?" he asked. His own nuptials were scheduled for the very end of October. "Will you and St. John return to St. Timothy with us?"

"We are not being married until next spring," Aurora told him. "It has all been decided by the dowager and Mistress St. John. Oh, George, I do wish you could persuade Mama to leave the island and come to England to be with Cally and me. The duke has said Cally may go back to London after she births her child, and she is planning to do it. If Mama were here, perhaps she would not be so restless."

"I will try," he said, and then, "Come on! I want to see Cally's face when she sees your betrothal ring. She'll be most envious. You know how she loves beautiful jewelry."

"God help you" was Cally's blessing on her sister's news. She was sitting up in her bed, drinking tea and eating sweetmeats. "Let me see the ring." She took Aurora's slender hand and peered closely at it. "He's generous," she noted, "but I've told you what he'll expect in return for his gifts. You would be wise to return the ring."

Shaking his dark head, George departed the room. His sister grew stranger every day, and made no secret of the fact she hated any intimacy with her husband.

When the door had closed behind him, Aurora said, "I am learning the pleasures of the flesh, little sister. St. John is quite passionate."

"My God!" Cally exclaimed. "You haven't been intimate with him and given away your virtue? Surely you aren't that foolish."

"We play love games," Aurora said, "but that is all."

"How can you bear it?" Cally said wearily.

"I like it," Aurora said. "I like his kisses, and I like his mouth on my skin, and I enjoy it when he fondles me, Cally."

Calandra shuddered. "You must be a wanton," she said.

"Because a woman enjoys the physical attentions of a man does not necessarily mean she is a loose jade. Of course, I do not mean she should encourage just any man," Aurora told her sister, "but it can be no sin with a husband, or an affianced husband. Why should a woman not take her pleasure too? I can find no wrong in it."

"Perhaps it is me," Calandra admitted. "I just don't enjoy being pawed and invaded by a man. *Any man*. It isn't just Valerian. While I was in London there were several gentlemen who approached me in a less than seemly fashion. I enjoy being admired and envied, but I will not be touched by a lustful man."

"I am astounded, then, that you are with child," Aurora spoke boldly to her sibling. She did not really expect an answer.

"My husband forced me," Cally said, surprising her. "He wanted an heir, and that I wasn't willing was of no importance to him."

Aurora was thoughtful as she considered her sister's words. If Cally didn't want her husband, how could he be aroused by her enough to spill his seed? She must ask St. John about such behavior. Perhaps the duke enjoyed resistance. It was a distasteful and frightening thought that a woman's desires and wishes were not paramount to such intimacy.

Aurora had no opportunity to inform her brother-in-law of her impending marriage, for the dowager had already told him, as she discovered when she sat down to dinner. The old lady had been so delighted, she could not contain herself long enough to allow Aurora to announce her own good news. The duke took the news impassively.

"I wish you happiness," he said.

"And you will give an intimate little dinner to announce Aurora's betrothal, Valerian," his grandmother said. "Just the immediate family and the Bowens, of course. Calandra is hardly even up to that, but we must do it for propriety's sake. Elsie Bowen will trumpet the news all about the county, I am certain. We will achieve our aim without incurring any vast expense in doing so," she chuckled. Then she turned to Aurora. "Of course, if your sister were not so fragile right now, we should have a very grand ball to announce your coming marriage, but we shall soothe everyone's feelings by inviting them all to the wedding. It will be the grandest occasion the county has seen in years. Valerian will, naturally, foot the expense, won't you, my dear boy?"

"Of course," the duke said dryly but without enthusiasm.

"Are you not happy for me?" Aurora asked him pointedly.

"If you are happy, Aurora, then I must be happy for you even if I believe you could do better" was the reply.

"*Better?*" Her voice was sharp. "With one of those London fops Cally was forever pressing upon me? I am astounded that you think so little of me, Valerian, to believe that I would be that shallow. St. John suits me quite well. He is a country gentleman, and I prefer being a country lady. *And he is very passionate!* His kisses set my heart afire! I am the luckiest girl in the world!" She glared at him, daring him to contradict her or criticize St. John.

"God deliver me from a romantic virgin in love for the first time," he mocked her. "I am assuming, of course, that you are still a virgin and have not been silly enough to let my cousin seduce you. He is quite a notorious rake, you know. Or perhaps you do not know. He has fathered at least three bastards to my knowledge."

"*Valerian!*" His grandmother's handsome face was flushed with her annoyance. "You are being deliberately provocative and most indelicate."

"How nice to know St. John's seed is so potent," Aurora said sweetly. "I am very eager to begin a family. Does he throw sons or daughters the most, Valerian?" She smiled brightly.

Mary Rose Hawkesworth gasped at the girl's boldness as George Spencer-Kimberly stifled his laughter. The duke and his grandmother were going to find out that Aurora was a formidable opponent when irritated, aroused, or otherwise annoyed. No one had ever called his sister a biddable female. He would miss her when he returned to St. Timothy with his bride, but Besty Bowen was a more predictable female, like his mother, and he far preferred such a girl for his wife.

"Be careful, my dear Aurora," the duke said coldly, "else you be mistaken for a coarse strumpet."

Standing suddenly, Aurora threw her wineglass at him and stormed from the dining room. The duke laughed, both amused and amazed by her actions. Then he nodded to Peters to see the disarray was cleaned up, and turned his attention back to his dinner plate.

"You are really quite impossible, Valerian," his grandmother remarked. "Frankly, I would have thrown the entire wine carafe at you. It was well within Aurora's grasp. She was rather restrained, I thought."

George could no longer contain his mirth, and burst out laughing.

The tension broken, the trio continued their meal, while upstairs Aurora was sending Martha for a tray, for she was ravenous, her anger and her excitement both fueling her appetite. When George stopped by later on to bid her good night, Aurora was just finishing her meal.

"He laughed at you, you know," George informed his sister.

"He can go to the devil," she muttered.

"You must restrain your antipathy toward Valerian, Aurora, lest people gain the wrong impression," her brother gently warned her.

"What impression could they possibly obtain other than the fact I dislike Valerian's arrogance?" she demanded.

"They might think that you were in love with him," George said with devastating forthrightness.

"*What?*" Aurora grew pink. "How can you say such a thing, George? It is ludicrous and shameful! I am in love with St. John!"

"I am pleased to know it," her brother responded in serious tones. "Now, listen to me, Aurora. You have always been headstrong and willful despite your charm and your good heart; but I would remind you of the deception we—you and Cally and I—have enacted upon the Duke of Farminster. I knew it was wrong, yet I allowed you to do it. Indeed, I aided you, and the results are disastrous for Valerian and Cally. While I am in love with Betsy, and will be happily married, while you are in love with St. John, and will be happily wed, they despise each other and are utterly miserable, and it is our fault to a great extent." He took Aurora's hand in his and kissed her fingertips. "I love both of my sisters. You should have been the duke's wife, and Papa would be very disappointed that I allowed myself to be manipulated by you, Aurora. Had I only known of Cally's abhorrence of physical love, I would have never allowed what has happened to happen."

"But she wanted to be a duchess," Aurora said weakly.

"Do you remember when we were young and that group of Spanish nuns took shelter on St. Timothy from a hurricane? Cally wanted to be a nun for weeks afterward. This was a similar situation, and I was too blind to see it because I love you both and wanted you happy. Look upon the results of my foolish indulgence, little sister.

"I will be brutally frank with you, Aurora. Whether you are willing to admit it or not, you are attracted to Valerian, and I believe he is attracted to you. Perhaps you don't even realize it, but I see it, and I know the dowager sees it too. Face it, and put it from you else it cause further disaster. Valerian is married to Cally, and they are, for better or for worse, expecting a child. You will marry in the spring, and that must be an end of it," George concluded.

"I am *not* attracted to Valerian," Aurora said firmly.

"Then cease asking him if he thinks you're pretty in this or that new gown. Stop baiting him, and taunting him with your *passion* for St. John. He and his cousin have always been rivals of a sort, and neither can seem to get over it. Are you certain that St. John cares for you, Aurora? Really cares for you? Not just lusts for you, for even I observe that he does lust for you. Tell me that there is more between you than just desire. Do you even know, or understand, that there must be more between a married couple than just physical hunger?"

"Yes, of course, I think so!" Aurora pulled away from her brother and sat down in a chair by the fire. "We amuse each other," she told George. "I know I like him, and I believe he likes me. If we are to live together as man and wife, shouldn't that be important?"

He sat himself opposite her while Martha, having returned to the room, bustled quietly about, listening. "You and St. John already have more than Cally and the duke," he said approvingly, "but there must be more. For instance, Betsy and I agree upon several things that will affect our married life. We are in concert in the matter of raising our children. We know that we would like two sons and two daughters. We have decided that even if the slaves have their own religion, we will still raise an Anglican church on the island and encourage them to attend. St. Timothy is going to change, Aurora. With the bottling facility that Valerian and I intend to erect, it shall become a more important island. Eventually trading ships will stop regularly, and we will not have to send our sugar to Barbados for transport to England. Betsy and I plan to work together to make certain that St. Timothy remains a good place, a happy place. It is up to you and St. John to set the goals that you wish to follow in your life together. Do not marry him just because you enjoy his kisses and like his hand up your skirt."

"*Master George!*" Martha's indignant voice interrupted them. "What a shocking thing to say to your sister. She's a good girl, she is! Don't you dare cast doubt upon either her purity or good character.''

George laughed, catching a hold of Martha's hand and pulling her down into his lap. "I know Aurora is a good girl, Martha," he said, "but I would not be a good older brother if I did not attempt to ascertain that she is marrying St. John for the proper reasons, and will be happy with her choice. Poor Cally is very unhappy with her choice." He kissed the servant's cheek.

Martha struggled to her feet. "Now, don't you go trying to wheedle me or confuse your sister. She has made her decision to marry that Mr. St. John, and he's a mighty good catch. She's going to be happy, and no mistake about it, Master George. Now, go along with you and let my poor mistress get some sleep. It has been a very exciting day for her, for us all." She shooed him from the room.

"Remember what I said," George called out to her as the door closed behind him.

"Young scoundrel," Martha muttered.

"He just wants to be certain that I am happy," Aurora said.

"Well, he shouldn't say such wicked things to you, brother or not. And he shouldn't be confusing you about Mr. St. John," Martha said.

"I'm not confused about St. John," Aurora assured her as Martha helped her to undress and get into her nightgown. She washed her face and hands and cleaned her teeth in the basin of warm water that Martha provided for her. Then, tying her nightcap on, she climbed into her bed. "I'm not confused about St. John at all. He's going to make me a wonderful husband, Martha. I really think he is."

Satisfied, Martha tucked the girl into her bed, and blowing out the candle on the nightstand, gathered up her mistress's discarded garments and left the room with a chirpy "Good night, miss."

Aurora lay quietly beneath the down coverlet. The fire in the fireplace blazed cheerily, casting dark, mischievous shadows upon the walls and hangings. She closed her eyes and attempted to rekindle her delicious memories of that afternoon. She had been waiting for hours, it seemed, to be alone so she might recall her sensuous little adventure with St. John. He really was quite wicked, and she had been very naughty, yet she felt not a moment's guilt over the matter. His mouth on her breasts. His fingers beneath her skirts. The look in his eyes when his love juices had erupted and he had turned his head to gaze at her. She sighed deeply, and then suddenly her eyes flew open. It had been Valerian Hawkesworth's face she had just imagined! It hadn't been St. John's at all! What was the matter with her? Was her brother right? Was she unknowingly attracted to the duke?

Aurora shivered. This was wrong. It was very wrong. How could she be attracted to Valerian Hawkesworth? She didn't want to be a duchess, and he was certainly the most irritating man she had ever met, not to mention his appalling arrogance. And what had he done to her sister that Cally so disliked the physical act of passion? And had Cally not said he forced himself on her so he might have an heir. This was a terrible man. She could not possibly be attracted to him! *She couldn't!* Was Cally right? Was she a wanton who enjoyed clandestine revels with her affianced and had secret thoughts about her sister's husband? What is the matter with me? she wondered.

Was she regretful that she had deceived the duke? Was her conscience bothering her over it? Did she feel guilty that Cally was so unhappy? Yes, she did, but no one had forced Cally to marry Valerian Hawkesworth. She had taken one look at his handsome face, considered the elevated social position she would attain, and agreed. I will not accept responsibility for my sister's unhappiness, Aurora decided.

That still left the problem of why she kept seeing Hawkesworth's face in her daydreams, even when she was contemplating the deliciously sensual St. John. Both were tall and lean. St. John had an attractive face with good features, but Valerian was extremely handsome, his face a combination of angles and planes. This is ridiculous, Aurora thought. It makes no difference what they look like. That cannot be the reason that I keep imagining Valerian instead of St. John in my dreams. Yet, I am not aware that I feel anything for the duke but irritation. I do not think I have ever met any man who so annoyed me. That is not love. Even with my inexperience I am wise enough to know that. I don't know why I keep thinking of him, but I will not do it any longer. *I will not!* It is disloyal to my dear St. John. George is wrong. St. John does love me. I am certain of it. Did he not say he had never felt for any woman what he felt for me? It must be love, and I will not allow Valerian Hawkesworth to spoil my happiness. *I won't!*

Chapter

❧ 10 ❧

George Spencer-Kimberly and Miss Elizabeth Bowen were married on the thirtieth of October. It was a bright and crisp afternoon. The villagers had gathered outside St. Anne's to catch a glimpse of the bridal party. It was almost like family, for the Bowens had lived in Farminster for eleven generations, and there were several of those standing in the crowd who had not only seen Betsy Bowen grow up, but her father, Sir Ronald, as well.

It was a small affair with only close friends and nearby family invited. Almost everyone was known to the villagers. The bridegroom arrived on horseback with Mr. St. John and the duke. The ducal coach stopped directly before the church path to debark the old dowager, quite regal in burgundy velvet trimmed in beaver. Her snowy hair was piled high and had two fine plumes in it. Miss Spencer-Kimberly followed the dowager, quite pretty in dark green velvet, her ringlets bobbing. But then, to the onlookers' surprise, an open sedan chair was brought up to the coach and the young duchess was helped out and into the conveyance that was then carried into the church.

"She don't look good," an anonymous voice in the crowd said.

The dowager's sharp eyes swept the crowd for the speaker, but suddenly all was quiet. Linking her arm into Aurora's, they proceeded into St. Anne's. Inside, the church was filled with an air of expectancy. The midafternoon sun streamed through the stained glass windows, casting multicolored shadows on the oaken pews and stone floors. Fine white linen and autumn flowers adorned the altar with its gold candlesticks containing pure beeswax tapers. The two women proceeded to the front ducal pew and settled themselves. Calandra's sedan chair had been set in front of the pew so she might see everything from the best possible vantage point. St. John joined them, a quick smile on his lips as he greeted Cally, the dowager, and Aurora. The duke was to act as George's best man.

Lady Elsie nodded to them from across the aisle. Her eyes were red from weeping, and she clutched a sodden handkerchief. Her look was so woeful that the dowager leaned over, whispering softly to Aurora, "You would think her daughter were being forced into marriage with a monster, the silly woman!" Before Aurora might reply, however, the organ began to play a stately anthem, and the congregation arose to watch as the wedding ceremony began.

From the sacristy the bridegroom and the duke came forth to await the bride. Down the aisle tripped Misses Isabelle, Suzanne, Caroline, and Maryanne Bowen in yellow and white striped gowns, wreaths of late yellow roses in their hair. Now came Master William Bowen, aged ten, escorting the bride, who was radiant in her creamy taffeta gown with painted blue forget-me-nots, her hair piled atop her head, dressed with silk flowers and strings of pearls and lightly powdered. And awaiting them before the altar with George and the duke was the bride's father, who would marry the couple.

The ceremony was elegant yet simple. It was only the second wedding she had ever attended, Aurora thought as she watched her brother and his glowing bride. The church was peaceful, and it all seemed so right. How different it was from Cally's wedding in the hallway of the plantation house on that long-ago early spring day. Perhaps with God's blessing George's marriage would be a happier one than Cally's. Aurora hoped so with all her heart, but then, she knew Betsy and her brother would be happy. They already were, and it could only get better between them as the years went by because they were so well suited.

The newlyweds came down the aisle, smiling, the service over,

their union formalized. They walked from the church to the cheers
and good wishes of the villagers, the rest of the wedding party, and
the guests following behind them to the vicarage, which was located
on the other side of the churchyard. Aurora walked next to her sister,
who despite her sedan chair looked exceedingly uncomfortable.

"Are you all right?" Aurora asked.

"How could I be all right with this creature inside me?" Cally
grumbled irritably. "Having to sit like this is horrible, and I can
only imagine that I look a fright!"

"You can recline on a settee at the vicarage," Aurora said soothingly. "George and Betsy are so happy that you made the effort to
come to the wedding, Cally."

"Why does George have to leave us?" Cally whined. "I don't
want him to go, Aurora. I am afraid without George."

"That is so much nonsense, Cally," her sister chided her. "You
were without George all those months before we arrived in England.
And you know why George is going. He must run the plantation.
Besides, do you want Mama left alone forever on St. Timothy?"

"I wish I could go with him," Cally whispered. "I wish it were
two years ago, that Papa were alive, and we had never heard of
Valerian Hawkesworth! If I had only known, Aurora, I would not
have agreed to marry him. What if this creature I carry is not the
son he wants? Then it will begin all over again, and I do not believe
I could bear it!" Her voice had begun to have a hysterical edge to
it.

"Calm yourself, Cally," Aurora said sternly. "This is our brother's
wedding day. It is a happy time, and I will not have you spoiling
it with an attack of the vapors! You will put a smile on your face,
and you will speak politely with all who greet you. If you do not,
I shall convince St. John, and believe me it will take little effort,
to elope immediately, and I will leave you! You will not enjoy being
alone with your dark thoughts and bad temper, I promise you!"

Calandra's defiance crumbled in the face of her sister's threat.
She forced a wan smile onto her face. "You are hard," she murmured.

The front and rear drawing rooms of the vicarage were decorated
with autumn flowers and branches of colored leaves and evergreens.

Here the bride and groom received their guests and the many congratulations offered them. In the dining room the table was set with antique Irish linen and lace, silver candelabra, a silver bowl of late roses, and the bride's cake in the center of the table. There was champagne served from the duke's own cellars. Sir Ronald, a man of modest means, was extremely grateful for the Hawkesworths' generosity. A usually reserved man, he was expansive today in his delight over his daughter's excellent marriage. Betsy's union now joined his family in a tenuous marital connection with the Hawkesworths. This meant that he might seek just a bit higher for his other girls.

The wedding cake was cut, served, and eaten. The toasts were drunk to the couple's good fortune and happiness. Betsy discreetly hurried upstairs to remove her bridal finery and get into her traveling costume, aided by her sisters and her still-weepy mother. George was also nowhere to be seen, having gone to change from his satin breeches into something more practical for the road. The young couple would spend the next few days upon the road, making their way to London, and the vessel that would take them to St. Timothy.

Again Valerian Hawkesworth had shown an openhanded munificence. George and his bride would travel in the duke's large traveling coach. A baggage wagon would follow, overseen by Wickham and Betsy's maid. The newlyweds would spend three days in London at Farminster House before boarding the *Royal George* for their trip to St. Timothy. The duke had paid the first-class passage for the bridal couple so they might travel in the utmost comfort and privacy on this, their honeymoon voyage.

Dressed for travel, George Spencer-Kimberly came to bid his two sisters farewell. Cally could not help weeping. "I feel that I will never see you again," she sobbed piteously, but he reassured her fear as he always had since they were children.

"We'll come for a visit in five years' time, little sister," he told her. "Perhaps we will even be able to persuade Mama to come then."

"And our children will get to know one another," Aurora said cheerily. "Mama will be in her glory with *all* her grandchildren gathered about her, don't you think, Cally?"

Cally sniffled, and nodded slowly.

George now turned to Aurora. "You are certain?" he said meaningfully, looking directly at her. "I want you happy with St. John, and not miserable like our poor Cally." His hands rested lightly upon her shoulders, his eyes filled with concern.

"I am as sure as any woman can be," she answered him. "It is a good match, and I believe we suit, George. What more can there be but that. At least I do not fear the marriage bed like our sister."

"No"—his hazel eyes twinkled at her—"you do not, I suspect, but more than that I do not want to know," he chuckled. Then he kissed her upon the forehead, hugging her to him. "Be happy, dearest Aurora!"

"I will, George," she promised him.

He turned his attention back to Calandra, pulling her gently to her feet and embracing her, kissing her upon both cheeks. "Try and be good, Cally," he said softly. "In the end you will find that hearthside and children are the happiest life for a woman."

"Nonsense!" Cally replied with a touch of her old spirit. Then she sat back down again heavily. "Give Mama my love."

"Together," George said. "Forever," Cally replied. "As one!" Aurora finished.

"The bouquet! Betsy is going to toss her bouquet!" came the cry from the hallway. "Come along, girls!"

Giggling, pushing, and shoving for the best position, all the unmarried ladies hurried into the hallway, where Betsy stood halfway up the staircase, the now slightly wilting flowers clutched in her hand.

"Come on!" George pulled Aurora by the hand and pushed her into the fray.

"One! Two! Three!" chorused the other guests, and then the bride pitched her bouquet, which seemingly by magic went directly into Aurora's outstretched hands. She caught it, laughing, and blew a kiss in St. John's direction.

"Oh, that's not fair!" Isabelle Bowen protested. "We all know that Aurora will soon be married! She already wears the St. John betrothal ring."

"You're too young to be married yet, Bella," the new Mistress Spencer-Kimberly said with a smile. "Whoever catches the bouquet must wed within a year, or no one else present can marry. That is the rule. Do you want every girl in the county waiting for you to make up your mind regarding some young man? We all know that you have a terrible time deciding things!"

There were nods and chuckles of agreement all around. Then, before Isabelle could protest, the bridal couple was making its final farewells, climbing into the coach and departing. As the vehicle made its way down the drive with both Betsy and George hanging out its window, smiling happily and waving, Lady Elsie burst into fulsome tears, joined by her daughters, who continued waving weepily at the retreating carriage.

"Good grief!" the dowager muttered. "Where is our transport? I do not intend to stand here and be drowned by the tears of that silly woman and her four remaining chits. Valerian! Fetch the coach!" She turned her attention to her host and hostess. "A lovely wedding," she murmured. "May I thank you on behalf of the entire family, but we must be going. The duchess cannot take any more excitement, y'know. It was quite an effort for her to come, you understand. Good-bye! Good-bye!"

She practically leapt into the carriage, followed by Aurora. Cally had already been ensconced inside as her brother and his wife departed. The dowager's agility was remarkable for one of her advanced years. The door to the vehicle slammed shut, and it moved off.

"Thank heavens!" Mary Rose Hawkesworth said with feeling.

Both Cally and Aurora giggled, unable to help themselves.

The dowager herself smiled a small smile, saying, "Elsie Bowen is a sweet creature to be sure, but a silly and sentimental one as well. Why on earth was she crying? Five daughters to marry off, and the dowries not particularly large, and Betsy marries a handsome young man with a good income and excellent prospects. What, I ask you, is there to cry about *that?* Not to mention that her daughter is now connected to our family by marriage. That should help that chit Isabelle when she is ready to go husband hunting. I know a most suitable young baronet who should be ready to settle down in another year or two," the dowager concluded, her eyes narrowing at the prospect of matchmaking again.

"Gracious, ma'am," Aurora replied with a small chuckle, "you will have Lady Bowen's daughters all married off before she knows what has happened, and then she will really drown us all in her tears."

"Heh! Heh! Heh!" came the reply, and the dowager settled down with a pleased expression as they were driven home to Hawkes Hill.

Cally retired to her room immediately, complaining that she felt even worse than usual. The dowager and Aurora settled themselves in the family parlor overlooking the gardens to have tea.

"I do not like the look of Calandra," the dowager noted. "Her hands and her feet are quite swollen, and she has become sallow. Perhaps we should call in Dr. Michaels tomorrow."

Aurora nodded. "I believe it might be a good idea to err on the side of caution, ma'am. I have never known Cally to complain quite so much as she has in recent months."

The day ended, and the house grew quiet. Extra quiet, it seemed to Aurora without George. For some reason, she could not fall into a deep sleep. It was almost as if she were waiting for something to happen. She would doze and then waken, doze and waken. Then, just as she was finally drifting into a deep sleep, there came a frantic knocking upon her bedroom door. Aurora struggled awake again even as Martha hurried from her little chamber to answer the frantic knocking. The servant flung open the door, and there stood Molly.

"It's her grace," Molly sputtered. "She says she's in terrible pain and wants Miss Aurora to come to her."

Aurora arose quickly, putting her robe about her. "Did you call the duke? What about the dowager? Perhaps we should send for Dr. Michaels." She pushed past the two servants, who followed after her.

Entering her sister's bedroom, she saw Cally was even paler than she had been earlier. There were droplets of perspiration beading her forehead, and her breathing was heavy. *"Aurora!"* she cried. "I am in the most dreadful pain. I think this creature may be coming early."

"You are certain it is not just something you ate, Cally?" Aurora queried her sister. "This is not a bit of indigestion?"

Calandra shook her head vehemently. "I drank no champagne but a sip to toast George and Betsy. I ate no cake, and have had no supper but for some tea with cream and sugar, for I have felt wretched all day. Ahhhhhh! I am being ripped apart by this thing!"

"Sally, wake Peters and have him send for Dr. Michaels," Aurora instructed the servant. "Then go to Browne and have him waken the duke."

"What about the old dowager?" Sally asked.

"Leave her sleep. There is nothing she can do to help us right now. Neither can the duke, for that matter, but it is his heir." She caressed Cally's swollen little hand. "It will be all right, Cally. This child will soon be born, early though he may be, and you will be a mother! How wonderful! I cannot wait until St. John and I produce."

Cally wrinkled her nose. "You will feel different when you are at my stage of life," she said. Then she brightened. "If the baby comes early, I shall be able to be back in London for Christmas. Perhaps it is all to the good. Ahhhhhhh! Nasty little beast! You don't think being born early will harm it, do you, Aurora?"

"Now, what would your sister, and her a maiden still, know about such things, your grace?" Martha said, and then she smiled at Cally. "Plenty of babies come early, and none the worse for it. Besides, 'taint that early. You had only a few more weeks to go."

Cally looked a bit more reassured, but then she said piteously, "Aurora, do not leave me. *Please!* I am so afraid."

"I won't leave you, little sister," Aurora said softly, and she sat down on the bed next to Calandra. "Do you know that in all the months you have carried your child, you have never once said what you would call him. What name do you favor?"

"I suppose they will want to call him after his father," Cally said glumly. " 'Tis tradition to call the Hawkesworth heir James or

Charles. Valerian is the duke's middle name. His first is James, like his grandfather. I don't really care."

"But if you did," Aurora persisted gently, "what would you name this baby if the choice was all yours?"

"Robert, after Papa," Cally said.

"And if it is a little girl?"

"God forbid!" Cally cried, and then, "Ahhhhh! Why does it hurt so much? I did not know it would hurt so!"

Aurora took a cool cloth that Martha handed her and lay it on her sister's head. "I am certain it is a boy, but if it were a girl? The poor little mite must have a name, and it cannot be Robert."

"Charlotte, after the queen," Cally murmured, ever mindful of the social consequences of naming a daughter after the king's bride.

The bedchamber door opened and the duke entered, coming over to the bed. "Is she in labor?" he asked Aurora.

"I think so, your grace," Martha answered him. "Miss Aurora couldn't know the answer to such a thing. She has never been around a woman in this condition. I have. It's early, but not too early."

"Dr. Michaels has been sent for," Aurora said reassuringly.

"Should you be here?" he asked her gently.

"No, she shouldn't," Martha said firmly.

"Cally wants me here," Aurora replied. "Just until the doctor comes? Please, Valerian. Cally is frightened. It cannot be good for her, or for the baby, if she is in terror." She placed a pleading hand upon the sleeve of his dressing gown, her look importuning him to acquiesce.

"Ahhh!" Cally moaned, and she began to cry. *"It hurts so!"*

He nodded. "Until the doctor says you must go," he told her. "I will await him downstairs." He leaned over and told Cally, "You are being very brave, my dear, and I thank you." Then he kissed her on the forehead and left the room.

"I hate him!" Cally exclaimed.

"Do not say it, I pray you," Aurora answered her sister.

"I do! If it were not for him, I should not be in such pain. I didn't want a child. I just wanted to be the Duchess of Farminster, and live in London, and give exquisite parties. I did not know I should have to do *this*. Ahhhhh!" She looked accusingly at her sister. "It is all your fault, Aurora! You did not tell me it would be like this!"

"Keep your voice down," Aurora warned Cally. "I did not tell you it would be like anything. I didn't know what it would be like to be the Duchess of Farminster. I just knew I didn't want to marry a stranger. You, however, were willing to do just that in order to be a duchess, Cally. I will share the blame, if there is any blame, but I will most certainly not take full responsibility for your actions!"

Calandra turned her head away from Aurora's gaze. They waited now in silence as the minutes ticked by, the laboring woman crying out when the pains overtook her, but there was little they could do until Dr. Michaels arrived. A kettle was brought from the kitchens, filled with water, and set in the coals of the fireplace to heat. Several stacks of clean cloths and clean linens were placed conveniently. The ducal cradle was positioned by the fireplace in readiness for its occupant.

Downstairs, the duke paced back and forth, nervously awaiting the arrival of Dr. Michaels. He was surprised when a total stranger was escorted into the house by one of his grooms. He was a tall, well-set gentleman with a ruddy complexion.

"Your grace? I am William Carstairs, doctor of medicine. I am Edward Michaels's cousin, and his new partner. Dr. Michaels has gone to York to see his ailing father. I was given to understand that her grace was not due to deliver until the end of next month, or possibly the middle of the following month."

"We do not even know if Calandra is in labor, but she is in pain," the duke said, holding out his hand and shaking that of the doctor. "Thank you for coming. It is our first child, and no one in the house except my elderly grandmother really knows about childbirth. We chose not to awaken the dowager, as she has had an active day with my brother-in-law's wedding to Miss Bowen. We had intended calling you in tomorrow at any rate, as Calandra has not looked particularly herself of late."

The doctor nodded. "Let us go upstairs, then," he said.

As he entered Cally's bedchamber, Martha's eyes grew wide with recognition. "Dr. Carstairs," she said, surprised.

"Martha? Martha Jones? What on earth are you doing here?" Then his eye spied Aurora. "And Miss Aurora?"

Aurora arose from her place upon the bed. "It is Cally, Dr. Carstairs. She is in terrible pain with this child."

The doctor nodded, and then said to the duke, "Take Miss Aurora from the room while I examine her sister."

Cally weakly protested, but was scarcely heard as the doctor turned his full attention to her.

"How do you know Dr. Carstairs?" the duke asked Aurora as he escorted her from the bedroom.

"He came from Jamaica with us when Mama married Papa. My father didn't want to lose another wife in childbirth for lack of proper medical attention," she explained. "He was with us for ten years, and in that time taught several of the more intelligent slaves and bondsmen the art of doctoring so we would always have someone to attend to our needs should there be illness or injury among us. Where is Dr. Michaels? Why didn't he come?"

The duke explained, and Aurora nodded. They stood silently for several minutes, and then the doctor joined them.

"Your wife is indeed in labor, your grace," he announced. "It is, however, a difficult labor, and the child is not quite turned properly, so I expect it will be some hours before she delivers." He turned to Aurora. "Go to bed, child. This is not the place for you now, although remembering your bravery, I know you would remain if I let you, Miss Aurora. I will not, however. Cally will be fine in my company, and I will keep Martha and Sally with me to help. We will send you word of your sister's progress as it develops."

"Let me say good night to her at least," Aurora begged, and the doctor nodded, escorting her back into the bedchamber.

"Why did you leave me?" Cally protested to her sister.

"Because the doctor made me," Aurora said. "You remember Dr. Carstairs, Cally? He only left St. Timothy when we were twelve. Dr. Michaels is away, and Dr. Carstairs will be delivering your baby. He will not let me stay, but Martha and Sally will remain."

"I am going to die," Cally said in a strangely calm voice.

"Nonsense," Aurora replied. "You are just frightened, little one. Dr. Carstairs will take excellent care of you."

"*I am going to die,*" Cally repeated firmly.

"Do not say such a thing!" Aurora begged her.

"I do not blame you," Cally continued. "I wanted to be a duchess, Aurora. I didn't have to do it. I do not blame you."

"Come along now, child," the doctor said, his hand on Aurora's shoulder. "It is time for you to get some rest."

"You will not die, Cally," Aurora insisted.

"I love you," Cally replied as her sister was taken away, and she watched with sad eyes as the bedchamber door closed behind Aurora.

"What a mean thing to say to your sister," Martha scolded Calandra. "Having a baby won't excuse you. Shame on you!"

But Cally said nothing, instead turning her face away from Martha as she had from Aurora earlier. The hours moved on slowly at first, and then with exceeding speed. It was dawn, and then midday. The dowager came to see how Calandra was doing, speaking kindly to the girl, and then leaving, strangely disturbed.

"Why is it taking so long?" she demanded of the doctor as he brought her from the bedchamber. "The child decides to come early, and then will not be born. What is the matter, Dr. Carstairs?"

The doctor shook his head. "I do not know, your grace, but while I am concerned, the young duchess has been in labor only about ten hours. That is not really too long. We can be patient yet."

"Indeed," grumbled the dowager to Aurora, who had joined them. "Trust me, my dear Aurora, if it were the man having the baby, nine hours ago would have been long enough. Patience! Hummmph!"

"Cally says she is going to die," Aurora said quietly.

"Now, now," the dowager comforted the young woman, "that is just your sister's fear and her sense of the dramatic speaking. By tomorrow she will be delivered, beginning to feel well again, and planning her triumphant return to London, I am certain." But Mary Rose Hawkesworth was not certain at all. Calandra had not looked right for several days now, and this early labor did not bode well. She could easily die. Childbirth was a dangerous business.

The afternoon faded into evening. Aurora had asked twice to be allowed to visit with her sister, but Dr. Carstairs would not permit it. Dinner was a silent affair, and afterward Aurora sought her bedroom. There she found Martha, who looked quite exhausted, sitting dozing by the fire.

Aurora shook her gently. "Martha, what has happened? How is Cally? Is the baby born yet?"

"Dr. Carstairs sent me and Sally away to rest a bit, miss," her servant said. "It ain't good. Oh, it ain't good. Poor Miss Calandra is getting weaker by the minute, and the baby won't be born. She's going to die, miss. I'm so sorry to say it, but she is!"

Aurora ran from her bedchamber and to her sister's room. The doctor came forward as she burst through the door, but with a surprising show of strength the girl pushed him aside and went to her sister's side. "Cally! Cally! Open your eyes this minute," she commanded.

Calandra's hazel eyes opened slowly. She looked at Aurora with a weak smile. "I knew you would come before it was too late," she said. Then she shuddered, and her look grew vacant.

"*Doctor!*" Aurora's voice was almost a scream.

He came quickly to the bedside, and taking Cally's wrist, sought for a pulse. There was none. He put his ear to her chest, but the young woman's heart was stilled. Looking up, he said to Aurora, "I am sorry, Miss Aurora, but your sister is dead."

"*The baby!* Is the baby dead too? Oh, God! Don't let Cally's death have been in vain! What of the baby?" Aurora cried.

"Fetch me my medical kit," he ordered her. "Will you faint at the sight of blood? Go and fetch Martha. *Hurry!*"

She practically flung the black leather bag that held the necessities of his doctoring skills at him, and then she dashed from the bedroom, sobbing wildly, calling for Martha. The servant stumbled from her chair and practically collided with her young mistress.

"It's Cally," Aurora wept hysterically. "*She is dead!* Oh, Martha! My sister is dead, and it is all my fault! Go! Hurry! The doctor wants you to aid him. He will try to save the baby."

Martha dashed into the duchess's bedroom, where the doctor

stood staring down in horror at the bed. "What is it, sir?" she asked him tremulously, attempting to see around his bulky figure.

"Come no farther!" he said sharply.

"What is it?" she repeated nervously.

He turned, white-faced. "Look if you will, but it is a terrible sight, Martha Jones. No wonder poor Calandra could not deliver her child. It is a monster, but praise God in his mercy, it is dead."

Determined but fearful, Martha gazed down upon Calandra, whose belly had been opened by the doctor in his desperate effort to save the duke's heir. "It's two babies," she said softly. "What's that about their necks, Doctor, and why are they so close together? Why, they look as if their poor little bodies are united." Then she gave a little scream. "God help us! They have but two legs! Oh, Doctor! What is it that poor Miss Cally has borne in her body all these months?"

He shook his head in his own wonderment. "I have heard of such a thing, but rarely. Had they been normally formed, they might have been twins, but of what sex, I cannot tell, for they are conjoined in such a manner to make it impossible. They have two heads and necks; each has a set of shoulders and an upper chest, and each has two arms, but the rest of their trunk is one, and there are but two legs. They have been strangled by their own cord, thank God! I will sew the duchess back up, Martha Jones, and we will tell the duke the child was dead in its mother's womb, which is no lie. There is no need to say what we have seen this day. There will be sorrow enough in this house, and as Miss Aurora is to be married herself in a few months, there is no need to frighten her with her poor sister's misfortune, eh, Martha?"

Martha nodded. The sight of Cally's monster would remain with her for the rest of her days. It was horrible. Then she had a thought. "They'll ask what the babe was, Doctor. Tell them a wee girl. There will be so much sadness over this as it is. The duke has been good to us. Don't let him think he lost a son as well as a wife."

"It is no son," the doctor said softly, "but I do not think it is a daughter either." Then he shook himself and said, "Go and fetch the duke, but I do not want him to come into this room yet. Ask him to await me in the library, Martha. And see to your mistress. She was here when her sister died. Calandra's last words were for her.''

As Martha left the room, the doctor began to sew up his patient's belly. He was astounded by what he had seen, and wondered what could have possibly caused Calandra to conceive such a creature. Shaking his head, he worked with swift, neat stitches. He didn't want anyone else seeing what he and Martha had seen. Poor girl, he thought. If she had lived, if the creature had survived, what would have become of them all? No mother could surely look upon such a monstrosity and love it. It might have driven her to madness.

Martha hurried down the hallway. Her first concern was for her mistress. The duke could wait. They all could wait. Aurora's earlier words had disturbed Martha, and she had to make her understand that she was not responsible for Calandra's fate. Cally had been offered a choice, and had willingly, nay, eagerly, accepted the responsibility of being Valerian Hawkesworth's wife. No. Not his wife. His duchess. Cally had not been a true or good wife at all, God rest the poor soul.

She could hear Aurora weeping bitterly even before she entered the bedroom. The girl was sprawled across her bed, sobbing as if her heart were broken, and in a sense, Martha realized, it was. Going to her mistress, she gathered the girl to her bosom and attempted to soothe her sorrow. "There, miss, there. It was God's will, and there's no standing against God's will now, is there?''

"Th-th-the b-b-b-baby?'' Aurora queried.

"Dead too, a girl,'' Martha said shortly.

Aurora cried all the harder. "It was all for nothing,'' she sobbed. "All for nothing, Martha. Oh, my poor Cally.'' She looked up at her servant, her lovely face all red and wet. "It's my fault Cally is dead, Martha. It's all my fault! Did you and Mama not warn me that no good ever came of deception? But I would not listen, would I? And now my sister is dead because of my selfishness!'' Her weeping began afresh, her whole body shaking turbulently.

Martha drew in a deep breath and then she grasped Aurora by the shoulders and looked her directly in the eyes. "It ain't your fault, miss. You didn't force Miss Cally into marriage. She had a choice, but the silly girl was so overwhelmed with the idea of being a duchess that she was just as headstrong and willful as you're wont to get. All Miss Cally wanted of her marriage was to be beautiful and acclaimed, wear fine clothing and drive in a magnificent carriage, and give parties that all the mighty would come to after fighting over her invitations. But we didn't know that, did we? Your parents set you both a good example of a Christian marriage, miss. Miss Cally knew what was expected of her, but she refused to be a good wife to the duke. None of that is your fault, and I won't let you blame yourself for it!"

"But I am to blame, Martha," Aurora said woefully. "My father arranged a fine marriage for me with his friend's son, and when I learned of it I spurned it, and would not do my duty. I tempted Cally because I suspected that she would adore the idea of being a duchess. I was right, and she took my place. By doing so, it has cost her her life. Had I done what my father expected of me and married Valerian Hawkesworth, my sister would be alive today. I do not hold myself responsible for Cally's behavior or actions, but I do hold myself responsible for my own."

"Well," Martha said in hard, practical tones, "you can't change what's done, miss. Miss Cally is gone, and that's a fact." She arose from the bed. "I got to go and fetch the duke for the doctor. Dry your eyes and wash your face. Then go find the old dowager. She'll need a bit of comforting to get over this shock." Martha stamped from the room, leaving Aurora alone once more.

The servant found the duke in his library and requested that he await Dr. Carstairs, beating a hasty retreat before Hawkesworth might ask her any questions. She met the doctor coming down the staircase as she was hurrying back up.

"Find the duchess's maids, Martha," he told her, "and do what you can to make her look presentable." Then he moved on down the stairs and entered the duke's library.

Valerian Hawkesworth came quickly to his feet, looking anxiously at William Carstairs. "My wife, the child?" he said, but from the look on the doctor's face, he knew the news would not be good.

"I am very sorry, your grace, but they are both deceased. The labor was extremely difficult for your wife. She was unable to birth the child, and her poor little heart just gave out. I opened her belly surgically to save the infant—it was a girl—but it was dead, its cord wrapped tightly about its neck. I sewed up the incision, leaving the child with its mother. You have my deepest sympathies."

The duke nodded silently. Vain, foolish Calandra, he thought. She is dead, and our daughter with her. Poor girl. At least she will never again have to endure my attentions. A daughter. I would have enjoyed a daughter, but I needed a son. "I understand, Dr. Carstairs," he finally said. "We could all see that Calandra was having a difficult time these past months." He walked over to the mahogany sideboard and poured two tumblers of whiskey, handing one to the doctor. "I hope her suffering was not too great. Sit down, Doctor. You look tired."

"I am" came the admission as the doctor sat opposite the duke in the chairs that flanked the blazing fireplace. The fire was warm, and between it, and the excellent whiskey he was sipping, William Carstairs asked the question of Valerian Hawkesworth that he had been dying to ask him ever since he had entered the house. "I was always given to understand, your grace, that you were to marry the heiress of St. Timothy, and yet your wife was Calandra Spencer-Kimberly. How, may I ask, did your marriage come about?"

"I did marry the heiress to St. Timothy," the duke said. The poor doctor was obviously tired and confused.

"No, sir, you did not" came the firm reply. "Aurora Kimberly is the heiress of St. Timothy. I lived on the island, in the Kimberly house, for ten years. I was the only white man of breeding with whom Mr. Kimberly could speak, and we did so each evening after the meal was over. We sat either on the veranda of the house or in his library, drinking fruit juice and rum, and discussing all manner of things. He confided in me the betrothal agreement he and his good friend, Charles, Lord Hawkesworth, had arranged between their children even before Miss Aurora was born. He had not told his wife of the matter, for he hoped to make an equally good match for Calandra one day, and he wanted no jealousy over Aurora's match until he had a marriage set for his stepdaughter.

"I came to St. Timothy from Jamaica with the Kimberlys when they were first married. It was hoped in those days that his third wife might give him the heir he wanted, and so he desired a doctor on the island for emergencies. There had been none when Emily Kimberly died. I watched both Miss Aurora and Miss Calandra grow up. I left the island only five years ago to return to England. I would know them if they were my own daughters, your grace. Your duchess was Calandra Spencer-Kimberly, Robert's stepdaughter, not Aurora, his daughter, and his heiress, of that I am absolutely certain."

Valerian Hawkesworth was numb with shock, and at the same time he felt a burning anger beginning to arise deep within him. What kind of a deception had been played upon him, and why? "I am as confused about this matter as you are, Dr. Carstairs," he said in a cool, even voice. "I was given to believe Calandra was the heiress, and certainly no part of her dowry was withheld from me. Mr. Kimberly is deceased, you may know. As I wished to marry and return to England as quickly as possible, a minister was brought from Barbados to perform the ceremony. My wife and I departed for home. Aurora and George came nine months later. Mistress Kimberly wanted them to seek out English mates. My brother-in-law married Miss Bowen yesterday, and they are even now on their way to St. Timothy. Aurora is to marry Mr. St. John in the spring."

"I did not know about Robert Kimberly," the doctor replied.

"I would request that you do not mention this matter to anyone," the duke said. "I will wish to investigate it myself, and I certainly desire no scandal at this time. My wife and child must be buried with dignity and honor. Nothing must detract from that."

"Of course, your grace," the doctor said, and finishing off his whiskey, he arose. "I must return to the surgery. With my cousin away, there may be another in need of my services." He bowed politely, and the duke nodded, standing.

"Thank you, Dr. Carstairs," he said, ushering him from the library and into the foyer of the house.

There Peters awaited with his long, dark cloak. Helping the

doctor to don his garment, he said, "Your coach is waiting outside, sir. The horses are rested and fed, and your coachman is ready." The butler escorted the doctor outside, and then, returning inside, shut the door behind him, certain in the knowledge that the man was being helped into his coach by the grooms assigned the task.

The duke was already climbing the stairs, and seeking out his grandmother. He found Aurora with her, comforting the old lady, and was torn between his anger and the pleasure he took in her kindness to Lady Hawkesworth. "Go to your room, Aurora," he said quietly. "You look exhausted, and there is nothing more that can be done tonight."

"George?" she said in a whispery voice. "Should we send after George and Betsy, Valerian?"

"I think not," he replied, looking to his grandmother for confirmation, and she nodded. "There is nothing they can do for poor Calandra, and I don't want to spoil their honeymoon. We shall send word on the next vessel bound for the western Indies. It will give them time to reach home and give your mother a little happiness before they must learn of this tragedy. Now, go to your room."

She curtsied to them and departed.

"What is it, Valerian?" his grandmother asked when Aurora was gone. "Something is distressing you, and it is not just the deaths that have happened in this house tonight. What is the matter?"

"Calandra was not the heiress to St. Timothy," he said, repeating what the doctor had told him.

"I know," the dowager responded when he had finished speaking.

"You know?" His look was incredulous. "You knew the deception perpetrated upon me and you said nothing? Why, Grandmama? Why?"

"I learned the truth only a few months ago," his grandmother said quietly. "From the day I met her, Aurora seemed familiar to me, and yet I could not understand why. Then, several weeks back, I was in the family portrait gallery when I came across the portraits of the first duke's two younger sisters. Catherine Hawkesworth was married to the Kimberly, who was given the grant of St. Timothy by King Charles II, and her sister, Anne, was wed to the Meredith who shared the island with the Kimberlys. Aurora is Catherine's image, and very much Anne's as well. I realized then why Aurora had seemed so familiar, and I confirmed it with her servant, Martha."

"*But why?*" he rasped, his head reeling.

"She didn't want to marry a stranger, and she didn't care if she was a duchess or not. She wants to wed for love," the dowager said softly. "Calandra, however, was not so particular, I fear."

"Aurora didn't want to be a duchess?" he said wonderingly. Then he shook his head. "There will be time to deal with that matter, but first we must see that poor Calandra and her daughter are buried decently in the family plot. She was my wife for all the deception. We can do no less, Grandmama."

"Leave it rest, Valerian," Mary Rose Hawkesworth said. "If Calandra had been safely delivered of her child, it would have been different."

"But she was not, Grandmama, and now, poor girl, she is dead," the duke replied quietly.

"It was a mismatch, and granted it was the wrong match, but nothing of the heiress's dowry was withheld from you, Valerian," his grandmother said. "Let it be, and bury your wife with dignity."

"We will bury Calandra honorably," he answered her calmly, "but then I will deal with that deceiving little bitch who should have been my wife. So, Miss Aurora Kimberly did not wish to be a duchess. She will shortly learn that the choice is not hers to make."

"Valerian," his grandmother said sternly, "Aurora is affianced to St. John. Their marriage is scheduled for May."

He laughed, and it was a hard sound. "I'm afraid if my cousin wishes to marry in May, he will have to find another bride. *Aurora is mine!*"

Chapter

❧ 11 ❧

Charlotte Calandra Hawkesworth, Fourth Duchess of Farminster, was laid to rest in the family plot on a hillside overlooking the estate lake. The funeral was private, the young duchess mourned by her husband, her sister, Lady Hawkesworth, and three servants. Sir Ronald said the Anglican service of Christian burial over the body, and at the duke's request agreed to explain to everyone that the family's grief was such that they could not bear the weight of a larger gathering.

"Understandable, understandable," murmured the cleric. "A terrible loss, the duchess and her child both." Then he left them to their mourning, grateful that Betsy and her husband had not been called back and their honeymoon spoiled. It had been generous of both the duke and his sister-in-law in their great trial and time of grief to think of the newlyweds.

"I must write to Mama," Aurora said when they had returned to the house after the burial.

"I will write her too," the dowager said.

"And I," the duke told them.

"I cannot remain at Hawkes Hill for much longer," Aurora said. "It is not proper with my sister gone."

"You will remain," Valerian Hawkesworth said firmly.

"I cannot!" she cried desperately.

"You can, and you will, and I think we both know why, Aurora," he said coldly. "Besides, you have my grandmother to chaperon you. No one will think ill of you for staying."

"St. John will not be happy," she told him.

"My cousin's state of mind should be of no concern to you," Valerian Hawkesworth answered her, "but I shall speak to him myself very shortly."

Aurora fled up the staircase to her bedroom, slamming the door behind her as if the devil himself were after her. *"He knows!"* she told Martha, pale and wide-eyed. *"He knows!"*

"Knows what, miss?" Martha was puzzled.

"That I am the one. The one he should have married!" Aurora replied frantically. "Oh, Martha! He looked like he wanted to kill me!"

"Oh, miss, how could he know?" Martha said. "Unless . . . oh, Lord help us! The doctor must have said something. He and your papa were good friends, being the only two of their kind on the island. The doctor must have known about your betrothal, and when he saw Miss Cally got curious as to why she was the duchess and not you."

"He is going to speak to St. John!" she said frantically.

"Oh, the duke wouldn't make you marry him when he knows you love Mr. St. John, miss. Besides, it would cause a terrible scandal, and Miss Cally only just dead with her poor child. You're over-wrought, miss. Now, you come and have a nice lie-down. I'll go get you some tea."

"No!" Aurora clutched at her servant's arm. "We have to leave Hawkes Hill, Martha. We must!"

"And where will we go?" Martha said in practical tones. "You can't go to Primrose Court even with Mr. St. John's mother in residence. It would cause a terrible calumny. Besides, your wedding is going to have to be postponed for a year. We're in mourning now, y'know."

"I could shelter with the Bowens," Aurora said desperately.

"In that rabbit warren of a house, and with all those daughters, not to mention that little devil, Master Willie? There's no room for you there, miss. Come, now, and lie down for me, dearie."

"Then we must go home to St. Timothy!" Aurora decided. "I have my mother's house! *He* cannot take that from me, and in a year's time St. John can come for me, and we will be married. We do not have time to get to London to catch the *Royal George*, but there will be another sailing of another ship in a few weeks' time. That's it! That's what we shall do, Martha! We shall go home!"

"Yes, miss, now, lie down and try to rest while I fetch you a little tea. You're all upset with Miss Cally's death." She settled the girl, and then, leaving the room, the curtains drawn, hurried to speak with the dowager.

"Poor child," the dowager sympathized. "My grandson would glower at her darkly, and frighten her."

"Does he know, ma'am?" Martha ventured. "Excuse my boldness, but I love Miss Aurora. I've raised her since she was a baby."

"The duke knows he was deceived," the dowager answered the servant. "What he will do, I do not know, but I promise you I will do my very best to protect Aurora from his anger and caprice."

"It was the doctor, weren't it?" Martha said. "When I first saw him I was so glad to see him, I didn't realize he might be the key to our undoing. How am I to keep my mistress calm, ma'am? How am I to keep her from running away back to St. Timothy?"

The dowager arose, and opening a small drawer in her desk, drew out a little ivory box. Opening it, she drew out a small, gilded round pellet. "Crush it and put it in her tea, Martha. It will make her sleep the night through, and after a good night's rest Aurora will certainly think more clearly and forget this nonsense of running away. Then I will speak to her myself tomorrow, and we will decide upon a course of action that will calm her fears."

"Oh, thank you, your grace," Martha said gratefully, curtsying. She departed the dowager's rooms and went to the kitchens, where she fixed a small tray with bread and butter, some dark, rich fruit-cake, and a small pot of tea. Then, carrying it, she returned to Aurora, finding her up and pacing the bedroom. Martha placed her tray on the piecrust table and said briskly, "Now, you sit down and have your tea, miss. Then I'm going to tuck you up in bed, and after a good night's rest we'll plan our journey, eh?" She smiled at the girl, drawing her to the table.

Aurora sat down, taking the saucer of tea from Martha, sipping it nervously, nibbling on the bread and butter, eating a small slice of the fruitcake. Gently Martha encouraged the girl to finish the tea, and poured her more, until the little pot was emptied. Aurora's eyelids grew heavy, and she did not protest when Martha helped her to her bed and tucked her in beneath the down coverlet. She was asleep even as Martha blew out the bedside taper. Taking the tea tray, the servant returned to the kitchens and then hurried back to her mistress. Entering the bedroom, she gave a small cry at the figure looming over Aurora's bed.

"It is only me," the duke said, quickly calming her fears. He turned to face her, and Martha thought how handsome he was.

"You shouldn't be here, your grace," she gently scolded him.

"She is so lovely," he responded. "Why is she sleeping so heavily, Martha? Is she all right?"

"Your grandmama gave me a little pill to put in her tea, your grace. Miss Aurora is heartbroken over her sister's death and wants to go home to St. Timothy. She would have tried to leave tonight if we had not stopped her. She ain't slept too good since Miss Cally died, and she ain't thinking clearly."

"Her home is here at Hawkes Hills," the duke replied.

"You ain't going to let her marry Mr. St. John, are you, your grace?" Martha asked him candidly. It was bold of her, but she had to know if she herself was going to decide what to do.

Valerian Hawkesworth shook his head. "Aurora was betrothed to me, Martha. That she and her family deceived me makes no difference. Under the law, Aurora is my betrothed wife. If poor Calandra had lived, if she had given me a son, it would have been a different matter altogether even if I had eventually learned of the subterfuge. Calandra, however, is dead, and our child with her. And Dr. Carstairs has exposed the trickery that was practiced upon me."

"But, your grace," Martha said softly, "you were married to *Charlotte* Kimberly, and you did receive her dowry according to the terms of the agreement your father and Robert Kimberly arranged all those years ago. Nothing was withheld from you."

Valerian Hawkesworth chuckled. "Indeed, Martha, but it was the wrong *Charlotte* Kimberly. The agreement between my father and Aurora's was made even before her birth, before he wed his third wife, Oralia Spencer, and adopted her two children. The Kimberlys have defrauded me by palming the wrong bride off on me. Should my cousin, St. John, learn of it, and be married to Aurora, he would attempt to claim the island for himself. Not because he really wanted it, but out of plain malice and mischief. I cannot allow him to do that. Besides, your mistress is, by law, mine. I intend to have what is mine." Then, in a great gesture of good manners, he nodded to her, and, turning, departed.

Martha was astounded by his politeness. After all, she was only a servant; granted, an upper-class servant, but a servant nonetheless. The duke had taken the time to speak with her at length, and answer her questions although he was certainly not bound to do so. She liked him. She had always liked him, and had never understood Aurora's antipathy toward Valerian Hawkesworth. Now, however, there would be war between the two. Martha decided then and there not to reveal a word of what had passed between herself and the duke tonight. It would only drive Miss Aurora to reckless actions, and even without knowing what Martha knew, her young mistress was going to behave in a hasty and foolhardy manner. Of that Martha could be certain.

The duke was the right husband for Aurora, and Martha had always believed it. Mr. St. John had been a good alternate, of course, but Martha suspected that he was as reckless and adventurous as Aurora herself. They might have been a good match, but on the other hand, it could have proved a disastrous marriage with St. John encouraging Aurora to hector the duke even as he did. Besides, Miss Aurora deserved to be a duchess even if she thought she didn't want to be. And it was what Mr. Kimberly, God rest his good soul, had wanted for his daughter. At that moment Martha decided that she would aid the dowager and her grandson to bring about the marriage between Aurora and the duke. It could be no betrayal of her mistress to do what Martha knew in her heart was the right thing. She had known it all along, as had George Spencer-Kimberly and his mother.

When she awoke in the morning, Aurora seemed calmer, Martha thought. She ate her breakfast, wrote to her mother, and complained of the headache, but she said nothing about leaving to return to St. Timothy. Perhaps, the servant thought hopefully to herself, she has given up the idea, and so she reported to the dowager. But Aurora kept to her bedchamber, claiming fatigue, and had both her later meals brought to her upon a tray as well. Her appetite, however, was quite good. She took to her bed early, reading until she fell asleep.

"Poor lamb," Martha said to herself as she snuffed the candles and banked the fires in the fireplace before seeking her own little room.

Aurora awoke as the clock struck three. lying quietly in her bed, she smiled to herself. Since childhood she had always slept seven hours exactly unless she was ill. She had deliberately gone to bed early so she might awaken in the middle of the night and effect her escape from Hawkes Hill. Martha, she sadly realized, could no longer be trusted. She was almost certain her maid had drugged her tea the evening before. Obviously Martha did not approve of her plans, and that was unfortunate. She would have to leave her servant behind, but she knew the dowager would treat Martha well and keep her in her employ, so she felt no guilt over her decision.

She slipped from her bed, shivering at the chill of the November night. She was going to London. Once there, she would find respectable lodgings and book passage on the next boat to the western Indies. She had more than enough money, most of what she had come to England with, for the duke had paid for all of her expenses since her arrival. There was a single public coach that came past the main road outside the estate early in the morning once a week. That morning was the day. The coach would take her to the town of Hereford, and from there she would be able to get the London coach. She was taking none of her possessions so that no one would suspect she had gone far until possibly the morrow, at which point it would be too late to find her. She would dress plainly so as not to attract attention, and carry only a small reticule with her funds, and a brush to keep her hair neat.

The dress she chose was a simple dark blue silk, respectable but not showy. She wore several petticoats beneath it, including a flannel one, and knit woolen stockings. She would buy whatever else she needed in London before sailing. Pinning her hair into a neat chignon, she picked up her fur-lined cloak and slipped from the bedroom. She walked carefully, tiptoeing down the staircase and across the foyer to the front door. Cautiously she drew back the bolts on the front door.

"And where, my dear betrothed, do you think you are going?" the duke's voice shattered the silence of the night.

Aurora whirled to see him in the dimly lit doorway of his library. "I am going home," she said. "You cannot stop me, Valerian!" *Betrothed!* He had called her his betrothed. So he really did know.

"I think not," he said coldly. Then he closed the distance between them, and snatching her cloak from her grip, flung it across the foyer. An arm reached out, wrapping itself tightly about her waist, forcing her body against his in a proximity that set her senses reeling. "Hawkes Hill is your home, Aurora. It was settled even before your birth, when our fathers pledged us in marriage. A marriage you sought to avoid with deception, putting your sister in your place."

"You got what you wanted!" she cried. "You got St. Timothy and a wife. What more do you want, Valerian? *What more?*"

"I want you, Aurora!" he said fiercely, and his hand caressed her face, his dark blue eyes scorching her with their intensity.

"Was not my sister enough for you?" she demanded angrily. "You mistreated her, Valerian! She told me so!"

"Calandra was a marble Venus, my dear Aurora," he said in hard tones. "She hated my touch, and I had to force myself upon my own wife in order to get her with child. She lay like a dead woman, her head turned from me, her body as cold as stone each time I took her."

"But you still managed to engage your lust, Valerian, didn't you?

Did you enjoy your rape of my sister? How could you do it?" Aurora demanded, her eyes filled with tears as she remembered Cally.

"*I thought of you,*" he said with devastating effect, almost pleased to see the shock in her aquamarine-blue eyes. "I aroused my baser instincts, as Calandra would have called them, by remembering the sight of your coming naked from the sea one day on St. Timothy."

"*Oh, my God!*"

"I am not proud of it, Aurora," he told her. "Do not ever think I was proud of what I had to do, but your sister hated the physical act of love, and I had to have an heir. Calandra was my wife, and that was her duty. I would have given her anything she wanted if she had only given me an heir. I quickly accepted the fact that she did not love me because I realized she would never love any man, nor would she cuckold me. She loved her position, and she loved my wealth and all it afforded her. It was all she sought, but she was too selfish to give me what I sought in return for what I gave her. I regret her death."

"Yet you are glad she is no longer here to trouble you!" Aurora accused him. "Do not deny it, Valerian!"

"I wished your sister no harm, Aurora, but she is dead, and no, I will not deny my relief at being freed from her. You would despise me if I did, for you would then know me as a liar, and I am not that."

"I despise you anyhow," Aurora declared angrily. "You cannot stop me, Valerian. I am going home to be with my family, and to wait out my year of mourning for Cally. But when that year is over, I shall marry St. John, as we have planned. I hate you! I will always hate you for what you did to my poor little sister!"

It was as if the small thread of sanity and reason that had been holding him together for these past months was suddenly snapped. "You deceitful little bitch," he snarled at her. "You are going nowhere, and as for my cousin, St. John will not have you, my dear, after I have finished with you!" Then he began ripping her bodice and her skirts.

With a shriek Aurora pulled away from him, turning and running for the stairs. Halfway up he caught her, his hands furiously shredding the fabric of her garments until she was virtually naked despite her valiant efforts to fend him off and escape once more. Finally Aurora attempted to scream, but he clapped his hand over her mouth even as he picked her up in his arms and continued on up the stairs and down the hallway to his bedroom. Kicking the door open and then shut behind him, he walked across the room, flinging her onto the bed as her hair came loose from its neat chignon, spilling about her shoulders.

She had to get up, she realized. She had to push past him and run for her very life. Yet she lay upon her back, watching with fascination as he yanked his own clothing off. Boots were kicked across the room, followed by breeches, drawers, stockings, and shirt. He stood over her, and she could not for the life of her stop staring. He was beautifully proportioned, but he looked hard as iron. I have to get up, Aurora thought desperately, yet her own limbs felt weakened and incapable of supporting her. She made a single futile attempt.

He pushed her back. Then, putting one knee upon the bed, he bent, cupping her face between his two big hands, and kissed her. It was a deep, slow kiss, his mouth warm and demanding upon hers, and betrayed by her own body, Aurora's lips softened beneath his. She sighed deeply, her mouth opening against the pressure of his. Their breaths mingled, and she could taste the whiskey on his. For a single moment in time, sanity returned, and she attempted to struggle away from him, but then his tongue slipped between her lips to touch hers. Emotions she had never really quite understood exploded within her. Their tongues entwined and caressed until Aurora was completely breathless and near to fainting.

He seemed to sense her state, and lifted his mouth from hers so she could catch her breath. Then slowly he began to kiss her face, his lips grazing softly and warmly over the skin. Delicately he touched the corners of her mouth, her cheeks, her chin, her eyelids, her forehead. Not just once, but several times over. Then, pushing her head back with the heel of his palm, he began to place warm kisses upon her straining throat, lingering momentarily in the beating hollow at the base of it. She almost screamed when his hot tongue began licking at the column of her neck, sweeping up the length of it and then back down again. Her silken flesh was utterly intoxicating.

"Oh, God," Aurora murmured. How could he do this to her? How could his passion have such an incredible effect upon her? She loved St. John, didn't she? Did she even know what love was? She was beginning to realize that she didn't. How could she feel this way about Valerian Hawkesworth when he was forcing her. *But he isn't,* the voice in her head said. *You want him. You have always wanted him.* Has it not been his face you saw in your dreams? "No!" she cried aloud.

"Yes!" his voice grated back at her. *"Yes!"*

Lying next to her now, he drew her into his arms. Gently he began to fondle her breasts. Aurora quivered with anticipation, desperate for the feel of his mouth upon her nipples, but instead he caressed the small rounds of warm flesh with delicate fingertips, brushing over the skin lightly, teasing at the little nubs until they darkened and grew taught with their rising excitement. Finally, when her breasts were swollen so hard that Aurora thought they would burst, he touched the very tips of her with his facile tongue, brushing against them quickly at first, and then each in its turn slowly. And at last he took a nipple in his mouth, sucking hard upon her until she gasped, feeling the wetness against her thighs.

Shyly, she touched the dark head upon her chest, not daring to stroke him, not even certain she should if she could get up the nerve. What was a woman supposed to do when a man made love to her? She remembered the bitterness in his voice as he spoke of her sister lying like a dead woman when he had exercised his husbandly rights. Still, she should not encourage him, for he had no right to make love to her. No right at all! *"Ohhhhhh!"* His tongue and his kisses were moving down her torso, and her belly was both aching and roiling with nervousness.

"You are so soft," he murmured, looking up at her a moment, the anger now gone from his eyes.

"Let me go, Valerian," she pleaded. "Why must you shame me?"

"You do not feel shamed, you little liar," he said, his voice tinged with amusement. "You know damned well I intend marrying you. Besides, you are as warm and as willing as your sister was cold and unwilling. I will never let you go, Aurora!"

"*Why?*"

"Because you are mine," he answered, and then his lips began to kiss her upon her belly, pushing his tongue into her navel to tease at her until, unable to help herself, she began to writhe beneath his attentions.

I will not be his, Aurora thought mutinously. *I will not!* Yet if she would not, then why did she lie in his embrace, enjoying his passionate attentions? Cally had once said she must be wanton. Was she a wanton? Yet Cally had also said Valerian Hawkesworth had abused her with his attentions, and Aurora did not feel abused at all by him. Still, she felt it her duty to make a further protest of his actions. "You will ruin me for St. John," she said low.

"You mean St. John has not ruined you for me?" he mocked her.

Aurora attempted to smack him, but he caught her hand, and kissed the palm. "I am a virgin," she snapped furiously.

"Then I shall certainly ruin you for St. John," he agreed.

"But why?" she demanded.

"Because you are mine," he repeated, piercing her with a hungry gaze. "You belong to me, Aurora. You feel the attraction between us every bit as much as I feel it, but you will not admit to it. St. John will not have you or St. Timothy," he said fiercely.

"But you already have St. Timothy," she said desperately.

"No, I do not. Not until its heiress is my wife, and you are its heiress. If my cousin learned of it, and you were his wife, he would take the island for himself."

"I will admit to deceiving you, and sign my property over to you," she said, half angry. This wasn't about her, or had it been about Cally. It was about land.

"No," he said.

"Why?"

"Because I want you," he answered her. "*I want you!*"

"You will never have me," she cried. "Not really!"

He laughed at her mockingly. "Oh, yes, I will, Aurora. You cannot

deny me, for the fires of passion run as hotly in your veins as they
do in mine. You are not your sister, cold and unfeeling. You are
warm, and loving, and I shall have you! *All of you!*"

"No!" she protested, but she knew that she lied not only to him,
but to herself as well. She could feel his member now pulsing
insistently against her thigh. She whimpered, but whether from fear
or eagerness she would never know. His big body slid over hers.

"Put your arms about me, Aurora," he whispered to her. "Hold
tight, my precious, and I will take you to paradise."

She felt the tears prickling behind her eyelids, and she could not
keep the words from her lips. "I am afraid, Valerian."

"No, my precious, not you!" he reassured her. "Trust me, Aurora.
Do you not know I love you, you little fool?"

"I don't believe you," she said, sliding her arms about him.

"You will in time," he reassured her.

She was so ready for him. He slipped just the head of his manhood
into her passage, and feeling it, she stiffened, but he caressed her
face and made soft, reassuring noises in her ear even as he moved
himself a little deeper. She could feel the walls of her channel
giving way reluctantly, opening before him, welcoming him. Then
suddenly he ceased his forward movement. She felt him pressing
against something within her that seemed to be impeding him. He
drew back and pushed against it. Aurora cried out, but he would
show her no mercy, and pulling himself back again, he thrust hard
within her, causing her to scream softly, and the tears to slide down
her cheeks.

It hurt! Dear God how it hurt! The pain swept up her body into
her chest, almost suffocating her with its intensity. It swept down
into her thighs, making them feel leaden and incapable of movement. She could feel him, hard and throbbing, now deep within
her. She sobbed, and he kissed the tears from her face even as he
began a rhythmic movement within her aching body. *And the pain
was gone.* As cruelly as it had overtaken her, it was now totally gone,
to be replaced with a wave of pleasure that swept over her, leaving
her gasping with surprise. Her body began to find his rhythm, and

imitate it with an instinct she hadn't even known she possessed until then.

"That's it, my precious," he encouraged her tenderly.

Aurora's hands found the flat of his back. Her fingers began to knead at him first, and then, unable to help herself, she was clawing at him. He groaned as if pained, but he seemed to be waiting for something. Slowly, Aurora felt a change taking place within her. There was nothing but an incredible, wonderful feeling claiming her, and she was drowning in it, and didn't care. Then suddenly her body convulsed, and she cried aloud, the pleasure so intense, she thought she would die. Half sobbing, she clung to him even as his member released its burning love juices within her, and they both slipped into a half-conscious state.

He rolled off her after a few moments, his arms wrapped tightly about her, holding her close. Aurora listened to the beat of his heart beneath her ear. His chest was smooth and warm. She felt very shy of him now. The intimacy between them had been more than she had ever anticipated, and she wasn't certain what to say.

"Did I hurt you badly?" he asked her softly, his hand caressing her as he spoke. It was as if he were attempting to quiet a skittish animal.

"It hurt terribly, and then it was wonderful," she answered. "Will it hurt the next time?"

"No," he said.

"Will it be wonderful again?"

"If you want it to be," he replied, smiling in the darkness at the ingenuousness of the question. Then, "I will see the magistrate tomorrow about obtaining a special license so we may be married right away."

"I will not marry you, Valerian," Aurora told him.

"Yes, my dear, you will" came his reply. "We are pledged."

"I will be your mistress if you will, but you cannot hold me to a promise our fathers made, Valerian," she insisted.

"I can, Aurora, and I will," he said in implacable tones.

"You cannot force me," she insisted.

"Oh, but I can. I could send a new overseer and manager for the plantation on the next boat to the Indies with orders to dispossess your mother, your brother, and his wife, Aurora.''

She pulled away from him, crying, "You would not be so cruel!''

"Will you test my resolve, my precious?" he asked her.

"But you said you loved me!'' She sounded betrayed.

"I do, which is why I will not let you behave foolishly. You could be carrying my child even now, Aurora.'' He forced her onto her back and played along her lips with his fingers, finally pushing one of them into the warmth of her mouth. "Suck it!'' he commanded her.

She couldn't help herself, and did as he bid her. There was something so sensual in the act that she was almost dizzy with excitement.

Finally he drew the finger from between her lips, and bending, kissed her slowly. "You will make me a most adorable wife, Aurora.''

"I hate you!'' she told him.

He laughed softly. "No, you do not, but if it pleases you to believe it, and soothes your conscience, you may think it.''

"You assaulted me! My conscience is clear,'' she told him angrily. "I feel no guilt whatsoever for my actions.''

He laughed again. "You are torn between knowing how much you enjoyed making love, and your guilt over St. John. Do not fear. I will explain all to him myself. He will dislike losing to me once again, but he will get over it, as he always does.''

"You are heartless, Valerian. St. John loves me,'' Aurora said.

"Has he said so? The words, I mean,'' the duke inquired.

"Well . . .'' She hesitated a moment, and then, "He said he feels for me what he has never felt for a woman before,'' she concluded triumphantly. "If it is not love, then what is it?''

"My cousin saw I was drawn to you, even though I had a wife. It gave him great pleasure to take you from me. To taunt me with the knowledge that he could have you when I could not. What a new and rare pleasure that must have been for him. Oh, he cared for you in his fashion. St. John is feckless, but not deliberately cruel, but love? No. I do not believe it. St. John has never given his heart to any woman. To give any part of himself to another would be to put him at a disadvantage, he believes. He will be angry and disappointed, but he will accept that you are mine, Aurora."

"Is everything a game between you two?" she wondered.

The duke considered a moment, and then said, "I have never thought of it that way before, but I suppose it is. I cannot tell you why, Aurora, but from our childhood St. John and I have rubbed each other the wrong way. He more than I, however, I believe." His fingers brushed her hair from her face. "I don't want to speak on my cousin any longer, Aurora. Have you any idea of how lovely you are? Your eyes are like the finest aquamarines, and your skin like silk. There is a necklace among the family jewels that would match your eyes. Although I realize it is no longer the fashion to wear such gems, they would be magnificent reflected by your eyes." He smiled wickedly. "Perhaps I shall dress your naked body with those pieces for my delectation, and mine alone." Leaning forward, he nibbled tenderly on her earlobe.

She caught her lower lip in her teeth. She ought to be absolutely embarrassed, and certainly ashamed of what had happened in the last hour, but she could not seem to muster up those emotions. She actually giggled to her acute horror as he teased at her ear. "Stop it!" she finally managed to say in what she hoped passed for a severe tone. "You are a fool, Valerian. Now, lend me a robe so I may gather up the shreds of my clothing that you have strewn all over the stairs and foyer. Then I will go to my room. I will not remain in this house another night. Since I will be unable to catch the public coach to Hereford, and then on to London, you must send me via your own transport. I shall return to St. Timothy upon the next available vessel." She pushed him away and attempted to sit up.

"I am going to have to lock you in your bedroom, aren't I?" he said wearily, pushing her back upon his bed. "You are going nowhere, my precious Aurora, except to St. Anne's Church, where you will marry me." He leaned over her, pinioning her beneath him again.

"No! No! No!" she insisted, pummeling his chest with her fists. "I will not marry you, Valerian! I won't!"

"Then I shall send a new man to St. Timothy to take George's place. He, Betsy, and your mother will be very grateful to you for being so selfish, Aurora. But then, you were being selfish when you deceived me with Calandra, weren't you? Think of what your self-centeredness has cost us all. Why do you persist in it?" His resolve almost evaporated when he saw her eyes fill with tears at the mention of her sister's name. "Ah, my precious, I am sorry," he amended his harshness, and he kissed her soft mouth lightly, once, twice, the third time his kiss deepening until their passions were well engaged once again.

She knew immediately what was happening between them, but she did not, she admitted to herself, want to stop it. Why am I fighting him, she wondered, but she knew. She wanted the decision to be hers and no one else's, yet he would insist upon attempting to master her. I will not be forced, she thought, but as he joined their bodies once again, she knew he was not coercing her. Tensing a moment as if there would be pain again, she was astounded to find he had told her the absolute truth. There wasn't any. Just an incredible feeling of fullness as his member thrust and withdrew, thrust and withdrew, until she was dizzy and breathless once more with the sudden and violent if temporary feeling of utter deliciousness their two bodies together seemed to engender.

"Damn you!" she gasped as she slid over the precipice.

When she finally awoke, she was to her utter amazement back in her own bed, her nightgown neatly tied at the neckline, the sun peeping through the draperies. Had she imagined it all? Was it a drug-induced dream brought on by Martha's tea? No. She had had no tea last night. She shifted herself beneath the coverlet, wincing at the sudden soreness between her thighs. *It had been no dream!* Valerian Hawkesworth had caught her running away, and he had . . . forced . . . seduced . . . made utterly incredible love to her! And he was going to make her marry him. Aurora burrowed down deeper beneath the bedding.

She had enjoyed it. Dear God, she had enjoyed it! It had been what she had been waiting for all her life. She had been totally and utterly wanton, practically encouraging his attentions. His lips had been so knowing against hers. His hands had touched her so tenderly, and she had let him. She hadn't really resisted him at all. He had called her his *precious*. He had said he loved her. And they had done *it* twice! She hadn't realized that you could do it twice in the same night. Damn him for a rogue! Would he tell anyone? Would others be able to tell by just looking at her what had transpired between Aurora Kimberly and Valerian Hawkesworth? *She was going to die!*

The door to her bedchamber opened slowly, and Martha entered the room. "Good morning, miss," she said brightly, and going to the window, she pulled the drapes. Then she put the painted screen about Aurora's bed. "The footmen is bringing the bath up now, miss. His grace has given orders that you're to be ready by eleven o'clock."

"Ready for what?" Aurora demanded, but Martha apparently didn't hear her mistress. Aurora could hear the footsteps of the servants lugging the tub into the room, setting it by the fire, pouring the buckets of hot water into the vessel. She smelled the honeysuckle and woodbine she favored permeating the air in the room. Martha bustled about, giving orders to unseen servants. Then it was quiet.

The screen was folded back. "Come along, miss, and hop out of your bed. I've got to do your hair too, and we've just got two hours."

"What is this all about, Martha," Aurora said as she climbed from the bed. "What is going on?"

"I don't know myself," the servant said honestly. "All I know is that the duke has ordered it, and told me what you're to wear, and that you're to be ready by eleven. He certainly ain't going to confide in a servant, miss. You'll have to ask him yourself." She whisked her mistress's nightgown off, laying it aside, helping the girl into her tub. If she noticed the dried blood on Aurora's thighs, she said nothing either by word or by look. Instead, she went to work washing the girl's brown-blond hair thoroughly, rinsing it, toweling it roughly, and wrapping a linen cloth about Aurora's head. "Now, don't dawdle, miss. We've got to dry your hair and style it properly, so wash quickly." She handed Aurora a sea sponge and a cloth along with a cake of soap.

Silently Aurora bathed herself, wondering as she did so what

Valerian Hawkesworth was up to, and why no one else seemed to know. Stepping from the tub, she let Martha dry her and wrap her in a large towel. Then she sat by the fire while her servant brushed her hair until it was dry, and then rubbed it with a piece of silk until it was shining. The door opened, and both Sally and Molly entered, their arms filled.

Martha yanked the towel from her mistress, and then snatched a garment from atop the pile Molly carried, sliding it over Aurora's arms. It was a small corset, and Aurora normally did not wear one, but so stunned was she by what was going on, she did not protest as Martha laced up the little garment, just enough to give her shape, but not so tightly that she couldn't breathe. She had seen women in London overcome and unable to breathe, so tight were their stays. Her breasts, however, threatened to burst from the garment.

The three servants pulled the girl this way and that as they continued dressing her in silk stockings with tight rosette garters, a hooped petticoat support made of bent wood covered with a flannel petticoat, two linen petticoats, and two silk petticoats.

"Let me do her hair before we put on the gown," Martha said.

The two younger servants lifted the hoop so she might sit, and Martha took up her brush and began to style her mistress's hair. Today there were no flirtatious little curls on either side of Aurora's head. Instead, Martha fashioned an elegant chignon which she dressed with a strand of little seed pearls and silk flowers. She pinned and brushed, patted and stared until she was completely satisfied. When she was finished, she nodded to the other two, and the dress was brought.

Aurora stared hard. "It looks like a wedding gown," she said.

"It does," Martha agreed.

"I'm not putting it on," she told the servants mutinously.

"Now, miss, there's no good fussing at me. I'm just doing what the duke and the dowager told me to do. He can be a hard man, the master. If you don't get into this gown right now, and I've got to go and tell him so, the three of us could be dismissed. Now, here's a good girl, miss. Where would me and Sally go without references? You wouldn't do that to us after all our years of faithful service to the Kimberly family, would you?"

"Oh, put the damn thing on me, then," she grumbled as they lowered the cream-colored velvet trimmed in ermine over her. The neckline of the gown, despite its edging of fur, looked indecent to Aurora, for the corset made her breasts swell dangerously over its edge.

Molly knelt before her, slipping her shoes with their decorative rosettes onto Aurora's feet. Rising, she stepped back and said, "Oh, miss, don't you look grand!"

Sally stepped forward. "His grace asked that you wear these," she said, proffering a box at Aurora.

Opening the slightly tattered leather case, Aurora gasped. Lying within upon a bed of yellowed white silk was an incredible necklace unlike anything she had ever seen. Each stone was cut in the shape of a heart and set in a pinkish gold. From the center of the necklace a large pear-shaped pearl hung. It was the biggest pearl she had ever seen.

"Why, them stones is the exact color of your eyes, miss," Martha noted, taking the necklace up and fastening it about Aurora's neck.

Aurora stared into the mirror. The necklace sat flat upon her chest beneath her collarbone, the pearl dipping toward her cleavage. It was probably the most beautiful thing she had ever seen in all her life. Then she blushed, remembering his remarks the previous evening about the necklace. She couldn't imagine wearing such a jewel in public. It was so sensuous and decadent.

Martha set a deep blue velvet cape over Aurora's shoulders and handed her a pair of long, creamy kid gloves which the girl drew on slowly. "Come along now, miss. The clock is about to strike eleven."

Downstairs, Peters greeted her politely. "The carriage is waiting for you, miss. Martha is to ride with you." He handed the serving woman her cloak and ushered them outside, where the footmen waited to help them into the vehicle.

The coach moved off. Aurora did not need to ask where it was going. She would have been a fool not to know. When they reached their destination, it would be St. Anne's Church, and indeed it was. The grooms jumped down from the back of the carriage where they had been riding, and opening the door, pulled down the steps and helped the two passengers out. The dowager and Lady Elsie were awaiting them upon the stone porch of the church.

"I am pleased by this," the dowager told Aurora, "but shocked by the haste with which my grandson has effected this event."

"He has given me no choice in the matter," Aurora replied. "My sister is hardly in her grave, and he is forcing me to the altar. You know the deception of which I am guilty, ma'am. If I had wished to marry Valerian in the first place, I would have done so."

"Oh, my dear," twittered Lady Elsie, "Sir Ronald will not marry you if you are being coerced. It goes against Christian law."

"As the duke has taken my virtue from me already, and has threatened to dispossess George's family from St. Timothy, Lady Elsie, I believe I must acquiesce to Valerian Hawkesworth's demands. Besides, there is the little matter of my betrothal, is there not? It is all, I fear, quite legal. His grace has the law on his side."

Lady Bowen grew beet red with the bride's indelicate admission. "Quite," she managed to say. Heaven forfend that Betsy and her dear husband suffer the consequences of this outrageous chit's unruly behavior!

The dowager's blue eyes twinkled. "Would you be so kind," she said to Lady Bowen, "to tell Sir Ronald that we are ready, m'dear?" And when the good woman had bustled into the church, she turned to Aurora, saying, "Do not let him bully you further, my child. By marrying him you right the wrong you previously committed against him. All debts are now paid in full, especially given your revelation of a moment ago. I will ask nothing, you understand," she murmured with a smile. "You look none the worse for wear. If he is like the rest of the men in the family, he is a vigorous lover. Now, let us get this business over and done with, Aurora Kimberly, so we can get on with our lives. And remember, I will be your ally in most cases. Men are charming, and an absolute necessity, but they are not always particularly intelligent." She then linked an arm in Aurora's and led her into the church.

Inside, an altar boy hurried forward to remove her cloak and hand the bride a small nosegay of white rosebuds tied with gold ribbons. She accepted them, smiling at the child, and then continued on with the dowager to the altar, Martha following them.

The church looked very much as it had a few days before, when George and Betsy had been married. Lace-trimmed white linen bedecked the altar with its gold candelabra burning beeswax candles. The duke awaited her dressed in cream-colored breeches, a flowered waistcoat, and a fawn-colored coat with silver buttons. Lace dripped from his sleeves and from the neckline of his fine cambric shirt. He was wearing a wig the dark color of his own hair, a small queue tied with a ribbon at the back of his neck.

Sir Ronald, however, did not look very happy with the part he was about to play. The duke had appeared in his home at ten o'clock that morning and presented him with a special license he had obtained from the local magistrate at the crack of dawn. He explained briefly the deception that had been played upon him, and said the whole matter would be corrected by his immediate marriage to Aurora Kimberly. When the minister had protested the unseemly haste and the scandal it would cause, the duke had shrugged. Then he had suggested that if Sir Ronald did not perform the ceremony, his eldest daughter's life could be changed for the worse. The cleric was outraged. He had never before imagined Valerian Hawkesworth capable of such harshness toward others, but he realized he had no choice in the matter.

The bride came quietly forward with the dowager and her servant, who would, along with Lady Elsie, act as witnesses. Sir Ronald then performed the ceremony that united Valerian Hawkesworth to Aurora Kimberly. When it was over, and the duke had kissed his bride, Sir Ronald softened his stance. It was, after all, not the bride's fault that her new husband was such a hothead, and he had, despite the unseemly haste, only righted a wrong, and they were, after all, family now. He shook the duke's hand and offered his genuine congratulations.

"There will be no further celebration," the duke said, "for we are in mourning for my wife's sister." Then with a smile in Lady Elsie's direction he escorted his bride from the church to the coach.

"You may not gossip about this until Sunday," the dowager told Lady Elsie sternly. "Not even to your girls. Especially not to your girls or your servants. St. John must be told first, you understand."

"Yes, your g-grace" came the nervous reply.

"If I hear so much as a whisper, I shall know where it came from, m'dear, and then I shall not introduce your Isabelle to that nice young baronet I have in mind for her. Such a handsome man, and two thousand a year plus a manor house and a hundred acres." She smiled toothily at Lady Bowen. "Good day, m'dear." Then she hurried off to get into the coach.

They returned to Hawkes Hill, Martha wiping her eyes all the way. The dowager sat with a pleased smile upon her face. Aurora and Valerian were silent for a time, and then he spoke.

"I have asked St. John to come after lunch," he said.

"I would be there," she answered.

"I do not think it wise," he replied.

"Nonetheless I will be there, else he obtain some foolish idea about this matter," Aurora responded firmly. "Please understand, Valerian, that you may be my husband now, but you are not my *master*. I will not be treated like a child, nor will I be dictated to by you. You wanted me, and so you must accept me for what I am. St. John is entitled to face both of us under the circumstances, and he will."

Mary Rose Hawkesworth could not help herself. She burst out laughing at the surprised look upon her grandson's face. "Well, my boy," she chortled, "you wanted her, you took her, and now you have gotten exactly what you deserved. Oh, my dears, I could not be happier! You are a perfect match!"

And Martha, in her corner next to the dowager, chuckled right along with the old lady.

Chapter

❧ 12 ❧

The ducal coach drew up before Hawkes Hill and the servants hurried to help its occupants out and escort them into the house. There, the entire household staff was lined up in the foyer.

"The staff wishes to offer you and her grace their congratulations, my lord," Peters said solemnly.

"God bless the duke and duchess," the servants dutifully chorused, and then they exited the foyer to return to their duties.

"Please convey to the staff our thanks, Peters," the duke said. "Is the luncheon ready? We will be expecting Mr. St. John about two this afternoon. Will you see he is shown into the main drawing room?"

"Of course, my lord," the butler replied. "Luncheon is served."

A footman came forward to take the ladies' cloaks. Martha had already gone upstairs to fill Sally and Molly in on the wedding.

"If it please your grace," Peters said as they entered the dining room, "I have had the table set en famille with her grace on your right and Lady Mary Rose on your left hand."

They were seated, the duke at the head of the long, mahogany table, the ladies on either side of him. The places were set upon heavy linen mats with beautiful silver and fine crystal. The service plates were snow white with a wide gold band edging them. Soup plates were brought, and the hot clear consommé served, a thin, round wedge of lemon floated upon the surface of the soup. Aurora lay her nosegay upon the table to her right, noting that the flowers upon the table matched them.

"What a lovely day for a wedding!" the dowager said, attempting to break the ice and bring a sense of normalcy to their gathering.

"I had not noticed," Aurora said. The soup was wonderful, and took the chill from her extremities. A footman poured wine into her goblet, and she sipped it for contrast.

"It's unusual for us to have so bright and sunny a day in November, and not a cloud in the sky," the dowager continued.

"I don't even know what day it is," Aurora replied, sipping a bit more wine as she finished up her soup.

"Why it is the fourth of November, my dear," the dowager said. "Certainly you will always want to remember this date."

Aurora couldn't resist a small chuckle. "Certainly the entire county will remember it, so I may have no need to, for there will be plenty of people to remind me. It will be recalled as the day that dreadful Duke of Farminster married his second wife, and his first not even cold in her grave a week! And, of course, the duchess is no better than she ought to be, y'know. Tossed over that fine Mr. St. John for a title, she did, the ambitious jade!" She looked directly at her husband as she spoke, her manner mocking and bold.

But the duke was not in the least intimidated. He equaled her rhetoric with a bit of his own. "And, my precious, should you deliver a child in less than ten months' time, nay, a year, I think, we will be accused of carrying on a passionate affair even while poor Calandra yet lived. I believe I should like that, wouldn't you?"

"Valerian!" his grandmother said. "You go too far."

"Do I, my precious?" he demanded of Aurora.

"Perhaps," she considered, and turned her attention to the meaty prawns that had been placed upon her fresh plate. They had been broiled in lemon butter and wine, and served upon a small patch of cress.

"The aquamarines suit you," he said softly, pleased to see her cheeks grow pink.

The trio now turned their full attention to the meal at hand. The fish course was followed by beef with small roasted potatoes, turnip, peas, a fat capon, a marrow pudding, and bread and butter. Aurora ate with her customary good appetite. When the plates had been cleared away, Peters brought a small bride's cake iced in white and topped with a fully blown white rose. He set it before Aurora and handed her a silver cake knife. "Will your grace do the honors?" he asked.

"Now, how on earth did Cook manage that?" the dowager said.

"A small, uncut fruitcake was found in the pantry, your ladyship," the butler replied. "It was quite fortunate, as it is the last of Cook's supply, and time to make them again for the year."

"Please thank Cook," Aurora said, "and tell her the meal was superb, especially given the short notice."

"I shall tell her, your grace," Peters replied. Now, this was a *duchess*. Not like the other lady, who never had a kind word for any of them, or ever said thank-you. And it had not been just his disapproving notice. His granddaughter, Molly, had had much to say to him on her late mistress. Moving sedately about the table, he poured champagne into the glasses provided.

The dowager raised her glass to her grandson and his bride. "To you both," she said. "Long life, happiness, and healthy children."

They drank, and then Valerian Hawkesworth raised his glass to Aurora. "To you, my precious, and to the truth, which you will always tell me from now on," he said, a twinkle in his eye.

"Perhaps," Aurora said, and then she lifted her glass, saying, "To Calandra."

The others raised their glasses solemnly, repeating, "To Calandra."

Aurora cut the cake, giving them all small slices of the dark, rich fruitcake. When they had finally finished, the dowager excused herself, claiming fatigue, but Aurora knew she did not wish to be there when St. John came to call. The clock in the foyer struck two o'clock as she and her husband entered the drawing room. Peters was already hurrying to open the front door, for St. John was always punctual. Aurora settled herself on a settee, her skirts spread about her.

"You look perfect, and are the most beautiful woman I have ever known," the duke said. Then he continued. "St. John will be quite piqued, I fear." He chuckled wickedly.

"If I did not wish to muss my attire," Aurora told him, "I should smack you, Valerian! If you expect St. John to act like a grown man, then you must stop behaving like a childish boy!"

He laughed even as the double doors to the drawing room were opened, and Peters announced, "Mr. St. John, my lord." Then, closing the doors behind the duke's guest, Peters left them.

Justin St. John's eyes went immediately to Aurora. They took in her attire, lingering a moment upon the necklace she wore. He was no fool. "Have you married her, then, Hawkesworth?"

The duke nodded.

"You bastard!" St. John replied, and turned angrily to go.

"Wait!" the duke called to him.

St. John turned. "Why? What more is there to say about it?"

"She is the heiress to St. Timothy, not Calandra," Valerian told his cousin, and then he went on to explain the deception that had been enacted, and how Dr. Carstairs, coming in place of Dr. Michaels, had revealed the truth to the duke after Calandra's unfortunate demise.

"Well, I'll be damned!" St. John chortled, his mood suddenly lightened. "So Aurora was your betrothed, and not Calandra. And if you had not learned of it, and I eventually had, then I should have been able to lay claim upon St. Timothy! Well played, cousin!"

Aurora stared at the two men, now embracing and clapping. *"Well played?"* She arose from the settee where she had been seated. "Damn you, St. John! Did you not love me? You said you felt for me what you had never felt for another woman!"

The two men turned to look at her, astounded. Only the duke really understood his bride's outrage. He grinned, and waited to see what she would do next. Poor St. John! He had no idea of how a woman who believed herself betrayed could behave.

"Why, my dear," St. John said, "I did not lie to you. I did feel for you what I had not ever felt for another woman, but that was because you were not like any other woman I had ever met. Each girl is different, and so, of course, I feel differently for each of them."

"So you did not really love me," she responded.

"I loved you in my fashion," he told her weakly.

"St. John, you are a seducer and a fool! I do not know which is worse," Aurora replied. "Why on earth were you prepared to marry me, then? To confound Valerian?"

"In part, yes," he admitted. "Could you not see how badly he wanted you, Aurora? And he could not have you! It was too delicious a situation to resist. The dowager saw a scandal in the making, and was very much on my side, and besides, it was time for me to start my nursery. My mother will be quite disappointed, for she desires grandchildren."

Aurora's fingers had wrapped themselves about a small vase upon the table next to the settee as he spoke. Now, as he finished with a small, apologetic smile, she grasped the vase and threw it at him with all the force she could muster. Surprise exploded upon his face as he ducked, but the vase slightly creased the side of his head before crashing to the floor and breaking into several pieces. The duke burst out laughing, then leapt across the space that separated him from his wife, who had obtained a second missile and was prepared to launch it.

"Now, my precious," he murmured at her soothingly, "you must not be rude to poor St. John. He has answered your questions as honestly as he knows how. Come, Aurora, and let us all make peace." He yanked a china figurine from her fingers and put a restraining arm about her.

Aurora stamped down upon his foot with all her might, and as he yelped in pain, she pulled away from him. "You may, the pair of you, go to hell!" she said, and then stalked from the drawing room.

"Spirited gel," St. John noted. "Perhaps you have done me a favor, cousin, by taking her off my hands. I don't think I could manage such a fierce firebrand, although I will admit," he confided wickedly, "that she kisses like an angel and has marvelous little tits."

"Do not honor me with your confidences regarding the lady who is now my wife, cousin. I might be forced to call you out, St. John," the duke told him pleasantly, but there was an undertone of menace in his voice. "Come, and let us have a whiskey before you ride home to break the news to your mother."

"Well," St. John responded sulkily, "I did leave her virtue intact, Hawkesworth. You might at least thank me for that. After all, we were to be married, and no one could have faulted me for breeching her." He accepted the cut-glass tumbler the duke handed him and sniffed at it appreciatively.

The duke laughed. "Very well, St. John, I thank you for leaving my betrothed wife's virginity for me to dispose of last night."

St. John laughed back. "Why, you devil! You were taking no chances, were you? I do believe that I am flattered, Hawkesworth." He raised his glass to the duke. "To her grace," he said.

Valerian Hawkesworth acknowledged his cousin's salute and lifted his own tumbler. "To her grace," he said, "and to you also, St. John. You are certainly the most gentlemanly cad I have ever known, even if we are related by blood."

The two cousins drank their whiskey in companionable silence for a few minutes, and then St. John said, "Who the hell am I going to find to marry, Hawkesworth? Mama is going to be furious, and there will be hell to pay. What about that tempting little Isabelle Bowen?"

"My grandmother has her marked for some baronet, but of course she has not introduced the two yet. I see no reason why you shouldn't make an attempt. Pretty wench. Modest dower, but the Bowens are quite respectable and a very old family. She would be most suitable, and she's innocent enough to be bowled over by your unctuous charms, St. John. Your mother would be quite pleased if you could pull it off. Best to catch Miss Bowen before she grows much older and discovers what a rogue you really are, cousin," he finished with a chuckle.

"I shall play the heartbroken lover," St. John said thoughtfully. "Young girls always adore comforting a man whose heart has been hurt by some other vixen. You don't mind if I suggest Aurora is a villainess, do you, Hawkesworth? Not a wicked one, of course, but a wee bit of a one. Tampered with my affections knowing all along how she had deceived you and was now deceiving me." His look was that of a saddened lover.

The duke burst out laughing. "Be heartbroken if you will, St. John, but do not make my wife out a villainess. The truth will serve you quite nicely. You must be generous in your crushing grief. It will play better, I suspect. Also, you will have to turn your talents to overcoming any objections that the Bowens have regarding your suitability as a son-in-law. Win Isabelle over first, however. Sir Ronald will not like losing a title for his daughter. I will assuage my grandmother's disappointment by reminding her that the next Bowen chit will be marriageable in just three or four more years. If the baronet is loath to settle down, a few more years should not matter to him."

"Why on earth would the Bowens object to me?" St. John asked. "I am young, healthy, extremely handsome, and rich. What more could they possibly want in a son-in-law, Hawkesworth?"

"My dear St. John," his cousin answered him, "you are indeed all those things, but you are also an undeniable rascal. You have broken any number of hearts, and if rumor is to be believed, you have at least two bastards to your credit."

"Three," St. John murmured, unabashed. "The daughter of the innkeeper at the Three Swans has recently presented me with a girl child. I do acknowledge the little ones, and pay their mothers a generous yearly stipend as well as seeing to their baptisms."

Hawkesworth laughed all the harder. "I am certain that Sir Ronald and Lady Elsie will be most impressed by your Christian charity. We get ahead of ourselves, however. First you must entice Miss Isabelle Bowen in your web of love. Once you have done that, the battle is half won."

"And if not, I shall have to go to London to see if I can find some sweet little debutante whose down-on-her-heels but utterly old family will not blink at my reputation, so blinded are they by my fortune and lands." Putting his tumbler down, he grinned at the duke. "I wish you more happiness this time, Hawkesworth, than you had with your last marriage. For all our rivalry, we are family and best friends."

The two men shook hands, embraced, and then the duke walked with his cousin out into the afternoon, where one of the grooms stood waiting with St. John's horse. Mounting the beast, St. John gave the duke a wave, and then rode off in the direction of Primrose Court. Hawkesworth watched him for a few minutes and then returned to the house. It was time that he and his wife began getting seriously acquainted.

Peters greeted him, saying, "Her grace will not allow us to move her things into the duchess's rooms, my lord."

"Nor should you, Peters. At least not until the rooms have been totally redecorated. You can understand that my wife would not want to sleep in the place where her sister has so recently died. Tell her servants to leave her grace's possessions where they are. I will discuss the refurbishing with my wife shortly."

"Of course, my lord," the butler said. "It was thoughtless of us to have attempted to move her grace under the circumstances."

The duke hurried up the stairs to Aurora's room, but she was not there. He went to his grandmother's room, where the dowager was sleeping. Where the hell could Aurora have gone to, he wondered as he entered his own bedchamber. Then he gaped in shock. She lay curled upon a hip in the center of his bed, resting her body upon an arm and an elbow, her heart-shaped face supported in the palm of her hand. She was stark naked but for the necklace of aquamarines about her neck. A fire crackled in the fireplace, the light of the flames mingling with the light from the setting sun.

"I have decided to forgive you, Valerian," she said, breaking the silence between them. "You were absolutely right about St. John. He is a scoundrel." She shifted her legs just slightly, allowing him a fine view of the thick thatch of tight brown-gold curls between her thighs. Then she ran the tip of her tongue along the top of her lip.

"How in God's name did you manage to preserve your virginity so long?" he demanded of her. He shrugged off his coat, and, unbuttoning his waistcoat, lay the two garments upon a chair. Moving back to the bedroom door as he undid his cambric shirt, he turned the lock, and spinning about, yanked off the shirt, saying, "I shall need your help with my boots, Aurora. Come here," he commanded, and watched with pleasure as she slid off the bed and walked toward him.

"What shall I do, my lord?" she murmured.

Seating himself in a chair, he said, "Straddle one of my legs, and then pull the boot off, my precious." Then he grinned, delighted at the sight of her pretty bottom. It was as round as a peach, and when she grasped his right boot and began to pull, he was unable to resist placing his left foot upon her and and pushing gently.

"Ooofff!" she grunted as the first boot slid off, and she set it aside, bestriding his other leg and drawing off the second boot.

He peeled his stockings off, and when he stood again, she began to undo his breeches. Shaking his head, he said, "If I had not sprung you myself, I should be in serious doubt as to your chastity."

"Don't you want to make love to me?" she said softly.

"Yes, I do," he admitted as she pulled the breeches over his hips, leaving him to finish the job, and slipped his drawers down to complete her task. "Tell me, did St. John light this fire in you?"

Aurora shook her head. "Since my childhood I have known how to pleasure myself," she told him. "I am wise enough to have known that I must keep this part of my nature secret, and not be called wanton, or shame my family, but the hunger was always there. Last night you were able to satisfy that hunger. I want you to do it again!" She pressed her naked body against his, slipping her arms about his neck. "Do I shock you? Calandra, I know, was my opposite. She told me she did not like *the act*. I do, Valerian. I like it very much. Can we do it twice again? I was so surprised that you could do it twice in one night!"

He wanted to laugh. She was wonderful! Ingenuous, innocent, and knowing all in the same moment. She was a gift after his marriage to her coldhearted sister. "This passion of yours," he said softly, his arms wrapping about her, "must be reserved for me, my precious. You do understand that, do you not?"

She nodded, and then her hand slipped down to push between

them and grasp his member. "It is so hard," she noted, and then loosed her grip upon him and began to caress it. "Do you like that as much as I like it when you stroke my breasts? You do not mind if I ask you such questions, do you? I want to please you as you have pleased me."

"Yes," he said slowly, "I like it when you touch me. There are other ways you can give my member pleasure besides petting it, but if you are fearful, or repulsed, I will understand."

"How?" Her tone was filled with curiosity.

"Kneel before me," he said softly.

"What?" Her voice was surprised.

"Kneel before me," he said, and when she complied with his request he took his manhood in his hand and rubbed it gently across her lips. "You can use your tongue on it, or suck on it," he told her.

Aurora's heart was beating wildly. There was something so exciting about the forbidden, and this was certainly a forbidden thing. She touched him with just the tip of her tongue. He said nothing. Emboldened, she licked vigorously about the ruby tip of him, and when he removed his hand she bent her head slightly and licked the length of him several times. Then, unable to help herself, she opened her mouth and took him into it, her tongue working fiercely as her own excitement level rose with each passing second. He was warm and hard, and smooth. The taste of him was musky and salty. She sucked on him, and felt his fingers kneading her head, encouraging her, and then he grated at her to cease, and when she could not seem to stop, he pulled her away, yanking her up to face him once again.

"Would you swallow me whole, my precious?" he demanded.

"Yes!" she said, her eyes bright with her desire.

He laughed, amazed at her capacity for lust. "Turnabout is but fair play, Aurora," he told her. "Let me show you." Taking her by the hand, he drew her over to the bed, sitting her down so that her legs were hanging over. "Lay back," he said, and when she had, he knelt and slowly drew her legs down and over his shoulders.

"What are you doing?" she cried out nervously.

He did not answer her, instead burying his face in the soft nest of curls and kissing her plump, warm mound. She did not protest, instead sighing with obvious pleasure. He then parted her nether lips with his two thumbs and touched her little pleasure button with just the tip of his tongue. He heard her draw a sharp breath, and smiled to himself. With his whole tongue he slowly licked the coral walls of her love grotto, pushing his tongue into her channel, withdrawing it to return to her pleasure button, which he then began to sweetly torture.

Aurora could not restrain herself, and she moaned with open enjoyment. "Ohhhh, Valerian, that is absolutely wicked. Don't stop. I beg you! Please, don't stop! I shall die of delight! *Oh! Oh! Oh!*"

Her love juices began to flow, and he lapped them up eagerly. "So you like it, you little wanton," he growled at her, and then he was mounting her and pushing himself into her. "Do you like this too, my precious?" He thrust hard, and she half sobbed, *"Yes!"* and hearing her, he began a fierce rhythm, thrusting and withdrawing, thrusting and withdrawing, until her head was thrashing wildly. "Put your legs about me," he said in a deep tone, and when she obeyed he was able to push deeper into her hot, wet sheath.

She could feel him inside her, throbbing and pulsing. He was such a fierce but tender lover, and she wanted him to go on forever. "Don't stop," she begged him. *"Don't stop!"* Her nails began to rake down his back as the pleasure overtook her. He groaned against her mouth, his tongue, ripe with her musk, arousing her as she had never before been aroused. Her body had joined him in the primitive passion, pushing up to meet his downward thrust. Her legs were wrapped tightly about his torso. I am going to die, she thought as she felt herself beginning to soar and spin out of control. Stars and moons were exploding in her head, and the pleasure was tearing her apart. She cried aloud.

He didn't want to stop. She was the most exciting woman he had ever known. He desired her above all women. He wanted her so badly that even in the act of possessing her his loins yet ached with longing. He was on the brink of death, and he didn't care. It was worth it. It had all been worth it just to possess that incredible creature who was his wife. He was falling into darkest space, and yet he could feel his manhood erupting its juices to flood her secret garden with life. He collapsed.

Together they lay gasping, struggling for breath, and when at last they had managed to quiet their raging hearts, Valerian Hawkesworth gathered Aurora into his arms, weakly drew the coverlet over them, and they slept.

They were awakened by a discreet knocking at the door, and heard Browne's voice calling. "My lord. My lord."

"Yes, what is it?" the duke asked sleepily.

"It is after nine o'clock, my lord. Will you and her ladyship be wanting supper before the staff retires?" the valet said.

"Bring a tray, whatever is available, and champagne too," Valerian Hawkesworth responded. "You may leave it outside the door, Browne. Just knock to let us know it's there."

"Yes, my lord." They heard the retreating footsteps.

"Do you think the servants are shocked?" Aurora wondered.

"Probably not," he said. "Why should they be? It is our wedding night, after all, and you, my dear duchess, are absolutely delicious!" He kissed her a deep, slow kiss. "I think we might manage it more than twice tonight, my precious. Would you like that?"

She grinned at him mischievously. "I believe that you are utterly insatiable, my lord," she teased.

"As are you, madam," he agreed calmly, and bending, nibbled at her ear. "You must be satisfied with me, however, Aurora. I will not countenance your taking lovers, as do so many fashionable women."

"Good God, Valerian, what do you take me for? Why on earth would I want a lover? I was not raised to be loose. A woman cleaves to her husband, unless, of course, he turns out to be an utter cad, in which case she poisons him quickly and becomes a merry widow," she finished with a wicked smile. Then she took his hand, and separating his fingers, began to suck them slowly, one by one. Her tongue rotated in leisurely fashion about each digit, and then she would draw upon the finger so strongly that he thought she might devour it.

"Fashionable women," he murmured, bending to nuzzle in the cleft between her two round little breasts, "take and discard lovers with little thought, as do their husbands. Had Calandra not been so coldhearted, I believe she would have followed the fashion quite willingly."

"I am not my sister, as you have already discovered," Aurora said, "and I have no need for another man in my bed as long as you are so attentive. You had best not take a mistress, my lord. Besides, if I never see London again, it will be too soon. I love living at Hawkes Hill, and I shall be most happy to remain here for the rest of my life." Finished playing with his fingers, she nipped at his knuckles.

With startling swiftness he pinioned her beneath him and kissed her until she was quite breathless and laughing. "Wanton witch," he accused her, but he was smiling.

She felt him already roused against her thigh, and said, "You are impatient, Valerian. I did not expect such passion from you."

"I cannot wait, my precious," he apologized, pushing himself into her wet, hot sheath. "Will you forgive me?" He began to move on her.

"Ummmmmmm," she replied, and she wrapped her legs about his torso once again. "Make me fly again, Valerian, and I will excuse this unseemly haste and your lack of finesse. *Oh! Oh! Yessssss!*"

"Little bitch," he groaned against her mouth. "I cannot get enough of you, *I cannot!*"

He was a sorcerer, she thought as she began to lose control of herself once more. His touch inflamed. His hard body excited her more than anything else she had ever known. Take a lover? Dear heaven, what other man could please her so greatly? Could reach so deeply into her heart and soul that she was overwhelmed with a plethora of emotions she hardly understood, and which threatened to overwhelm her. She would never take a lover. Husbands could be such fools, she considered as she soared from the pinnacle once more. "Ahhhhhhhh, my darling!" she cried.

He lay atop her, drained and gasping for breath. Her sweetness and her intense passion would certainly be the death of him. The elusive fragrance that was Aurora assailed him, and he sighed with pleasure. Mistress, indeed! She had, in a day's time, spoiled him for all other women forever. She shifted beneath him, and immediately he rolled off her. "I think I may kill you," he said low, "for all the time you cost us with your stubborn nature, my precious." He took her hand and squeezed it hard. "I think I fell in love with you the day I saw you coming from the sea, but I put it from me. Then, when you arrived in England, I was tortured by the thought you would wed another and I could not have you. And when you chose St. John, I wanted to kill him!"

"Hush, Valerian." She leaned over him, stopping his mouth with her own for a moment. Then she continued. "I can never forget that my selfishness caused Cally great unhappiness, and cost her her life. I must live with that the rest of my life even as I experience the joy of loving you. It seems so unfair that I should be happy and poor Cally will never know happiness."

"Then you love me as I love you?" he said, his voice breaking.

"Of course I love you, you fool," she replied. "When I would daydream, it was your face I saw, and never St. John's. I did not understand it until now, but I realize that I was in love with you although I could not admit it for fear of being disloyal to my sister. After all, it was not right that I love Cally's husband, Valerian, but I may certainly love my own husband, may I not?"

There was a discreet knock upon the bedchamber door, and Browne's voice said softly but distinctly, "Supper is served, your grace." Then they heard him retreating down the hallway.

"Are you hungry?" he asked her. *She loved him!*

"Ravenous, my lord," she assured him, her look smoldering, and then she amended, "for food also, my darling!"

Laughing, he arose and crossed the room to open the door and bring in an enormous tray which he placed upon a large rectangular table set against one of the paneled walls. He tossed two more logs upon the fire, coaxing the flames higher. Then he took the bedside taperstick and used it to light several other candles upon the table and about the bedroom. "What shall I bring you?" he asked her.

"What is there?" she responded.

Removing the silver domes covering the dishes, he said, "Raw oysters, capon, cold asparagus from the greenhouse, bread, cheese, butter, and fruit. And champagne."

"Everything!" she told him eagerly.

He filled her plate and brought it to her. She had plumped up the pillows and drawn the coverlet up modestly over her breasts. Taking the plate from him, she began to eat with great gusto, swallowing down six raw oysters and then attacking a piece of capon breast. Joining her with his own full plate, he found himself being aroused as she ate her asparagus, sucking the vinaigrette from her fingers, licking her mouth with her facile tongue. He averted his eyes and concentrated upon the consumption of a dozen oysters. He was obviously going to need their restorative powers.

"We have no champagne!" she cried, and putting her plate aside on the coverlet climbed from the bed and padded across the room to pour them two crystal gobletsful. She brought him his, bending first to dip a nipple into the sparkling wine, and then offering it to him mischievously. "Is it to your grace's taste?" she inquired innocently.

"It will do," he replied, licking her nipple with a grin and taking the goblet from her.

She climbed back into their bed with her own narrow crystal, sipping it decorously. "Delicious," she pronounced. "Do do you think we could dip your . . ."

"No!" he said, and he began to laugh again.

"Why not?" she demanded. "Have you done it before?"

He shook his head. "It is not advisable, Aurora. You know what will happen if we begin such love play, and then there will be champagne and oyster shells all over the bedclothes."

"Oh, very well, Valerian, but one day when we are not so encumbered we must try it. Perhaps I shall bathe in a tub full of champagne, and you may lick me dry," she tempted him.

"How can a girl who was a virgin until a day ago have such lascivious and libertine thoughts?" he demanded of her.

"Are women not supposed to think of *it?*" she asked him. "Even after they are wed? That is not fair! Certainly men think on *it*, and for that matter, men get to do *it* without any criticism before they are married, and ofttimes after with other women."

"But we will not do *it*," he said, "with anyone other than each other, Aurora." Rising from the bed, he took their plates and then brought her a wet cloth with which he wiped her face and hands before doing his own. "Would you like some dessert? Cook has sent up some lovely grapes, and little meringues."

"Bring the champagne, and we shall make our own dessert," Aurora told him. "I have a great many more licentious and salacious thoughts to share with you, my husband. Perhaps I shall even convince you to act upon them, *or perhaps I shall act upon them*," she teased him.

"You have it in your head to kill me," he said. "Don't you?"

Aurora chuckled. "Only with love, Valerian, and only if you promise to slay me with your love too."

Shaking his head, he refilled her crystal goblet and his own. Then he joined her in their bed, the burning look in his dark blue eyes matching the passion in her aquamarine-blue ones.

Part III

ENGLAND, 1762

Chapter
⚜ **13** ⚜

"**Y**ou will have to leave Hawkes Hill for a short time," the dowager said to Valerian and Aurora. "The scandal is too new, and will not die if you remain here for the gossips to feast upon."

"Just because no one came to call at Christmas," the duke began, but his grandmother cut him short with a wave of her hand.

"People call at Christmas, even to a house in mourning," Mary Rose Hawkesworth explained. "They did not call at Hawkes Hill because of your unseemly haste in marrying Aurora. The apparent lack of good manners you have both shown toward Calandra's memory is considered both outrageous and shocking. I will need time to erase that notion among our neighbors, and I cannot do it if you are both here. It gives the appearance of recalcitrance on your part."

"I don't give a damn what our neighbors think," Valerian said in strong and unrepentant tones.

Aurora laughed at her husband's stubbornness. "I do," she said, "and you should also. If we continue to be ostracized by our neighbors, with whom will our children associate as they are growing up, and how shall we arrange suitable marriages for them one day? Not only that the truth will become blurred as time passes unless we can contain it, and stop the slander before it is out of control. It will spread beyond the county, and we shall truly be avoided. No, my darling, your grandmama is correct. We must go off until the gossip dies and the truth be spread about.''

He glowered at the two women, but neither seemed taken aback by his dark look. In fact, both looked rather amused. "Oh, very well," he finally agreed, "But I am not happy about being discommoded by a cackling group of fancy hens. I suppose we could open Farminster House and go up to London for a few months."

"An excellent idea," his grandmother said. "You have not yet had the opportunity to pay your formal respects to the king. Your grandfather died around the same time as the old king, then you were off to collect your bride, and then Calandra was *enceinte*, so you missed the royal wedding and the coronation both. I think it would be a very good thing if you were to visit London for a time."

"Will we get to meet the king and queen?" Aurora asked.

"Of course, child," the dowager assured her. "I was once friends with the Earl of Bute's mother, and knew him as a boy. Valerian has met him also, and, I believe, sold him some breeding stock for his cattle herds, did you not, dear boy?"

"Yes, about three years ago," the duke replied.

"The earl stands high in his majesty's favor," the dowager continued. "He was the king's tutor, and quite close to the king's mother, I am told. He will certainly arrange an introduction to their majesties for you and Valerian. I shall write him tomorrow."

"You must tell me how many servants we will need to run Farminster House properly," Aurora said, and the two women put their heads together, chattering away, much to the duke's chagrin.

He did not want to go up to London, and he would wager that Aurora didn't want to go either. She was simply being good-natured about their rather sticky social situation. Damn his nosy neighbors! What did they know of his misery, or Calandra's, during the months of their marriage? And they most certainly did not know that Aurora was the bride he should have married, and not her sister. His grandmother, with the willing help of the silly Lady Bowen, however, would manage to get everything straightened out eventually.

"We will be home May first," he announced to the two women.

"You are not giving me a great deal of time, are you, Valerian?"

his grandmother said, "But I expect I can manage to wipe away most of your sins by then, and as Aurora was but your innocent victim, yes, the first of May will be all right." She chuckled at the outraged look on his handsome face.

Messages were dispatched the following day to the Earl of Bute and to Farminster House. The trunks were packed and the baggage cart filled up with everything they would need for their stay in London. There would be a carriage for the duke and duchess, and one for their servants. Several riding horses would travel with them so Valerian and Aurora might have an alternate means of transport when they chose not to travel within the confines of their coach. A rider had already been dispatched ahead to arrange for their accommodations in local inns. There would be an armed guard to protect them from highwaymen.

"You are being very good about this," the dowager said to Aurora the evening before their departure.

The younger woman smiled ruefully. "How well you know me, Grandmama," she responded. "Yes, I should rather remain here, but I know if we are to regain our reputations we must go up to London for a time. There were those who knew Cally there, and I shall be nothing but honest with them regarding this startling change of duchesses," she chuckled. "If I am not, we shall just get in deeper."

"Be honest," the dowager agreed, "but clever, my child. You need only say your sister died in childbirth, and that when Valerian learned it was really you he should have wed, he did before you might escape him again. Say it lightly, and make it amusing. There will be those who will be shocked, but mostly society will accept the situation with a wink and a chuckle. They have heard far worse tales, and as long as you and your husband are reconciled to each other, where is the harm? You will be readily accepted, and quite presentable to their majesties. Then, after you have amused yourselves for a few months, return home to us at Hawkes Hill. Certainly a new scandal will have arisen by then to overshadow this one." She kissed Aurora on both of her cheeks. "Oh, I shall miss you, my dear child!"

"Come with us!" Aurora begged her.

The dowager smiled and shook her head. "No," she said. "I must remain here to make things right again for you and my grandson. Besides, I think it is time you had a honeymoon, don't you? Grandmothers do not belong on honeymoons with their grandchildren," she finished with a small chuckle. And the next morning she waved them off with a brave smile, knowing even as she did so how empty and lonely the house would be for the next few months while they were away.

The trip to London was uneventful. The roads remained dry, to everyone's amazement. The inns were comfortable, if dull. Finally the spires and towers of the city could be seen in the yellow-gray haze that hung over London during the cold months, a result of the coal fires burned in each house to keep its inhabitants warm. Finally the carriages and baggage coach turned into Grosvenor Square, moving around to the west side of the common, where Farminster House was located. Almost immediately after they had stopped, the door to the brick mansion was thrown open, and a column of footmen hurried out to aid them in disembarking and to take the baggage.

"Welcome back to London, your grace, and the staff's felicitations on your marriage," Manners, the butler, said, bowing elegantly. "And welcome to her grace as well." He bent himself in Aurora's direction.

"Our thanks," the duke acknowledged with a smile. "Is dinner ready? I think her grace and I should like something to eat, and then to bed. It has been a long day, and our trip was tiring."

"Immediately, my lord," the butler replied. "There are several messages for you that have come in the last day or two."

"And you have seen to my instructions?" the duke asked.

"Of course, my lord," Manners replied in plummy tones that suggested he was slightly offended his master did not understand that an order given was one obeyed. "Shall I bring your grace his messages?"

The duke nodded. "Please," he said, and then turned to Aurora. "I have a surprise for you if you will but wait a moment." Then he turned without waiting for an answer and took the messages from the silver salver the butler proffered. "Bute," he told her, noting the seal on the first missive. He broke the seal, and opening it, scanned the contents quickly. "The earl welcomes us to London and will arrange for us to meet their majesties," he said, laying the note aside and reaching for the next one. "This is addressed to you." He handed it to her.

Aurora snapped the sealing wax on the paper and opened it. "Oh, Lord," she said. "It is from Trahern for Cally. He doesn't know she is deceased and wants to call on her."

"How I wish we could arrange it," Valerian said wickedly.

"What am I to do?" she demanded. "It is not amusing, Valerian!"

"I'll send a footman around to Trahern's lodging to say the Duchess of Farminster will receive him in the morning. It's just the sort of thing Cally would have done. She wouldn't have bothered to write," the duke noted.

"And when he arrives?" Aurora said.

"We will both receive him," her husband replied, "and explain the situation. Trahern will have our arrival trumpeted throughout polite society before tomorrow is out. How the hell did he know we were here anyway?" Valerian wondered. "I must remember to ask him."

"More than likely, one of his servants is friendly with one of the servants in this house," Aurora noted. "Now, what is my surprise?"

He laughed, and kissed her mouth quickly. "You are such a greedy creature," he teased her, and then, turning to the butler, he said, "Send a message to Lord Trahern that we will receive him tomorrow at eleven o'clock in the morning." Then, without waiting for an answer he took his wife by the arm and escorted her upstairs. "Knowing your aversion to your sister's things, I have had the duchess's rooms redone for your arrival," he told her, flinging open the doors to what had been Cally's suite.

Stepping inside, Aurora clapped her hands in delight. It looked nothing like the rooms Cally had commanded. The woodwork was painted in a pale golden-cream color—the moldings, the chair rails, and below the chair rails. Above, the walls were covered in peach-colored silk painted with hummingbirds and butterflies. Only the mural on the ceiling remained the same, but Aurora didn't care. She had always thought the ceiling painting of Venus and her band of cupids charming. The furniture was of polished mahogany, and the upholstered pieces were done in gilt, silks, and velvet. The chandelier, the wall sconces, and the candelabra were all sparkling Waterford crystal. Coral-colored velvet drapes with gold rope tiebacks hung from the windows. The polished wood floors were partly covered with a magnificent Turkey carpet in gold and blue.

Aurora hurried through to her bedchamber and sighed with pleasure. Here the walls were decorated in gold silk with cream and gold butterflies, and cream-colored lilies with their narrow leaves just touched with a grayish green. The woodwork was cream, and the ceiling filled with pink, lavender, and white clouds floating in a blue sky amid a troupe of plump cupids. The draperies at the windows were the blue of a southern sea, their tiebacks heavy gold ropes.

There was a mahogany Chippendale chest of drawers over which hung a carved and gilt Chippendale wall mirror crested with two Argus pheasants. In the curve of the window was a gilt wood settee upholstered in the identical blue as the draperies. The bed, which had been placed opposite the fireplace, was also from Mr. Chippendale's shop. It was richly carved with spiraled urns and acanthus leaf, its border backed by a Chippendale scroll with rosettes, its wooden canopy with a Greek motif, its feet voluminously carved with a wide bracket. The bed furnishings were of cream and gold silk. On both sides of the bed were small mahogany nightstands with silver candlesticks and snuffers. Near the dressing room door stood a mahogany cheval mirror with a delicately cut and etched frieze panel. Attached to the sides of the mirror were two small silver candle holders. Also within the room was a lovely piecrust table, and two wing chairs upholstered in wide cream and sea-blue stripes.

Aurora whirled about and said to her husband, "How on earth did you create such a miracle, Valerian? These are not Cally's rooms at all! Oh, I shall be so happy here!"

"I suspect the paint may still be wet in places," the duke told her with a smile. "When I sent word to Manners that we were coming, I also sent instructions for these rooms to be redone immediately, and all the furniture replaced. I did not want you unhappy, my darling."

"Oh, Valerian, I have been such a fool!" Aurora declared.

"We were both rather foolish," he agreed, "but we are luckier than most, for we have been given a second chance. Let us make the most of it, Aurora. I promise you that our few months of exile will be good months, and then we will go home to Hawkes Hill and live happily ever after."

She threw herself into his arms, pulling his head down to her, kissing his mouth passionately. "I hate traveling," she murmured. "There is never any privacy in those poky little inns with the servants snoring on their trundles, and separate rooms for his grace and her grace. It seems like forever since we've been together." She nibbled upon his earlobe provocatively. "I miss our cuddles." She began to undo the buttons upon his flowered waistcoat.

"Madam, you are showing a complete lack of decorum," he scolded her gently, his fingers undoing the laces upon her gown. "Dinner is almost ready." With a sigh he buried his face in her perfumed cleavage.

"Are you hungry?" she purred back at him.

"Yes," he said, tipping her back onto the bed and falling atop her. He pulled her bodice aside, and his mouth fastened upon a nipple, biting gently upon it, then sucking it. "Mmmmmm," he murmured. "A most delicious hors d'oeuvre, madam. I must have more!" Then he moved to her other breast, licking and nibbling upon it.

There was a discreet cough beyond the bedchamber in the salon, and they heard Sally say, "Manners says that dinner is served, your grace. Shall I tell him you will be coming down?"

"Damnation," growled the duke.

Aurora giggled, her eyes twinkling at his discomfit.

"We will be there directly," Valerian called to the maid.

Sally hurried from the room and down the staircase. "His grace says they're coming down," she informed the butler. Then she lowered her voice. "They were at it again," she confided in him. "Miss Calandra, the old duchess, she weren't much for con . . . con . . ."

"Conjugal?" the butler supplied dryly.

"Aye," Sally said, "that's the word I want. Well, she weren't much for conjugal relations with his grace, but Miss Aurora, why, she and him can hardly keep their hands off one another. They're at it all the time, they are. All the servants talked about it at Hawkes Hill. It's practically a scandal, it is!"

"It is hardly a scandal that a man cleaves to his wife, Sally, and at Farminster House we do not gossip about the master and the mistress," the butler said with strong disapproval in his voice. "I am quite surprised that Mr. Peters allowed you such liberties. I will not. Now, go about your duties, girl, and tell Martha that I want to see her when she has finished her duties later this evening."

"Yes, Mr. Manners," Sally said, and darted off. "Old goat," she muttered beneath her breath as she went.

The butler watched her go, thinking, a troublemaker if I ever saw one. I recognized it last time when she was with us. The young duchess doesn't seem the type to keep such a girl on, but then, she did come from St. Timothy, and perhaps the young duchess feels a loyalty to the jade. She will have to mend her ways, she will. Then, hearing footsteps upon the staircase, the butler remembered himself, and greeted the duke and the duchess as they descended. Her grace's hair was just a trifle in disarray, and she was prettily flushed, Manners thought, remembering Sally's words. But the duke looked happier than the butler could ever remember seeing him look, and that was all that mattered.

The following morning the butler opened the door at precisely eleven o'clock to find Lord Charles Trahern standing there. Lord Trahern's bobtailed coat and high wig, topped with a small tricorn hat, proclaimed him a macaroni. "Good morning, my lord," Manners said.

"I am calling upon the duchess," Trahern said.

"If you will follow me," the butler replied. He only wished he could see this poppinjay's face when he learned the Duchess of Farminster was not the duchess he was expecting, but he would listen at the door after he had announced Lord Trahern.

"Has her grace produced the desired heir, then?" Trahern asked as they moved toward the morning room.

"Her grace, I regret to say, miscarried of her child," the butler replied coolly.

"And Hawkesworth let her return to London?" Trahern said incredulously. "I suppose he thinks to get on her good side for another try, eh, Manners?"

The butler ignored the crass familiarity with which Lord Trahern was addressing him, as he opened the door to the morning room, and said. "Lord Trahern, my lord, my lady."

Trahern brushed past the butler. "Calandra, *mon ange,*" he began effusively, and then stopped, surprised.

Manners closed the door behind him, and then, looking about to ascertain that he was not being observed, listened at the door to the morning room to hear what was transpiring within.

Charles Trahern gaped, astonished. Before him stood the farmer duke, as he had always called Valerian Hawkesworth behind his back, and by his side was Calandra's sister, the sharp-tongued Aurora. "Where is Calandra?" he demanded of them. "I was told the Duchess of Farminster would receive me this morning. Good Lord, Hawkesworth, you can't be jealous! Have you forbidden Calandra my wicked company, and having found no victim in the country, are you about to foist your sister-in-law upon me? Calandra always did say we would be a good match."

"I wouldn't marry you, Trahern, if you were the last virile man upon this earth," Aurora told him acidly, "and besides, I am already married. You asked to see the Duchess of Farminster, and behold you see her. What may I do for you? Valerian, my darling, a whiskey for Trahern, please. He looks a bit green about the gills."

Charles Trahern fell back dramatically upon a satin striped settee. *"Where is Calandra?"* he gasped. "What have you done with her?"

The duke placed a tumbler of whiskey in their guest's hand and sat himself opposite Trahern while Aurora settled herself next to the astounded man. "Calandra died in childbirth, Charles," he said quietly. "The infant was too large to be birthed naturally. When the doctor attempted to remove it surgically, he found the child dead in its mother's womb, the cord about its neck. It was a daughter."

"When did this happen?" Trahern asked.

"On the last day of October," the duke said.

"And you married Aurora?" Now even the unshockable Lord Trahern was shocked. *"When?"*

"On the fourth of November," Hawkesworth replied calmly.

" 'Pon my soul, Hawkesworth," Lord Trahern exclaimed, "You have scandalized even me! Something I surely never expected you to do. Granted, neither you nor Calandra had any real feeling for one another, but that is not so unusual in a marriage between people of our rank. Yet your wife is not even cold in her grave when you turn about and marry her sister? 'Tis shocking! Simply shocking!" Trahern gulped down his whiskey and held the crystal tumbler out to be refilled.

Aurora arose from her place by his side and walked across the room to fetch the decanter back to where their guest sat, almost sprawled with his trauma upon the settee. "Are you going to have an attack of the vapors, Trahern?" she asked him, amused, as she poured the smoky liquor into the crystal. "Oh, do explain, Valerian, or our reputations will be ruined in polite society." She placed the decanter on a side table and rejoined the gentlemen.

"It is really all quite simple, Trahern," the duke began. "Calandra was not the heiress to St. Timothy. She was not born a Kimberly, but, rather, a Spencer. She was Robert Kimberly's stepdaughter, but she wanted to be a duchess, and Aurora, who is the true heiress, did not. Since both girls bore the identical first name, *Charlotte*, they decided to switch identities. After all, Calandra lived practically her entire life upon St. Timothy. It was not difficult even for her."

"You did not wish to be a duchess?" Poor Lord Trahern was astonished with his disbelief. What girl wouldn't want to be a duchess?

"Actually," Aurora elucidated, "I didn't wish to marry a stranger. If Valerian had come to St. Timothy and courted me, it might have been different." She turned and smiled at her husband.

"Of course it would have been different," he replied, returning her smile. "The minx didn't even give me a chance. So believing that Calandra was my bride, I married her, with even as you will admit, Trahern, disastrous results. Calandra loved my wealth and my position and all the things it entailed. She did not, however, love me."

"She didn't have to," Trahern interrupted, "as long as she produced an heir or two for you, Hawkesworth. How many wives actually love their husbands? Oh, some may, and others may harbor an affection for their mates, but most women of our class dislike their husbands intensely. We marry for land and power, not love. It is a wife's duty to give her husband children, preferably *his* children. Only then is she free to pursue her own pleasures. How on earth did you find out the deception that had been played upon you?"

The duke explained.

"But why the scandalous haste to remarry?" Lord Trahern asked when the duke had concluded his account. "Aurora was in your charge as long as she remained in England. Did you think she would flee you?"

The duke chuckled. "She tried to," he replied. "But of more importance was her engagement to my cousin, St. John. She was so pigheaded that she was determined she was wildly in love with him, and would marry him, and no one else."

"Well, I do harbor an affection for St. John," Aurora answered mischievously. "He has great charm, Trahern. Have you ever met him? I do believe that you would do quite well together. He may be coming up to London, wife hunting. No title, of course, but he is outrageously wealthy with a magnificent estate. I do believe I shall put him in your charge. Would you do me that favor?"

" 'Pon my soul!" Lord Trahern exclaimed.

"Well, Valerian and St. John have this ridiculous rivalry, and have had, so the dowager tells me, since they were boys. I do not think my husband will be content until St. John has his own wife, Trahern, and I know absolutely no one in London other than yourself. You do know *everyone* of importance, my lord," Aurora flattered him.

"A truth, a truth," Trahern admitted dryly, and then, "So, Hawkesworth, you married Aurora to prevent her running off with your cousin, and thereby cheating you of St. Timothy. An outrageous explanation, but perfectly reasonable under the circumstances. Since neither of you really likes London, I suppose you have come up from the country to ride out the scandal your actions have caused. 'Twas wise of you."

"Oh, Trahern!" Aurora said enthusiastically. "I am so glad you understand, and will aid us! Cally was right. You really are a fine fellow. I know your friendship meant much to her, my poor sister."

"*Did it?*" Trahern's voice quavered a moment. "She was such a beautiful girl. She had style and she had elegance. I believe she could have been one of London's most famous hostesses, given the opportunity."

"Oh, yes," Aurora agreed with him. "Cally was socially clever."

"Indeed!" Trahern assented. Then he turned to the duke. "Have you the aegis to meet their majesties? The queen is delightful. Ingenuous, and perhaps a trifle unsophisticated for my taste, but the king adores her. She is quite to his taste, I fear, and one must step carefully these days at court. Unlike the previous two reigns, morality rules."

"The Earl of Bute has arranged our introduction," the duke responded.

"*Bute?* Well, well, Hawkesworth, you surprise me. Bute is quite the closest to the king other than the queen. How on earth do you know Bute? He's no insider, and quite disliked by the Whigs, although the Tories will side with him even if they like him no better."

"His mother and my grandmother knew each other," the duke answered Lord Trahern. "I sold him some breeding stock a few years ago, and have some small acquaintance with him, but it was really my grandmother's connection that made the arrangement," Valerian admitted.

Lord Trahern nodded. "One uses what one can to get ahead socially," he said, "but don't rely on Bute for too much. It is unlikely he will be around in any capacity of power for very long." Setting his empty crystal tumbler down, he arose. "I really must be going," he told them. "I am meeting friends at Boodles."

"Boodles?" The duke cocked his head curiously.

"A new club," Trahern said. " 'Tis over in St. James's Street. The food is quite good and the gaming great sport. You must have a membership if you are going to remain in London for even a short time, Hawkesworth. I shall sponsor you myself. There are quite a number of country gentlemen like yourself who belong." He picked up his tricorn and settled it on his head.

Aurora stood, offering her hand to Lord Trahern. "You are really so generous, my lord. I know Valerian is most appreciative too, aren't you, my darling?"

"Oh . . . yes," the duke replied, forcing a smile.

Lord Trahern kissed Aurora's hand. "While I am quite devastated by the news of Calandra's death, I am so pleased we are to be friends, my dear Aurora." He smiled toothily at her.

She gently extracted her hand from his grip, smiling back. "It is wonderful to know we have such a good friend, my lord. I know my dear Cally would be happy to know it too."

Together the ducal couple escorted their guest into the main foyer of the house. Manners opened the door, and Lord Trahern, blowing a kiss to Aurora with his fingertips, departed. His haste to hurry forth and spread the word of what he had just heard was patently evident.

Valerian Hawkesworth turned to his wife. "You are extraordinary," he said admiringly. "You have missed your calling, Aurora. You would be a most superb actress."

"Being an actress is hardly as respectable as being a duchess," she replied pertly.

"I thought you did not want to be a duchess," he teased her as they returned to the morning room.

"I have changed my mind," she said calmly. "I adore being a duchess as long as I can be your wife, Valerian."

"Sometimes," he said, "I want to strangle you." And then, "You were quite good with Trahern, my darling. How do you manage? He is really a dreadful little toad."

"But a gossipy toad," she replied, "and since he will gossip, I should prefer he be our friend rather than our enemy, Valerian. I spoke the truth when I told him he knows everyone of importance. He does. Cally saw it immediately, and that is why she latched on to him, for he was her ticket to those heady social heights she so longed to climb. He will tell our tale cleverly and with wry humor. Some will be shocked, but most people in the ton will, as your grandmother so wisely observed, be amused by your haste to marry me and secure my dowry. With Trahern on our side, there will be no scandal in London."

"But we want to be at Hawkes Hill, and there is scandal there," the duke observed.

"It is only temporary, my darling," she reassured him. "There is bound to be another scandal in the district soon enough. Don't forget that St. John is once more a footloose bachelor. Heaven only knows what mischief he will get into before the spring." And then she laughed.

Chapter

⚜ 14 ⚜

The Earl of Bute was giving a ball, and it was there that Valerian and Aurora would be presented to their majesties.

"You will beggar me with your extravagance," the duke groaned when he saw Aurora's ball gown. "You are no better than your sister, I fear, and will certainly put me in the poorhouse."

"Oh, pooh, my lord!" she responded sharply. "You are a rich man, and I have brought you a rich dowry. You certainly cannot want me to greet their majesties looking like a milkmaid."

"A prize heifer would be of more value to me than that gown you are wearing," he grumbled.

"Fiddlesticks!" she snapped back. And then, "Have you seen my dancing shoes, Valerian?" She presented him with a pointed foot, shod in a silk shoe decorated with a rosette in whose center was a glittering diamond.

"Is it real?" he demanded, half shocked.

"Of course," she replied calmly. "You surely would not expect me to wear a false jewel. Do you like the length of my gown? It is the newest rage, and ever so practical for dancing."

"Indeed," he remarked, noting the gown's hem ended just at her neatly turned ankle. Then he allowed himself a small smile. She looked absolutely spectacular. Her gown was of lavender satin, its cream-colored underskirt embroidered in peach, blue, lavender, and pink flowers with pale green stems and leaves. The U-shaped neckline was edged in delicate silver lace and lavender silk bows sewn with tiny seed pearls. The bodice had a ladderlike decoration of ribbon bows known as echelle. Silver lace engageants dripped from the fitted sleeves. "You will turn heads, Aurora," he graciously admitted. "Just remember I am a jealous man where you are concerned, my darling."

"I can be jealous too," she told him, her eyes sweeping over his form. He was incredibly handsome, and looked every bit a duke. Because it was a formal occasion, he was garbed in cream satin breeches with silver buckles at his knees. His matching stockings were silk, as was his shirt. His waistcoat was a scrollwork pattern of black and gold on cream, his dress coat lavender satin to match her gown. His dancing shoes had jeweled buckles.

"Are they genuine?" she teased him.

"Of course," he mocked her. "You surely would not expect me to wear false jewels." Then he drew a velvet-covered box from his coat pocket. "These are for you, Aurora."

She opened the small case to reveal a pair of fat pear-shaped pearl earbobs set in gold, and a matching pearl choker from which dangled a delicately filigreed gold cross. "How lovely!" she exclaimed. Handing the case to Martha, who was beaming her approval, she fastened the earbobs into her ears and then lifted out the choker, handing it to him. "Will you put it on, please?"

He complied, explaining, "The Hawkesworth vault is filled with jewelry, and it is yours, Aurora, but most of it is from another time. It is old-fashioned, and to my eye a trifle gaudy. I purchased these especially for you. There, now turn around so I may see you."

When she did, she asked him, "Did you ever buy Cally jewelry?"

"No," he said quietly.

"You both look just grand!" Martha said enthusiastically, smoothing away the awkwardness that had suddenly arisen betwixt husband and wife. "Now, your ladyship, you remember your manners," she cautioned. "After all, this is our king and queen you're to meet tonight."

"Yes, Martha," the duchess answered her servant dutifully, and then she and the duke chuckled along with Martha.

The ball was to be held at St. James's Palace. Many of their neighbors about the square would also be going to the ball, and their coach joined a line of vehicles heading toward the palace. Aurora felt as if a colony of butterflies had suddenly taken up residence in her tummy. The few balls she had attended previously would surely pale in comparison with this affair. And she didn't know anyone. And what if the king and queen didn't like her?

Valerian Hawkesworth noted how pale his wife had become. He reached over and took her gloved hand in his, squeezing it gently. "They are only two people. A young, newly married couple like ourselves," he comforted her.

"Have you ever met the king?" Aurora asked her husband.

"No," he answered. "We do not travel in the same circles, for I am a country man, as you know. I have heard, however, that the king is much interested in agriculture."

"And Trahern says the queen is a simple girl," Aurora remarked.

"They are our sovereigns, and we will greet them with respect and affection," the duke replied.

Their carriage reached St. James's Palace, and exiting it, they followed along with the crowd of similarly garbed ladies and gentlemen, moving up a wide staircase, and finally to the impressive entrance of a magnificent ballroom. The duke murmured softly to the liveried majordomo.

The majordomo called out in stentorian tones, "His grace, the Duke of Farminster, and her grace, the Duchess of Farminster."

As they passed into the ballroom, Aurora wondered if anyone had even heard the majordomo. The noise of several hundred chattering voices was incredible. Looking about, she suffered a brief moment of panic and wished that they hadn't come at all. There were no familiar faces at all. They were in a sea of strangers. She clutched Valerian's arm tightly and hoped that her nerves didn't show.

"Hawkesworth! I say, Hawkesworth!" A pleasant-faced young man pushed his way beside them.

"Mottley," the duke replied, and then, turning to Aurora, he said, "My dear, this is Lord Robert Mottley, a former school chum. Mottley, my wife, Lady Aurora Hawkesworth."

Lord Mottley bowed politely, kissing Aurora's hand. "Your grace," he said, "I am honored." Then, before Aurora might even reply, Lord Mottley turned to Valerian, saying, "What on earth are you doing here of all places, Hawkesworth? I thought it was your custom to eschew London and high society."

"It most certainly is," the duke chuckled, "but I was unable to pay my respects to the king last autumn when he was married, and then later coronated. I felt it my duty to do so now."

"You'll like him, Hawkesworth," Lord Mottley said with a twinkle in his eye. Then he lowered his voice. "We call him Farmer George, for he does love all things pertaining to country life, and the little queen does too. They are well matched. The rumor is, although, of course, it has not yet been officially announced, that her majesty is with child, but her waist seems as slim as it was on her wedding day, I vow, so who knows what truth there is in the rumor. Who is sponsoring your introduction to their majesties, or have you no one?"

"The Earl of Bute," the duke answered.

"*Bute?* Well, Hawkesworth, you do have high connections. I would not have thought so, but put no faith in Bute. He will not last long, for the Whigs hate him and the Tories but tolerate him. An introduction is about all he is good for, I fear."

"Aurora, *mon ange*, you look divine," she heard Charles Trahern murmur in her ear, and then he popped about into her view. "Hello, Mottley, how are you? Still looking for a wife? Not much available tonight in this room for a baronet of modest means," Lord Trahern snickered. "I will wager, however, that Aurora might know some sweet country lass of good breeding who can fill your nursery."

Lord Mottley bowed stiffly to them, and moved off.

"Trahern, you have a tongue like a rusty knife," Aurora said. "Not only do you cut, you leave infection behind. What on earth do you have against poor Lord Mottley?"

"The man's a bore," Trahern said offhandedly. "Were you at school with him, Hawkesworth?"

The duke nodded, amused. Robert Mottley was a good-natured fellow, but Trahern was right. He was a bore, and Trahern did not suffer fools easily, or gladly. "And have you enjoyed yourself spreading our little scandal about London?" he faintly mocked Trahern.

"I spread it only with the people who count," Trahern replied, slightly offended. "It does no good to gossip indiscriminately, my dear fellow. I would have thought you knew that. Have you presented yourselves to Bute yet?"

"We have only just arrived, and I haven't been able to find him in this crush, Trahern," the duke replied.

"Of course you haven't," Trahern answered. "He is in the Blue Drawing Room with their majesties, presenting newcomers. Come along, and I will show you where it is." He hurried off.

They followed dutifully behind, Aurora's eyes gazing at everything in sight. The ballroom was a magnificent place, all carved gilt, and walls painted with lush romantic themes. Plaster medallions gilded in gold and silver framed the painted ceiling with its depiction of ripe-breasted goddesses and half-naked gods at play. The crystal chandeliers and the gilt wall sconces twinkled with a thousand beeswax tapers. Gilded wood chairs and settees upholstered in crimson velvet lined the room at one end of which a dais for the musicians had been set up. Everyone was dressed beautifully. How Cally would have loved it all, Aurora thought, and all I want to do is go home to Hawkes Hill. I do not like London. It is much too big and noisy.

They exited the ballroom, following Lord Trahern down a picture-lined gallery. At its end was a double door. The two footmen standing on either side of the door flung it wide, allowing them to pass through into the Blue Drawing Room, so named for its blue velvet draperies and blue upholstery. Immediately a tall gentleman with a long, aristocratic face came forward, his hand outstretched in greeting. He did not smile, but his demeanor was a pleasant one.

"Hawkesworth, my dear fellow, I am delighted that you were able to join us this evening," the Earl of Bute said politely.

"I am grateful for your lordship's patronage in this matter," the duke replied. He drew Aurora forward. "May I present my wife to you, sir? Aurora, this is the Earl of Bute."

"The *true* heiress?" The Earl of Bute's blue eyes twinkled mischievously for a moment. "Madam, I am honored to make your acquaintance. I hope you will soon be able to return home, although the court will be at a loss for your departure." He kissed her hand and bowed gallantly.

Aurora curtsied prettily. "I thank your lordship for his kindness to my husband and myself. This is a great honor. I cannot wait to write to my mother to tell her of this evening."

"Come along, then, and let me present you to their majesties," the earl said, and drew them over to where the king and queen stood.

The king was a handsome young man with a fair complexion, blond hair, and slightly protruding blue eyes. He was the first of the House of Hanover to have been born and raised entirely in England, a fact of which he was extremely proud. Unlike his grandfather, George II, and his great-grandfather, George I, he had no German accent, English being his first tongue. The young queen, while not a beauty, had a pleasant little face, sparkling blue eyes, and reddish-blond hair. She was only seventeen, while the king was twenty-three.

"Your majesty," said the Earl of Bute, "may I present to you Valerian Hawkesworth, the Duke of Farminster, and the Lady Aurora, his duchess. They were unable to be at your majesties' wedding, or coronation last autumn, and have come up to London especially to pay their respects to your majesty. The duke, like your majesty, has a deep love of agriculture, and spends his time down in the country, overseeing his estates. He raises excellent cattle and horses."

The king's face lit up immediately. "You farm?" he said.

"Yes, your majesty, I do," replied the duke with a bow.

"Where are your estates?"

"In Herefordshire, your majesty" was the response.

"We must come and see one day," the king said. "Would you

believe that I envy you, Hawkesworth? I should like nothing better than to farm my lands."

"But England needs you, your majesty," the duke told the king graciously. "You will rule this land with equity and justice."

"You have a courtier's tongue to match your farmer's heart." The king chuckled. Then he turned to his wife. "May I present her majesty to you, your grace. My dear, this is the Duke of Farminster."

The duke greeted the queen while King George turned his attention back to Aurora, who immediately curtsied to him.

"I am told, madam, that you are a *petite cause célèbre*," he said. "What on earth did you do to earn such a reputation. You would appear to be a respectable and sensible young woman."

With a pretty blush that immediately convinced the king of her honesty, Aurora briefly explained, concluding, "I was very foolish, I fear, your majesty."

"Indeed you were," the king scolded her, "but the good Lord has given you a second chance, your grace, and you have taken it, and are happy, I can see. Do you like your country life?"

"Oh, yes, your majesty!" Aurora said enthusiastically. "I love Hawkes Hill, and miss it so! It will be a wonderful place to raise our children. Children thrive in the country."

"And you desire children, your grace?"

"Oh, yes!" she told him.

The king smiled. Whatever waywardness this young woman was accused of, she had obviously repented, and would be a good wife to her husband and an excellent mother to their children. King George approved of such a woman. He wanted an England full of them. "Let me present you to the queen," he said to Aurora, and did so.

Aurora curtsied to Queen Charlotte, and was rewarded with a smile. "You were not born here," the queen observed cleverly.

"No, your majesty, I was born on the island of St. Timothy, in the Caribbean, where I lived until I came to England a little over a year ago. St. Timothy was a grant to my family from King Charles II."

"How do you live on an island?" the queen inquired, curious.

"We raise sugar cane, your majesty," Aurora said.

"Do you have slaves?"

"Yes, we do, for you cannot raise sugar without them. The labor is intense and difficult," Aurora explained. "We do not mistreat our slaves, however, your majesty. They are as valuable to us as the cane itself."

"I have heard that is not the case on the other islands," the Earl of Bute noted.

"No, it is not. Most of the planters treat their slaves as if they were expendable because they can easily obtain more. My family did not feel it was a Christian way to act, and besides, it takes longer to retrain new slaves than to treat the ones you have decently. We harvest as much sugar as any other plantation our size. Our cost to do so is less because we aren't always replacing our labor with new labor, and our profits are therefore greater."

The king chuckled again. "Hawkesworth, I do believe you have yourself a most practical little wife. You are very fortunate."

Valerian Hawkesworth smiled broadly. "Yes, your majesty, I certainly am, and I suspect your majesty shares my good fortune in the queen." He bowed gallantly to Charlotte.

The queen's eyes twinkled, and she was obviously quite pleased with the duke's compliment.

The Earl of Bute now stepped forward once more. "Your majesties, I do believe it is time for you to formally open the ball," he said quietly.

The king nodded, then said, "Follow along behind us, my dear Farminster. I will want to talk with you one day soon about an idea I have regarding the land. You will be in London until spring?"

"Yes, your majesty," Valerian Hawkesworth said.

They reentered the ballroom, walking directly after the royal couple. Behind them, the Earl of Bute came along with Lord Trahern, who could scarcely contain himself with delight at this temporary elevation in his status.

The musicians began to play, and the king led the queen onto the floor along with the Duke and Duchess of Farminster. As the minuet began, the other guests joined them. The king danced the second dance with Aurora, while Valerian partnered the queen.

"Your success is assured in high society now," Lord Trahern assured her later in the evening as he escorted her to the buffet for a glass of champagne. "They may gossip their tittle-tattle down in the country, but you are a triumph here in London, *mon ange.*"

"And what exactly does a *triumph* do in London, Trahern?" Aurora asked him. "One cannot attend balls all the time."

"Heavens, no!" Trahern exclaimed. "There are routs, and racing, picnics, and boating, gambling for the gentlemen, cards for the ladies, and, of course, one makes calls and leaves cards. You do have cards, my dear Aurora, don't you?"

"Cards?" She looked confused. "What sort of cards?"

"No cards?" Lord Trahern looked scandalized. "Oh, my dear, it will simply not do. I shall call upon you tomorrow, and we shall go to Mr. Dove's shop. He is the finest cardmaker in London, nay, I lie, in all of England. You absolutely must have cards if you are to make calls, *mon ange.*"

Aurora took a sip of her champagne. "Upon whom shall I call?" she asked him. "I know absolutely no one in London. Is it not forward for me to call upon people I do not know, Trahern?"

"Mon ange, after tonight, they will all be eager to call upon you, for have I not said you are a triumph? Not only are you one of the most beautiful women here; you are dressed exquisitely; you have both been recognized by their majesties, you have danced with the king, and your husband with the queen. For a provincial ducal couple from Herefordshire, this is astounding. Therefore everyone will be eager to know you, especially given your rather unique history." Trahern gulped his wine down and continued. "Once you have been called upon, you must return the calls, leaving your card to indicate that you have called."

Aurora helped herself to a second flute of champagne that was being offered by a footman. She did enjoy champagne. "Why must I leave cards when I call on people? Will they not receive me, Trahern?"

"Most will when they see your card, but others may not be

receiving when you call, or may be out calling upon others," he told her. "As for you, *mon ange*, I will tell you whom to receive immediately and whom to not. You must not seem overeager to gain the approval of the ton."

"Actually, Trahern, I don't care if I do or not," Aurora told him frankly. "We are in London for the winter, and only because we could not remain at Hawkes Hill. Once we return home, I doubt we will come to London at all."

"Be that as it may," he said, "while you are here you should meet, know, and associate with only the *right* people. Remember that one day you will want to make an alliance for your son."

"I don't have a son," she responded laughing.

"But you will," he replied quickly.

Aurora told her husband of her conversation with Trahern as they lay abed later that night, and he laughed.

"Trahern is a silly fool," he said. "Do you intend to retain his company?" He fingered a brown-gold curl, kissing it.

"He is not as great a fool as he makes out," Aurora said. "But he does amuse me. Not as he did Cally. She was impressed by him. I am not. Still, we cannot sit alone by ourselves in Farminster House until the spring, Valerian. You have been accepted into Boodles and can run off to your club when you are bored. I have no such luxury, and so I must rely upon Charles Trahern for my entertainment."

He slid his hand into the open neckline of her nightgown and fondled a small, plump breast. "I will amuse you, my darling," he murmured seductively, nibbling upon her earlobe.

"Be serious, Valerian," she scolded him.

"Why?" he demanded of her, and then his mouth fastened upon a trusting nipple, and he began to suck upon her.

She sighed, her fingers stroking the nape of his neck. "Because . . ." she began, but his rising passion was too distracting.

He pushed her nightgown up to her hips, but she stopped him, drawing it off instead, and then reaching out to help him out of his nightshirt. "Better," he groaned, wrapping his arms about her. "Much, *much* better."

"Ummmmmm," she agreed. She loved the feel of skin on skin.

He was so warm against her. Very warm, and very hard. Why was it that a man was so hard and a woman so soft, she wondered. He began to kiss her throat and her shoulders, leaving her breast bereft. His lips were tender and very exciting against the silk of her skin. Aurora considered that it was really a miracle that a woman did not grow tired or bored with a man's lovemaking. After all, when a couple had been together for a period of time, there were few surprises left. And yet despite their married state she enjoyed Valerian's attentions. No. She craved them.

Her fingers stroked the back of his neck, moving on to his shoulders and back. He was so beautifully formed, she thought. She could feel his musculature beneath her hands. It rippled smoothly with his every movement. His head was buried in the soft curve of her neck. Reaching out, she caressed his buttocks, her fingers stroking the taut flesh beneath them. He groaned with his pleasure, and she felt a riffle of anticipation race through her.

"Witch," he murmured against her ear. "You will not have your way with me until I am ready to have my way with you." Moving sinuously, he buried his face between her breasts, inhaling the perfume of her satiny body. He began to tongue her, his fleshy organ laving first the twin mounds of her bosom, then moving lower, until her excitement was so great, she thought she would explode with the feeling. Her breasts felt swollen and tight, her nipples near to bursting with sweetness. Her lower belly ached, almost painfully with the expectancy.

"Please!" she gasped softly, her breath coming in short little pants. And then she cried out with pleasure as his face brushed against her golden-brown bush. *"Please!"* she whimpered more urgently.

Slowly he ran his tongue up her furred slit. Even more slowly he opened her, smiling at the creamy coating already upon the coral flesh. Her breath was ragged to his ears. Her pleasure spot almost throbbed visibly beneath his hot gaze. He slipped between her thighs, drawing her legs up and over his shoulders. Then, spreading her open again, his tongue slid from between her lips, the tip of it just touching the pulsing nub. She moaned desperately, needing far more than he was giving at that moment.

Raising his head, he said low, "You are so utterly wanton, my precious. I fear that one day I shall not be able to satisfy you."

"*Never!*" The word burst forth. Then, "In the name of heaven, Valerian, do not stop now!"

He lowered his head again, inhaling the delicate sexual fragrance of her. The scent intoxicated him, and his own lust increased. His tongue flicked relentlessly back and forth until she was almost sobbing with her desire. Her open hunger was so great, he decided he might initiate her into a new position of passion. Turning himself about so that his head was still between her thighs, he offered her the same opportunity of which he was availing himself. To his delight, she needed no encouragement at all. She licked at his love pouch with all the enthusiasm of a starving woman, her tongue hot and eager. Then, taking him into her mouth, she began to tease his rod with her tongue and her teeth.

He almost exploded with his own desire, but catching himself, he instead began to caress her moist flesh with his own tongue, pushing it into her hot passage, simulating her for several moments, then, taking her little pleasure nub between his lips, he sucked hard on it until she screamed her delight, sucking even harder upon his member, her body convulsing several times.

"Release me," he managed to growl, and when she had reluctantly done so, he turned about again and thrust fiercely into her pulsating body over, and over, and over again until he could actually feel the spasms rocking her so hard, he could not prevent himself from erupting, his juices so copious that they flooded her womb, and filling her, oozed out, dampening the bedding. Her body shook in his embrace until they were both weak with their satisfaction. Rolling off her, he caught her hand in his, bringing it to his lips to kiss passionately. "You are totally magnificent," he said when he was finally able to find his voice once more.

Turning his hand about, Aurora brought it to her lips and returned the kiss. She was yet speechless. When at last she found her own voice, she murmured low, "That was wonderful! I could have never imagined such a thing. Can we do it again? What else are you keeping from me, my lord?"

He laughed weakly. "I can see I shall have a terrible time keeping you satisfied, madam, but I shall enjoy fulfilling your wanton nature, Aurora. Just see you allow no other man such liberties."

"You are my husband," she reassured him. "You must not even say such things to me, Valerian. I would never betray you! This is not the first time you have suggested such a thing. Why do you do so? Do you not believe I love you?" Turning slightly, she took him in her arms, his dark head resting upon her breasts. "Men are supposed to be stalwart and brave. They are not allowed to show pain of any kind, yet your marriage to my sister was painful not just for Cally, but for you too, wasn't it, Valerian? I believe you feared that one day Cally, for all her coldness, might betray you with a lover because it was the fashionable thing to do. You know as well as I do that my sister would have died rather than appear unfashionable to society, even if it meant doing something she found distasteful, and we both know passion was unpalatable to Cally. But I am not my sister, Valerian. I rejected you initially, as you well know, out of fear of the unknown, of both you and England, and of being a duchess. I reject none of it now, for I have come to love you even as you love me. I can say it no more plainly than that, my lord. You will believe me, or you will not, but never again suggest that I would betray you with another man! Certainly not after the wonderful hour we have just shared."

Raising his head, he looked into her eyes. "I apologize," he said softly. "I am a fool, I fear, driven by my love for you."

"As I was once driven by my own fears," she responded. "Let us both stop being foolish, my darling husband."

He nodded against her bosom, and then she could feel him sliding into sleep. Aurora smiled. She could never have imagined such happiness two years ago as she was now experiencing. If only her happiness had not come at such a high price. She gently caressed his dark head, and he murmured low. She closed her eyes, and slept.

In the morning Trahern arrived as he had promised to take Aurora to Mr. Dove's shop for her cards. She had breakfasted with her

husband, who had then gone off for a ride in the park. She had
had to decline his invitation to accompany him, knowing Charles
Trahern would fuss at her if she did not go with him to Mr. Dove's.
The elegant little establishment in St. James's was a revelation to
her. Under Lord Trahern's watchful eye she ordered ivory vellum
cards with the Farminster ducal monogram, and her title, *The Duchess
of Farminster*, in elegant black calligraphic script. Enthusiastically
she added cards for Valerian, and notepaper with her monogram as
well, telling Mr. Dove to deliver her purchases to Farminster House
as soon as possible.

"Within the week, your grace," Mr. Dove said, bowing low.

"I should hope so," Trahern interjected. "Her grace cannot make
any calls without her cards, and lives too far from London to send
back for them. Her foolish undermaid did not pack her ladyship's
writing box. A country girl, y'know," he concluded with a broad
wink at the stationer. "Eager, but not quite bright." He tapped the
side of his head with his finger knowingly.

"I shall have at least three dozen cards for your ladyship by
tomorrow morning," Mr. Dove responded with a smile. "You cannot
be unavailable to your friends at the height of the season, your
grace. Why, such a thing is utterly unthinkable." He bowed again.

Aurora nodded graciously, and taking Trahern's arm, departed
the shop. "Thank you, Trahern," she said, her eyes twinkling at
him.

"You picked up my direction quite quickly, *mon ange*," he told
her, thinking that while she was quite lovely, she was not the beauty
Calandra was with her ivory skin and black hair. Calandra, of whom
he had had such high hopes, and who had been so generous with
her purse when he had lost at the cards, which was more frequently
than not. Cool and elegant Calandra. Had Valerian Hawkesworth
really done all he could to save her life, or had his desire for Aurora
overpowered him? Especially when he learned that she was the true
heiress of St. Timothy and not beauteous Calandra. There had been
a doctor, and yet she still had died. It seemed very odd to him, but
he was certain that Calandra should not have died.

"Trahern, you have quite gone away," Aurora said.

Remembering himself, he helped her into her carriage, saying, "I was contemplating if you had ordered enough stationery, but I believe that you have. After all, you will not be remaining in London for very long. Too soon, *mon ange*, you will hurry back to the bucolic pleasures of your Hawkes Hill, will you not? You and your farmer duke, although I will admit that your husband is not a bad fellow."

"How kind of you, Trahern," Aurora teased him. "I shall certainly remember to tell Valerian that you said so. As for my notepaper, I can use it in the country too. In fact, from now on I shall order all my paper goods and cards from Mr. Dove. After all, you have assured me his is the most fashionable stationer's shop in London."

"*Mon ange*, I am beginning to have hope for you," Lord Trahern responded with a chuckle. "I do believe you are showing promise."

"Take me home, Trahern," she said. "Valerian will be back from his ride in the park and wonder why a little shopping is taking so long. He is quite jealous, you know."

"Then I shall invite him to lunch with me at Boodles and assure him that I look on you as your dear brother, George, would," Lord Trahern answered her. "Did he ever find a bride, by the way?"

"Indeed he did," Aurora said, and filled Lord Trahern in as the coach made its way along the streets of London.

"A parson's daughter," Trahern laughed. "Well, if her bloodlines are as good as you say, I suppose a country girl would be better suited to life on a Caribbean plantation than one of those city misses who dangled themselves before George last season."

"Betsy will make my brother a perfect wife," Aurora replied. Then she said, "And what am I to do while you take Valerian off for luncheon, which will certainly end in several hours of cards?"

"Why, *mon ange*, you must make yourself beautiful for this evening's festivities. The Duchess of Devonshire is having a grand ball, and I know you have been invited. You must promise me a dance. What fun we shall have. And tomorrow afternoon there is a marvelous horse auction at Tattersall's over at Hyde Park Corner. The three of us will go, of course. I know your husband will be most interested."

"And I was worried that I should, perhaps, hire a social secretary.

I see now I shall not have to with you about," Aurora teased him, laughing. "It all sounds quite exciting, Trahern, but when does the ton rest itself from all these exertions?"

"*Rest?* There is plenty of time to rest when one is old, or in the grave, *mon ange,* but we are all young, and should enjoy life!"

The ducal carriage drew up before Farminster House, and a footman ran out to help Aurora from the vehicle. Trahern bounced out behind her, following her into the house.

"Has the duke returned from his ride?" she asked Manners as he took her fur-trimmed cloak.

"He is in the library, my lady," the butler said. "Shall I tell him you are home?"

"No, I shall tell him myself," Aurora replied. "Please show Lord Trahern into the Morning Room, Manners." She hurried off to the library, slipping through the door with a sigh. "Charles Trahern is absolutely exhausting," she announced to her husband. "It is your turn to amuse him now, Valerian. He wants to take you to lunch at Boodles, and he has invited us to Tattersall's for a horse auction tomorrow afternoon. I shall enjoy that. I have never been to a horse auction."

"Good God!" the duke swore. "He wants to take me to lunch? It will end up on my tab, I assure you, my darling, and not Trahern's. Have you noticed what a sponge he is? I will wager his fascination with Calandra was half the money she put in his pocket. I always thought her constant need for coin odd. She could never manage to live on her allowance, and I was really overgenerous."

"Be kind, my love," Aurora said. "We are so happy, and it is quite obvious poor Trahern is not. He is amusing, and we really know so few people in London."

The duke smiled at her, and coming over to where she was standing, kissed her mouth softly. "You have a good heart," he said, "and to please you I shall trot off to Boodles with Trahern. He will rope me into cards afterward, I warn you. God knows when I shall return home to your loving arms."

"Just in time to dress for the Duchess of Devonshire's ball," she reminded him, laughing. "I know I can trust Trahern to get you home for that, since he is going too."

Valerian Hawkesworth groaned. "I am beaten," he said.

"And if you are very good," she promised him, "we shall end our evening as we did last night." Her aquamarine-blue eyes twinkled at him, and she ran a pink tongue swiftly over her lips.

"We could spend the afternoon that way, and send Trahern on his way right now," he tempted her.

Aurora laughed. "I should be far too exhausted to attend the Duchess of Devonshire's ball if we did, my love."

"Do you really want to go to the ball?" His eyes were dark with his rising passion.

"Yes!" she said, laughing again. "I will not let you make a recluse of me, Valerian. We are in London, and we are going to take advantage of it, because it is very unlikely we shall ever come back once we are home. I really don't like the city, but since I am here, I shall sample the wonderful variety of amusements London has to offer, for until our eldest daughter is ready to make her debut, I see no need to come up to town."

"If we spend the afternoon the way I want to," he said with perfect reason, "we might have that daughter sooner than later."

"We must have a son first," Aurora said. "Now, go and find Trahern. He is in the Morning Room, eagerly awaiting your arrival."

"I have no doubt," the duke responded dryly. He drew her into his arms and nuzzled at the top of her head. "Are you certain that I cannot change your mind, Aurora, my precious?"

"No, I am not certain, so you must leave me immediately," she told him with a smile. "I do not know if Trahern is ready to believe that you would rather rodger your wife than go to Boodles with him. Have we not created enough scandal?"

The duke burst out laughing, and kissing her atop her head again, he said, "Very well, Aurora, for the sake of our reputations I shall go to Boodles with Charles Trahern, but I really would rather remain at home and rodger my wife!"

"Let him win a little bit off you, Valerian. I think his pockets a bit shallow right now," she called after him.

Turning about he grinned. "Of course, my darling. I think Trahern a bit of a doodle, but I am not insensitive to his finances." He blew a kiss to her, and then was gone through the library door.

Chapter

🙢 15 🙠

"I don't understand why the queen is spending so much time with the Duchess of Farminster," sniffed Lady Jarvis.

"Perhaps because they are both young and newly married," the Duchess of Hamilton suggested. "It is only natural that the queen would want the company of someone her own age, and Aurora Hawkesworth is only a year older than her majesty."

"But she is a *colonial*," Lady Jarvis replied spitefully.

"It is true that she was not born in England," the duchess responded, but then, neither was the queen. It is another thing that they have in common, becoming used to their new homeland. It helps her majesty to acclimate, and now that she is expecting a child, do we not want her to be especially happy? Come now, Estella, do not be jealous. Lady Hawkesworth will soon be gone, and very unlikely to return to London for some time. She is admittedly a country woman as opposed to a city woman, and does not really enjoy the court."

"Well, it is a fact that the court is duller now than in the old king's time," Lady Jarvis said. "All this high moral tone is irritating, and the strong emphasis on family that the king is promoting is amazing, especially considering his own background. King George I was always at odds with his son, the second George, and the second George was at odds with his eldest son, whom we all called *Poor*

Fred. Both these previous Georges flaunted their German mistresses, but, by God, the court was fun then! I wonder if *Poor Fred* would have had his ladies, too, had he become king, but alas, he died when his son was thirteen, and now that lad is our king, and a man grown who claims that the family and the land are everything that a good Englishman needs to be happy. Gracious! What sort of thing is that for a king to say?"

"Vhat is dat you say about the king?" young Queen Charlotte said, just catching a vague reference to her husband.

"I was saying that his majesty rightly believes that one's family and one's lands constitute complete happiness, your majesty," Lady Jarvis responded quickly.

"Indeed, yes," the queen replied with a smile, and then she turned to Aurora, who was seated by her side. "You are so fortunate to live in the country, your grace. I love our little house in Kew, but it is said of it dat it is not majestic enough. His majesty is purchasing Buckingham House in Pimlico for us because there have been complaints dat our dear Dutch House is much too simple." She lowered her voice. "I do not like grand houses. You cannot get comfortable in a grand house, and there are too many prying eyes in a grand house. Do you have a grand house?"

"Hawkes Hill is a large home, your majesty, and set most beautifully in its own park and woodlands, but I do not think it palatial, although it is certainly larger than my home on St. Timothy."

"Do you miss St. Timothy?" the queen asked.

"I miss my family, and the sunny, warm days," Aurora said thoughtfully, "but my home is wherever Valerian is now."

The queen nodded, then said shyly, "Do you love him?"

"Yes," Aurora answered simply.

"Good! Dat is very good. I am coming to love my George. He is a fine man, but of course none can know him as I do because he is the king." She sighed. "It is very hard to be a king, you know. Everyone vants your attention, your favor, and for the king to do things *their* vay." Her blue eyes twinkled, and she gently patted her belly. "Poor little *Liebling*, this baby of mine. He vill not have an easy life. Do you vant *Kinder* . . . children?"

"I may be with child now, your majesty," Aurora confided. "I cannot be certain because I have no one to advise me if my symptoms are those of a breeding woman. Martha, my serving woman, might know, for she was my mother's servant, but she cannot keep a secret. I might ask my husband's grandmother, but she is at Hawkes Hill."

"Has your link vit the moon been broken?" the queen queried.

"Yes."

"Are your breasts beginning to feel fuller? Are your nipples sore?" the queen continued in a soft voice.

"Yes."

"Do you feel a revulsion for certain foods, or a desire for others?" Aurora nodded. "I do!"

"Then more than likely you are vit child, your grace. Vould you like me to arrange dat you see the royal physician?"

"I would be most grateful, your majesty," Aurora said. "We are not due to arrive home until May first. I do not want to wait until then to consult Dr. Carstairs. I would know now."

"I vill arrange it," the queen said. Then she giggled. "Do you think dat Lady Jarvis looks like her spaniel?"

"I do," Aurora agreed, and the two young women were overtaken by a fit of conspiratorial laughter.

"Such silly creatures," Lady Jarvis murmured to the other women. "I do hope that the queen will gain a more regal manner as she grows older. Young women are so impossible."

"I think the queen and Lady Hawkesworth most charming," the Duchess of Hamilton said. "Their youth is infectious, and it keeps us all younger by association. I know I like that!"

The doors to the queen's drawing room opened, and the king entered with Valerian Hawkesworth by his side. They bowed to the ladies, and then the king said to his wife, "Lotte, Hawkesworth has been telling me the most fascinating things about his village mills. The cotters weave their own cloth to his specifications, from his own wool and the additional wool he purchases. He then sells the cloth and allows them to share in the profits!"

"Vhy do you not keep all the profits for yourself, your grace?" the queen asked curiously.

"Because by allowing my tenants to share the proceeds of their own labor, they become more involved in that labor. Our cloth is finer than others because my people know the better the cloth, the higher the price. By allowing them to partake a bit of the profits, they work harder to gain me a better cloth which sells at a better price, your majesty," the duke explained. "The extra income they gain gives them a better life for their families. I have even allowed certain of the families to put money aside for the purchase of their cottages, although I retain the land beneath those cottages. That, in turn, absolves me of maintaining those particular dwellings, although I insist upon a certain standard of maintenance and with-hold moneys from those who do not make the proper repairs and keep their cottages whitewashed neatly."

"You are, it vould seem," the queen said, "a strict master but a fair one. Dat is good, is it not, George?"

"Aye," the king agreed. Then he said, "Will you join me at bowls upon the lawn later, Hawkesworth. I am much interested in your breeding methods for cattle. Bute says they are superior, and result in strong stock."

The duke bowed. "I should be delighted to share my knowledge with your majesty," he replied.

"Farmer George, and the farmer duke," Lady Jarvis said low, her tone scathing. "What will happen to the country with such a ruler?"

"I think England will be a far better place when this king leaves it than when he took up his scepter of office," the Duchess of Hamilton said softly.

"Cattle breeding and weaving," sniffed Lady Jarvis. "What on earth is the world coming to, I wonder." Her tone was less discreet than it had been before, and the king overheard her.

"You enjoy a good dinner of beef, my dear lady," he said sternly, "and without weavers of cloth you should be as naked as a newborn babe, madam. Thank God, I say, for the land, and all that it produces, and thank God for the English yeoman farmer!"

Publicly censured, Lady Jarvis looked most uncomfortable, especially as the queen and the Duchess of Farminster had begun to giggle at the mention of nakedness. She flushed irritably, but wisely held her tongue for the moment.

Because Aurora wanted to surprise her husband with the news of a possible heir, the queen arranged for the royal physician to examine the duchess privately at the Dutch House on the same day the doctor paid her majesty his weekly visit. He confirmed Aurora's suspicions with a smile.

"Indeed, your grace, you are most definitely with child. From my examination, and from the information you have supplied me with, I should say the heir is due around Martinsmas in November. You are a healthy young woman, and should have no difficulty."

"Will it be safe for us to travel back to Herefordshire at the end of April?" Aurora asked him. "Or should we depart now?"

"It is only the matter of a few weeks, your grace," said the doctor. "I see no reason for you to disrupt plans already made. I presume you have a well-sprung and comfortable traveling coach? And the trip must be made in gentle stages, of course."

"May I ride? The coach is so confining, and I have begun to feel quite queasy of late from motion," the told him.

"As long as you are extremely careful, do not subject yourself to undue jolting—no galloping, madam—and do not become overtired, I see no reason you cannot ride an hour or two a day. The queasiness will pass, your grace, I promise you. And when you reach home, you are to inform your own physician of your condition. You do have a doctor in your vicinity?"

"We do," Aurora assured him. Then she said, "Please do not tell anyone that I am with child, sir. I would surprise my husband. His first wife, my half sister, died in childbirth. I may wait until we are home to announce my condition. He will only worry unduly, and I am not like Cally at all. I am going to have lots of babies!"

The royal doctor smiled. "A good attitude, and a happy heart are most important when a woman is in your condition, your grace. My lips are sealed." He bowed to her, and departed.

The queen hurried into the room. "Vell?" she demanded.

Aurora nodded, beaming happily.

"Vhen?" Queen Charlotte was smiling too.

"November," Aurora said. "Only you and the doctor know, your majesty, and he has agreed to keep my secret. I hope you will too. I don't want to tell Valerian until we reach home. We will be leaving soon, and he will just fuss at me, remembering Cally's difficulties. My sister hated being with child, but I am joyful! History will not repeat itself in this case."

Impulsively the queen hugged Aurora, kissing her on both cheeks. "I vill keep your secret," she promised.

When Aurora had returned home that afternoon, she found Trahern awaiting her. "I have someplace special to take you," he said. "Will you let me escort you this evening?"

"What about Valerian? she asked him.

"I have already spoken to him," Trahern said. "He is having supper privately with the king, who wishes to quiz him further on matters relating to agriculture." He sighed dramatically. "I am utterly astounded by the king's hunger for such knowledge. I cannot imagine where he gained such a leaning. He would do better to become more interested in matters relating to his government. Bute encourages him in his passion for *divine right* instead of advising him to mediate what will shortly be a serious confrontation between the Whigs and the Tories. Divine right or no, the king cannot rule without the politicians. We are in modern times now."

"I shall ask Valerian if he objects to my going alone with you," Aurora said.

"He will not object," Trahern assured her. "I shall pick you up at nine o'clock, *mon ange*. Wear something spectacular." He kissed her hand and left her.

Aurora, nonetheless, did ask her husband if he would mind her accompanying Lord Trahern that evening. "He did not say where we were going, but he said I should dress for an occasion. Have you any idea where we might be going?"

"There are any number of balls being given," the duke said in an offhanded manner. "Go along and enjoy yourself. I should rather speak to the king on farming than have to attend another of those dull affairs. Just a few more weeks, my darling, and we shall return to Hawkes Hill. My grandmother writes that while the scandal of our marriage has not entirely died, we will be welcomed back."

"Thank goodness!" she replied. "I haven't really made any friends here in London, except for the queen. I just don't seem to have a great deal in common with the court ladies. Lotte and I are of an age, and both strangers to England. Her upbringing was much like mine, with a loving family and less formality."

"You call the queen *Lotte?*" He was quite surprised.

"Only when we are alone together," Aurora replied. "If any of the other ladies heard me, they would be furious, and even more jealous than they already are of me. Especially that sour Lady Jarvis. Lotte prefers informality, however, and with me she may be freer than with the others."

"It cannot be easy to be a queen," the duke considered. "She is fortunate in her husband, however. The king has come to love her dearly, a miracle for such a marriage."

"You have come to love me, and I you," Aurora pointed out.

"Another miracle." He kissed the tip of her nose.

"I do not know if I really want to go with Trahern," Aurora said. "I could be just as happy remaining home and going to bed early. I am tired with all these late nights they keep here in London. I shall be relieved to go back to the country, where we can keep sensible hours, Valerian. Besides, I have missed your grandmother."

"So have I," he agreed, then, "If you send your regrets to Trahern now, he will have a fit of the sulks and complain at me when we meet at Boodles tomorrow. He is worse than a woman, my precious. Go for my sake, I beg you."

"Oh, very well," she acquiesced.

"What will you wear?" he asked her. "Nothing too tempting, Aurora, for I would not have other men ogling you too greatly."

"I think the rose silk with the gold and rose striped petticoat," she told him. "I have not worn it before, and I am not certain it is not a bit too peacockish and showy, but Trahern asked that I wear something *spectacular*, and this certainly fits the bill. I wonder where he is taking me, Valerian. I shall not let him keep me too late, however."

"I shall be gone before you, and home probably just after you leave," he told her. "You know the king keeps to a strict schedule. He leaves the card table at precisely ten o'clock, and goes to bed."

"A lucky man," Aurora responded.

The duke laughed. "You really are a country lass," he teased her. "I suppose you shall be up with the birds, and to bed as soon as the sun has set, but then"—his arms slipped about her—"I shall not mind it if we retire early." He kissed her softly, little kisses all over her face.

"Ummm," she sighed contentedly. "Oh, Valerian, let us remain home this evening. I shall send a note to Trahern, and you will tender your regrets to the king. Say you have the headache."

He held her close, breathing the soft fragrance of her hair. "We cannot," he told her regretfully. "This small friendship I have forged with King George may be of value to our family one day. Shortly, we will be gone from court, my precious, and we both know it is unlikely we will come again to London soon. The king is usually overly suspicious and mistrustful of people's motives, or so Bute has told me. With me, however, he is not. I do not want to disappoint him in any way, Aurora. He is truly interested in my agrarian knowledge, and wants to learn. You know there are no others among the court who can speak with him on such matters. They have already begun to make fun of him behind his back, calling him Farmer George, even as they call me the farmer duke, but he will eventually win them over. He may be a solemn and very moral man, but he is kind and good-hearted. Eventually all of England will respond to his sweet and decent nature. We have little time left here. Let me serve the king as best I can while we remain."

She sighed and nodded. "You are right," she agreed.

"I must leave in another hour or so for Kew," the duke told his wife. "I will wait up for you, my precious."

"And I shall come home as early as I dare," she replied with a small smile at him.

"You're a wicked, wanton chit," he said, kissing her hard.

"Aye, sir, but I am *your* wicked, wanton chit," she answered, kissing him back, her tongue slipping between his lips to tease him. Then, slipping from his arms, she ran upstairs.

"Well," Martha said as she entered her apartment, "what are we doing this evening, my lady?"

"Valerian is leaving for Kew to be with the king, and I am going to some ball or other with Trahern," Aurora answered.

"Going to a ball? *Without your husband?*" Martha's lips were pursed in a disapproving manner.

"Valerian says if I don't go, Trahern will complain at him tomorrow at Boodles," Aurora laughed. "I should far prefer to remain at home, Martha."

"And so you should in your condition!" came the sharp reply. "Have you told his grace yet, my lady?"

Aurora looked at her servant, surprised. *"You know? How?"*

"Well, it weren't that difficult to figure out, my lady" came the retort. "Don't I see your laundry gathered up for the laundress? Well, you ain't had any show of blood in weeks, and I've noticed of late that your appetite is a bit peckish and your gowns is getting a bit tight in the bosom. It weren't really that hard."

"You haven't told anyone, have you?" Aurora fretted.

Martha looked mildly aggrieved that her mistress would even ask such a question. "Yer certain?" was her response.

"I've seen the queen's physician," she replied, "But I don't want to tell Valerian until we get home to Hawkes Hill. He'd only worry, and the doctor says I am healthy, and happy, and that is good for me right now. Oh, Martha, I'm not Cally, and I don't want Valerian to be afraid. Having a baby is the most natural thing in the world! I cannot wait to hold my child in my arms!"

"Yer mama, the real one, I mean, was just like that," Martha said. "She loved children, and you do too. I won't tell his grace, my lady. We'll be home shortly, and that's time enough for him to know. *But,* I don't want you overexerting yourself now!"

"I won't," Aurora promised the faithful Martha.

"What are we wearing this evening?" the servant said.

"The rose and gold, I think" was the response.

"That flamboyant thing? I don't know why you had it made in the first place," Martha huffed. "Do you really want to be seen in public in that gown?"

"Trahern said wear something spectacular, and I believe the rose and gold qualifies. It may be the only chance I get to wear it. I don't know why I had it made either, but the material seemed so interesting before it became a gown," Aurora remarked.

Martha nodded. "Aye, that sometimes happens. Well, I'll get it out and see that it's pressed, my lady. At least it won't go to waste before it goes into the back of the wardrobe," she giggled.

A bath was brought for her grace, and Aurora enjoyed a long and leisurely soak, for she had plenty of time before Trahern would call for her. The water was perfect, and the scent of honeysuckle and woodbine filled the air. Sally had found the most interesting little chemist's shop nearby that made the fragrance up in a bath oil. It was a clean yet sensual smell, and Valerian liked it. There was even soap to match it. Picking up her bath cloth, Aurora soaped it and washed herself. The bath was so relaxing, and she was beginning to get sleepy.

"There's time for a nap and a wee bit of supper before you go," Martha said, helping her from the tub. "If you're going to be up tonight instead of in your bed, where you belong, then you need your strength. How about a bit of chicken, bread, and butter?"

Aurora nodded, and lying down, was asleep almost before her head hit the pillow. Martha awakened her at eight, and after nibbling a bit on the contents of the plate her servant had brought her, and drinking some sweet golden wine, she was ready to dress. Wiping the chicken grease from her face and washing her hands in the basin Sally held for her, she at last stood up. Her maids bustled about her, dressing her in her undergarments, stockings, and petticoats, until finally Molly and Martha lowered her gown over her head, and Sally, kneeling, settled the skirts of the garment over her mistress's petticoats.

"Take a deep breath," Martha ordered, and began lacing up the gown with skillful fingers. Aurora had a naturally small waistline, and the servant was careful not to pull the laces too tight. Many a tightly laced woman fainted in her desire to be ultra-fashionable.

Aurora stared at herself in the long mirror. Her bosom was certainly threatening to swell over the neckline of the gown, which was edged in gold lace. She tugged at it in an attempt to draw it up in order to give herself a more modest countenance.

Martha shook her head. "There ain't no help for it," she said dourly, and Sally giggled, only to be silenced by a furious look from the upper servant. "We had best choose another gown, my lady."

The clock on the mantel struck nine o'clock. "There is no time," Aurora said. "You know how prompt Trahern always is. Fetch the deep blue velvet cape, Molly." She turned back to Martha. "I have no intention of staying out too long, at any rate. I'll be back before anyone has had the time to dwell on this gown," she promised. Then she fitted her pear-shaped pearl earbobs into her lobes and gave her hair a final pat. "Do you think it looks all right without the twin curls on either side, Martha?"

"I like the chignon, my lady. It gives you a sophisticated look, and besides, a change now and then is good," the servant reassured her mistress. She handed Aurora her cloth-of-gold reticule. "Your handkerchief and little painted fan are inside."

Aurora exited her apartment, Molly hurrying behind with her velvet cloak.

Trahern, at the foot of the stairs, looked up, his eyes widening. "I say!" he blurted out.

"Well, Trahern, you did say *spectacular*," she mocked him.

His eyes fastened a moment too long upon her bosom, then met her gaze boldly. "I would not have expected such a garment existed in your wardrobe, Aurora. In Calandra's, yes, but not yours."

"The color is better suited to Cally," Aurora admitted. "I don't know why I chose this material, but it fitted your instructions."

Molly set the cape over her mistress's shoulders and fastened the silver frog closures.

"Where are we going?" Aurora asked her companion as they settled themselves in his carriage.

"You will soon be leaving London," he said. "You have seen the

court with all its pomp and decorous behavior. But before this young
king with his priggish mannerisms took the throne, we had two less
genteel Georges. They were kings who openly kept a series of
mistresses, and despite their insistence upon a certain royal etiquette, we had a much freer lifestyle. That lifestyle still exists today,
albeit hidden away from prying eyes and the censure of those prudish
members of the court who would not approve of it. I am taking you
to the Brimstone Club. Calandra visited it with me several times,
and quite enjoyed it."

He was lying to her, and Aurora realized it almost immediately
when she entered the nondescript mansion off of St. James's Park.
Cally, with her distaste for the sensual, would have detested the
unbridled passion taking place within the Brimstone Club. The
footmen opening the door to the club, and taking coats were actually
nubile young women. They wore powdered wigs, and their flowered
satin waistcoats were cut so that their bare breasts hung out. When
they turned about, Aurora was shocked to see their white breeches
had absolutely no backs so that their naked bottoms were fully
revealed. The men servants, offering glasses of champagne from
silver trays, were no better dressed. They wore no coats or shirts at
all, and their bare skin appeared to be oiled. Their tight breeches
were cut out to reveal both their genitals and their tight backsides.
All were very handsome, but their faces were impassive beneath
their powdered wigs.

"I am appalled you would bring me here," Aurora said softly
in angry tones. "Call for your carriage immediately, and take me
home!"

"Oh, do not be such a little Puritan, *mon ange,*" Trahern said.
"You do not have to remain if you do not want to, but at least let
me show you about before you flee this deliciously wicked place."
His grip fastened upon her arm, and he drew her into a richly
decorated salon. Within, perfectly attired musicians sat upon a small
dais, playing quietly. About the room were properly garbed women,
some masked, and others not. "In this room," Trahern said, "ladies
who wish for a tiny bit of adventure outside the bonds of matrimony
come, and sit to await their cavaliers. Look over there, *mon ange.*

The lady in crimson velvet with the jeweled mask. Look closely, Aurora. It is Lady Estella Jarvis, and the gentleman seeking to escort her to a private room abovestairs is Lord Bolton, the prominent Whig politician. Ah, his plea has been successful. Come, we will follow. There are peepholes where we may observe."

"Are you mad, Trahern?" Aurora attempted to pull away, but his grip was very firm, and she doubted a cry for help in this place would do her any good. Still, she was horrified by the debauchery and drunkenness about her. As they reached the staircase, she yanked her arm from Trahern's grasp, and, turning, almost ran for the front door. "My cape!" she snapped to the attendant, who quickly complied. A servant flung open the door, and Aurora stepped forth back into the cool night. "Have Lord Trahern's carriage brought around at once," she commanded the liveried linkboy awaiting arrivals at the curb.

"Gracious, *mon ange*, you are far more proper than I had anticipated. I assumed it was a masquerade as it is with so many proper ladies," Trahern said, coming to her side.

"How dare you escort me to such a place!" Aurora said angrily. "I would tell my husband, except that he would call you out, and I wish no scandal to touch the Hawkesworth name. What on earth ever made you think I would enjoy such bawdy entertainment?"

"Your sister did," he replied.

Aurora climbed into the coach, settling her skirts irritably about her. "Trahern, you lie," she said bluntly to the man now sitting opposite her, smirking.

"Calandra was my mistress," he continued.

"Another lie!" Aurora snapped.

"How can you be so certain," he challenged her mockingly as the vehicle drew away from the Brimstone Club.

"My sister hated the physical requirements of marriage," Aurora said with surprising candor. "Making love was anathema for her. That is one of the reasons she ran away from Hawkes Hill and came to London. She would not accept the responsibilities that being the Duchess of Farminster entailed. Valerian had to bargain with her in his attempt to gain an heir. Had she birthed her child successfully, she was to be allowed to come up to London again for a season. The marriage was a nightmare for both of them, and I blame myself. Had I not tempted my sister with a ducal crown, she would not have married Valerian, nor been so unhappy, nor died in childbirth. Valerian and I would have been married back on St. Timothy, and we should have probably had a son by now. You may have lusted after Cally, Trahern, but you had nothing of her, I know, but a chaste kiss on the cheek, or the forehead. I do not understand why you should assume I would enjoy the Brimstone Club. You have made an error in judgment, I fear. I will pardon you, for your friendship has been invaluable to both me and to my husband these past months we have been in London. I would ask you, however, not to call upon me for the next few days."

He was struck silent by her words, astounded to learn that the divinely beauteous Calandra had been a cold and hollow shell. He knew Aurora Hawkesworth well enough to realize that she was not lying to him. He felt himself filled with icy anger. He had been taken in by the little colonial bitch. Calandra had been nothing more than a garden-variety coquette. She had carelessly trifled with his heart, hoodwinking him in the cruelest manner possible to believe that there was hope for him, when there had never been any hope at all.

Trahern knew now that the dramatic scenario of Hawkesworth murdering Calandra in a jealous rage was nought but the product of his fevered imagination. The bitch had died in childbirth just as they had said, and Hawkesworth, fearful of losing St. Timothy, had dragged Aurora to the altar. It was just that simple, and the wicked revenge he had concocted in an attempt to redress the wrong he thought done to Calandra was now useless. Or was it? Why should he not be revenged? Had Calandra not victimized him? Had not the farmer duke and his sharp-tongued wife used him in an effort to gain entrance into polite society here in London? His grievance against the Hawkesworths was justified. *He would be revenged!*

"I apologize to you, *mon ange*, and I shall certainly honor your request not to call for several days," he said calmly. *Bitch!* He would never call upon her again, but she needn't know that now.

Lord Trahern's coach drew up to Farminster House, and a well-trained footman was there to open the door. "Good evening, your grace," he said, helping her from the vehicle.

"Please do not bother getting out, Trahern," Aurora said, turning about and dismissing her escort rather sharply. "Good night." She hurried into the house without a backward glance. "Is his lordship home yet?" she demanded of Manners.

"Yes, your grace," he replied smoothly, noting her irritation.

"Good night, then," Aurora replied, and swiftly ascended the staircase, moving down the hallway to her apartments.

Martha was waiting for her, dozing lightly in a chair by the fire. She awoke immediately, saying, "You are home early, my lady," and then, seeing the look upon Aurora's face, asked, "What has happened? You're pale, and angry, I can tell it."

"Help me out of this horrid gown," Aurora said. "I will tell you as I undress," and she did.

"The cheek of the man!" Martha said indignantly. "I hope you'll not receive him again, my lady. He's a cad and a bounder for certain. I can only imagine what his grace will say."

"My husband is not to know, Martha. Valerian would only become angry and call Trahern out. Then we should have another scandal. I was not at the Brimstone Club for more than fifteen minutes. It just isn't worth all the fuss that will be made over it. I am not hurt, only angry."

"What will you tell your husband when Trahern finally calls again—if he dares, I mean," Martha wondered.

"If he does not come, so much the better," Aurora said. "If he does call in a few days' time, I will receive him, but as far as I am concerned, my friendship with Trahern is over. Not just because of his behavior tonight, but because of what he said about Cally. His mistress, indeed! If he had ever dared to approach her in *that* way, she would have repudiated him immediately."

"Indeed, she would have," Martha agreed. "She were spoiled, and sometimes arrogant was Miss Calandra, but her heart was good, and she was a lady like her mother." She helped Aurora on with her nightgown, and then, gathering up her finery, said, "I'll give these things to Sally and Molly to put away. Then we can all go to bed."

"I'll brush my own hair," Aurora said. She exited her dressing room, and walked across her bedroom to sit down at her dressing table and pick up her silver brush to brush her hair. In the mirror she saw the reflection of her husband, fast asleep in her bed. She smiled and pulled the pins from her hair. Running the brush through her long brown-gold hair, she thought how good it would be to be back in the country. That evening's experience had been most distasteful. What had she ever done to make Trahern assume that she would enjoy the Brimstone Club? The brush raced vigorously through her tresses. She had done nothing. Trahern was simply a strange man.

"You're back." The duke's voice came sleepily from the bed. "What time is it, my precious?"

"Just after eleven," Aurora said.

" 'Tis early," he replied. "Where did you go?"

"Trahern took me to some private party in St. James's. I knew no one, and I found it a wretched bore. I stayed but a few minutes, and then insisted he return me home. You know I did not want to go anyway." Putting her brush down, she crossed the room, and, pulling her nightgown off, slipped into bed beside him. "This is where I want to be, Valerian."

His arms wrapped about her. "Good," he said, pressing himself against her, "because this is where I want you to always be, Aurora." Then he kissed her, and it was, Aurora thought, all right again.

Chapter

⚜ 16 ⚜

"'Tis an odd question to be certain," the Earl of Bute said to the Duke of Farminster, "but do you know where your wife was last night, Valerian?" John Stuart poured himself and his guest crystal tumblers of smoky whiskey, brought down from his own Highland still in Scotland. He handed one to the duke, and keeping the other for himself, sat down opposite Valerian Hawkesworth. They were in the earl's private apartment in St. James's Palace. A cheerful fire burned in the stone fireplace, warming the spring chill off the room.

"Aurora was with Trahern," the duke said, "Why?"

"Do you know where it is they went?" Bute queried.

"A party near St. James's, I believe my wife said," the duke told him. "What is this all about, John? Why on earth would you be interested in Aurora's social life?"

"There is a terrible rumor making the rounds this morning, Valerian, and it involves your wife," the earl told him. "That she was with Trahern partly confirms the rumor, for he is very much a part of the gossip burning everyone's ears."

"From the seriousness of your demeanor, John, I think you must tell me what it is the tattletales are saying," the duke answered, and he slowly sipped the whiskey, appreciating its fineness.

John Stuart gazed deeply into his tumbler, then, taking a deep breath, he raised his head and looked directly at his companion. "Your wife was at the Brimstone Club. It is reported that she disported herself publicly, and in a manner both lewd and shocking."

"The Brimstone Club? I didn't know it was still in existence," the duke said, "and I am astounded that anything should be considered lewd or shocking in that fancy stew. Good God, John, you know the sort of randy shenanigans that go on there, and at the Hellfire. Aurora would have no part in such antics. Besides, she was home quite early, and very out of sorts with Trahern."

"Your wife is said to have auctioned her clothing off piece by piece until she was totally naked. Then Trahern offered her favors to any man who would take her publicly. Several men took him up, and used her. The debauch ended with Trahern whipping her buttocks red while she sucked Lord Bolton dry. Then Trahern sodomized her. When he had finished, she thanked the gentlemen involved for a delightful time, and covering her nakedness with a cloak, departed the Brimstone."

His temples were pounding, but Valerian Hawkesworth managed to retain a semblance of calm. "And just why is everyone convinced that this wanton creature was my wife?" he asked. "Certainly being in Charles Trahern's company is not enough."

"The woman was masked," the Earl of Bute said, "but many had seen your wife arrive in a rather striking gown earlier. She obviously donned the mask later on in an attempt to conceal her identity, but that rose and gold gown gave her away."

"My wife did go out with Trahern last night," the duke said, "and indeed she was wearing a rose and gold gown. But she was home quite early, and we spent the night together. It cannot have been Aurora, John. The question is, who was it, and why are they attempting to defame my name?"

"The incident did take place quite late," the earl said thoughtfully. "I know that because the men involved in the episode are several of the most fashionable men in society. They would not be caught at the Brimstone before midnight. The time is easy enough to check, but we must clear up this scandal quickly before it reaches the king's ears. If it does, neither you nor your wife will be allowed in their majesties' presence ever again. You know what *he's* like, and the queen will obey his directive even if she disagrees with him."

"What do you suggest?" the duke asked.

"I believe I shall begin by making discreet inquiries of the parties involved, and even though you believe your wife innocent of such behavior, you should question her. After all, she was with Trahern, and she was seen entering the Brimstone earlier in the evening," the Earl of Bute replied. "We must first ascertain that it was not the Duchess of Farminster, as the gossips believe. Then we shall seek to find out who it was, why they were masquerading as your wife, and most important, who began the rumor so quickly. It is very unusual for the members of the Brimstone to boast of their adventures publicly."

Valerian Hawkesworth returned home to Farminster House. He found his wife in the Writing Room. "To whom are you writing?" he asked her, sitting down near her.

"My mother," she answered him. "I have not heard from her since I wrote her about Cally's death. Betsy has written to say that she is heartbroken, but Mama has not answered any of my correspondence to her. She holds me responsible for Cally's demise. I know she does! Still, I will continue to write her in the hope that she will eventually forgive me."

"Were you at the Brimstone Club last evening?" he said. He made his query a direct one so she might not lie to him.

"I never imagined such a place existed. It was awful!" Aurora replied. "As soon as I saw the kind of place that Trahern had brought me to, I insisted he bring me home."

"Why did you not tell me the truth when I asked you where you were last night?" the duke pressed his wife.

"You know the sort of place it is, Valerian. I feared that you might be angry at Trahern and call him out. I did not want another scandal. There was no harm done, as I departed quickly. I have told Trahern he may not call on me for several days. I am really quite put out with him that he would assume I should enjoy such entertainment. He said he had taken Cally there, which I know to be untrue. Cally would have been even more horrified than I was. He also had the temerity to claim that Cally was his lover. Another lie! I believe we have misjudged Lord Trahern. He is no gentleman," Aurora concluded. Reaching over, she put her hand on his. "Promise me you will not call him out. He is not worth the fuss, my love."

"I have just come from Lord Bute's. He informed me there is a terrible rumor making the rounds, involving you and Trahern," the duke said to his wife.

"What sort of rumor?" she asked. She was beginning to look angry. Not guilty. Not fearful. *Angry.*

He told her everything John Stuart had told him, watching her closely as he spoke for the least little sign of culpability. There was none.

Instead, Aurora grew pale with shock. A wave of disgust overcame her countenance, and then her anger burst forth. "How dare anyone assume that some masked strumpet in a rose and gold gown was me!"

"Where is the gown?" her husband asked.

"Manners! Fetch Martha here at once," Aurora called to the butler, and when her maid stood before her, she asked, "Where is the gown I wore last night, Martha?"

"Why, in the wardrobe, my lady. Remember, I give it to Sally to put away," Martha replied.

"Fetch it, please," Aurora said.

The three of them ascended the stairs to Aurora's apartments. Martha hurried into the dressing room to seek out the requested garment. She returned some minutes later, a puzzled look upon her face. "I can't find it, my lady. It ain't where it should be, and it ain't anywheres else. I give it to Sally with clear instructions. She was to brush the gown and put it in the wardrobe."

"Fetch Sally," the duke said.

"I will skin the wench if she is behind this," Aurora said furiously. "She was Cally's maid, and I kept her on because of it, but I have never really liked her. She is too sly by far."

The duke nodded. "Manners has spoken to me about her on more than one occasion. She's too pert."

Martha returned with Sally. "I ain't told her nothing," the older servant said.

"Where is the rose and gold gown I wore last night, Sally?" Aurora asked the servant.

"Why, it's in the wardrobe, m'lady," came the too-quick reply.

"It is not," Aurora said.

"Well, then, I ain't got no idea where it might be," Sally retorted, but not once did she look directly at her mistress.

"To whom did you give the gown, Sally? And do not lie to me, girl," the duke said sternly. "The truth now!"

Sally shifted on her feet nervously, eyes lowered. "I don't know what you mean, your grace," she said.

"You're lying," Valerian Hawkesworth said, and he grasped the maid hard upon her upper arm.

"Owwwww!" Sally struggled to break his grip. "Yer hurting me, yer grace! Let me go!"

"Not until I learn the truth of this matter," he said harshly. "Now, once again, girl. What did you do with the gown?" He gave her a shake, glaring angrily into her face.

Sally began to cry. "Yer ladyship! Are you going to let him treat me like this? And after all the time I been with your family? Ain't you got no gratitude?"

"If I had my way, Sally," Aurora said in a hard voice, "you'd be beaten until you couldn't walk! You are a bold baggage, and you have, for whatever reason, stolen my gown. I want to know why, and if you do not tell me, I shall have you trussed up like a pig ready for market and tossed in the river!"

"Ohhhh, yer lordship, you wouldn't let her do that, would you?" Sally wailed. "That would be murder!"

"You are her grace's servant, girl, and hers to do with as she pleases," the duke answered. "Besides, who would look for you? What is one bad servant more or less to London?"

"Have the footmen bind her," Aurora spoke.

"Owwwww! I'll tell! *I'll tell!*" Sally screeched. "Don't kill me, please!"

"Very well," the duke replied, releasing his hold on her arm. "Speak, girl."

"It was Lord Trahern! I give him the gown! But he promised to return it, he did, the liar!" Sally sobbed. "You wasn't to know, my lady. He said he wanted it to play a joke on someone, and that he would bring it right back, but he didn't."

"When did Trahern ask you, Sally?" Aurora queried her.

"A few days ago I went to the chemist to get you yer soap, my lady. He come upon me in the street, and tells me he is taking you to a special party on Tuesday night, but that he doesn't think you'll like it so you'll probably come home early. Then he says he wants the gown you wear that evening to play a jest, and says he'll bring it right back. I waited for him all night downstairs by the kitchen entrance, but he never come. I was going to ask him when he came calling on yer ladyship again. I didn't think you would notice the gown gone 'cause you really didn't like it so's you wouldn't be looking for it anytime real soon. How did you find out so quick?" She sniffled, wiping her runny nose with her arm.

"Lord Trahern has indeed played a jest, Sally, but it is a rather wicked one that threatens to destroy my good name," Aurora told the sniveling maid. "If, however, you repeat your story to a certain person, then I shall not dismiss you from my service, but you will no longer serve me personally in your present capacity. If you do not cooperate with me, then you will go out on the street this very night in naught but the clothing you are wearing, and no reference as well."

"I'll do whatever you want me to, your ladyship," Sally said. "I really didn't mean to cause no trouble, but Lord Trahern promised me half a crown when he returned the gown. I ain't likely to see that much money all at one time again. I didn't think a gentleman would cheat a poor servant," she finished piteously.

"Leave us," Aurora ordered the servant. "Martha, go with her and remain with her until I need you."

"Yes, my lady," Martha said. She was openly puzzled by all the proceedings, and looked quizzically at her mistress.

"I will explain shortly," Aurora said, catching her look.

Martha nodded, and escorted the chastened Sally from the room, giving her a slap as they went.

"So we now have the answer to how your gown returned to the Brimstone Club," the duke said.

"What do we do next?" Aurora asked her husband.

"Bute is discreetly interviewing the participants in last night's proceedings. We need to know at what hour the events took place. Manners and the other servants know at what time you returned home, and at what time you left with Trahern earlier. Why, I wonder, has he perpetrated such a hoax? I shall have to call him out."

"Please don't, Valerian!" she begged him. "So far this scandal has not spread or become open. Trahern has appeared for all the world to see as our friend, and even, in some eyes, our sponsor. If you force him to a duel, it will all come out. There are many who would believe me guilty of this shameless behavior because they enjoy thinking ill of others. They would claim our servants lied to protect us, to protect their places in our household. We would never be believed. But if we can keep this from going any further, then our good name will be saved. Please, I beg of you, do not allow your anger to overrule your good sense, and challenge Trahern."

"Very well," the duke promised his wife, "but I cannot bear the thought of him getting away scot-free with such a hoax."

"I, too, want revenge," Aurora admitted.

"What would embarrass Trahern and make him the unhappiest of all, I wonder," Valerian considered.

"Marriage to an unsuitable woman. A marriage he could not get out of that would put him beyond the pale of the court, and of polite society. Charles Trahern is such a snob," Aurora said, "that he could not bear it if he were no longer a part of our world."

"I want Trahern to suffer, not some innocent woman," Valerian replied. "I don't mind making him miserable, but not a poor woman with whom I have no quarrel, my darling."

"It doesn't have to be some retiring creature unable to defend herself against Trahern," Aurora said. "Let us find the whore he hired to impersonate me. I'll bet she'd jump at being *Lady* Trahern, and if she's as bold as they say she was last night, she is perfectly capable of defending herself, isn't she?"

"You are diabolical," he told her admiringly. "Yes, it might work, my precious."

"I am certain the Earl of Bute will secretly help us, and the public disclosure of such a marriage will put Charles Trahern very much at a disadvantage. A man who would marry such a woman and keep it secret can hardly be either reliable or truthful," Aurora finished triumphantly.

"Agreed," her husband responded, "but first we must make certain that your reputation is not tarnished. I shall immediately return to St. James's Palace and tell the earl of our findings."

"I will go with you," Aurora said.

"No, my darling, you will not. If you are to appear to be the innocent party in all of this, you must not be involved," the duke replied, kissing his wife atop her head.

"If it will help any, Valerian, I saw Lady Jarvis at the Brimstone. I do not know if she saw me. She went upstairs with Lord Bolton, who, you have told me, was later involved with the woman in the rose and gold gown." '

"I will tell the earl," he said, and then he departed Farminster House for St. James's.

"I have managed to pinpoint the time of the incident," John Stuart said as the duke rejoined them. "It was between one and two o'clock in the morning. Two of the gentlemen involved remember hearing the mantel clock in the room where they were gathered strike two as Trahern began his final act of debauchery on the woman. And both say they did not arrive at the Brimstone until just after one."

"And I have discovered that my wife's undermaid was bribed by Trahern to give him the gown Aurora wore last night. When we sought for it, it was gone, and the wench was forced to a confession.

She waited up all night for him to return it, and give her her half-crown."

"So the bounder didn't even make good on his debt," John Stuart said, shaking his head in disapproval. "Well, our next step is to find the whore Trahern used for this masquerade."

"How on earth can we do that?"

The Earl of Bute smiled wickedly. "When playing at politics, my dear Hawkesworth, it is always wise to have a friend or two in the London underworld. They are little different than we are actually. They want the same things. Power and wealth. We play our games within the boundaries of the law, and they play them on the other side of the law. Both of us are equally ruthless in our manipulation of the populace, but we do so under the guise of proper society. They rely on no such niceties. Even as you and I speak, the woman we seek is being sought. She will brag to someone about her little adventurous escapade, and we shall find her, I promise you."

"Aurora has concocted a delicious revenge upon Trahern," the duke said, and then he told the earl.

John Stuart laughed aloud, then said, "What a wonderful way to rid ourselves of that obsequious little toad! By Jove, we shall do it, Hawkesworth! I know a not-too-respectable clergyman, not yet defrocked, who will perform the ceremony. I shall give you his name, for, of course, as the king's closest adviser, I must not appear to be involved in the slightest."

"Trahern will have to be quite drunk," the duke said. "Will your parson cooperate under such circumstances?"

"A gold piece and a bottle of whiskey will gain you whatever you seek from this man," the earl assured him with a laugh.

Suddenly a hidden door opened in the paneled wall, and a man stepped into the room. He was dressed respectably, but so anonymous in appearance was he that the duke thought you would not be able to pick him out of a group. The man bowed, saying in a gruff voice, "Good even', your lordship. I got what you want, and I come as quick as I could, as you say it's a matter of importance."

"Good evening to you, Mr. Wiggums. May I introduce my friend,

Valerian Hawkesworth, the Duke of Farminster. Will you have a
whiskey?" He was already pouring a tumblerful as he asked.

"I will, and thank ye," Mr. Wiggums replied, taking the tumbler
and bolting it down. "Ye've got the finest whiskey in all of London,
yer lordship, and that's no lie. I doubt even the king's whiskey is
as good." He smacked his lips appreciatively, putting down the
crystal with a thump.

"You are right, Mr. Wiggums, it isn't," the Earl of Bute said.
"Now, what have you for me?"

"The wench you want goes by the name of Merry Maybelle.
Rather fancies 'erself too, I can tell you. She ain't got no pimp, nor
madam fronting for 'er, and she don't walk the streets. She's got
two wee rooms in Tanners Alley, near the river. Some young lord
brought 'er to London from the country a few years ago, and when
he deserted 'er she was smart enough to move on to another young
fellow of means. The word is she's a clever wench, and saves 'er
money so she can entertain 'er gentlemen callers privately. She also
sells flowers at the theater, which gives 'er a chance to flirt and spot
prospective marks," Mr. Wiggums explained.

"What number in Tanners Alley?" the earl inquired.

"Third 'ouse on the left. Merry Maybelle is on the second floor,
in the rear, overlooking the river. There's no way out but the way
you come in, yer lordship."

"I want the girl here within the hour, Mr. Wiggums. Can you be
discreet?" the earl said.

"Ain't I always, yer lordship?" the man said, and then without
another word he turned about and disappeared through the hidden
door, which shut silently behind him.

"We have only but to wait," the earl said pleasantly. "Do you
fancy a game of cards, Hawkesworth?"

When the hidden door reopened exactly one hour later, Mr.
Wiggums entered the room again, drawing a young woman with
him. While Aurora was of medium height, this girl was tall, but she
had dark blond hair that dressed properly might have passed for his
wife's color in the right light. Her proportions, while not overlarge,
were generous, and in keeping with her height. The amber eyes

darting about the room, observing the two gentlemen, were intelligent.

"Please wait, Mr. Wiggums," the earl said, and then he turned his attention to the girl. "Now, Mistress Maybelle, I am far more powerful and dangerous than the gentleman who hired you for last night's performance at the Brimstone Club. Please answer my questions honestly, and no harm will come to you. There may even be a small something in it for you if you tell the truth. Do you understand?"

"Yes, m'lord," the young woman answered.

"Do you know the name of the gentleman who hired you last night?"

"Yes, m'lord, it were Lord Trahern" was the answer.

"Did he tell you why he was hiring you?" the earl said.

"Just that he was playing a trick on a lady friend of his," Maybelle responded. "I thought it was a rather odd trick, but he wasn't asking me to do anything I hadn't done before, and he promised me two gold crowns if I went along with him. He give me one when I agreed to help him, but he never give me the other when it was over," Maybelle said indignantly. "Said he would have to owe it to me! I don't give credit. If I did, I'd be in the street!"

Valerian Hawkesworth swallowed back a laugh and saw from the look on John Stuart's face that he, too, was struggling manfully with his own amusement, but to laugh would have offended the woman before them, who in her own way was quite ethical.

"Did Lord Trahern give you a gown to wear?" the earl continued on with his gentle interrogation.

"Oh, yes!" Maybelle said enthusiastically. "I were real upset he made me auction it off piece by piece. It were by far the prettiest gown I ever wore. I'd have taken it off, if he asked, without selling it," she said mournfully.

"Did you know any of the gentlemen involved other than Lord Trahern?" John Stuart questioned the girl further.

"Two of them, but I never spoke except at the end to thank the gentlemen nicely as Lord Trahern had instructed me," she told him.

"Which two?"

"Lord Shelley and Sir Roger Andrews, and I seen Lord Bolton once at a party I was invited to, but I was never introduced formal-like," Maybelle explained.

"Did Shelley or Andrews recognize you?" the earl queried.

"Sir Roger might have," she replied. "He kept looking at me real close, over and over, while I was there. It really began to make me nervous, I can tell you," Maybelle said.

"Sit down, Mistress Maybelle," the earl told the girl. Then he turned to Mr. Wiggums. "Do you know Sir Roger Andrews?"

"Aye, m'lord, I do. I've lent 'im a wee bit of coin on occasion. 'E always pays on time. A real gentleman, 'e is."

"Fetch him!" the earl snapped, and Mr. Wiggums was quickly gone.

"Will you have something to drink while we wait, Mistress Maybelle?" the earl inquired solicitously.

"Wouldn't mind a tad of something" was the reply.

"Whiskey or sherry?" he asked.

"Whiskey, sir," she said.

"Valerian?"

The duke shook his head.

The earl, to be polite, joined his female guest in liquid refreshment, and they sat quietly awaiting the arrival of Sir Roger. When he arrived, coming through the hidden door with Mr. Wiggums, the young peer's jaw dropped, recognizing both the earl and the duke. He bowed politely, and then his eye went to Maybelle.

"So it was you last night!" he said. "I thought so! And Trahern, that outsider, insisting that it was the Duchess of F. Your pardon, my lord! I meant no offense."

"Which is why we are here, Andrews," the earl said. "A lady's reputation is at stake, as is her family's good name. You are certain it was not the lady Trahern insists it was?"

"Good Lord, no! At first, of course, I didn't know, and then I wasn't certain, but then this morning I woke up and knew it was Maybelle. She wears this violet perfume, and I don't know any other lady who does; and she's got this heart-shaped birthmark on her left breast, just above the nipple. Not another one like it in the world, I'm quite certain!"

"Do you think any of the other men involved know who it was, Andrews?" the earl asked him.

"Lord Shelley was certain it wasn't the duchess, despite Trahern. He said her hair wasn't that color, and her perfume was entirely different, more like country air, and less exotic. Shelley said he danced with the duchess at several balls, and her eyes are blue, not brown like Maybelle's here. We couldn't figure out Trahern's game, but we surely did have a good time."

Maybelle giggled coyly. "Why don't you come and see me, then, Sir Roger? Number three, Tanners Alley, second floor rear."

The young man grinned back at her.

"You will sign a statement to that effect, Andrews?" the earl said quietly. "And you, Mistress Maybelle, if we write down your story, will you put your mark to it?"

"I can sign me name," Maybelle said proudly.

"Excellent, my dear," the Earl of Bute replied with a smile. Then he reached out and drew upon the bellpull. A moment later a young man entered the room. "Franklyn, I would like you to take down several statements. Please get your writing box."

The statements were drawn up, and read over by both Sir Roger Andrews and Maybelle. Both signed without hesitation. Mr. Wiggums had been dispatched to fetch lords Shelley and Bolton. Sir Roger and the girl were told to be seated and remain quiet. They sat on a far and slightly darkened side of the room. Lord Shelley arrived first, explaining that Mr. Wiggums had said he was wanted by the Earl of Bute over at St. James's Palace. One quick look around the chamber at its other occupants, and he knew immediately why he had been sent for.

Lord Shelley bowed to the earl and the duke. "This is about last night at the Brimstone, I presume," he said.

The earl nodded. "We cannot allow Hawkesworth's good name or his wife's reputation to be compromised by such a nasty prank. Sir Roger says you know it wasn't the duchess. Will you sign a statement to that effect?"

"Of course," Lord Shelley replied. "But why is it even necessary? Certainly no one there really believed it was Lady Hawkesworth, my lords. Granted the wench was an excellent fuck, but her skin had not the fine texture of a lady's. No one was fooled."

"Trahern has developed a grudge," the duke said briefly. "He is attempting to spread the rumor, and if it reaches the king's ear, both my wife and I could lose their majesties' friendship if we have not the means to repudiate such a nasty rumor."

"The man is a lowlife, a hanger-on, a scoundrel," Lord Shelley said. "If he were an animal, I would put him out of his misery for all our sakes. Pity he ain't."

"Lord Trahern will regret his actions, I promise you," the duke replied grimly.

Lord Shelley signed his statement, and then joined Sir Roger and Merry Maybelle on the darkened side of the room.

Suddenly the hidden door opened and Lord Bolton, protesting, was pushed into the room by Mr. Wiggums. "Bute!" he snarled. "Is this your doing? You had better have a damned good explanation!"

The earl quietly explained.

"Don't have the slightest idea of what you're talking about," the Whig politician said. "I would never go to the Brimstone."

Valerian Hawkesworth gritted his teeth angrily. The Whigs were currently out of power, and were making strenuous efforts to thwart the king and the Earl of Bute at every turn.

"Bolton, a lady's good name is at stake," the earl said.

"Has nothing to do with me" was the reply.

Lord Shelley and Sir Roger stood up and came forward.

"Both Percy and I saw you quite plainly," Sir Roger said.

"And if you say so, you'll damn yourselves with his majesty," Bolton said smugly. "We all know what a prig he is in matters concerning morals. Makes no difference to me that the farmer duke's wife is slandered or not. Anyone who consorts with that bounder Trahern gets what they deserve."

John Stuart reached out a hand to calm the Duke of Farminster. "We can, of course, call Lady Jarvis, my lord. I do not believe she would jeopardize her place with the queen, or with her husband, to save you from scandal," the earl replied.

"L-Lady Jarvis?" Lord Bolton stuttered slightly.

"Do not deny it, Bolton. You were seen," the earl told him. "Now will you cooperate with us?"

"But the king will see," Bolton protested.

"No, he will not," the earl promised. "If this matter comes to the king's attention, and he takes it seriously, then and only then will the statements be brought forth for his eyes alone. There will be two copies. One with your full name, and the other with only an initial. That is what I will show the king. The other documents will remain in my safe, to be destroyed after the king is satisfied as to Lady Hawkesworth's innocence."

"Very well," Lord Bolton grumbled. "I suppose I must trust you, Bute. Never trusted a Tory before."

"You should embrace each new experience with eagerness," said the Earl of Bute dryly.

When Lord Bolton had signed his statement, the earl dismissed the three gentlemen with his thanks, and the admonition not to speak of that evening's events. All agreed. Now the earl and the duke turned their attention to Mistress Maybelle, who had begun to look a trifle nervous to find herself again alone with them.

"How would you like to be *Lady* Trahern, my dear?" the earl began. "After all, the cad owes you, does he not?"

"It would not be an easy marriage," the duke quickly interposed. "You realize that you are quite unsuitable for him, and he will be very angry to find himself bound to you in most legal and holy wedlock."

To their surprise, Maybelle came from the shadows, poured herself another tumbler of the earl's whiskey, and then, sitting down, looked them both in the eye, saying, "What's in it for me? This is how yer going to revenge yerself, ain't it, yer lordship? Well, the truth of the matter is that I quite fancy being a *lady*. A *real* lady, not just some tricked-into-marriage wife for yer convenience."

"What do you want?" the earl asked her.

"Well," Maybelle told him, "I know I ain't a bad-looking female.

With the right clothes I might look the part, but I don't know nothing about being a lady. Because I'm a whore don't mean I don't want to better myself. I weren't born a whore. I was born a farmer's daughter in Essex, and foolish enough to listen to the master's younger son when he said he loved me. But when he left me, I didn't go to pieces. I saw quick enough once we got to London how it was going to be, and him always delaying the wedding. I made certain I had enough to live on before he went off. I've picked and chosen the men I wanted to protect me, but it ain't no easy life, and I'm twenty-five now, and here in London ten years. I got to think of my old age now, I do. I'll help you, but you got to help me. I want a sum of money put aside with a goldsmith of my choosing first off, and then I want lessons in how to be a lady."

"How much?" the duke asked her.

"Five hundred pounds, yer lordship. I can live comfortable the rest of my life on that, and it ain't, I suspect, that much to you. Call it my dowry"—she smiled—" 'cept the bridegroom ain't going to get it to gamble away. Don't think I don't know Lord Trahern ain't got a pot to piss in, because I do know."

"Why do you want *lessons* in being a lady?" the earl asked her, quite curious by the request.

"Yer little lordling will eventually drink himself into the grave or desert me," Maybelle said. "Once he weds me, his own kind won't want to have anything to do with him, will they? Well, when he's gone I can set myself up with a nice dress shop, and while I won't get the gentry for customers, I'll get those just below them on the social ladder because I'm a damned good seamstress, but only if I knows how to talk right, and have nice manners, yer lordship," the girl finished.

"I will pay your dowry, Mistress Maybelle," the duke said quietly. "Is it only the money that convinces you to help me?"

"Nah," she told him. "Look, yer lordship, I'm tired of being a whore. I knows better, but how on earth am I ever going to be able to get out of the life I've made for myself, and into a new life, if I don't take a chance. Yer offer is a heaven-sent opportunity."

"Trahern will not be easy," he warned her.

"I know he won't," Maybelle replied. Then, "Does he own any property at all? I mean a place I can call home."

"He has a small house down in Suffolk somewhere," the duke said, "and, of course, he keeps rooms here in London."

Maybelle nodded. "Any family?"

"A younger sister married to a clergyman and a younger brother in the army," John Stuart supplied. "The brother is out in India, and unmarried, I believe."

"So he'll get the title one day when my Charlie kicks the bucket," Maybelle said thoughtfully.

"Unless you give Trahern an heir," the earl said, smiling.

"Don't want no brats fouling up my life," she replied, "unless, of course, that house in Suffolk is entailed on the title. His rooms here in Suffolk he'll be renting."

"The house could be in debt," the duke warned.

"You'll find out for me, my lord?" Maybelle turned to the Earl of Bute. "I'll marry the devil whenever you want me to, but I'll need to know sooner than later if the house can be mine one day without having a kid. You understand. I got to take care of meself 'cause I don't have anyone else who will."

"You don't have to do this," Valerian Hawkesworth said, feeling guilty already, but the young woman soothed him immediately.

"Listen, yer lordship, I'd marry old Scratch himself for five hundred pounds. Don't you feel sorry for me now. I knows just what I'm getting myself into, and I can handle his lordship."

"Very well, then, Mistress Maybelle," the Earl of Bute said. "Hawkesworth, do you have a plan?"

"I do" came the solemn reply. "Oh, I most certainly do."

Chapter

17

Charles Trahern was astounded to receive an invitation to the Duke and Duchess of Farminster's farewell ball. At first he thought it must be a mistake, that the duchess's social secretary had forgotten to strike his name from their list of welcome guests, but no retraction came. Then a few days later he received a note penned in Aurora's own hand saying although she was still quite piqued at his taking her to that *awful* club, she would forgive him, and was looking forward to seeing him at their ball. He was amazed.

Had they not heard the rumors about her? Come to think of it, no one had heard the rumors he had sought to have spread. All the gentlemen involved in that delightful night of debauchery, rather than bragging about it, were astonishingly silent on the matter. Of course, none of them had been that drunk, and when he reconsidered the whole affair, he realized that none of them were fooled. It had probably been put down to a wicked prank on Trahern's part. On one hand, he was relieved, and on the other, a bit disappointed. And now the Hawkesworths were leaving London. He knew it was not likely he would meet up with them again. So, he would go to their ball. It was to be a masked and costumed affair, and he did love such spectacles!

"I shall go as Romeo," he said aloud to himself, and then he sat down and wrote a note to Aurora accepting the invitation and telling her of his costume plans.

Aurora laughed when she read Trahern's missive. "Make certain you run into him at Boodles," she told her husband, "and be sure he doesn't change his plans. We have the perfect Juliet for him, my darling, don't we?"

The white and gold ballroom at Farminster House was turned out vigorously over the next few days. The paint and the gilt was touched up. The parquet floor was waxed until it shone brightly. Even the gilt ceiling moldings and the painted ceiling of the ball-room itself were inspected for damage and repaired where necessary. The crystal chandeliers were carefully lowered, and each individual arm, candle saucer, and teardrop washed and carefully polished, as were the matching crystal and silver sconces attached to the walls. Each of the lighting fixtures was neatly fitted with beeswax candles that would burn evenly and not smoke too greatly. The windows were cleaned both inside and out. The sky-blue satin draperies hanging from those windows were brushed free of cobwebs and dust, their heavy gold rope tiebacks replaced with new ones.

A dais was set up at one end of the room for the musicians. The musicians had been hired, and carefully instructed in their duties. The ball would be opened and closed with a minuet, but Aurora also wanted lively Scotch reels, the contredanse, the écossaise, and other English country dances played as well. This would not be a dull and stuffy evening like so many balls. Her guests would have fun.

As for the invitations, they were hard to come by, as the ballroom at Farminster House could comfortably contain only about one hun-dred and fifty people. Since King George and Queen Charlotte had accepted their invitation, the Hawkesworths' farewell ball had become one of the last real social events of the season. There were many who felt to be left out was to lose social standing. Consequently, many of the lesser families departed London for their country houses in an effort to appear as if they had important business elsewhere and couldn't possibly attend another ball this season.

There was a rectangular room next to the ballroom known as the Buffet Room. It, too, was turned out, and an enormous mahogany table covered in Irish linen and lace was set up to contain the refreshments which would, of course, include an unlimited supply of French champagne. Small gilt chairs upholstered in rose and cream tapestry as well as chairs done in pale blue velvet were set all about the ballroom and the buffet. There would be a cloakroom, and two rooms set aside for a ladies' necessary and a gentlemen's necessary. Favors were chosen to give the guests. Small silver gilt snuffboxes for the gentlemen, and pomander balls tied with gilt ribbons for the ladies. A menu was chosen for the midnight buffet; the flatware, the candelabra, and serving pieces were polished; and all was in readiness. Fresh flowers would be brought in to be arranged and set about on the day of the Farminster ball.

Maybelle, whose last name it turned out was Monypenny, was brought discreetly to the house several times to be fitted for her costume. She was quite a pretty girl, mannerly, and quiet-spoken. She had already begun her lessons in deportment. She watched carefully as the seamstress fitted and pinned the costume, making one or two gentle suggestions to the woman, which were at first received with surprise, and then gratitude, for Maybelle obviously knew her way with a needle, and the seamstress said so approvingly.

The Juliet gown was of creamy velvet, fitted beneath the bosom, the sleeves long and coming to a point at the wrists, the narrow skirt falling in graceful folds about its wearer's feet, which would be shod in flat satin slippers. The neckline of the gown was trimmed with dainty lilac-colored silk flowers, and there would be a gold brocade girdle about Maybelle's hips. Her dark blond hair would be confined in a golden caul, and her swansdown feather mask would be decorated in tiny pearls and diamanté. When the final fitting was done, Maybelle looked every bit the lady she wanted to be.

The king and the queen would be coming as two of their royal ancestors, King Edward III and his queen, Phillipa of Hainault. Valerian and Aurora had decided on simpler costumes, that of a Roman general and his wife, a proper Roman matron. As they stood greeting their guests on the night of the ball, both the duke and the duchess were delighted by the variety of costumes that entered Farminster House, passing up the staircase to the receiving line. There was a Henry VIII and all of his six wives; a Richard, Coeur de Lion; Robin Hood and Maid Marian; Turkish sultans and sultanas; lords and ladies of bygone eras; a Louis XIV in his red high heels; several devils; two cardinals; seven medieval monks; pirates, Gypsies, and some ancient British warriors. Sir Roger Andrews came as a colonial frontiersman, Lord Shelley as a harlequin, the Earl of Bute, a Scots warrior.

Because the king rarely varied his bedtime hour, the handwritten invitations read "eight o'clock." The royal couple arrived at a quarter to nine, and the ball officially began with the Duke of Farminster partnering Queen Charlotte, and his wife, King George, in the stately figure of the minuet. As they danced, the king said, "Madam, I have lately heard a most unpleasant rumor, which I was relieved to learn was naught but that. Do you know of what I speak?"

"My husband has mentioned that Lord Trahern attempted to play a rather naughty jest upon me, but was stopped. Valerian would not go into detail, your majesty, for he said the jest was in such poor and dreadful taste that a decent woman should not hear of it. I was, of course, quite put out that our friendship should be repaid in so unkind a manner, but I have forgiven Trahern for my dear late sister's sake. She was always quite fond of him."

"A most charitable and Christian attitude, my dear lady," the king said approvingly. "And the duke was quite right not to divulge the full extent of Lord Trahern's perfidy. The slander was not one fit for a lady's ears. It was quite poor judgment on Trahern's part, and I shall personally admonish him myself, madam."

"I thank your majesty for his kindness and his friendship," Aurora replied sweetly, "but most of all, I am grateful that your majesty would reach out to protect my good name. It is a comfort to know I have two such fine knights such as yourself and my husband."

"Quite so, madam! Quite so!" the king said, bowing gracefully to her as the dance came to an end.

"Excellent," the duke told his wife when she had repeated her encounter with the king. "He heard, was assured it was false, did not believe anyway, and is suspicious of Trahern. Now Trahern's marriage cannot help but destroy him and his credibility in the eyes of polite society. I am very pleased by this turn of events."

The king and his wife departed exactly an hour after they had arrived, but the ball went on into the wee hours. More and more of the lively country dances were played. The champagne flowed more freely than at any other ball that season, it was noted by those who kept track of such things. The Duke of Farminster's hospitality could not be faulted in the slightest. The guests began to depart, warmly thanking their host and hostess for a most enjoyable evening. Finally only Sir Roger, Lord Shelley, and Trahern remained. The musicians had been paid, and were packing up their instruments.

"More champagne!" Trahern called to a passing footman, who obliged as he had been instructed. Charles Trahern was quite drunk and slightly confused. Not once had Aurora danced with him that evening, and he could not understand why after her conciliatory note to him. Each time he had approached her she had disappeared into the crowd, and several times she had insisted that rather than dance with him, he dance with a mysterious lady garbed as Juliet. The lady had simpered and giggled at him, and even permitted him to steal a kiss, but not once had she spoken to him. Now she appeared out of the shadows of the ballroom and plunked herself down in his lap.

"Hello, Charlie," she said to him, and provocatively wiggled her ample bottom against him.

He slid his hand boldly down her neckline, giving a rather big breast a good squeeze and tweaking the nipple. "You're nice," he mumbled, nuzzling her neck. "What's your name?"

"Why, Juliet, my Romeo," she answered him.

"Wanna fuck?" he said crudely.

Maybelle giggled. "You're bold! Have some more champagne, Charlie. Juliet's a virgin, and don't fuck without a wedding band."

Lord Trahern stood up, almost dumping the woman on his lap upon the floor. "Then le's get married," he slurred drunkenly. "I saw lots of monks here tonight. Any left who can marry us?"

The single footman filled Trahern's glass again, and he drank it down quickly, holding it out for another refill.

"The man's a fool," murmured Sir Roger. "Closing the trap on him's almost too easy. Ain't no sport in it at all."

"The fun comes when he realizes what he's done and that he can't get out of it," Lord Shelley said, laughing softly.

"Where's the priest!" Trahern half shouted. "Can't fuck Juliet till she has her marriage!"

"Why, Charles, you rogue," the duke said, coming forward with a cleric. "So you want to wed this pretty creature, do you?"

"Aye, your grace, I'll marry her, and then we get to fuck!" Lord Trahern said enthusiastically. "Where's your good lady. She can be Juliet's witness!"

"Here I am, Charles," Aurora said, coming forward.

"Wouldn't dance with me this evening," he muttered. "Why wouldn't you dance with me, Aurora?"

"Poor Charles," she said. "I'm sorry, but my duties as your hostess just overwhelmed me. I promise you two dances at the next ball we attend, all right?"

Trahern quaffed down his glass of champagne, saying, "Le's get married, Juliet!"

The ceremony was duly performed, and then Trahern signed the papers put before him by the duke, his hand guided by the clergyman, for it was shaking as his excesses of the evening began to overtake him. The Duke and Duchess of Farminster along with Lord Shelley and Sir Roger signed the marriage papers as witnesses. The minister was paid most generously, and departed with his bag of coins and two bottles of French champagne. While Aurora distracted Trahern, the duke took the new Lady Trahern aside.

"I had your husband sign two sets of the papers. If he should ever find yours, come to me for the duplicates," Valerian Hawkesworth told Maybelle.

"He ain't going to find 'em," she said firmly. "After he sobers up and sees 'em, I'll give 'em to the goldsmith to keep safe. My witnesses will speak up for me, won't they?"

"They will, your ladyship," the duke said, and he kissed Maybelle's hand. To his surprise, she did not giggle or simper.

"Thank you for your friendship, your grace," she said quietly.

The three men loaded Trahern into the duke's coach, the duke giving his coachmen instructions to help her ladyship get her husband into his house, and his bed, before departing. The carriage rumbled off, and the three men reentered the house where Aurora was awaiting them with a celebratory glass of champagne.

"Gentlemen," she said, raising her glass to them, "I thank you for your help in protecting my good name. You will always be welcomed at Hawkes Hill by my husband and me. We are in your debt."

"Actually, madam," Sir Roger said, "it was rather fun," and he grinned mischievously.

"Never liked Trahern anyway," Lord Shelley said. "Man's a damned scoundrel. Actually feel sorry for the wench."

"You need not," the duke promised him. "Lady Maybelle Trahern is quite up to the task of handling her husband."

"Can't wait to brut it about tomorrow at Boodles," chortled Sir Roger. "I imagine if Trahern dares to show his face, he'll have quite a head. Ha! Ha!"

"We'll take our leave, then," Lord Shelley said. "It was a grand party, ma'am." He kissed Aurora's hand.

Sir Roger then kissed her hand and thanked Aurora.

When the door had closed behind the two gentlemen, Aurora and Valerian looked at each other and burst out laughing.

"I can't believe that we actually pulled it off!" she said.

"Shelley was right," Valerian replied. "There really wasn't much sport in it. At least not quite yet."

"You will go to Boodles tomorrow afternoon?" she asked as they walked hand in hand up the staircase.

"My only regret is that you won't be there," he answered her. "I shall report it to you in careful detail."

"I intend going with you," she said.

"Women are not allowed in Boodles."

"I'll dress myself as a boy, and you will pass me off as your cousin, St. John," Aurora told him.

The duke was about to protest, and then he laughed. "All right, my darling," he agreed. "Why not? You deserve to be there at the kill, and if any notice, they will remain silent in agreement. Men like Trahern cannot be allowed to stain any woman's reputation unfairly." Entering the ducal apartments, he drew her into his arms. "Revenge really can be sweet, Aurora, can it not?" His lips brushed hers.

"Ummmmm," she murmured, and ran her tongue along his lips. "Very, very sweet, my lord."

"I like your Roman matron's costume," he said softly in her ear, loosening it so that it fell away from her body.

"And I adore your conquering general," she replied, unfastening his sword and scabbard and sliding her hand beneath his tunic as it clanked to the floor.

He pushed her back against the closed doors of their bedchamber, and sliding his hands beneath her buttocks raised her up, then lowered her upon his rock-hard lance. Aurora put her arms about his neck and kissed him passionately, allowing him to guide their lovemaking to a torrid peak. The walls of her silken passage clutched at him, arousing him to an even hotter lust. Holding her, he walked slowly to the bed, never once breaking their conjunction as they collapsed upon the down comforter. Her legs were wrapped tightly about his torso. Pressing her back into the mattress, he moved himself slowly and with great deliberation, delving deeply into her depths. And when she finally spasmed sweetly, his own desire exploded rapturously.

"You are perfect!" he said several minutes later when he had finally managed to come to himself again.

"As are you, my lord," she told him contentedly. She really did have to tell him soon about their baby. After tomorrow, Aurora thought sleepily, rolling over onto her side with a drowsy sigh.

He drew the coverlet up over her, smiling softly. What a woman she was! Not simply beautiful, but clever and intelligent as well. Neither his father nor hers could have known it when they matched their children all those long years back, but it really was the perfect marriage. They had begun badly, but thank God they were now on a straight path. He smiled to himself. Not so Charles Trahern. Come the morning, when he was sobered up, he was in for quite a shock. And would he come to Boodles tomorrow afternoon? Yes, the duke decided. He would come because he wouldn't believe Maybelle despite her marriage lines. He would think it a jest being played on him in retaliation for his attempt to slander Aurora. So he would come to Boodles and learn that he was indeed married to one of London's finest whores, Merry Maybelle Monypenny. And the Duke of Farminster and his duchess would both be there to witness their revenge.

And indeed at four o'clock the next afternoon the duke and his *visiting cousin*, St. John, were seated in the bow window of Boodles, awaiting the arrival of Lord Charles Trahern, who always arrived promptly at five past four each day, if he hadn't come earlier for luncheon. Lord Shelley and Sir Roger had already spread the news of Trahern's precipitous marital union with Merry Maybelle. Many of the club's members were in proximity to the front door and the bow window.

"He comes," the duke murmured as Trahern stepped briskly down the street. He was attired, as always, in the height of fashion. His breeches were black and fitted above the knee. His stockings had not a wrinkle in them, and his shoes sported square silver buckles. His coat was buff, the patterned waistcoat beneath it a lavender and white. There was lace at his throat and at his wrists. His powdered wig was topped by a tricorn hat with gold braid, and he carried a long walking stick ornamented with an amber knot. He looked a bit under the weather, but the duke knew Trahern would never vary his daily routine.

As Lord Trahern stepped into the club, he was suddenly surrounded by its members all congratulating him upon his marriage.

"Nonsense!" he said. "I've not gotten married. 'Twas only a jest, gentlemen." His eye spotted the duke. "Was it not, Hawkesworth? A fine jest that you played on me."

"*A jest?*" the duke drawled. "I played no jest upon you, Trahern. You are a married man these—" He paused, and drawing forth a round silver hunter's case from his watch pocket, snapped it open and peered closely at it. "Twelve hours and six minutes. Yes, that is it. Your bride is well, I trust? You have certainly made a most interesting choice in a wife, Trahern."

About them there was a flurry of knowing snickers, and Lord Trahern flushed.

"*I am not married to her!*" he said emphatically.

"But, my dear fellow," Valerian Hawkesworth said pleasantly, "I am afraid that you are. I witnessed it, as did my wife, and both Sir Roger Andrews and Lord Percival Shelley. Are you calling us liars?"

"*I can't be married to her!*" Trahern protested.

"Bridegroom's nerves after the fact, Trahern? You were certainly eager enough last night." The duke smiled, and the other club members crowding about the two men laughed aloud.

"It is a trick!" Trahern cried desperately. "You have tricked me into this position, and it is not legal! I shall hire a lawyer to protect me in this matter."

"There was no trick," the duke told him. "No one initiated the marriage but you yourself. You insisted upon marrying the wench because, as you so succinctly put it, your Juliet wouldn't fuck without a wedding ring. The ball was over, and most of our guests had taken their leave, and you demanded we fetch a man of the cloth to marry you to Maybelle Monypenny. You cannot fault us for following your orders, my dear Trahern. You are a married man now, and we have witnesses to that fact."

"*I was drunk!*" Trahern wailed. His life had suddenly become a nightmare, and if this marriage was indeed legal, he was ruined. While some of his male acquaintances might continue to associate with him here at the club—if indeed the club allowed him to retain his membership—no respectable hostess would invite him, nor would their majesties invite him. Not a man married to a notorious whore!

"You are quite frequently drunk, Trahern," the duke said smoothly. "I have never before known it to impair your judgment."

Charles Trahern's eyes almost bulged from his head. He suddenly had the look of a trapped rat. The duke was adamant in his insistence that he was a married man, and both Andrews and Shelley were in his line of view, and they were grinning at him like smug loons. Maybelle had shown him the marriage lines, and these very respectable men were silently telling Trahern that they would go into court and swear to the validity of his marriage. They would not perjure themselves, he knew, especially not Valerian Hawkesworth, who prided himself on his ethics. "You bastard!" he snarled at the duke. "You did this! I know you did!"

His antagonist's eyes were suddenly cold with disdain as he scathingly dismissed Charles Trahern. Valerian Hawkesworth turned to his companion. "Come, Cousin St. John," he said. "It is time to go home now." Graciously he acknowledged Sir Roger, Lord Shelley, and the other gentlemen as they moved through the path opening for them amid the crowd. At the front door of Boodles the duke lifted his hat to the members and stepped forth onto the street where his coach awaited. His companion, catching Sir Roger's eye for the briefest of moments, winked mischievously.

Sir Roger Andrews burst out laughing as in a flash he recognized Aurora in the young man's garb.

Hearing him, Aurora grinned with satisfaction as she joined her husband in their carriage and it moved off into the London traffic back to Farminster House. Trahern, they learned the next morning as they prepared to leave, had gotten himself gloriously drunk, and when Boodles had finally closed the previous evening, Mr. Almack, its owner and founder, had asked several of the gentlemen to escort Lord Trahern home, where his wife, Lady Maybelle, was awaiting him with some very harsh words. This was reported to them by Sir Roger, who had come by to wish them a safe and speedy journey. The entire ton was alternately shocked, fascinated, and titillated by Charles Trahern's marriage, Sir Roger said, and he was already bestruck from the guest lists of English society. Mr. Almack, however, had a kinder heart than London's prime hostesses. As long as

Lord Trahern paid his chits within a reasonable time, he would remain a member of Boodles.

"Almack says a fellow's got to have a place to escape the old ball and chain, even an unsuitable one," Sir Roger stated as he took his leave of the Duke and Duchess of Farminster, never once alluding to Aurora's masquerade the previous day, for Sir Roger prided himself on his gentlemanly behavior. And he also secretly believed that the young duchess had deserved the opportunity to see the downfall of the man who had attempted to slander her name in so vile a manner.

Their journey home to Hawkes Hill was a pleasant one, for England was experiencing a spate of fair weather and the roads were hard and firm, not dusty with drought or muddy with rain. Their armed escort assured that no highwaymen would accost them or their baggage coaches. When Hawkes Hill came into view, the coach suddenly stopped, much to the duke's surprise, and a footman opened the door of the vehicle, lowering the steps for their descent. The duke looked puzzled, but as he opened his mouth to speak, Aurora spoke instead.

"I have asked to have the carriage stop here," she said. "Do you mind if we walk the rest of the way home. We can see the house, and it isn't really far, Valerian."

"If it would please you," he said, curious, and leaping out, turned back to help her descend. "Go along, Mainwaring," he said to his coachman when they were clear of the coach. "Her grace would like to walk."

Aurora slipped her hand through Valerian's, and they walked together as their transport rumbled past them and across the greensward toward Hawkes Hill. The air was sweet and warm, as they passed through a nearby field covered in rock rose, poppies, and daisies. "Ohhh, it is so good to be home," she said. "I will never leave again no matter what," Aurora declared vehemently.

"What is it?" he asked her intuitively.

"What is what?" she teased him.

"You have something to tell me," he said. "I sense it, my darling.

I am so attuned to you, Aurora, that you will never be able to keep anything of import from me." He stopped and looked down into her face questioningly.

"We are to have a baby," she said, laughing. "Oh, Valerian, I am so happy! A baby! Our first child! How I have longed to give you an heir. I never realized it until suddenly I realized that I was with child. Martha knew immediately. And when I told Lotte, she insisted that her own physician examine me, and he said yes!"

He had grown pale with shock. *"No!"* he said in a strangulated voice. "My God, Aurora! What have I done to you in my lust for you?"

She was startled. "Don't you want our baby?" she said.

"Not if it means losing you," he cried desperately, catching her to his chest. "I love you, Aurora, and I do not want you to die as your sister did! I could not bear to lose you, my darling!"

Aurora burst out laughing and pulled away from him. "Oh, Valerian, I am not Cally. I want this baby. I am overjoyed to be carrying this child. The queen's physician says I am in excellent health and spirits. He says I should have a houseful of babies with no danger to my health. *I am not Cally.*"

"But your own mother died in childbirth," he said.

"Many white women in the Indies do, Valerian," she said. "We have no medical assistance, and must depend upon our women servants, who are as ignorant there as they are here. St. Timothy is a small island domain. Perhaps if we had lived on Barbados, or Jamaica, my mother would not have died. I am not my mother, and I shall have a doctor to shepherd me through my confinement. I will not have you worrying until November, Valerian. *I won't!*"

He kissed her, his mouth softly caressing hers, and then he swept her up in his arms and began walking toward the house.

"What on earth are you doing, Valerian Hawkesworth?" she squealed. "Put me down this instant, my lord!"

"You must not overtax yourself, my darling," he said seriously.

"You are a great fool," she laughed, snuggling into his embrace and laying her head against his shoulder.

"What has happened to Aurora!" The old dowager came hurrying toward them. "Is she all right, Valerian? Why are you carrying her?"

"I am to have a baby, madam, and this great fool has gone mad, I believe. Come, my lord, put me down. I will not endure another scandal at your hands now that I am at last safely home."

"Put her down at once, sir!" his grandmother commanded, and the duke obeyed with a grin. Then she turned to Aurora. "My dear, I am so happy for you both!" She kissed Aurora on both her pink cheeks. "And you also, my lord. How was London?"

"Crowded, dirty, noisy, and scandalous," the duke replied. "I am home to stay, dear madam. Scandal or no, *we* are home for good, and nothing will convince me otherwise."

"Their majesties are well? What is she like?" the old lady inquired.

"Delightful," Aurora said. "It was the queen's physician who confirmed my condition. She, too, is with child, and will deliver England's next king in August, madam."

"How wonderful!" the dowager replied as they entered the house, Peters hurrying forth to take their cloaks.

"Welcome home, your grace," the butler said to the duke. "Welcome home, your grace." He bowed to Aurora. "Tea is being served in the Yellow Salon."

They hurried into the sunny room and settled themselves.

"And has the scandal of our marriage died down yet, my dear grandmother?" the duke said, pouring himself a sherry in lieu of the tea the old woman was now serving.

"Of course," she said, "although for a while I thought it would not what with the reports of your riotous living up in London returning to titillate the district."

"*Riotous living?*" Aurora burst out laughing. "Someone has a rather fertile imagination, Grandmama. We lived a most circumspect life, I fear. I became friends with the queen, who is really a sweet little hausfrau, as am I. I think anyone else would have been bored to death. Several of the queen's ladies were, in fact, quite put out by our friendship. I was not, I fear, grand enough for them, and quite dull in their eyes, what with my talk of preserves and soapmaking."

The dowager chortled. "Well, my dears, you have at last been supplanted by a far more shocking scandal. It should be some time before it dies down, I am happy to say, at which point you and Valerian will be considered a respectable married couple, especially as you are to have an heir before the year is out." She chortled again, her blue eyes dancing with merriment.

"Well," the duke said, sounding just slightly aggravated, "are you going to tell us, Grandmama, what this new and obviously delicious scandal is?" He sipped his sherry.

"It does involve the family," the dowager teased him.

"*St. John!*" Aurora guessed. "It has to be St. John. Only he would have the ability to cause a greater scandal than we did."

The dowager laughed aloud now.

"Well, dammit, madam, what has my cousin done?" the duke demanded irritably. "I am astounded that he would try to outdo our alleged calumny, but then, St. John always must have the last word!"

The dowager laughed harder, tears coming to her eyes. "Well, dearest Valerian, he has indeed outdone you this time, and the entire district is talking about it, will be talking about it for months to come. What a rascal St. John is, but this time he has bitten off a tiny bit more than he can chew, although his fate is a better one than he deserves, I can tell you."

"*Well, what has he done?*" the duke almost shouted.

The dowager managed to compose herself. "St. John," she said, "eloped two days ago to Gretna Green with Miss Isabelle Bowen!"

Epilogue

ENGLAND, 1770

On June 6, 1770, the Dowager Duchess of Farminster celebrated her eightieth birthday privately, with only her family as guests at a small party. The back lawns of Hawkes Hill, overlooking the magnificent gardens now abloom with roses, were manicured perfectly. A tea table was even now being set up with fine linen, the silver tea service, and the new porcelain dessert set from Dr. Wall's pottery in Worcester town. There was to be a cake with sugar icing filled with cream and strawberries.

Mary Rose Hawkesworth sat comfortably ensconced in a large high-backed chair that had been brought from the house. Bright-eyed and still sharp of wit, she watched as her great-grandchildren played upon the lawns with their St. John cousins. There were five great-grandchildren so far, and Aurora was shortly to deliver a sixth. Isabelle St. John with her four would deliver a fifth in July. The old lady smiled contentedly, thinking that while she might not be as agile as she once was, this was possibly the best time of her life.

Her eye went to her grandson. Valerian was slightly heavier than he had been several years earlier, but he was thirty-seven now. They had celebrated his birthday just two days before. He was a happy man, and she thanked God for it. He stood now, speaking with his eldest son and heir, seven-and-a-half-year-old George. George's twin sister, Charlotte, was vying for her father's attention.

The birth of the twins had been a great surprise, for never before had twins been born into the family. Then had come Robert, James, and little Calandra. Aurora was certainly keeping up with the queen, or at least trying to keep up with her. Queen Charlotte had delivered her seventh child, a third daughter, to be named Elizabeth, just the previous month.

"How are you feeling, Grandmama?" Aurora inquired solicitously. She settled herself in the chair next to the dowager.

"Quite well, considering my years," the dowager said wryly. "And how are you feeling with your great belly, my dear. Is it a son or a daughter you carry this time? What think you, Aurora?"

"Oh, I hope it is a daughter, Grandmama" was the reply. "We already have an heir, a son for the navy, and one for the church. What would we do with another boy? I suppose we could buy him a commission in the army." She sighed. "Daughters are easier. All you have to do is find them suitable husbands, and a duke's daughter with a generous dowry will have no trouble making a good match."

"Unless, of course, she favors her mama in her temperament, and then even a duke will not be good enough," the dowager teased her granddaughter-in-law, a smile upon her lips.

Aurora laughed. "I was really quite the fool, wasn't I?" she said. "I still feel guilt over Cally's untimely death even if it did bring me all this happiness. I am only grateful that my stepmother finally found it in her heart to forgive me. It pained me to hurt Oralia, for she was always so good to me, and really the only mother I ever knew. I'm sorry she will not come to England, but her fear of the sea is far greater than her desire to see my children."

"She has Betsy and George's children," the dowager comforted Aurora. "I imagine those three little boys keep her quite busy."

"Perhaps we shall go to St. Timothy next winter," Aurora said thoughtfully. "I would like to see the islands again."

"St. Timothy. The island snatched from me by my greedy cousin, the duke," St. John said teasingly, coming up to where the women sat. He kissed his wife, who was seated on the other side of the dowager, upon her cheek.

Isabelle smacked his hand lightly. "Behave yourself, St. John!

You are worse than the children, I vow. Have you spoken to Frederick about teasing his sister, Caroline? It really must stop! When Augustus and Edward see him begin, they join in, and poor Caroline is quite overcome by them. Well, have you taken Freddie to task yet, St. John?"

Aurora arose quietly and walked across the lawns toward her husband. St. John had really, as the dowager remarked more than once, bitten off more than he could chew when he married Isabelle Bowen. He had indeed gotten his just deserts in a loving martinet of a wife, as Isabelle had turned out to be. She utterly adored him, and to his amazement St. John felt the same way about her. She ran his house with an iron hand, and bore him beautiful children; but she expected total obedience from her husband, her children, and her servants. She had totally engineered her courtship and elopement, the dowager said. Poor St. John had never realized he was being taken in hand until the ring had been placed upon Isabelle's dainty finger—and in St. John's aristocratic nose.

Coming up to her husband, Aurora slipped her hand through his arm. "What a perfect day," she said. "Could it be any better?"

He smiled down at her. "No," he agreed. "It could not."

"Mama!" Her eldest son tugged at her skirts. "Mama! There are new puppies in the stables! May I have a puppy? *Please!*"

"How many puppies are there, Georgie?" she asked him.

"Five, Mama! They are liver and white, and Franklin says they'll be ready to leave their mother in eight or nine weeks. Their eyes aren't opened yet. They are so tiny, Mama. I may have one, mayn't I?"

Aurora looked up at her husband. "If Georgie gets a puppy, the others will want one too," she warned him, and then she laughed at the look on his face. "Oh, very well," she said, and she looked down at her son. "Yes, Georgie, you may have a puppy. And so may your brothers and sisters too."

"But I get to pick first because I am the eldest," the boy said. "I am the eldest, and I am the heir."

"I was born five minutes before you were," his twin sister, Charlotte, said. "I don't want a puppy, Mama. I want one of Pusskin's new kittens, and so does Cally. If he gets a puppy, I get a kitten."

"Cally isn't old enough for a kitten," Georgie said. "Or a puppy either," he concluded. "You just want two kittens, Lotte."

"You're just jealous because I was born before you were," his sister replied. "Cally will want a kitten if I get one, Mama."

"You may be older," the boy replied, "but I am the heir. I will be Duke of Farminster one day, and I shall banish you to a nunnery, Lotte."

"You can't do that!" she cried. "What's a nunnery, Mama? He can't do that, can he?"

"A nunnery is where ladies who have decided to devote their lives to God live, Lotte," her mother said, "and no, Georgie cannot banish you to a nunnery. One day you shall fall in love, and marry."

"And I shall marry a duke who is even richer than you will be," Charlotte Hawkesworth told her brother smugly.

"Will not!" he cried.

"Will too!" she replied.

"Sheep face!" he insulted her.

"Frog's head!" she taunted him, and giving him a quick smack she ran off, her twin in hot pursuit to gain his revenge.

The duke looked into his wife's face. His deep blue eyes were dancing wickedly. Tenderly he patted her belly. "Nonetheless," he said, "I do love children, my darling, and I love you even more than the day I married you. I think our life together a fairy tale."

Georgie Hawkesworth had caught up with his sister. He grabbed at her curls, and catching one, yanked hard upon it. Lotte shrieked so loudly that the sheep in the nearby field scattered madly.

The duke began to chuckle.

"And they lived happily ever after," Aurora replied, and then joined her husband in merry laughter.

Bertrice Small lives in the oldest English-speaking town in the state of New York, which was founded in 1640. She writes her novels in a light-filled studio surrounded by the paintings of her close friend, cover artist, Elaine Euillo; as well as the many momentos of the romance genre she has collected. Married almost thirty-five years to her husband, George; she is the mother of, Thomas, a sportscaster; mother-in-law to Megan, a wonderful daughter; and the doting grandmother of Chandler David, who is almost three. Longtime readers will be happy to know that Nicky, the charming Cockatiel who is now ten; Checquers, the fat black and white cat with the pink ears who is now fifteen; and Pookie, the long-haired greige and white feline, aged three, are still her dearest companions. Readers are invited to write the author with their comments at:

P.O. Box 765
Southold, NY 11971-9765